"A woman came to see me today," Kate said.

"A prospective client?"

She nodded. "She saw the CNN interview I did last week and thought I might be able to help her."

Mitch's blue gaze was lit with curiosity. "What did she do?"

"Nothing. The one who needs my help is her fiancé. Apparently he's the number one suspect in a murder he says he didn't commit."

Mitch continued to watch her. "So why send the fiancée? Why didn't he come himself?"

Kate's throat felt dry, her chest tight. "He can't. He's in hiding. He...fled before the police could arrest him."

This time the easygoing smile faded. Silence stretched out. When he spoke again, Mitch's voice was controlled. Not a good sign. "This prospective client has a name?"

"Todd Buchanan."

Mitch stood very still, his expression now neutral, impossible to read. They were only a couple of feet from each other, yet suddenly they seemed miles apart.

"Tell me you aren't actually considering representing my sister's cold-blooded murderer."

"A master at creating taut, romantic suspense."
                                                —*Literary Times*

CHRISTIANE HEGGAN

MOMENT OF TRUTH

MIRA®

ISBN 0-7394-2280-4

MOMENT OF TRUTH

Printed in U.S.A.

For Jeff and Nancy
with all my love

Prologue

The one-story roadside motel stood alone, stark white against the northern Virginia night sky. In the surrounding darkness, a red neon sign with the word "Vacancy" flashing on and off provided the only light.

Silently, the dark Mercedes pulled into the motel parking lot and slid into an empty space. The man behind the wheel did not turn off the engine but let it idle as he surveyed the area. His gaze stopped on the window of Room 12 at the end of the building. Weariness mixed with excitement. He still wasn't sure this meeting was a good idea. There hadn't been enough time to investigate the girl, make sure she was what she claimed to be—a chat room enthusiast looking for a few hours of hot, mindless sex.

She had joined *Spider's Web* only two weeks before, and from the moment she had logged on under the pseudonym of Guinevere, he had felt an irresistible attraction to her. Though admittedly new to sex chat rooms, she was no slouch in the erotic talk department. In fact, she was downright filthy at times—which thrilled him beyond description.

For some odd reason, she had singled him out, flirting openly and shamelessly with him, explaining that because of their respective pseudonyms—Guinevere and Black Knight—they shared a special karma. On her first night in the chat room, she had contacted him privately, through the instant message feature, and told him they should get together for a little fun and games. When he had brushed her off, she had asked again. And again.

That was the reason he had taken a short absence from *Spider's Web* last week. The woman was getting to him in ways no other ever had, and that worried him. From the moment he had discovered *Spider's Web* three years ago, he had made it a point to thoroughly investigate the backgrounds of the women he chose to meet in person. Guinevere, however, had refused to tell him anything about herself, claiming that the mystery surrounding their identities was part of the thrill—otherwise, why bother? The only information she had provided was that she lived in Delaware and was willing to travel.

His indifference to her repeated requests had made her even more determined. Only yesterday, she had teased him mercilessly, calling him a bad boy and scolding him for playing hard to get. Much to the pleasure of the others in the chat room, she had told him, in scorching detail, what she would do to him once they finally got together. She had talked as though she knew him intimately, knew what he wanted, what he craved.

Common sense had told him to ignore her and move on to another chat room. There were plenty of women out there willing to meet him on his terms. This girl was too wild, too much of a thrill-seeker. At the same time, the danger she presented had brought his arousal to new levels. Little by little, his resistance had begun to ebb, as her messages got hotter and hotter, conjuring a series of images that made it impossible for him to focus on anything but those incendiary words.

He drew a deep breath. There was nothing to be concerned about, he reasoned. This place, which he had used before, was completely safe, catering mostly to long-distance truckers who were too damn tired to worry about what went on in the next room.

His gaze swept over the parking lot one more time as he tried to guess which of the three sedans belonged to her. None had a Delaware license plate, which meant she had either rented a car to come here or borrowed one. He nodded approvingly. She was cautious, too, and that pleased him. Experience had taught him that the women who had the most to lose were the least likely to cause trouble.

With a shiver of anticipation, he turned off the engine, got out of the car and walked quickly across the parking lot.

The drapes of room 12 were drawn but for a crack in the middle. It was enough to give him an ample view of the room and its occupant. What he saw caused him to take a sharp breath. She was there, her back to him. Except for a black thong and black leather boots, she was naked, moving around the room with total abandon, her long platinum hair cascading over her shoulders, hiding half her face.

Rooted to the spot, he took in the sensuous hips, the round behind, the long, shapely legs. He waited for her to turn around so he could see the rest of her, but she didn't. Did she know he was there, watching her? he wondered. Had she left that opening in the drapes for that purpose?

He thought of waiting her out and showing her who was in charge, but as she bent to take a bottle of champagne from a cooler at the foot of the bed, he felt a strong, familiar jolt and knew he wasn't up to playing games.

At last, he walked over to the door and opened it. "Hello, Guinevere."

As she spun around, a look of utter shock on her face, his heart gave one powerful thump. He tried to speak but was unable to utter a single word.

Though she was just as stunned, she recovered quickly and reacted in typical fashion. She threw her head back and burst into laughter.

"Shut up." Having finally regained his voice, if not his composure, he closed the door and assumed a stern tone. "Do you want to wake up the entire building?"

She flipped her hair—a wig he now realized—behind her shoulders, clearly not intimidated. "You can't blame me for being amused, can you? This is truly priceless." She put her hands on her hips while she assessed him, slowly, from head to toe. "Not a half-bad disguise." She waved a finger above her upper lip. "I particularly like the Errol Flynn mustache. It gives you a certain...*je ne sais quoi.*"

"Shut up and listen," he said sharply. "I'm going to walk out this door, and you'll get dressed and do the same. As far as we're both concerned, this meeting never took place. Do you understand?"

"No way, José." She let out a bawdy laugh. "This is too good to pass up." She walked toward him in a slow, suggestive way that, under different circumstances, would have set him on fire. At the moment, all he experienced was cold, undiluted fear.

"Wait until the people at *Spider's Web* find out who Black Knight is," she scoffed. "You, my friend, will be the topic *du jour* for weeks to come."

"You will not mention one word of this to anyone!"

"And deprive myself of all this fun?" She shook her head. "Not a chance. I can't wait until all of Washington finds out exactly what kind of pervert you are."

She started to walk around him, chuckling. "Who would have thought," she said in a low, sexy voice, "that you had such a hot spark burning deep inside you." Her hand trailed across his back. "I like it, you know." He felt her mouth brush against his ear. "It turns me on," she whispered.

He pushed her off. "Get dressed."

"Why? Don't you like this little number?" She pirouetted in front of him, batting her eyelashes. "I bought it just for you." Her tone was mocking now. "You're aroused, aren't you. Come on, admit it. You want me. I can read it in your eyes, feel it in the way you're holding your breath."

She inched closer, pressing her chest against his. Her mouth was only a breath away, red, ripe and lethal. To his disgust, he felt a stirring.

"I brought some of those toys I told you about." She ran the tip of her tongue along her upper lip. "Wanna play?"

He followed her gaze to a chair where several

bondage items—ropes, handcuffs, blindfolds—had been laid out.

"What's the matter, lover? Lost your tongue?" Her smoldering eyes filled with lust. "We wouldn't want that now, would we?"

His mouth felt dry. The blood pounded so hard in his ears, he thought they would burst.

"Oh, come on," she teased. "Don't be such a spoilsport. We came here to have fun, remember?" She gave him an exaggerated wink. "If you're as good as I think you are, I'll give you a great recommendation. Nothing beats good word of mouth. Maybe I'll even call the *Post*. They'd love a juicy story like this, don't you think?"

The thought of seeing his name plastered over the front page of the *Washington Post* made him sick. The bitch was going to destroy him. All those years of hard work would be for nothing, the dream as unreachable as a distant planet.

Another woman might have listened to reason, accepted money. Not this one.

He knew as surely as the sun would rise tomorrow that the only way out of this mess was to silence her. Permanently.

Obviously unsuspecting of the direction his thoughts had taken, she continued to watch him, the tip of her index finger in her mouth. It would have been so easy to wrap his hands around that delicate white throat and squeeze until she had breathed her last breath. Easy but risky. Her instincts would be to fight back, to pry his fingers loose, perhaps even to scratch him, leaving blood and skin residue under her fingernails.

He would have to find another way. As his mind worked feverishly, his gaze stopped on the bottle of champagne on the bedside table.

She caught his look and smiled, clearly into the game now. "Why don't you go ahead and pop the cork, lover? I'll get the glasses."

As she turned away from him, his heart began to thunder. This was his chance. He couldn't screw it up. Without wasting another moment, he grabbed the bottle of champagne by the neck, brought his arm back as he would if wielding a baseball bat, and, with all the force he could muster, slammed it against the back of her head.

He heard the *thunk* as it connected with the woman's skull. Simultaneously, her legs folded under her, making her look like a disjointed puppet. She fell onto the bed, facedown. In the sudden stillness of the room, the only sound was that of his ragged breathing as he stood looking at her. Blood had begun to trickle from her mouth, seeping onto the cheap yellow bedspread.

Was she dead? He kept staring at her, unsure. He could already feel the first signs of panic rising through him. What if she was only unconscious? What if he had to hit her again?

Moving was an effort, but he forced himself to put the bottle down and take a tentative step toward the bed, then another. He bent over her. "Molly?" When there was no response, he seized a handful of fake hair, turned her head and jumped back.

Lifeless blue eyes stared at him.

He wasn't sure how long he stood there, waiting for the shaking to stop and for his mind to start functioning again. When it finally did, his first thought was to get out of there. Quickly. But not yet. Not until he had taken care of a few details.

Calmer now, he pulled a handkerchief from his pants pocket and proceeded to wipe everything he had touched, or thought he had touched—the bedside table, the chair with the sex paraphernalia, and, of course, the champagne bottle.

When he was finished, he gave the room one last sweeping glance, trying to ignore the motionless figure on the bed. But even in death, she was like a magnet, pulling him in, forcing him to look. The sight made him shiver. At that angle and with her eyes wide open, she seemed to be staring right at him, mocking him.

After what felt like an eternity, he tore his gaze away and backed out of the room, pausing at the door long enough to wipe both knobs, inside and out. Then, after making sure no one was outside, he stepped out and hurried into the night.

One

Two years later

"Oh, Kate!" As the judge rose from behind his bench and walked away, his black robe billowing behind him, Melanie Riley threw her arms around Kate Logan and gave her a warm hug. "I don't know how to thank you. You performed a miracle."

Greatly relieved they'd gotten the verdict she'd wanted, Kate returned the embrace while watching Melanie's ex-husband storm out of the courtroom. "The credit is all yours, Melanie. You did a wonderful job on that witness stand. Your love for your daughter radiated from you like warm sunlight. The judge saw that and ruled accordingly."

Melanie released Kate and wiped a tear. "But you're the one who dug into my ex-husband's past and exposed him for the bully he really is. If you hadn't, Joe could have been awarded joint custody of Pru."

"But he wasn't," Kate replied cheerfully, taking her client's arm. "So why don't we put those past two weeks behind us and get out of here? I'm sure you've seen enough of this courtroom."

"I have, but first…" She reached into her purse and pulled out a thin envelope.

Kate stopped her. "Put your money away, Melanie. This one is on me."

The young woman gave a vehement shake of her head. "No, Kate. I told you I'd pay you a little each week, and I intend to do just that."

Even though Kate was short of funds herself, she had no intention of taking money from a single mother who worked so hard to support her little girl. Melanie's husband, a bum in every sense of the word, had walked out on her when Prudence was just a baby. He had reappeared three months ago, threatening to sue for custody of their daughter unless Melanie sold the house, which belonged to her, and gave him half of the equity.

Family law wasn't Kate's area of expertise, but when the young mother, who worked as a secretary in Kate's building, had walked into her office looking so frightened, Kate hadn't had the heart to turn her away.

"I have a better idea," she said, when Melanie tried to put the envelope in her hands. "Why don't you put the money toward that new bedroom set for Prudence. The one you saw at Hecht's the other day. I know how badly you want it."

"But all that time you spent—"

Kate cut her off with a wave of her hand and steered her toward the exit. "Didn't anyone tell you to never argue with your attorney?"

A smile—her first—brightened Melanie's pretty face. "Yes, your secretary."

"Listen to her. Frankie knows what she's talking about."

Melanie gave a sigh of resignation and dropped the

envelope back into her purse. "All right, Kate. We'll do it your way. But I won't forget," she added, with a shake of her finger. "Somehow I'll find a way to repay you for all you've done."

"All I want is for you and Prudence to be happy," Kate replied. She meant every word. A single mother herself, she couldn't help admiring Melanie's inner strength and proud demeanor.

Outside the courthouse, the two women hugged again and promised to keep in touch. Then, after one last wave, Melanie walked to her car, while Kate headed for her office, just off L'Enfant Plaza. Although the late March weather could sometimes be brutal, the past couple of days had been amazingly balmy. As a result, the streets of Washington were jammed with people taking advantage of the warm sunshine and tourists who had come to see the cherry trees in bloom.

As usual at this time of day, there wasn't a cab in sight. Glad she'd had the good sense to wear comfortable shoes, she started down Seventh Street, walking briskly.

As Kate crossed the National Mall, the grassy, gravel-pathed strip that stretched from the Capitol Building to the Lincoln Memorial, she glanced at her watch. It was almost noon, which meant it was one p.m. in the British Virgin Islands. If she called the yacht now, she'd get Alison before she sat down for lunch with her father and his new bride.

Cell phone in hand, she dialed the fourteen-digit number she had memorized over the past ten days. Alison picked up on the third ring.

From eighteen hundred miles away, her daughter's voice came through loud and clear. "Hello?"

"How's my girl?"

"Oh, Mom, I wish I could stay here longer. I'm having so much fun."

Kate felt a small stab of disappointment. After ten days away from everything that was familiar to her, Alison, she had thought, would be anxious to come home, but apparently that prospect didn't seem to thrill her daughter. Ashamed at her own selfishness, Kate scolded herself. Why shouldn't a thirteen-year-old have fun on the trip of a lifetime?

"I'm glad you're having such a good time, sweetie," she said, trying to sound cheerful. "What did you do this morning?"

"The captain took us to Mosquito Island, where we swam and went out looking for shells. And after lunch, Dad and Megan have arranged for us to tour the island on motor scooters."

Kate could hear the alarm in her own voice. "Make sure you wear a helmet."

Alison laughed. "Oh, Mom, they don't wear helmets in the BVI."

Kate started to ask to speak to Eric, then thought better of it. The last thing she wanted was to create tension between her and her daughter. There had been enough of that at the time of her divorce from Eric, which Alison had blamed entirely on Kate.

"How are you getting along with Megan's niece?" Kate asked instead. The sixteen-year-old, whose parents lived and worked in London, had joined the cruise just three days ago. Kate had been concerned the teenager might be a tad too old for Alison, who was at an impressionable age. Megan, however, had assured her there was nothing to worry about. Candace was a very responsible girl and completely trustworthy.

"Candace's so cool, Mom. Did I tell you she speaks three languages? And she can do everything— scuba dive, water-ski, parasail—"

"You're not going parasailing, Alison." This time Kate made sure her tone of voice left no room for an argument. "Or scuba diving."

"I know. Dad already said I was too young for that, but water-skiing is okay, right? We're planning to go tomorrow, on our last day here. I'll be wearing a life vest," she added quickly.

Kate bit back another negative response. In spite of Eric's shortcomings as a husband, he was a good father, and Megan was a responsible young woman. They wouldn't let anything happen to Alison.

"Of course," she said, trying hard not to show her concern. "Just be careful."

If she has so much as a scratch on her head, Eric, you're a dead man.

"I will." Kate could hear the excitement bubbling anew in the girl's voice. "I bought you a present. Mitch, too, but don't tell him, okay? It's a surprise."

Kate smiled. The relationship between Alison and Mitch had taken a while to develop over the past four months, but once it had, they'd become the best of pals. "My lips are sealed."

"Got to go, Mom. Lunch's ready. We're having my favorite today—lobster. The captain caught them fresh this morning. Did you know that Caribbean lobsters don't have claws?"

"No, I didn't." Silently, Kate scratched off the meat loaf dinner she had planned for Wednesday night to celebrate Alison's return. She'd have to think of something more interesting, though she didn't know what would hold its own against freshly caught lobster from the Caribbean Sea. "Have a great day tomorrow, Alison. I love you."

"Love you, too, Mom."

After Alison hung up, Kate held the phone against her chest for a moment. It was silly, but she was suddenly filled with nostalgia. Her little girl was growing up by leaps and bounds and becoming more independent every day, especially now that she spent so much time with Megan. Not that Kate resented the role Eric's new wife played in Alison's life. Megan was a good person, and she loved Alison, but there was no denying that the newlyweds' affluent lifestyle was starting to affect the teenager. In the past, always so careful with her allowance, she now spent it indiscriminately, knowing that when the money was gone, Megan would simply give her more. In fact, the young woman's generosity had gotten so out of hand that Kate had felt it necessary to put an end to it, something Alison deeply resented.

And when Eric and Megan, who had planned their honeymoon around spring break, had asked Alison to join them on a ten-day chartered cruise through the British Virgin Islands, Kate had had a dozen reasons for not wanting to let her daughter go, none of which Alison had understood. Or Eric, for that matter.

In the end, it was Mitch who had gently reminded Kate that her refusal would only give Alison another reason to pick a fight.

Mitch had been right. Kate was acting like an over-protective mother. Overprotective and maybe just a tiny bit jealous of the bond that was forming between Alison and Megan.

And speaking of Mitch... Forcing Alison out of her mind, for now, Kate dialed Mitch's number at Metro PD. The sound of his voice as he said, "Calhoon" lifted her mood considerably. "Hi, handsome."

"Hi, yourself." She could almost picture him tilting his chair back and running his fingers through his light brown hair, pushing back that stubborn strand that kept falling over his forehead. "How did it go in court?"

"We won, and you know what that means, don't you?"

"You want to celebrate."

"In a big way. My house for dinner?"

His tone turned playful. "Why don't we skip dinner and go straight to the celebration part?"

"You're bad, Calhoon."

"What do you expect? I've barely seen you these past two weeks."

Kate sighed as her gaze rested on a young couple sitting on a bench, necking. "It's this case, but it's over now. I should have more time on my hands from now on."

"With Alison coming back day after tomorrow? I doubt it."

"All the more reason to make the most of tonight, don't you think?" she asked in her sexiest whisper.

"Keep talking like that, and I'll come to your office right now and make mad passionate love to you on your new carpet. We could call it an overdue christening of the place.''

''Stop that,'' she said, aware that passersby were looking at her with amused expressions on their faces. ''You're getting me all hot and bothered right here in the middle of the National Mall.''

''Tempted?''

''Yes. No! Oh, you're incorrigible.''

''Okay, I'll let you off the hook. For now. Just greet me at the door in that little number you wore the last time I was there.''

Kate felt herself blush, remembering the red lace teddy she had bought on impulse one afternoon as she had walked by a Victoria's Secret window on Connecticut Avenue. That sex kitten side of her, carefully concealed until then, had delighted Mitch. ''Maybe this time, I'll great you at the door with nothing on.''

He laughed. ''Promises, promises.''

She said goodbye and dropped the phone into her purse, her mind already focused on a four o'clock appointment with a potential client. Charged with killing his business partner, Ed Gibbons now sat in the downtown jail claiming to have no recollection of the shooting. In his own words, he had suddenly found himself in Peter Brink's office, holding a .38 revolver—*his* revolver—though he had no idea how it had gotten from his safe at home to 600 New Hampshire Avenue.

Unhappy with his two previous lawyers, he had fired them both and was now considering hiring Kate. Whether or not he would depended on how well she could convince him that his only defense was to plead insanity, which, so far, he had refused to consider.

She prayed Gibbons would not cancel their appointment as he had the previous one. The sooner they got this case under way, the sooner she'd get her retainer.

She hated that money had become such an issue in her life. It shouldn't have. With all the media attention she had received when she left Fairchild Baxter, she had expected the momentary fame to translate into a handsome client base. Unfortunately, being associated with a prestigious law firm, even one shrouded in scandal, was more important for some than being represented by a competent attorney. And then there were Douglas Fairchild's old friends, staunch supporters of her former father-in-law, who actually resented Kate for tarnishing the reputation of a man they had admired for so long.

Exposing Douglas had been one of the lowest points in her life. Next to her father, the renowned attorney had been the only man she had ever looked up to. Finding out four months ago that he and a Washington madam had ordered the death of two women and almost caused Alison's own death, had been a devastating blow to her. After Douglas's arrest, she'd had no choice but to leave the law firm, even though Douglas's partner, Charles Baxter, had wanted her to stay, offering her a full partnership as an incentive.

Instead, Kate had chosen to open her own practice, secure in the knowledge that her friends and family supported her wholeheartedly. Even her ex-mother-in-law, Rose Fairchild, who had remained in seclusion following her husband's arrest, had stood by her, assuring Kate she was making the right decision. Rose had even offered to finance the venture.

"You've done so much for me, Kate. Let me do this one little thing for you. We're family, after all."

Kate had turned her down gently, assuring the woman she didn't need the money, which, of course, was a lie.

There were times when she wished she had chosen another profession. Criminal law was such a competitive field, especially here in the nation's capital. Yet, from the moment she had attended her first class at Georgetown Law fourteen years ago, she had known that this challenging field was her destiny.

She had graduated in the top five percent of her class and could have had her pick of any law firm in Washington. Instead, she had joined the overworked, underpaid team at the U.S. Attorney's office. She had been full of ideals in those early days, eager to make a difference in a system she felt was sometimes unfair.

"I want to serve the people," she had told her father. "And to do that I need to put criminals behind bars, not help set them free."

Her father had understood, but not Eric Logan, whom she married while she was still in school. He couldn't understand why she had settled for such an unrewarding, low-paying job when his stepfather had offered her a position in his prestigious law firm along with a significant five-figure salary.

Eventually the pressure had been too much. Foolish enough to believe that a bigger paycheck would mend her ailing marriage, she had accepted Douglas's offer, only to realize that money wasn't the panacea she had expected.

And now she had reached another milestone in her life, one that was fraught with new challenges and pitfalls. As a solo lawyer, her greatest expenditure was the rent. It probably would have been wiser to choose a more affordable building, but she hadn't been able to resist the location of the small but well-appointed office on Maryland Avenue, only a few blocks from the courthouse where she spent much of her time.

An optimist, she believed business would eventually pick up. All she needed was one big case to show prospective clients she could handle the challenge on her own, without the backing of a large, prestigious firm. Attracting attention was exactly what she had in mind when she had agreed to be interviewed by CNN last week. The seven-minute segment had been brief but had touched all the high points of her career, including the Washington Madam case. Unfortunately, except for Ed Gibbons, no one seemed anxious to break down her door.

She had almost reached the Sculpture Gardens when she heard someone call her name. She turned around. An attractive young woman stood just behind her. She had light brown hair that curled softly at her jaw and hazel eyes that studied Kate with a mixture of hope and apprehension. She wore an elegant gray suit, a pink silk blouse and gray pumps that were not meant for walking. A gold cross in an unusual design hung around her neck.

Kate shielded her eyes from the sun. "Yes," she said. "I'm Kate Logan."

"I know this is a rather unconventional way to approach you." The woman moved closer. "I called your office first, but your secretary said you were in court and wasn't sure when you'd be back. I didn't want to miss you, so I decided to go to the courthouse and wait for you. I would have approached you sooner, but you were walking so fast, I lost track of you, until now."

"May I ask who you are?"

"My name is Jessica Van Dyke. And I desperately need your help."

That much was clear. The woman was obviously under a great deal of stress. "Wouldn't you prefer if we talked in my office? It's only a five-minute walk from here."

"Actually—" she glanced up and down the Mall "—I'd rather stay here." She motioned toward a vacant bench. "Do you mind?"

Kate shrugged. She'd had stranger requests. "Not at all." Once seated, she turned to face the young woman. "What can I do for you, Ms. Van Dyke?"

The woman moistened her lips. "Will this remain between you and me?"

"Discretion is my middle name," Kate said, hoping to make the woman smile. "However, just to reassure you, why don't you give me a dollar?"

"Excuse me?"

"The dollar can be my retainer. That way I'll be bound by attorney-client privilege, which prevents me from repeating anything we discuss."

"Oh." Ms. Van Dyke searched her purse, found a crumpled dollar bill and handed it to Kate.

Kate dropped it into her own purse. "Now, what kind of trouble are you in?"

"I'm not here for myself," the young woman said hesitantly. "It's my fiancé. He... The police think he killed someone."

"Has he been arrested?"

"No." She met Kate's gaze. "He fled before they could arrest him."

A fiancé on the run. No wonder she was so jittery. "How did you hear about me?" Kate asked gently.

"I saw the interview you did on CNN last week. I thought, and so did my fiancé, that you were the right person to look into his...situation." She leaned forward, her expression earnest. "He didn't do it, Ms. Logan. I know what you're thinking, that my judgment is influenced by my love for him, but that's not the case. I do love him," she added quickly. "But that has nothing to do with my beliefs. My fiancé really is innocent."

Kate had seen that expression before—a mixture of unconditional love and absolute trust. The problem, she had found, was that too often such blind devotion wasn't justified.

"If he's innocent, why didn't he stay to defend himself?"

"He was scared. He didn't know what to do, so he ran."

The survival instinct. That, too, was something Kate was familiar with. "Who was the victim?"

"His former wife." She met Kate's gaze without flinching. "Her name was Molly. Molly Buchanan."

Kate stiffened. "Did you say Buchanan?"

"Yes. My fiancé is Todd Buchanan."

Kate let out a long, slow breath. The "situation" had just become a little more complicated. Molly Buchanan was Mitch Calhoon's sister.

Two

Kate gave herself a few seconds to recover from the shock. She hadn't known Mitch at the time of his sister's death, but as an attorney she had followed the case with the same professional curiosity as every lawyer in the Washington area.

Todd Buchanan, a well-known television sportscaster, was the youngest son of Supreme Court Justice Lyle Buchanan and the brother of Terrence Buchanan, a former international law professor at Georgetown Law School and now provost at Jefferson University.

Todd had been known as a smart-ass, a rich boy with a taste for trouble and a habit of using his father's name whenever he found himself in a jam, which was often. Therefore, it hadn't come as a great surprise when the police brought him in for questioning following the discovery of his wife's dead body in a northern Virginia motel room two years ago.

It had been the consensus at Fairchild Baxter that the police had been a tad too anxious to pin the murder on Todd and may not have looked at all the facts. A little payback, perhaps, for all the stunts the former playboy had pulled over the years.

Her initial surprise over, Kate cleared her throat. ''Since you heard the CNN interview,'' she said, "you must know that Mitch Calhoon and I are friends." She paused. "Close friends."

"I do. And to be frank, your relationship with Mitch is why Todd was so much against my coming here at first." She smiled. "Fortunately he changed his mind."

Lucky me, Kate thought.

"Actually," Jessica went on, "I see your relationship with Mitch as an advantage rather than a handicap."

"How so?"

"I figure that if Todd can convince you of his innocence, you, in turn, will be able to convince Mitch."

"You give me more credit than I deserve, Ms. Van Dyke. I didn't know Mitch at the time his sister was killed, but I do know there's a great deal of animosity between him and Todd."

"Only on Mitch's part. Todd had only good things to say about Mitch." Jessica paused. "Except for his unfair accusations the day Todd was taken in for questioning."

"You can hardly blame him. If I recall, the evidence against Todd was fairly strong. And when he fled—"

"He made things worse." Jessica nodded. "Todd realizes that now. As for the evidence, it's purely circumstantial. There were no fingerprints at the crime scene, and the motel clerk was unable to make a positive ID. The only thing he was sure of was that the person he saw, probably a man, came out of room 12. The suspect's description—medium height, medium weight—could fit thousands of people in Washington alone.''

Kate couldn't hold back a smile. She always found it amusing when clients tried to interpret the law. Most of them didn't have a clue what they were talking about. Not Jessica Van Dyke. The woman had done her homework, and, for the most part, she was right. No matter how repeatedly the police had questioned the motel clerk, they hadn't been able to get him to change his statement.

Jessica was watching her intently, playing with her little cross. ''Do you agree?''

''To a point.''

Hope flared in the lovely hazel eyes. ''Then, you'll take Todd's case?''

''Ms. Van Dyke, without a face-to-face meeting with your fiancé, I'm afraid—''

''I've taken care of that.'' She reached inside the leather bag she had placed on the bench between them and retrieved a videotape. ''I made this tape of Todd just before I left,'' she said, handing it to Kate. ''Please look at it, Ms. Logan. Listen to what Todd has to say. And then make your decision.

''Please,'' she said again, when Kate made no move to take the tape. ''All I'm asking for is twenty minutes of your time. If after viewing the tape you decide you can't represent Todd, I'll take the first plane out of Washington, and you'll never see me again. If, on the other hand, you believe Todd is innocent and agree to represent him, a hundred-thousand-dollar retainer will be immediately wired into your account. If that's not enough, just tell me what your fee is and we'll pay it. Money is not a problem.''

Kate had waited four long months to hear those words, and now that she had she was hesitating, torn between her need to take this case and her concern for Mitch. How could she represent, and possibly defend, a man he believed had killed his sister? A man he had spent a lot of his own time pursuing.

"If clearing your fiancé's name was so important to you, why did you wait this long before contacting an attorney? Obviously you've known about Todd's situation for some time."

"When Todd told me about Molly, my first impulse was to hire an attorney. Todd wouldn't hear of it. He was convinced no one would believe him. Then we saw the CNN interview you did not too long ago and knew you were different." Her eyes suddenly lit up. "You might say that the timing of that interview was like a sign."

"A sign?"

The young woman gave her a serene smile. "The day I saw you on television is the day I learned I was expecting a baby. Todd and I are going to be parents."

Lost for words, Kate just looked at her. No wonder Jessica wanted to clear her fiancé's name. What woman wanted to bring a little baby into the world and have such a dark cloud hanging over his, or her, head?

Ending the meeting, Jessica laid the tape on the bench and stood up. "I'm staying at the Mayflower Hotel," she said. "And this is my cell phone number." She handed Kate a slip of paper with the hotel logo on it. "My plane leaves at nine-thirty tonight. I hope to hear from you before then."

Kate took the video, slipped it into her briefcase and rose, as well. "I'm not promising anything," she said.

"I understand." Jessica smiled again before walking away.

"That dirty, spineless, two-timing dog!"

Standing outside her office door on the top floor of the Bellevue Building, Kate winced as the words, uttered by her secretary, were followed by the sound of breaking glass. Another boyfriend bites the dust, Kate thought, unable to hold back a smile.

Francine Morgano, better known as Frankie, was one of the best legal assistants Kate had ever had. She was bright, efficient and totally devoted to her job and to Kate. She had only one flaw. She had deplorable taste in men.

Because Kate was used to such outbursts, she remained unruffled by it, and walked into the reception room in time to see Frankie toss another framed photograph of her latest beau into the wastebasket.

She perched a hip on Frankie's desk while taking a handful of phone messages from her box. "Problems with Roméro?" she asked, flipping through the pink slips of paper.

Frankie gave her a dirty look. Not pretty in the true sense of the word, her face nonetheless possessed an exotic quality that never failed to make heads turn. She had large, almost transparent blue eyes, thin, outrageously arched brows and a heart-shaped mouth always painted a vivid shade of red. As always, her black hair was weaved into a tight braid she adorned with a different comb every day of the week. Today it was mother-of-pearl.

"Don't ever mention the name of that snake again," she warned.

When Kate wisely nodded, Frankie hit the desk with her fist. "Did you know that he was seeing his ex-girlfriend behind my back?"

Kate, who had never met Roméro, shook her head.

"I caught him having lunch in a little hideaway he had sworn was ours alone."

"I'm sorry," Kate said truthfully. "I thought this one would last longer."

"So did he, I'm sure." Frankie gave a disdainful sniff. "And why shouldn't he? I cooked his meals, did his shirts and picked up the tab when we went out. And how does the little slime repay me? By screwing his high school sweetheart, that's how."

She gave a vicious kick to the wastebasket and sent it sliding across the room. "Well, I've learned my lesson. I'm done with men." She brushed one palm against the other. *"Finito."*

Kate smiled. At Fairchild Baxter, where Frankie had followed Kate from the prosecutor's office, the secretary's romantic misfortunes had been the subject of constant speculations. Fortunately her frequent heartaches had never interfered with her job. If anything, Frankie was at her best when she was suffering.

Now, as she seemed to put her personal problems aside, she looked at Kate. "Enough about my crappy love life. How did it go today?"

Kate glanced at one of the messages and let out a sigh of frustration. It was from Ed Gibbons. "The judge ruled in favor of Melanie,'' she replied. ''She was awarded full custody of her daughter. The father will have one supervised visit every two months. My bet is that he won't even bother. All he wanted from Melanie was money. He never cared about Prudence.''

A light shiver shook Frankie's shoulders. ''That man gives me the creeps. I'm glad Melanie is rid of him.'' She waited, as if expecting Kate to say something more. When she didn't, she raised an eyebrow and asked the question Kate had expected. ''Did Melanie pay you?''

''She tried. I wouldn't let her.''

Frankie threw her arms up in the air. ''Why? You gave her a break on the fee already. Why couldn't you stick to the agreement the two of you had made— a hundred dollars a week until you were paid in full?''

''Because she works two jobs and used every cent she had to pay for the private investigator I hired to run the background check on her husband. In other words, the woman is broke.''

Frankie rolled her eyes heavenward. ''And you're loaded?''

''I know things are a little tight at the moment—''

''A little tight?'' Frankie took a handful of invoices from her desk and held them up. ''The rent on this palace is due on the fifteenth. So are the bills for the furniture, the computers and the phones. Unless you know a good fairy who's going to add a few zeros to your bank balance, we're in shitville.''

''We'll be okay. I should collect Ed Gibbons's retainer check any day now.''

''Don't count on it.'' Frankie's chin dipped toward

the message Kate still held. "Dollars to doughnuts, that's another postponement." She gave a disapproving shake of her head. "Face it, boss. The guy's a wacko. He gets his kicks from jerking lawyers around."

Before Kate could comment, she added, "A woman called here earlier. She seemed anxious to talk to you, so I sent her to the courthouse. Did you see her?"

"Yes. She caught up with me at the Mall."

Frankie looked at her expectantly. "Prospective client?"

"Her fiancé might be. He's suspected of a murder he claims he didn't commit."

Frankie's mood improved visibly. "Does he have money?"

"From what M.s Van Dyke told me, money is no object."

"Music to my ears." Frankie leaned forward. "So, who'd the guy ice?"

"The victim was his former wife."

"From around here?"

"Alexandria, but the murder took place in Fairfax." She waited for a reaction. When there was none, she added, "The woman was Molly Buchanan."

Frankie's huge, round eyes got even bigger. "Mitch's sister?"

Kate nodded. "Ms. Van Dyke believes her fiancé is innocent. She's willing to give me a one-hundred-thousand-dollar retainer, if I take the case."

Frankie let out a long, slow whistle. "A hundred grand. Wow. That puts you in the big league, boss."

"Yes, well..." Kate glanced at the rest of her messages—four in all. "I haven't given her an answer yet."

"You're worried about Mitch."

"I have good reason to, don't you think?"

"Oh, I don't know," Frankie said confidently. "Mitch is an understanding guy. He won't let business interfere with personal feelings."

An optimistic statement if she'd ever heard one. The problem was, Kate didn't believe a word of it.

Three

Kate sat in one of the deep, teal upholstered chairs in her office and watched the picture on the television screen go in and out of focus for a few seconds before it finally steadied. If she hadn't known the tanned, muscular man with the long blond hair was Todd Buchanan, she would have never recognized him. It wasn't just his appearance that had changed, but his demeanor, as well. After six years as a television sportscaster, no one was more comfortable in front of a camera, or more natural, than Todd Buchanan. Yet, on this tape, he seemed unusually self-conscious, frequently glancing beyond the camera, probably at Jessica, as he tried to find a comfortable position on the sofa where he sat.

"Hi."

His awkward grin brought a smile to Kate's lips. He reminded her of herself when she was being filmed.

"I guess if you've gone this far," he continued, "you know who I am and that I'm suspected of having killed my wife, Molly." He smoothed down his jeans before looking up again. Kate heard a soft prompting, then Todd nodded, cleared his throat and started talking in a stronger, more assertive tone.

"Okay. Here it goes. I've never done this before, so please bear with me."

He looked straight at the camera, his expression serious. "It's no secret that Molly and I weren't getting along. We did at first, but after about a year, she changed and seemed to lose interest in our marriage. She started to go out at night and wouldn't tell me where she went or with whom. She swore she wasn't cheating on me, but when I searched her purse one night, I found a pack of condoms and knew she was lying."

He looked down at his folded hands and fell silent. This time there was no prompting from the other side. After several seconds, Todd looked up, his gaze once again direct, unflinching. "What our housekeeper said to the police was true. Molly and I fought a lot, and we did have an argument the afternoon of the murder. An ugly one that ended with me telling Molly that if she didn't stop acting like a slut, I'd kill her."

His expression remained calm. "I didn't mean it as a threat. I just blurted out the words in a moment of rage, without thinking, without suspecting that less than eight hours later those same words would be used against me."

There was another pause, and this time he did glance to the side, his expression apologetic. "In spite of all you may have heard about me, there is one thing you may not know—not too many people did. I was crazy about Molly. That's why I wouldn't divorce her. I kept hoping that whatever she was going through was just a phase and it would pass. I was wrong. It got worse. If you don't believe me, talk to her best friend, Lynn Flannery. She knew Molly better than anyone. Just be careful with her and take what she says about me with a grain of salt. The woman hates my guts. From the moment she heard about Molly's death, she was determined to make me the fall guy. I wouldn't put it past her if she left out some vital piece of information about Molly that could have led the police to the real killer.

"You may wonder why Molly didn't divorce me herself." He let out a small chuckle. "The truth is, she was as hooked to that sick relationship of ours as I was, partly because she got such kicks out of watching me suffer, and partly because she had gotten used to the money and the good life."

A few seconds passed. "After a while, I pretended that I didn't care and started going out, too, but I never cheated on her. Not even that night when I was so bummed out and said those things to her." He let out a dry laugh. "I wish to God I had cheated. At least I would have had an alibi. But instead, I went out with a friend of mine. We made the usual rounds, bars and strip joints.

"I've no idea how I managed to drive home afterward, but I did. Molly wasn't there, but that was nothing unusual. I went to bed with my clothes on, and at eight o'clock the following morning, the housekeeper woke me up to say that the police were downstairs and wanted to talk to me. That's how I found out that Molly had been killed."

He ran his hand across his mouth, hesitated and then continued, his voice huskier. "She was found in a roadside motel room, her skull fractured. Whoever killed her wiped the place clean. The only fingerprints the police found were Molly's and those of the mo-

tel's maid. I couldn't account for my whereabouts after I left my friend, so the police took me in and
started questioning me.

"They treated me like a murderer right from the
start. Not that I was surprised. I gave those northern
Virginia cops a pretty hard time for a while. So in a
way, they were getting back at me. I knew I was
going straight to jail, so I asked my friend Jake to lie
about the time he and I left that last bar. He couldn't
do it, and I ended up looking even more guilty."

He looked down again. "I know that taking off the
way I did was a stupid thing to do. My father raised
me to believe that sooner or later justice prevailed. I
guess that night I was too afraid to believe it. I made
things worse for myself and I hurt my parents." He
paused. "And my brother. He worked so hard all his
life and he was finally going to be rewarded, and I..."
He shook his head. "I ruined everything for him."

Kate knew what he was referring to. Three weeks
prior to Molly's murder, the newly elected president
of the United States had asked Terrence Buchanan to
become his national security advisor. When the news
of Molly's murder and Todd's disappearance broke,
Terrence withdrew his nomination.

Todd's expression softened as he glanced off-
camera again. "The only good thing that came out of
this mess was Jessica. She's a beautiful woman, inside and out." He laughed, a little self-consciously.
"And damn convincing. But you already know that."

He was serious again. "I know you're in a difficult
position, because of Mitch. He's not an easy person
to deal with, and he loved Molly. But you're my last
hope, Ms. Logan."

Apparently finished, he nodded at the person behind the camera, and the screen went black.

Kate sat in silence for a long time, staring at the blank screen while the tape rewound. After eleven years as an attorney, she had learned to spot a liar from a mile away. A part of her had wanted Todd to lie, because if he had, it would have made her decision a lot easier. If there was one thing she could not tolerate it was a client, or a potential client, lying to her.

Todd Buchanan had surprised her, though. He had stated the facts simply, and, if her instincts were correct, truthfully, which could only mean one thing. Someone else had killed Molly Buchanan.

Not one to make impulsive decisions, Kate decided she needed more facts, and those, she knew, she would find on Nexis, the newspaper database that could, with a click of the mouse, bring up everything ever written about virtually any subject.

She walked back to her desk and booted up her computer. Within moments, she was scrolling through a number of articles, most of them from major newspapers such as the *Washington Post,* the *New York Times* and the *Chicago Tribune.* Normally, the murder of a young woman, even one connected to a wealthy family, wouldn't have attracted national attention. But when that young woman was the daughter-in-law of a United States Supreme Court Justice and that justice's son was a murder suspect, the press quickly picked up the scent of a titillating story.

As expected, the details were all there, confirming what she remembered of the case. As well as questioning Todd, the police had also talked to Lynn Flannery, a furniture designer with a studio on K Street. Molly had worked there for the last two years of her life, in charge of marketing and advertising. Prior to that, she had tried her hand at a little bit of everything—copywriting, public relations, sales. In 1996, she had opened her own PR consulting business, but after a year, and not much to show for her efforts, she had turned her attention elsewhere.

Her hobbies were as diverse as they were numerous. In school, she had been a champion swimmer, an accomplished equestrienne and a sculler. Far from taming her, her marriage to one of Washington's most eligible bachelors had taken her need for adventure to new heights.

Another click, and Kate was reading Justice Buchanan's impressive bio. A former judge on the U.S. Court of Appeals before being appointed to the Supreme Court, Lyle J. Buchanan had the dubious honor of being one of the most hated justices in the history of the Court. He was a tough conservative with an ideology he had inherited from his late father, a district judge, and his grandfather before that. His outspoken views on abortion, prayers in schools and gay rights had generated much anger and so many death threats that the director of the FBI had assigned not one but two FBI agents to guard him at all times. Three months later, annoyed by the inconvenience, he had dismissed them both, saying he could take care of himself. So far he had.

In reading further, Kate learned that the detective in charge of Molly's murder had been Frank Sykes, a veteran of the Fairfax County police force. He was also a friend of Mitch's, which meant he might or might not cooperate.

There were other hurdles. Not the least of them the Buchanans. The attorney they had hired to represent Todd was one of the top litigators on the east coast and a senior partner in a law firm that employed more than a hundred-and-fifty attorneys. Kate could only imagine the Buchanans' reaction when they heard that Todd had hired an attorney who ran a one-woman practice.

The last hurdle was no less intimidating.

Mitch.

With a troubled sigh, Kate stood up, walked over to the window and gazed at the famous dome of the U.S. Capitol. This town was where her romance with Mitch had begun—badly at first because they had been on different sides, she trying to keep her ex-husband from going to prison and Mitch hell-bent on doing exactly the opposite.

But even then their attraction for one another had been undeniable. Kate could still recall his first official visit to her house, his suspicions that she was helping Eric, the subtle way he had warned her, and the way their eyes had locked.

So much had happened since that cold December day, yet she could recall every detail of their budding romance. And of their first night together, the way he had scooped her up in his arms and carried her upstairs to her bedroom. The following morning she had awakened to the rattle of pots and pans and the smell of sizzling bacon.

The sight of Mitch in her kitchen, preparing breakfast, had brought a knot to her throat. When was the last time a man had cooked for her?

It wasn't until days later that he had mentioned Molly, how her death had nearly killed his mother and how he had gone after his sister's killer, traveling to many of the places he believed Todd might have run to, hoping to find him.

And now fate had brought them all together—the man she loved on one side, and the one who needed her on the other.

And Kate in the middle.

At last, she pulled away from the window and went to stand in front of the TV set. After hesitating for a moment, she picked up the remote and pressed play again.

Four

As it turned out, Frankie had been wrong. Ed Gibbons had not called to postpone their meeting but to tell Kate that, after careful consideration, he had decided to hire her.

Now, sitting in his cell, surrounded by grimy walls and the stench of urine, Kate studied her new client—a diminutive, harmless-looking man, except for his bulging eyes that were overly bright and seemed to get even brighter when he was excited. With a slight shiver, she remembered Frankie's words: *He's a wacko, boss. He gets his kicks out of jerking lawyers around.*

He had certainly done that, not just with Kate but with his two previous counsels. The reason she had hung in there until now was that she needed this case, but also that she felt sorry for the man. Although the assistant U.S. attorney claimed that Gibbons was faking his insanity, Kate believed that the computer analyst had a severe problem separating fact from fantasy. A court-appointed psychiatrist had been called to assess his mental condition and had agreed with Kate that Ed Gibbons needed help.

"Thank you for coming." Gibbons fixed her with

that disturbing gaze of his and sat on the cot against the wall, leaving her the only chair.

"I'm your attorney now, Ed. You call, I come." She kept her voice cheerful, hoping to lighten up the charged atmosphere in the cell, but the humor was lost on him.

"Okay." He clasped his hands on his lap. "Let's just get to it, then. You do understand that I didn't kill Pete."

"I understand that you have no recollection of killing him," she said cautiously.

"That's because I didn't do it."

"You told the police you hated him."

"He was a sneak and a dirty thief. He stole money from the business."

"And that made you angry."

Cold black eyes flashed. "Wouldn't you be?"

"Yes," Kate replied in a low, even tone. "Very."

A thin smile appeared at the corner of his mouth as he leaned forward. "I wanted to kill him," he said in a whisper.

Startled, she pressed her back against her chair, away from him. "Is that why you bought a gun on March twenty-eighth? Because you wanted to kill him?"

He didn't flinch. "Are you trying to trick me? Like the other lawyers?"

Kate shook her head. "I'm trying to understand what happened, Ed."

"Why?"

"So that I can prepare a proper defense."

"By telling them I'm crazy?" He had taken a corner of the brown wool blanket and was twisting it, coiling it around his index finger.

Kate kept her gaze on Gibbons and tried not to show her uneasiness. "By showing that you were temporarily out of control. It's your only chance, Ed."

"I don't want to be locked up with a bunch of loonies."

Patiently, Kate explained that if he didn't agree to the plea, he would be locked up, anyway, for a very long time, and with some very unpleasant people. It took her nearly half an hour to convince him, and though there were moments when she felt like walking out, she didn't. By the time she left the jail, it was too late to go back to the office. Briefcase in hand, she headed for the nearest metro station.

Kate let herself into her house, which was much too quiet without Alison, and went directly to the kitchen, inhaling the tantalizing aroma of rosemary chicken roasting in the oven.

Thank God for Maria, she thought, opening the oven door a crack to make sure the bird was cooking properly. On days like these, when an unexpected meeting kept her well beyond her nine-to-five schedule, the loyal housekeeper was a godsend. Even more so when Alison was home, though the thirteen-year-old was beginning to balk at the idea of a baby-sitter.

Humming softly, Kate began setting the table for two in the little kitchen nook that overlooked her small garden. For a moment, she debated eating in the dining room, then changed her mind. Too formal. Mitch liked simplicity.

And this candle, she thought, putting the white taper and the silver holder back into the hutch drawer, reeked of a setup. What she had to discuss with Mitch might be unpleasant, but she wasn't about to sugarcoat the subject by creating a romantic atmosphere before dropping her bomb.

In fact, she wouldn't even wait until after dinner. She'd let him pour the wine and then she would tell him about Jessica's visit. And pray he would keep an open mind.

She was at the sink, scrubbing two baking potatoes, when she heard Mitch come through the front door, which she had left unlocked.

"Mmm...something smells mighty good in here." Strong arms wrapped around her while warm lips nuzzled the back of her neck. "And it ain't the food."

Kate breathed in the scent of Irish Spring. Clean, crisp. "You've been away too long."

"Tell me about it." Another nip. "What happened to our little deal?"

She turned her head sideways and leaned against him a little. "Deal?"

"You weren't supposed to be wearing all these clothes." His hands cupped her breasts.

Kate laughed. "Stop that. You're making me lose my concentration."

His hands moved lower, sliding inside her waistband. "How much concentration does it take to scrub a potato?"

Heat pulsed through her body. "At the moment, more than you know."

She dropped her knife in the sink and turned, wrapping her arms around his hips. He wore snug blue jeans, a red polo shirt open at the neck and a navy jacket that seemed to make his dark blue eyes even bluer. He was tall, a full head taller than her five feet seven inches, and lean, yet there was an underlying strength about him that made him appear as solid as a rock.

They kissed, a long, heated kiss that made her feel as though she ought to rearrange her priorities—fun now, talk later? No. That wouldn't be right. There was no question she wanted him as badly as he wanted her, but her heart wouldn't be fully into love-making when her thoughts were so weighed down.

With a little sigh of regret, she splayed her hands over his chest and gave a gentle push. "I have a chicken waiting to be—"

"Let him get his own girl."

"Be serious. I need to talk to you."

He pulled her back, holding her tight. "Later."

"No." She touched the upturned corner of his mouth, wondering how long that little lopsided smile would last, once he knew how she had spent part of her afternoon. "This can't wait."

"That serious, huh?" After one last kiss, this time on the tip of her nose, he let her go, walked over to the hutch and started rummaging through the drawer. When he found the corkscrew, he opened the bottle of Chardonnay he had brought with him. "Something happened after we talked?"

She watched him pour the wine into two long-stemmed glasses she had set on the counter. He was still smiling, but now those wary blue eyes were a trifle sharper and more attentive. No matter how re-laxed he was, the cop in him was never very far away.

She accepted the glass he handed her and took a fortifying sip. "A woman came to see me today."

"A prospective client?"

She nodded. "She saw that CNN interview I did last week and thought I might be able to help her."

His gaze was lit with curiosity. "What did she do?"

"Nothing. The one who needs my help is her fiancé. Apparently he's the number-one suspect in a murder he says he didn't commit."

Mitch continued to watch her. "So why send his fiancée? Why didn't he come himself?"

Kate's throat felt dry, her chest tight. She took another sip of the wine but couldn't really taste it. "He can't. He's in hiding. He...fled before the police could arrest him."

This time the easygoing smile faded. Silence stretched out. When he spoke again, Mitch's voice was controlled. Not a good sign. "This prospective client has a name?"

The wine wasn't helping, so she put it down. "Todd Buchanan."

Mitch stood very still, his expression now neutral, impossible to read. They stood only a couple of feet from each other, yet suddenly they seemed miles apart.

"Todd Buchanan is here? In Washington?"

"No, his fiancée came alone, and before you ask, I don't know where Todd is."

"What about the woman? What's her name? Where is she staying?"

Although Kate had expected the question, she answered with a small, nervous laugh. "Come on, Mitch. You know I can't tell you that."

"Why the hell not?" She could sense the anger building just below that layer of self-control he was trying to hold on to. "She's an accessory after the fact, and if she and Todd are living together, she's also harboring a fugitive. Did you explain to her the consequences of aiding and abetting?"

"I didn't have to. She knows what she's doing."

He put his glass down without even trying the wine. "What about you, Kate? Do you know what you're doing? You're an officer of the court. You have to tell me where she is."

"No, I don't. First of all, there is a matter of attorney-client privilege—"

"You took him on as a client? Without discussing it with me first?"

"You don't have to shout," she snapped. "I'm not deaf." Then, chastising herself for losing her temper when she had sworn not to, she took a deep breath and counted to five. "No, I didn't take him on as a client. I wanted to talk to you first, calmly and rationally. But I did give Todd's fiancée my word that I would not divulge her name or her whereabouts until she had left Washington."

"Tell me you aren't actually considering representing a cold-blooded murderer."

"Correct me if I'm wrong, but to my recollection Todd Buchanan was never charged with any crime."

"He killed my sister!"

"I don't think he did it, Mitch."

His eyes narrowed. "How did you arrive at that conclusion?"

"Todd's fiancée brought me a videotape Todd made just before she came here. I watched it twice. I didn't want to believe him, either. I wanted to find holes in his story. I expected him to sound insincere, hesitant, even devious. He was none of those things. He's just a frightened man who felt he had no choice but to flee."

"He had a choice. He could have stayed here and faced the charges."

"How could he, when his own attorney didn't believe him?"

Color flooded Mitch's cheeks. "He didn't believe him because Todd's story didn't stand up."

"Or maybe the Fairfax police wanted to nail him for the murder. I never mentioned this to you before, but the consensus at Fairchild Baxter at the time of Todd's questioning was that he wasn't given a fair shake."

"That's bullshit."

"Is it, Mitch? Are you denying that the entire Fairfax police department hated Todd and that Detective Sykes may have been a little too hasty in his conclusion?"

"I won't deny that Todd wasn't one of their favorite people, but to imply that the police would allow their feelings to taint their judgment is ridiculous and insulting. The evidence was there, Kate, cold and damning."

"And completely circumstantial."

His temper flared anew. "He ran, dammit! He couldn't have looked more guilty if he'd been carrying a billboard with the word printed on it in big, bold letters."

"He panicked. He had seen it happen so many times, Mitch, innocent people being put on death row for a crime they didn't commit, only to be released years later with an apology and nothing to look forward to. That's why he ran. Not because he was guilty but because he wanted to survive."

She let a few seconds pass. "May I tell you what he said on that tape, without you blowing my head off?"

She had hoped for a small smile, a warming of that hard blue stare, something to show that he wasn't mad at her, just at the circumstances. Her hopes faded quickly, as Mitch's expression remained stony.

Pushing her wounded feelings aside, she repeated Todd's words to the best of her recollection. She explained why she had slowly begun to believe him and why that feeling had deepened with each passing minute. Todd had nothing to gain by fabricating a lie and coming to her for help, she pointed out. He was happy where he was, and he was safe. If it weren't for his fiancée, he would have never come forward.

There was a long silence broken only by the rhythmic *tic-toc* of the grandfather clock in the foyer. Gently, she asked, "Were you aware that Molly was cheating on him?"

"I read the police report, Kate. He was lying."

"She was dressed in a thong when they found her, Mitch. She had brought champagne and glasses and sex toys with her. She was expecting someone, and it wasn't Todd."

Jamming his hands in his pockets, Mitch leaned against the island and gave her a dark look. "So

Molly wasn't perfect. Did she deserve to be killed because of it?''

"No, but if she was seeing other men, or even one man, don't you think there could be someone else out there with a reason to want her dead? Someone who felt threatened by her?''

"The police looked into that. They didn't find anything. Or anyone. Todd is lying. My God, Kate, you're a smart lawyer—can't you see he's manipulating you?''

The remark almost made her snarl. He knew better than to assume she could so easily be conned. "Give me some credit, will you? I can recognize manipulation when I see it. And when I saw that videotape—''

"A videotape he and his fiancée had probably rehearsed a dozen times.''

Kate shook her head. "I don't believe they did, Mitch. You won't, either, after you see it.''

"I've got a better idea.'' He nodded toward the phone on the wall. "Why don't you call that woman, wherever she is, and tell her you won't be representing her fiancé.''

It wasn't an order, more like an ultimatum. "You want me to turn down the biggest case of my career? At a time when I need it most?''

"Is that what this is all about? Money?''

This time it was she who raised her voice. "No, it's not about money! Although I do have bills to pay and a daughter to support.''

"I offered to help you. You wouldn't let me.''

Kate let out a sigh of sheer frustration. Why was it so difficult for some men, even the good ones, to

understand that financial independence was as important to a woman as it was to a man? "I don't want
your money, Mitch. I want your support." Then, before he could answer, she added, "Look, before the
evening is a total bust, why don't we have dinner,
some harmless conversation, then later, over coffee,
we'll—"

He interrupted her. "You won't back down from
this case?"

"No—"

"Then, forget about dinner," he said rudely. "I
just lost my appetite."

Stunned, Kate watched him storm out of the
kitchen. Seconds later, the front door slammed shut.

Five

With the Panthers playing away from home tonight, the boys' gym on Kalorama Road in the Adams-Morgan section of Washington was empty. That suited Mitch just fine. In fact, a little solitude was the reason he had headed straight here after storming out of Kate's house.

Using his own key, he let himself in and flicked the switch on the wall. The basketball court, with its gleaming hardwood floor and three rows of bleachers on both sides, was immediately flooded with bright overhead lights.

This was the one place where Mitch felt truly at home. Here he could unwind after a long shift, play out his frustrations, or, if he was lucky, even work out a problem or two. Knowing he had financed the indoor court made the place even more special.

The idea of doing something worthwhile for underprivileged boys had come to him three years ago, when he had left his lucrative employment at Vargas Worldwide Investigations and returned to Washington with more money than he would ever spend in a lifetime. Rather than move to tony Georgetown, as one Realtor had suggested, he had chosen this lively, ethnic neighborhood with its smorgasbord of people and culture, each more fascinating than the next. On moving day, he had met Timothy O'Malley—Father Tim to his parishioners. The two men had quickly become friends, and it wasn't long after that that Mitch offered to finance a gym for the troubled boys the young priest counseled.

At first the teens, who had made a career of popping in and out of juvenile court, had been suspicious of the cop whose motives they didn't understand. Then little by little, as Mitch had volunteered his time, coaching basketball and showing up at their games, the boys eventually learned not only to accept Mitch but to trust him, the same way they trusted Father Tim.

Still feeling the tension of his argument with Kate, Mitch grabbed one of the balls lined up against the wall and started the familiar routine—dribble, aim, shoot, dribble, aim, shoot.

He tried to keep his mind blank, concentrating on the ball. But in spite of his determination, his thoughts drifted back to Kate and the way she had looked standing in her kitchen, her red hair gleaming in the overhead light, her green eyes wide with shock at his angry reaction.

The fifteen-minute drive to Adams-Morgan hadn't helped. He was still angry. No big surprise there. For the past two years, he had obsessed over finding Todd Buchanan and bringing him back to Washington. Now the only person who could make that happen was Kate. And she wasn't talking.

He took another shot, but tonight his aim was off. The ball hit the backboard with a loud *thud,* missed the basket and bounced back to him.

I should have killed the bastard when I had the chance.

He would have, if they hadn't stopped him.

Mitch had been out on a case when his friend Tom Spivak at Metro PD had called him with the news that Molly had been found murdered in a roadside motel. Mitch had gone straight to the police station in Fairfax, Virginia, where Todd was being questioned.

Driven by sheer rage, he had grabbed Todd by the shirt collar, thrown him against the wall and pummeled his face with his fists. He would have killed him, if two officers hadn't intervened.

Twenty-four hours later, arrest warrant in hand, the police had returned to the Buchanans' house in Alexandria. It was too late. Todd was gone.

Undeterred, Mitch had taken a leave of absence from Metro PD and embarked on a time-consuming, exhaustive hunt, flying to his brother-in-law's favorite haunts—Belize, Acapulco, Jamaica. He had talked to dozens of people, visited every luxury hotel he could think of and waited patiently for someone to point him in the right direction.

But the break he had been hoping for never came. Three weeks after leaving Washington, he had returned home defeated—but still hopeful that someday Todd would pay for killing Molly.

"Is this a private game, or can anyone play?"

At the sound of Tim's voice, Mitch turned. "Hello, Tim."

Tim O'Malley was a handsome young man with curly black hair, a dazzling smile and the patience of a saint. "I saw the light from the rectory," he said, catching the ball Mitch threw him. "And figured it had to be you."

"How did the boys do?"

"They lost, but Jamal scored eighteen points and T.J. fourteen, so the team is in good spirits." He aimed the ball and sank the shot. "What about you? What brings you here at this time of night?" As Mitch caught the ball on the rebound, Tim stole it from him and dribbled away. "Problems?" he asked, when Mitch didn't answer.

"You could say that."

"In that case—" he charged the basket, doing a perfect layup "—why don't we go to the rectory and talk? Mrs. Sorensen stopped by this afternoon with another pound cake—the kind you like, with the lemon icing on top."

Mitch smiled as he walked back to the bench to pick up his jacket. St. John may be a modest parish, but its people knew how to take care of their priest. Not a day went by without one of them repaying Tim for the many services he rendered throughout the year. As a result, the rectory was always clean and orderly, the pantry full, and every appliance in perfect working order.

"Padre, you've got yourself a deal. Anything is better than watching you show off."

Tim laughed. "You're just jealous."

The rectory was a plain, square brick building with a fully equipped kitchen, a living room that doubled as an office and a small bedroom in the back.

Over hot tea and generous slices of Mrs. Sorensen's pound cake, Mitch confided in his friend, knowing their conversation wouldn't go any further.

Tim listened quietly, waiting until Mitch was finished before pushing his plate away. "Feel better now that you've vented all those frustrations?" he asked.

"Not really. And if you're about to tell me that I'm being unreasonable, save your breath."

Tim smiled. "Oh, I would never accuse you of being unreasonable. Hotheaded, perhaps. Passionate, certainly. Maybe even impulsive, but not unreasonable. The fact that you're here, discussing the problem, proves you're already weighing both sides of the situation."

"There's only one side—the side of the law."

Tim picked up a cake crumb with his finger and ate it. "You don't think Kate has a professional obligation to take this case? She is, after all, a defense attorney."

"Kate can't resist being the champion of the underdog. The only reason she is considering taking the case is that she feels sorry for Todd's fiancée."

"So she's compassionate."

"And stubborn."

"But not foolish. You yourself have praised her investigative skills, her commitment to her profession, her undisputable integrity." He glanced at his friend. "Not to mention that she's an excellent judge of character. At least, from my standpoint."

"When she doesn't let her emotions get in the way."

"What about you, old friend? Are *your* emotions getting in the way?"

"Molly was my kid sister. I'm entitled to be emotional about her killer."

Tim nodded. "Yes, I suppose you are. But feeling

angry and frustrated shouldn't keep you from being objective. I think that's all Kate really wants from you, Mitch. She's not asking you to write Todd off as a suspect. She's asking you to consider the possibility that there may be another.''

Mitch drank his tea in silence, too stubborn to admit that Tim might have a point. Yet, as he drove home half an hour later, his friend's words kept drifting in and out of his mind, refusing to be ignored. And if the woman he loved, the woman whose opinion he respected, thought Todd Buchanan might be innocent, shouldn't he at least look into the matter? If for nothing more than to prove she was wrong.

Back at the town house, he went straight to his bedroom, where he found the police report on Molly's murder in a bureau drawer. Then he propped himself against the bed pillows, which smelled of Kate's perfume, and, fully clothed, he started to read.

In the two hours since Mitch had stormed out of Kate's house, she had called him twice, once at home and once on his cell phone. Both calls had remained unanswered, as had her two messages.

Now, standing in her kitchen, a mug of hot chocolate in her hand, she stared at the wall clock, aware that Jessica Van Dyke's plane would be leaving shortly. She could almost see the young woman sitting at her departure gate, glancing anxiously at her watch, perhaps checking her cell phone to make sure it was turned on. How many times had Kate been in a similar situation, sitting in her office on pins and needles, waiting for a verdict call to come in? Or that awful day four months ago when she had waited to hear the fate of her kidnapped daughter. She knew, better than anyone, how agonizing waiting could be.

Picking up the kitchen extension beside the refrigerator, she glanced at the number Jessica had given her and dialed it, not at all surprised when the phone was answered on the first ring.

"Hello?"

"Jessica, this is Kate. I'm sorry I waited so long to call. There were...complications."

"Mitch?"

"Yes."

There was a short silence before Jessica said hesitantly, "Does that mean you've decided not to help us?"

"No, not at all. I am taking the case, Jessica."

Kate heard the sigh of relief at the other end. "Thank you," Jessica said in a whisper. "Thank you so much."

Kate glanced at her watch. "I know you'll be boarding soon, so I'll make this brief. Would you ask Todd to call me? I'll need to talk to him on a regular basis, to let him know how I'm progressing."

"I'll tell him."

"It's best if he calls me on my cell phone." She gave the number and waited until Jessica had written it down. "Tell him to call me on Saturday at noon—my time. Is that possible?"

"Yes, no problem."

"That's all, then—for now. Have a safe flight, Jessica."

"I will. Thanks again."

Kate slowly replaced the phone in its cradle. There,

the decision had been made. Good or bad, she would have to live with the consequences.

She prayed that those consequences would not include losing Mitch.

Six

By noon the following day, one-hundred-thousand dollars had been electronically transferred from a Swiss bank into Kate's checking account at First Security. A beaming Frankie had given her the good news, adding, "I've got good vibes about this case, boss. It's going to put you on the map. Mark my words."

Her enthusiasm had strengthened Kate's resolve, if not her spirits. Mitch still hadn't called, and though the phone was like a magnet, begging her to pick it up, she didn't. If time was what he needed to realize what an ass he was, so be it. She had her own problems to worry about. And right now, a case to investigate.

First on her agenda was Detective Frank Sykes, who, fortunately, was on duty and at his desk when she arrived at the Fairfax County police station a half hour later.

The detective, whom she had met through Mitch last year, greeted her warmly. "Kate," he said, rising from behind his desk, as she walked in. "What a pleasant surprise." He was a medium-framed man with graying blond hair and heavy bags under very sharp brown eyes. As always, he wore a string tie and one of his pearl-button shirts. Having lived in Texas during his youth, he had never gotten the Lone Star State out of his system. Even his accent still held a trace of Southern drawl. It was J. R. Ewing without the Stetson.

"Can I get you anything?" he asked. "A cup of coffee? Some tea?"

"Nothing, thank you." She gave him a sweet smile. "All I want is your cooperation, Frank."

"All right, then, pretty lady." He waited until she was seated before returning to his chair. "You just tell ol' Frank what you need, and then consider it done."

"For starters, you could give me a copy of the police report on Molly Buchanan's murder."

He raised an eyebrow. "Molly? Why?"

"I'm investigating the case."

This time Sykes frowned. "On whose behalf?"

There wasn't much sense in not answering the question. The news that she was representing his prime suspect would be out soon enough. "Todd Buchanan."

"I see." He was silent for a moment while he digested the information. "Does Mitch know?"

"Yes."

"Then, you don't mind if I give him a call?"

She would have much preferred informing Mitch of her decision to take Todd's case herself, but thanks to his pigheaded attitude, that wasn't an option. "No, not at all."

Kate listened to Frank's side of the conversation, which was brief, and hoped Mitch wouldn't put a stumbling block between her and the detective. She didn't think he would, but in the mood he had been in last night, anything was possible.

"What did he say?" she asked, when Frank hung up.

"In his own words, 'Give the lady what she wants.'"

Relieved, Kate leaned back in her chair and watched Frank pick up the phone again and punch a number.

"Eddy, this is Frank," he said in a brisk, businesslike tone. "Make me a copy of the file on Molly Buchanan, will you? Yes, the photographs, too. We have an extra set somewhere. Thanks.

"What's going on, Kate?" he asked after he hung up. "Why would you want to represent a scumbag like Todd Buchanan when you know as well as I do that he killed Mitch's sister?"

"That's just the point. I don't think he did."

"I investigated the case myself. Todd is guilty as hell."

"Isn't it possible that certain details were overlooked?"

"What kind of details?"

"A newspaper photograph shows that the motel parking lot is divided by several grassy strips, one of them directly in front of room 12. Someone in a hurry could have crossed that strip in order to get to his car faster. Were footprints found? Or didn't anyone bother to check?"

She saw him bristle. "I know how to conduct a crime scene investigation, Kate, but since you seem to doubt my abilities, yes, I did check. Unfortunately, we didn't find any footprints."

"What about bloodstains on Todd's clothing? Or in his car?"

"Todd hadn't been arrested at the time of his questioning. Therefore we had no legal right to seize his clothing or search his car. If we had done it, the evidence obtained would have been inadmissible in court."

"But you did get a search warrant after he fled."

"Yes." He waited a couple of seconds before reluctantly admitting, "We found no evidence of bloodstains, in his car or on his clothing."

So the Fairfax police hadn't been as lax as she had first suspected. In fact, if Frank was telling her the truth—and she had no reason to believe otherwise—they had been quite thorough.

A knock at the door made her look up. A uniformed officer with a blond brush cut and freckles dropped a thick file on Frank's desk. "Here you are, Frank. Need anything else?"

"Not right now." Frank opened the file, shuffled through several typed pages and a dozen or so black-and-white photographs, before closing the folder and handing it to Kate.

"Thank you." She set the folder aside. "Would you mind answering one more question?"

"Shoot."

"What makes you so certain Todd is guilty, when all you really have is circumstantial evidence?"

"The evidence may be circumstantial, but it was enough for a judge to issue an arrest warrant. For God's sake, the guy asked his friend to *lie* for him so he'd have an alibi."

"That was a stupid mistake. He was scared."

"And fleeing the country? Was that another stupid mistake?" He shook his head. "No, Kate. That was a well thought-out, perfectly executed escape, one he probably had planned before he even killed his wife, just in case we didn't buy his little act."

He leaned forward, his gaze suddenly hard. "Now let me ask *you* a question. Do you know where Todd Buchanan is?"

"No."

"You expect me to believe that?"

"Just as much as you expect me to believe you went by the book."

She caught the brief twitch at the corner of his mouth. "Touché."

She tucked Molly's folder into her briefcase and snapped the lid shut. "Thanks again, Frank."

"You're welcome." He started to walk her out the door, but the phone on his desk rang.

"Go ahead and answer it," Kate said. "I'll see myself out."

Sitting at his desk, Mitch kept gazing at the phone, thinking about the brief conversation he'd just had with Frank Sykes. Kate certainly hadn't wasted any time—in making her decision about Todd, or in starting her investigation.

But why should he be surprised? Kate wasn't the type to drag her feet. And it didn't take a rocket scientist to see how badly she wanted to take the case, or how committed she already was to a client she hadn't even met.

He'd been awake half the night, reading and re-reading the police report, studying the photographs of his dead sister. What in God's name had she been doing in that motel, dressed like that? Who had she been waiting for?

By the time he finally turned off the light, he had convinced himself he was partly to blame for Molly's death. If he hadn't been so damn preoccupied with his job and paid a little more attention to his kid sister's problems, maybe she wouldn't have ended up dead in some sleazy motel. He had known her marriage was on shaky ground, so why hadn't he done something about it?

He glanced at the yellow pad beside him and the three names he had jotted down last night—Syd Willard, Todd's former attorney; Mike Banaki, the night clerk at the Lost Creek Motel, and Jake Weitz, Todd's drinking buddy the night of the murder.

All three had made sworn statements to the police. Even if Mitch questioned them again, what more could they say? Yet, he had written their names down and gone to the trouble of finding out their current addresses. Why?

He felt a vague sense of déjà vu about all this. He had been in this position before, unwilling to help Kate and at the same time compelled to do so.

Not this time. No matter how badly he felt about storming out of her house and not answering her calls, he wouldn't let her sucker him into joining forces with her again. If she wanted to waste her time on a hopeless quest, that was her business. But he would not help her. He had too much to do—three unsolved homicides, a court testimony to prepare for and a report to type.

He picked up his pencil and with a point that he

had sharpened while he'd talked to Frank, he began tapping over the three names, little stabs that left black marks on the paper.

After a full minute of this, he threw the pencil down, then, with a groan of frustration, he picked up the phone to call Todd's former attorney, Syd Willard.

Back in her office, Kate kicked off her shoes and propped her aching feet on the little stool she kept under her desk. She opened the file on Molly Buchanan. One of the first statements was from Adele Houser, the Buchanans' maid. She had told Frank Sykes about the frequent arguments between Molly and Todd, and had quoted, word for word, that infamous threat made the day of the murder.

The motel clerk's statement was there, as well, though he hadn't had much to say other than that the room had been paid for in cash by the victim. He remembered her vividly because of her long, platinum hair, which covered the entire right side of her face, and her dark red, shiny lipstick. A film noir buff, he had been reminded of Veronica Lake, the *femme fatale* actress who, back in the 1940s, had made the peekaboo hairstyle as famous as her name. Twenty minutes later, Banaki was about to step out for a cigarette break, when a shadowy figure hurried out of room 12. He hadn't thought anything of it at the time. In his establishment, men and women coming in and out of their rooms at all hours of the night was hardly an oddity.

As for the man himself, all the motel clerk could recall was that he was of average height and weight.

Kate made a mental note to talk to Mike Banaki soon. At the same time, she jotted down Lynn Flannery's address. Molly's best friend was a well-known furniture designer with numerous awards to her credit and exhibits in several major U.S. cities.

Questioned the day after the murder, she told the police that Todd was insanely jealous, even violent, backing her allegations with the claim that Molly had showed up at Lynn's studio one day, her face badly bruised, and told Lynn that Todd had beaten her up. Lynn had immediately taken photographs of Molly, hoping her friend would use them against Todd. When the police had searched the Buchanans' house and Molly's office at Flannery Designs, however, they hadn't found a single photo.

Kate stopped reading and bit on the end of her pencil. Todd had made no mention of a beating. A deliberate omission? she wondered. Or was Lynn Flannery lying?

There were other statements, as well, from Todd's family—his parents and his older brother, Terrence Buchanan. It was clear, at least to Kate, that Detective Sykes had gone out of his way to spare the Buchanans embarrassment and unwanted publicity. And he had made no reference to an unfounded rumor that Justice Buchanan might have helped his son escape.

The police photos, all taken at the crime scene, showed Molly sprawled across the bed, on her stomach with her face turned to the side, her eyes wide open. She had died instantly, from severe trauma to the head.

Molly had worn nothing except a thong and black high-heel boots. On the nightstand stood the murder weapon—a bottle of Dom Pérignon that had been wiped clean, as had other areas of the bedroom.

The champagne had been traced to a liquor store on Leesburg Pike, where the owner remembered the woman who had bought it—a "hot little number" with long blond hair, a black leather coat and leather boots.

The last photograph was a close-up of a chair with a number of bondage items displayed on the cracked vinyl seat. The assortment of handcuffs, whips, blindfolds and a studded leather choker left no doubt as to what kind of games Molly had been into.

With a sigh, Kate closed the file. Feeling a headache coming on, she pressed her eyelids with her thumb and forefinger and stayed that way until the intercom on her desk buzzed. It was Frankie, reminding her that Alison would be landing in a little over an hour.

Excited at the thought of seeing her daughter, Kate tucked the folder in a drawer, grabbed her purse and hurried out of her office.

Seven

Kate stood on her tiptoes and watched the throng of travelers walk out of Customs and into the busy terminal at Dulles International Airport. After what felt like an eternity, Alison finally appeared, followed by Megan. Behind them, a deeply tanned Eric, looking very dapper in gray trousers and a navy blazer, struggled to keep a cart piled high with designer luggage on a straight path.

"Alison!" Kate waved frantically to catch her daughter's attention.

"Mom!"

Kate pushed her way through the crowd and embraced her daughter. "Oh, baby, I've missed you so much." She held her at arm's length. "Look at you. You're almost as tall as I am."

"It's the platform shoes." Alison held out her right foot to show a black clog with a three-inch platform. "See?"

In one quick sweep, Kate's motherly gaze went from the shoes to the orange miniskirt and Alison's very blond hair.

"You're looking at my hair," Alison said with a laugh. "Do you like it?" She fluffed it with her hand.

"Megan took me to the beauty parlor to have it high-lighted."

Megan, who had stood quietly aside during the mother-and-daughter reunion, came forward, a smile on her lips. Tall and almost too thin, Megan Holl-brook was rather plain-looking, though she had a lovely smile and an inner beauty that made her lack of good looks totally unimportant.

"Hello, Kate." She gave Kate a hug. "It's all right, isn't it? About Alison's hair, I mean. When she saw Candace with her highlights, she had to have them, too."

"I suppose so," Kate said reluctantly, annoyed that the decision to dye Alison's hair had been made by her twenty-seven-year-old stepmom. And without Kate's approval. "It's just that…it makes her look so much older."

"That's what I said." Eric stopped to catch his breath. "But Megan swore to me the dye job would go away in six weeks."

"It's not a dye job, Daddy," Alison corrected. "I had a few strands highlighted, that's all. Why is everyone making such a big deal about it?"

"Yes," Kate said brightly. "Why, indeed." She gave her daughter's waist a squeeze. "You look lovely, Alison." Then, her gaze sweeping over the swarm of travelers that kept pouring out of Customs, she added, "Where is Candace?"

Alison turned, just as a stunning-looking girl with long blond hair, too much makeup and a skirt that was even shorter than Alison's walked out, her arms around the waist of a handsome, dark-haired young man.

"There she is. I'll introduce you, Mom. That is, if I can pull her away from Dimitri."

"Dimitri?"

"He's an exchange student she met in Tortola. He'll be going to Georgetown University, so I guess they'll be seeing a lot of each other." She waited until Candace had reached them before making the introductions.

Kate shook hands with the girl and with Dimitri, and learned that Candace's father, a London-based IBM executive, had been transferred to Washington but would be staying in England until July. Eager to join an American school, Candace had elected to come ahead of her parents and stay with Megan and Eric.

"Isn't that great?" Alison said excitedly. "Now I can see her every day if I want to."

Kate managed a smile. The prospect of Alison, who was only thirteen, developing a close friendship with a precocious sixteen-year-old didn't thrill her in the least. But now was not the time to show her disapproval.

"It was a pleasure to meet you both," she said to Candace and Dimitri. Turning to Megan, she added, "Thank you for inviting Alison on the trip, Megan. And for taking such good care of her. This will be a spring break she'll never forget."

"We loved having her," Megan said with a sincerity Kate didn't doubt. "In fact..." She threw Eric a quick look. "Now that my niece is here, we were wondering if Alison could stay with us on weekends. I didn't think you'd mind, since you so often work on Saturdays."

Kate felt a stab of annoyance. The truth was, she liked the visitation arrangements with Eric just as they were—two weekends a month, two weeks in the summer and Christmas Eve, unless something came up, such as the Caribbean cruise. To her knowledge, Eric had never had any problems with the schedule. In fact, before he married Megan, he hadn't been very good at fulfilling his fatherly obligations, always coming up with one reason or another why he couldn't see his daughter. Megan, on the other hand, possessed a strong sense of family values, even though she was a single child.

"Oh, Mom, can I?" Alison gave Kate one of her cute, pretty-please smiles.

"Why don't we discuss it later?" Kate said diplomatically. "Right now, I'm sure everyone is anxious to get home."

Taking hold of Alison's suitcase, which Eric had pulled out of the pile, she gave them all a bright smile and steered her daughter toward the exit.

"Alison, will you please slow down," Kate said with a laugh. "You make me dizzy just watching you."

Seated on Alison's bed, Kate watched her daughter pull out clothes from her suitcase and throw them helter-skelter across the bed.

"I told you I'm looking for something. Ah, here it is—" Grinning, she handed Kate a flat square box, tied with a yellow ribbon.

"For me?"

"Of course for you. Open it."

Knowing how much Alison loved giving presents,

Kate quickly untied the ribbon and opened the box. At the sight of the contents, she let out an exclamation. "Oh, Alison, it's beautiful." She took the lovely pink and gray silk scarf out of the box and held it in front of her. "Those are my favorite colors."

"I know. I picked it all by myself," Alison said proudly.

"I want to say you shouldn't have, but I won't. I love it too much."

"Good." Alison dove into the suitcase again. "And this—" she said, taking another package, "is for Grandma. Megan helped me with that one." She dug deeper and came up with two more packages. "This one is for Maria. And this one," she said, holding a small gold box, "is for Mitch." Her eyes glistened with happiness. "It's a set of silver cuff links with an antique African design on them."

Kate's smile faded. "Silver cuff links? They must have been very expensive."

Alison shrugged. "Megan gave me the money. Do you think Mitch will like them?"

"I'm sure he will." Kate made a mental note to speak with Megan again.

"Can we call him and ask him to come over? I thought he'd be at the airport with you."

Kate averted her eyes. She had wondered when Alison would come around to asking about Mitch. "He's working tonight," she improvised. "But I'm sure he'll stop by very soon."

"I can't wait to show him the shells I brought back." She put the little gold box on her bureau next to the other packages. "Mom, about you and Mitch..."

Kate started to gather the dirty clothes Alison had tossed on the bed. "What about Mitch and me?"

"Before I left for the BVI, I heard you tell Maria that you didn't have a lot of time together."

"I wasn't aware you were listening."

"I didn't mean to eavesdrop, Mom, honest." She emptied the rest of her suitcase, looking very grown-up. And very tall. "And you were right. You and Mitch don't have a lot of time together."

"That's because we're both very busy. Mitch has irregular hours and I have a new practice—"

"I know." She beamed. "And I have the solution."

"You do?"

"Yes. I could go and live part of the year, say six months, with Dad and Megan. That way, you and Mitch could have all sorts of time together and not worry when I'm going to pop into the room and spoil everything for you."

No doubt Alison was referring to that afternoon, shortly before Christmas, when she had caught Kate and Mitch kissing under the mistletoe. All three had felt a little awkward for a while, until Mitch, with his usual flair, had said something silly and made Alison laugh.

"You've never spoiled anything for me, Alison."

"But wouldn't you like to have a little more privacy sometimes?"

"No, I wouldn't. I like things just as they are."

"But—"

"In the first place," Kate continued, "there's the matter of your school."

"That's not a problem. Megan already said she would drive me."

"You've discussed this with Megan?" Kate asked, unable to conceal her annoyance.

"Only after I found out that Candace would be staying with them. And I talked to Daddy, too. He said that if it was okay with you, then it was okay with him."

It was time to put her foot down, firmly. "Well, it's not okay with me, Alison. Your visits to your father's house will remain just as they are."

"Why?" Alison whined.

"Because I'm your mother and I said so." Then, before Alison could tell her what a dumb answer that was, she tucked the pile of dirty clothes under one arm and wrapped the other around her daughter's shoulders. "It's our first evening together in ten long days, so let's not fight, okay? I made a wonderful homecoming dinner—lamb chops with those French paper hats you like so much." She had looked all over Washington for those little suckers and couldn't resist a little bragging.

Totally unresponsive, Alison followed her down the stairs.

Eight

By morning, Alison was in a slightly better mood, excited at the prospect of going back to school and telling all her friends about her trip.

As Kate was getting ready herself, she turned her thoughts to her new case—Molly Buchanan's murder—and how she would proceed in her investigation. Since she still hadn't heard from Mitch and obviously couldn't count on his help, she would have to call on her ex-mother-in-law, Rose Fairchild. Before Douglas was arrested for fraud and conspiracy to commit murder, Rose had been an active member of several organizations. Particularly close to her heart was Children's Hospital, where she had served as fund-raising chairman for many years. And if Kate's memory was correct, Hallie Buchanan had served on that committee, as well.

Hopeful that Rose could help her, Kate waited until Alison had boarded her bus, then walked back inside to call Rose.

Twenty minutes later, she sat in her car, gazing at the imposing white colonial she had once called home. She had spent eleven years in that house—some good, some bad—until she hadn't been able to ignore Eric's blatant infidelity anymore and walked out. She hadn't wanted to move into the Fairchild mansion in the first place. Like all newlyweds, she had expected she and Eric would start their married life in their own apartment, no matter how modest. Eric, who had lived in Douglas's house since he was fifteen, had been adamant about staying there.

"Why should we struggle to make ends meet," he had said with his very own brand of logic, "when we can live here, in the lap of luxury—for free?"

And while Douglas had nothing but contempt for his lazy, opportunistic stepson, he, too, had insisted the newlyweds live with them.

"It makes perfect sense to me," he had told Kate. "Potomac is only a twenty-minute drive from Washington. Besides," he had added with a fatherly wink, "I want you close to me, Kate, so that I may better convince you to come and work for me after you graduate from law school."

It wasn't until a little over a year ago, when she had caught Eric in *flagrante delicto* with a buxom blonde, that she decided she'd had enough. Ignoring his claims the girl meant nothing to him, Kate had packed her and Alison's belongings, moved out of the Fairchilds' house and immediately filed for divorce.

That first year as a single mother had been more difficult than anything Kate had ever experienced, especially since Alison blamed Kate for the breakup and found new ways of challenging her at every turn.

As the memories slowly faded, she stepped out of the car and headed for the house. As expected, Rose had taken advantage of this unusually warm March day to putter around her garden. Her knees on a green cushion, she was weeding a flower bed already blooming with brilliant purple and yellow pansies.

The ordeal with Douglas had changed her. Always a little plump, Rose was thinner now, and the lines around her eyes were more pronounced, making her look older than her sixty-two years. Deep down, though, she was still the same person Kate knew and loved—warm, generous and supportive.

At the sound of Kate's footsteps on the graveled path, she looked up, squinting against the sun. The frown quickly gave way to a smile Kate knew was completely genuine. Though devastated by the role her husband had played in the scandal that had rocked Washington four months earlier, she was deeply grateful to Kate for clearing Eric of a murder charge.

"There you are!" Rose exclaimed. Grunting a little, she braced her hands on her knees and pushed herself up. "Did Alison get back all right?"

Kate kissed her on the cheek. "Yes. And she looks radiant—tanned, bubbly, and I swear an inch taller."

Eyes the same blue as Eric's danced with amusement. "She's only been gone ten days, Kate. She couldn't possibly have grown that much." She motioned toward a patio table shaded by a white Italian market umbrella. "I know this weather can't last, but shall we pretend it's summer and ask Joseph to make us some iced tea? He's always complaining he doesn't have enough to do these days."

Joseph was the Fairchilds' faithful man-of-all-trades—butler, housekeeper, cook and chauffeur. Alison adored him. And so did Kate. "Maybe some other time, Rose. I can't stay long."

Rose removed her gardener's gloves and gave her

former daughter-in-law a sidelong look. "What's wrong, dear? You look troubled."

Kate chuckled. "It's that obvious, huh?"

"It is to me, but then, I know you better than most people, don't you think?" She moved her chair so she wouldn't be in the sun. "It's not Mitch, is it?"

Was that a random guess? Kate wondered, or did she actually have the word *heartbroken* pasted on her forehead? "No," she said. "It's not Mitch."

"Alison?"

Kate let out an involuntary sigh. "What's that saying?" she said quietly. "How are you going to keep them down on the farm now that they've seen Paris?"

"Ah." Rose nodded. "You're afraid that after cruising the Caribbean with Eric and Megan, she'll find Cleveland Park a little...bland?"

"Something like that."

"You're not giving your daughter enough credit, Kate. In the first place, Alison is no longer the little brat she was at the time of your divorce from Eric. In the second place, she adores you. No matter how much fun she had on her trip, I know she's glad to be home."

"She wants to live with Eric and Megan six months out of the year," Kate said flatly.

"What?"

At Rose's startled expression, Kate nodded grimly. "That was my reaction exactly."

"But what brought that on? Was it Eric? Did he put her up to this?"

"No. Alison is the one who came up with the idea. And, of course, Eric didn't do anything to discourage her. On the contrary, he told her that if it was okay with me, then it was okay with him.''

Rose gave a disapproving shake of her head. ''I can't believe him. He and Megan don't have the faintest idea how to raise a thirteen-year-old girl.'' She brought her gaze back to Kate. ''Do you want me to talk to him?''

Kate was tempted to say yes. Even though Eric seldom took his mother's advice and had made tons of mistakes as a result, he listened to what she had to say, and occasionally, she got through to him. This particular problem, however, was one Kate preferred to handle on her own.

''I'd better talk to him myself. You know how he is. He'll think we're conspiring. And, anyway, I didn't come here to bend your ear about Alison. I need your help with something.''

''Of course.''

''What can you tell me about Lyle and Hallie Buchanan?''

Rose laughed. ''They ain't the Waltons.''

Kate smiled. It was good to see that Rose was beginning to regain her sense of humor. ''Strange people?''

''Not strange. Just...complicated.''

''You are still on the fund-raising committee for Children's Hospital, aren't you?''

''Yes. That's one thing I could not bring myself to give up after Douglas was arrested.''

''And if I recall, Hallie Buchanan serves on that same committee.''

''Served. Past tense. She resigned shortly after her daughter-in-law was murdered. I suspect she didn't want to have to answer questions that were bound to pop up. And they do, believe me," she said with a knowing look.

"So you know her well."

"We spent a lot of time together during her years as program chairman, but I wouldn't say I know her well."

"Did she ever talk to you about the murder? Or her son fleeing?"

"No, and I didn't ask. She and Lyle value their privacy, even more than Douglas and I did. Neither ever gossiped, and they expected as much from others."

That was true. Kate remembered a news broadcast showing Justice Buchanan at the cemetery, helping his wife into a limousine. The press had been there, waiting for a statement, a word or two they could have used on the six o'clock news. He had given them nothing. Not even when a reporter had suggested that Todd might have been framed by one of Lyle's many enemies.

"On the other hand," Rose continued, "if you want rumors, I have plenty of those."

Kate leaned forward. "What kind of rumors?"

Rose watched her intently. "Why the sudden interest in the Buchanans, Kate?"

"I'm investigating Molly's murder."

Rose's eyes grew wide. "Oh, dear." Then, as the initial shock wore off, she added, "Why?"

"Because I've been asked to."

"I see." There was a short pause before she asked the same question Detective Sykes had asked. "Does Mitch know?"

"Yes. He wasn't very happy about it." She didn't tell Rose that he had walked out and she still hadn't heard from him.

"Well, I'll be glad to help you in any way I can, though a lot of what I know is just someone else's opinion."

"I'll keep that in mind."

Rose was thoughtful for a moment. "Like I said, Hallie was always very private, but from what I heard here and there, neither she nor Lyle were very fond of Molly. They tolerated her because she was Todd's wife, but that was about it. The girl was a bit of a wildcat, you know, and didn't fit the Buchanans' image of a daughter-in-law."

"Todd was no saint himself."

"Ah, but Todd was the prodigal son. He could do no wrong. At least, in his father's eyes. Hallie told me that much herself, in a rare moment of frustration. She frowned on the fact that Lyle brushed off Todd's escapades with a 'boys will be boys' attitude, which was quite different from the way he had brought up his older son, Terrence."

"Did Terrence resent Todd for getting away with so much?"

"Oh, I don't think so. Terrence was always the most sensible one of the two. And, anyway, Hallie made sure Terrence was compensated in other ways. He was *her* favorite, you know. She would do anything for that boy."

"I see."

Rose rolled her eyes. "The way she talked about him. Terrence this, Terrence that. She was convinced he would run for president someday, and win. Needless to say, she was devastated when he lost that wonderful opportunity.''

''You mean the Cabinet position as national security advisor.''

Rose nodded. ''That was a crushing blow to Terrence, but an even greater one to Hallie—though I must say, she was gracious about the whole thing. Much more so than her husband, who was very critical of the new administration.''

''You don't like Justice Buchanan?''

''I don't like what he did when Todd was about to be arrested.''

''What did he do?''

''You know.'' She leaned forward and lowered her voice, as though she was afraid to be overheard. ''Some believe he helped Todd escape.''

''Oh, Rose, I doubt that's true. The press probably started that rumor, hoping it would incite Justice Buchanan to come forward and talk about his son's disappearance. When the ploy didn't work, the rumor stopped.''

''But if it *is* true,'' Rose insisted, ''he and Todd would be responsible for what happened to poor Terrence. I don't think the nomination would have been withdrawn if his younger brother had stayed to face trial, do you?''

''That's hard to say.''

Rose had painted a lovely picture of Terrence Buchanan, the older brother who had so stoically accepted his misfortune. Wouldn't it be interesting, she thought as she drove back to town, to see if that picture held true or if it was just a put-on.

Nine

Kate had just reached the outskirts of Washington, D.C., when her cell phone rang. Though she had hoped it would be Mitch, she wasn't surprised to hear her ex-husband's voice, instead. He was so predictable.

"Kate," he said, without even bothering with a hello, "we need to talk."

She decided to play dumb. "What about?"

"Alison. Can you come to my office—"

"No, Eric, I can't come to your office. I'm working."

"You can't take a half hour to discuss your daughter's welfare?"

Welfare? Determined not to let him get to her, Kate allowed herself a couple of seconds before answering. "If you're referring to Alison's suggestion to live with you and Megan for half the year, we have nothing to talk about. The answer is no."

"It's what she wants, Kate."

"The only reason she wants to live with you is because you cater to her every whim."

"What's wrong with that?"

"Everything!" Kate said in exasperation. "A thirteen-year-old shouldn't be given unlimited funds.

And she shouldn't be allowed to stay up until all hours of the night, or highlight her hair, or dress like Britney Spears.''

She heard Eric snicker. ''So that's it. You resent Megan's influence.''

Oh, for God's sake. Kate slammed on the brakes as a traffic light turned red. Why did she put up with him when she no longer had to? ''I don't resent Megan's influence,'' she said as though talking to a five-year-old. ''In many ways, she's a good role model for Alison. But when it comes to money, she goes overboard and you know it. The three of us have had this conversation before.''

''Okay, okay, I'll talk to Megan about the money. How's that?''

''The answer is still no.''

''Look, Kate, this isn't fair. I've changed. I'm no longer the irresponsible wanderer I once was. And now that I have some stability in my life, is it so unreasonable for me to want to spend more time with my daughter?''

''You never complained about the arrangements before.''

''I told you, I'm a different man now. I have a wife I love and who loves me, and I want Alison to be a part of that.'' He paused. ''And...I worry about her.''

Kate's good intentions to not let him get to her were quickly slipping away. ''Where is that coming from? What do you have to worry about?''

''Her safety. You have a dangerous job, Kate, especially now that you're on your own. Don't deny it,'' he said, as she started to protest. ''I know about that weirdo you're defending—Ted Gifford.''

"Ed Gibbons. And he presents no threat to me whatsoever, so don't you dare put those thoughts in Alison's head. You know how impressionable she is."

"I'd feel better having her here," he said stubbornly. "I haven't forgotten what happened to her last year when she was kidnapped by a madman."

"If your memory is so good," Kate snapped, "then you'll remember that that madman was connected to *your* case, Eric. Alison wouldn't have been kidnapped if *you* hadn't gotten yourself involved with a call girl and if I hadn't been trying to save your ass. I didn't hear you complain then, did I."

"That was different. Alison was careless—"

With a cry of sheer frustration, Kate disconnected and threw the phone on the passenger seat.

One of the first calls Kate made when she got back to her office was to Provost Buchanan at Jefferson University. His secretary put her on hold, and came back on the line a few minutes later, deeply apologetic. Mr. Buchanan was very busy and would not be able to talk to her.

"May I call back in a few days?" Kate asked, sensing a brush-off.

"I'm afraid that won't do any good. This is a very busy time for members of the faculty. I hope you understand. Good day, Ms. Logan."

Kate was still trying to digest this very obvious rebuff, when Frankie buzzed her on the intercom. "Boss, Ted Rencheck is here to—" Then, in a louder voice, "Hey, you can't just barge into her office—"

Assistant U.S. attorney Theodore Rencheck, with

whom Kate had battled in and out of the courtroom for years, ignored Frankie's angry protest and pushed Kate's door open. He was a small, pretentious man with big political ambitions and an ego to match.

"What the hell do you think you're doing?" he asked with his usual bullishness.

Kate looked up. Clearly this wasn't her day. "Good morning to you, too, Ted. What put you into such a snit?"

"As if you didn't know."

She did, but decided to yank his chain a little. He made it so easy. "Why don't you sit down and tell me."

He sat down but remained on the edge of the chair, his feet solidly planted on the blue carpet, his hands clasped and hanging between his knees. "I heard you're reopening the Molly Buchanan murder case."

She wasn't surprised that he had already found out. He had been the assistant D.A. of Fairfax County at the time of Molly's murder, and still had friends there.

"I've been making inquiries," she said vaguely.

"Why?"

"I don't believe it's any of your business."

"It's very much my business. That case was mine. What do you know about Todd Buchanan? Where is he?"

"I have no idea."

"I don't believe you." His accusatory tone, which he used indiscriminately in and out of the courtroom, had always grated on her. Today was no exception.

"I repeat," she said, carefully enunciating each word, "I don't know where Todd Buchanan is, and even if I did, I wouldn't tell you."

"Need I remind you that the man is a fugitive? And that you could be disbarred for withholding evidence?"

Kate exhaled a thin breath. She was getting tired of people quoting the law to her, especially Ted Rencheck. The man was still fuming over his humiliating defeat four months ago when she had uncovered Douglas Fairchild's involvement in the Washington Madam case. Soon after, the conviction of the man Ted had prosecuted was overturned, destroying his chances of becoming the next U.S. attorney, a position he had been coveting for years.

"Threats won't get you anywhere, Ted, so do yourself a favor and save the theatrics for the courtroom."

But he wasn't ready to give up just yet. "Does Mitch know you're sneaking behind his back, trying to get his sister's killer off?"

She gave him a disgusted look. "You do have a way of reducing everything to its lowest common denominator, don't you, Ted. I'm not *sneaking* behind Mitch's back. He knows."

Rencheck scoffed. "I bet he's thrilled."

Kate leaned back in her chair. "Why are you so interested in Molly's case, anyway? You may have been the D.A. of record, but the case is out of your jurisdiction now."

An expression she couldn't read flickered briefly in his eyes. Instead of the snappy reply she had expected, he remained silent. Before Kate could speculate about this uncharacteristic behavior, he stood up and started for the door. Halfway there, he turned.

"About Ed Gibbons," he said. "My offer is still

on the table. Voluntary manslaughter instead of murder one. I don't believe you got back to me on that.''

A little startled at how quickly he had changed the subject, she played with the top button of her blouse. ''That's because I have no intention of taking your offer. The man is sick, Ted. He needs psychiatric help. The only way he'll get it is if he's tried on an insanity plea.''

He shrugged. ''Have it your way, then.''

Kate stared at his back until he had walked past Frankie's desk and out of sight, her fingers still playing with her button.

Ten

Kate was surprised not to see Maria's car in the driveway when she came home that evening. Then she saw the white Ford Taurus parked along the curb and grinned. Mitch was here.

A delicious aroma greeted her, along with the sound of laughter—Alison's laughter, which, considering her mood lately, was an accomplishment in itself. Walking quietly, Kate approached the kitchen and stood under the archway, watching the little domestic scene unfolding in front of her.

Both had their back to her. Mitch must have had the night off, because he wore his favorite tan Dockers and a hunter-green sweater with the sleeves pushed up to the elbows. He was bent over the stove, stirring a pot filled with the tomato sauce Maria had prepared earlier, while Alison, remarkably competent all of a sudden, was putting together a salad. On the counter, a bottle of Chianti classico and two balloon glasses waited.

"When do we put the pasta in?" Mitch asked, still stirring.

"Not until Mom gets here." She started to quarter a tomato. "The chef on the *Bahia* says pasta waits for no one, which means it must be served as soon as it's ready.''

Kate stepped forward. "I bet that chef doesn't hold a candle to the two I have right here in my kitchen.''

"Mom! You weren't supposed to get here until six-thirty.''

Kate glanced at Mitch, whose expression was half apologetic, half amused. "I was anxious to come home and be with my girl.''

Mitch put the wooden spoon he had been holding on the counter. "I hope you don't mind me stopping by.'' He flashed a lopsided grin. "Alison called and made me an offer I couldn't refuse—a home-cooked meal and a present from the Virgin Islands.''

"She did, huh?''

Alison kept tearing up a lettuce while looking at Kate from the corner of her eye. "It's okay, isn't it, Mom?''

"Of course.'' Kate kissed her blond head before taking the glass of wine Mitch handed her. "I would have invited him myself,'' she said, holding his gaze. "But for some strange reason his voice-mail wasn't working.''

She watched his lips move as he mouthed a silent *I'm sorry.*

She thought of mouthing a quick *It's okay,* then changed her mind. He had put her through hell. Let him sweat.

She watched Alison move around the kitchen with the efficiency of an accomplished homemaker, filling a pot with tap water, setting it on the stove, taking out a pack of spaghetti from the pantry. "Can I help?'' she asked.

"Nope." Alison shook her head. "I'm doing it all myself." She waved a paring knife toward the family room. "Why don't you two take your wine in there? Mitch made a fire. I'll call when dinner's ready."

Mitch lifted his shoulders. "You heard her. Come on." He took Kate's hand and led her into the adjoining room, where a cozy fire crackled, spreading its warmth throughout the room. Relieved at this sudden turn of events, Kate sat down beside him on the sofa.

"Alison told me all about her trip. She seems to have had a great time."

Kate listened to the sound of dishes being set on the kitchen table. "She did. So much so that she now wants to divide her time equally between her father and me. Six months in Georgetown and six months here."

"What brought that on?"

"She says you and I need more privacy."

"And you suspect something else."

"What I suspect," Kate said with a little pinch in her heart, "is that she's having a better time with her father than she's having with me. Eric is in the money now, and when Alison is around him she doesn't have to constantly hear 'this is too expensive' or 'it isn't in our budget.' He takes her to fun places, while I work like a dog trying to make ends meet." She sighed. "I'm whining, aren't I."

Mitch smiled. "Only a little." He took a sip of his wine. "What did you say about her proposed arrangement?"

"What do you think I said? A flat no. She pouted

the entire evening. That's why I came home early. I was hoping we could patch things up.''

Mitch glanced toward the kitchen. ''Have I spoiled things for you by coming here?''

''No, not at all. On the contrary. You seem to have greatly improved my daughter's mood.'' Kate smiled. ''You do have a way with her, Mitch. There's no denying it.''

He took the glass from her hand and set it on the coffee table next to his. ''I'd rather have a way with her mother,'' he said, pulling her to him.

''That might take some doing, considering how horribly you behaved the other night, storming out of here, not returning my calls, getting me crazy with worry.''

''Would it help if I admitted to being a total jerk?''

''Hmm.'' For a brief moment, she thought about torturing him a little by pretending to be angry. She might have pulled it off, too, if he had kept his hands to himself. He didn't. When they slid around her waist, tugging her even closer, her only impulse was to lock her arms around his neck. ''I must say, you're doing a very good job of redeeming yourself.''

''You think so?'' His hands cupped her buttocks, sending a flutter low in her belly. ''I've missed you, Kate. These past forty-eight hours have been hell.''

''Ever heard of the telephone? You know, that little invention that Mr. Alexander Graham Bell—''

His mouth came down, meeting hers with the softest brush. The tenderness of his kiss nearly made her heart stop.

''What was that about Mr. Bell?'' His mouth moved to her throat.

"Mr. who?"

"Kate, Kate," he whispered against her mouth. "You do drive me crazy. If it weren't for Alison in the next room..." He pressed his mouth to her ear and told her what he wanted to do to her. His voice was soft, his breath warm, his words intoxicating.

She had an instant image of the two of them in bed, moving fast, breathing hard. "God, Mitch, stop."

"Not until you say you forgive me."

"I didn't hear you apologize, did I?"

"I apologize. I'm sorry. *Mea culpa.* I was wrong to blow up at you the way I did."

"It took you two days to figure that out?"

"Some men are more hardheaded than others."

He waited a beat, as though unsure of what to say next, which was not at all like Mitch. "I went over the police report on Molly. I had read it before, many times, but I wanted to refresh my memory."

She hadn't expected that, but was pleased nonetheless. "Did you learn anything new?"

"No. Todd is still the best suspect we have, for the same old reasons. He lied to the police about his alibi, he asked his friend to lie, and then he ran. You can't blame me, or the police, for being more than a little suspicious."

He picked up his glass again and stared into it. "Having said that, I went and talked to a few people."

Another surprise. "Who did you talk to?"

"Todd's former attorney, for one. Syd Willard is retired now and lives in Richmond, but I was able to track him down. He's very bitter about the way Justice Buchanan treated him. Apparently the man didn't pull any punches. He flat-out accused Syd of mishandling the case, and fired him.''

''I don't understand why Syd Willard's firm was hired in the first place. Isn't Justice Buchanan close friends with Jacob Winters?''

''Winters was away on a safari, and Syd knew he was only to be an interim counsel. He would have been fired the moment Winters was back from his trip. As I said, Syd is bitter, but he was nice enough to give me his notes. I left them on your desk, but there's very little in there I found helpful.''

Stunned, Kate could only say a weak thank you.

''The motel clerk was an equal waste of time,'' Mitch continued. ''I was hoping he'd remember something...the make of the car, perhaps, or specifics about the man he saw coming out of room 12—his approximate age, a limp, a hump on his back.''

Kate smiled. ''He'd remember a hump, wouldn't he?''

''You'd think. Unfortunately the man he described to me sounds identical to the one he described two years ago to Frank Sykes. On the other hand, Jake Weitz—that's Todd's buddy—was a little more forthcoming. He was afraid of legal consequences, so it took some doing to make him talk.''

''What did he have to say that he hadn't already told the police?''

''Apparently, Todd was so drunk that night that when he and Jake came out of the last bar they were in, Todd couldn't find his car, so Jake helped him look for it. Then, worried that Todd might get himself in an accident, Jake followed him home, even though he wasn't in the best shape himself.''

Kate felt vaguely disappointed. ''That's nothing new, Mitch. It's all in the police report.''

''But what's not in the report, because Jake never said it, is that Todd was barely able to make it home. In order to kill Molly, he would have had to turn around again, drive to the Lost Creek Motel, some twenty miles away, commit the murder, and then drive back home. In Jake's opinion, that was just not possible.''

''Why didn't he say anything when he was questioned?''

''He doesn't know. He says the events of that night were fuzzy because they were drinking so damn much. The following day he had a bitch of a hangover, and the police had threatened to press charges against him for lying about Todd's alibi. It just didn't occur to him to give his opinion.''

''Did you give that information to Frank?''

Mitch nodded. ''I passed it on, but as I said, I don't know how much good it will do at this stage. Frank hasn't said a word about reopening the investigation.''

Kate studied Mitch's profile. ''I can't believe you did all this.''

''Why? You don't think I can be objective?''

''Not about Todd.''

''Yeah, well.'' He gave a little self-conscious laugh. ''I guess I surprise myself, too, sometimes.''

''And I think you're simply amazing.''

''Don't give me *all* the credit. I wouldn't have been

so quick to see the light if it hadn't been for some...divine intervention, shall we say?''

Kate laughed. ''You talked to Father Tim?''

''Who else could hammer some sense into this stubborn Irish skull of mine?''

A call from the kitchen brought their conversation to a halt.

''Dinner's ready, guys! Come and get it.''

Though Alison had balked a little about going to bed, she had finally agreed to call it a day, but not until Mitch promised to take her to Baltimore in the morning for the most awaited basketball game of the season—the Adams-Morgan Panthers against the Stone Harbor Falcons.

Alone once again, Kate and Mitch went back into the family room, where, with no prompting on her part, Mitch started to talk about Molly, their childhood, her years as a rebellious teenager, the crazy stunts she pulled from time to time.

''She was a good kid,'' he said, staring at the fire. ''Full of spunk and mischief—the quintessential girl next door. When my dad died and my mother moved to Florida, she and I assumed Molly would go with her. But Molly had just turned eighteen and was looking forward to making her own decisions. There was only one thought on her mind—to attend Georgetown University with her friends.''

''Was your mom worried?''

He laughed. ''She was out of her mind with worry, especially since I was working with Vargas Worldwide at the time and was rarely in Washington.'' He pulled his gaze from the flames and picked up the videotape, turning it around in his hands. "I didn't start seeing more of her until I left Worldwide and joined Metro PD three years ago. By then, she was married to Todd and doing her own thing."

"You never liked Todd, did you."

"Not one bit. He was such a smart-ass—flaunting his money and his dad's power, boasting about the sport celebrities he met, passing around free tickets to Super Bowls or World Series games like they were lollipops." After a few seconds of silence, he held up the tape. "I guess I'm ready to take a look at this now."

Without a word, Kate walked over to the VCR, slid in the tape and came back to sit on the sofa. She pressed the remote, watching Mitch's face as Todd appeared on the screen. Mitch showed no emotion, made no comment. From time to time, as Todd talked, Mitch would get up to poke at the fire, or to pour himself another cup of coffee, but Kate knew that even without looking at the screen, he was listening to every word.

Just as Kate had done at her office, he sat silent for a long time after it ended. She didn't interrupt his thoughts. Quietly, she picked up the remote and pressed the rewind button. She didn't eject it, though she doubted Mitch would want to watch the tape a second time.

When she couldn't stand the silence anymore, she looked at him. "Well? What's the verdict?"

Mitch put his cup down. "I still think he could have rehearsed that little speech of his a dozen times until he perfected it."

"He could have, but I don't believe he did. And I don't think you do, either."

"I never liked him," he said in lieu of a direct reply. "He was irresponsible, arrogant, and a hopeless womanizer."

"Molly must have seen something in him."

"I guess she was dazzled by his charm. But deep down she knew he wasn't right for her. She just married him to—"

Kate unfolded her legs from under her. "To what?"

"Nothing. Never mind." He walked over to the fireplace and threw another log on the dying embers. Orange flames shot up, casting a golden glow over the entire room. He wasn't telling her everything, she thought, watching his rigid back. He had let something slip, then caught himself. Why? What did he know that he couldn't share with her?

"There's something you're not telling me," she said, talking to his back.

"It's not important."

"If it has something to do with the case—"

"Kate, please." He turned. "Drop it, all right?"

His sharp tone startled her. She almost snapped back, but didn't. He had made a lot of concessions in the past forty-eight hours. Why push it? She spread her hands in surrender. "It's dropped." She watched him walk back to the sofa. "Is there *anything* we can talk about? Any safe ground about this case?"

He drew a long breath. "Todd has changed."

"I noticed. I mean, I never met him personally, but I've seen him on TV. He seems to have…matured, I guess, is the word."

Mitch was silent for another half minute, then asked, "What's Jessica like?"

"Pretty, refined, well-mannered. Not at all the kind of woman I thought would be attracted to a man like Todd Buchanan, but then again, that's what I said about Megan when she fell in love with Eric, and they seem to be blissfully happy, so what do I know?"

She remembered Jessica's serene smile just before she walked away. "She's also pregnant," she added.

Mitch shot her a quick look but made no comment.

"The baby had a lot to do with Todd's decision to contact an attorney," Kate continued. "Though I understand he was reluctant at first."

"I imagine he would be."

"Why do I have the feeling you're not totally convinced Todd didn't kill Molly."

"I'm not. For one thing, he didn't say a word on that tape about getting physical with Molly."

"Lynn Flannery could have lied about that. Or someone else could have beaten Molly. Maybe the same man she was meeting the night of the murder."

"Or maybe Todd conveniently left out that little detail."

"We'll see. I'm expecting a call from him tomorrow at noon. I'll ask about the beating, and I'll ask Lynn, as well. I have an appointment with her first thing in the morning. Which reminds me." She glanced at her watch. "Since you're taking Alison for the day, I won't be needing Maria. Let me give her a quick call."

By the time Kate returned to the family room, Mitch had ejected the video and turned on the evening news. She only half listened to the report, as Mitch helped her gather the coffee cups and remains of an apple pie, then abruptly looked up when she recognized a familiar voice.

Mitch did the same. "Well, if it isn't our mouthy prosecutor."

"What is he up to now?"

"Seeking his fifteen minutes of fame, what else?"

The previously recorded segment showed Rencheck in front of the courthouse, surrounded by a half-dozen reporters, all shouting at him.

A woman in the front row pushed a microphone in his face. "How do you feel about Kate Logan's decision to represent Todd Buchanan?"

"Does she know where he's hiding?" someone else asked.

"Will she have to reveal his whereabouts?"

"Will Todd Buchanan be returning to the U.S.?"

Obviously pleased by all the attention, Rencheck raised his right hand, looking like a witness being sworn in. "At the moment, I know very little, except that Kate Logan has taken Buchanan's case, and no, she is not bound, at least not legally, to reveal his whereabouts."

"Has there been an active effort on the part of the Fairfax police to find him?" The question had come from Eddy Povich, an insufferable tabloid reporter whom Kate despised.

"Not at the moment, though there was for a while. That's how we traced him to Mérida, Mexico."

"Any chance he's still there?"

Rencheck shook his head. "I doubt it. My bet is that he went to Europe and is probably living the good life in a country that has no extradition treaty with the U.S."

"Does that mean he'll never be found?"

"Oh, I wouldn't say that," Rencheck said with a confident look. "If *I* were on his trail, I'd start with that woman Todd Buchanan was supposed to have befriended in Mexico. You all know that famous saying, don't you?" He let out a bawdy laugh. "*Cherchez la femme* and you'll find her man."

Pleased with himself, he walked away, reporters in tow.

"Jerk." Kate shut off the TV set. "Why didn't he follow that *cherchez la femme* lead when he had the chance?"

"Because he couldn't find her. But I did," Mitch added, as he carried a tray into the kitchen. "Though by the time I got there, she was long gone."

"Who was she?"

"Her name is Pilar Fontana, a single mother of three who made her living selling straw hats at a local market. When I arrived, I learned that a day or two before, she had packed up her cart and moved to another town. I spent three days looking for her. No one could—or would—tell me where she was."

"How does she fit in?"

"From what I gathered, she had connections and supplemented her income by providing phony IDs for drug traffickers. She could have done the same for Todd. He spoke fluent Spanish and had a pocket full of American dollars. In Mexico, that will buy you just about anything."

He stole a morsel of pie crust and ate it. "I'd better go. It's late and tomorrow's a full day." He took his leather bomber jacket from the back of a chair and slipped it on. "You'll have Alison ready?"

"She'd never forgive me, if I didn't."

He pinned her against the kitchen counter. "When am I going to have you all to myself?"

She slid her hands beneath the jacket and ran them up and down his muscled chest. "Soon."

He kissed her, hard this time. "I'm holding you to it."

Eleven

Todd Buchanan stood on the bow of the *Ainara,* one of the many fishing boats returning to the busy seaport of Saint-Jean-de-Luz after a long day at sea. Though the sun was behind him, its reflection on the water was blinding, and he had to squint as he tried to pick out Jess from the dozens of people on the quay.

She had been gone only two days but, to him, that short absence felt like two years. He couldn't remember ever missing anyone so much—not even Molly.

He had fallen for Jess the moment he had seen her, standing on Place Louis XIV, eating an ice-cream cone. Maybe it was the way her brown hair had turned golden under the setting sun, or how totally absorbed she was in her task, licking the ice cream with great gusto, her tongue catching it as it dripped along the cone.

Afraid she'd disappear, he had jumped off the *Ainara* before it was completely docked and had fallen in the murky water, much to the amusement of the other fishermen.

Undeterred, he had taken off at a dead run, catching up with the young woman on rue Gambetta, the pedestrian thoroughfare that went through the center of town. He could still remember her startled expression as he stood there, dripping wet, and tried to explain in his less-than-perfect French the effect she'd had on him.

From the looks he was getting from passersby, he'd half expected her to either call the cops or walk away with that expression of disdain some French women seemed to have perfected.

She did neither. Instead she laughed and told him she was an American, a kindergarten teacher from San Diego, and that if he wanted to go home and change, she would wait for him.

He had settled for sitting on a sunny bench. Then, as she finished her ice-cream cone, he had told her, in his best British accent, the story he had stuck to since arriving in Saint-Jean-de-Luz. He was from Manchester, England, and had come to southwestern France in search of adventure.

In turn, she had told him about growing up in San Diego with a nagging sister and two wonderful parents, both of them teachers, which was the reason she had chosen that profession. Six months ago, on her twenty-ninth birthday, she had realized there was more to life than a classroom full of overactive five-year-olds and had taken off for Europe.

After spending a month traveling through Spain, she had arrived in Saint-Jean-de-Luz and was so taken by the charming seaport town that she had abandoned her plans to visit England and stayed here. Within a week, she had found a place to stay and a job as an English teacher at the local high school.

Two weeks after their momentous meeting, Jessica had moved in with him, making Todd the happiest man on earth. For the first time in years, he was in love again. His feelings for Jessica were different from those he had experienced with Molly. Jess brought out a side of him, a tenderness, he didn't know existed. He wanted to protect her, to do things for her, things he had never done before, like hang curtains, plant flowers or build a toolshed, even though he had never swung a hammer in his life.

It took him almost six months to find the courage to tell her the truth about himself. What if she didn't believe he hadn't killed Molly? What if she got scared and left him? Or turned him in to the police? *What if, what if, what if.* He drove himself crazy imagining things that, in the end, never happened.

Her eyes moist, Jess had listened quietly as he told her about his relationship with Molly, the events of the night she died, and his ultimate flight to Mexico where he had bought himself a new identity. Three months later, under the name of William Adler, a British citizen, he had left the coastal town of Mérida, where he had been hiding all this time, and flown to Geneva. He had stayed in Switzerland long enough to open a bank account and have the money he had smuggled into Mexico transferred there. From Geneva, he took a train to Bordeaux, then another bound for Marbella, a resort town in the south of Spain that he knew well.

His train had broken down unexpectedly in Saint-Jean-de-Luz, and, though it was quickly repaired and ready to go by the end of the day, Todd never reboarded it. After spending four hours walking through the picturesque town with its red-tile-roof houses and brightly colored boats bobbing in the water, he decided this was where he wanted to live.

He liked the people, too—friendly men in black berets and women in gaily printed dresses, whose language and sounds were unlike those of any other tongue in Europe. The Basques, he learned, were proud, private people who minded their own business and expected others to do the same. That suited Todd perfectly. In his situation, curiosity would have been disastrous.

He was lucky enough to find a job on a fishing boat, the *Ainara,* which meant the "Swallow" in Basque. In the wintertime, he earned money fishing for sardines, and in the summer, he went after the big catch—the tunas.

Not only had Jess believed him about Molly's death, but was convinced he should try to clear his name. "Why should you live the rest of your life with that terrible suspicion hanging over you?" she had told him. "It isn't fair."

"I'll trade fairness for safety," he replied. "Here, everyone believes I'm Will Adler of Manchester. If I thought I had a chance to convince a jury that I didn't kill Molly, I'd return to the U.S. in a heartbeat. But there's no way anyone will believe me now, so why should I risk losing my freedom? And losing you."

Then last week, while tuned to CNN, they had watched an interview with Kate Logan, a Washington, D.C., attorney, who, with the help of a local homicide detective, had recently solved a case that had stumped police for months. To Todd's surprise, the homicide detective was none other than his former brother-in-law, Mitch Calhoon.

Impressed by Kate Logan, Jess began to toy with the possibility of hiring her. Todd had balked, a little more forcefully this time. The fact that Mitch was Kate Logan's boyfriend was a disaster waiting to happen. Not only was the man a brilliant detective, but he was relentless. What if Mitch picked up his scent again and came after him? Just as he had two years ago.

He hadn't counted on Jess's determination, or the ace card she played that same night at the end of a romantic, candlelit dinner. Eyes glowing, she told him the news she had learned that very morning. She was pregnant.

Momentarily stunned, Todd stared at her, lost for words. A baby. He, Todd Buchanan, who had never done anything right in his entire life, was going to have a baby. It couldn't be. It was a trick. He hadn't heard right. Then, as tears of joy filled Jess's eyes, he realized that it *was* true. He was going to be a father.

Delirious with happiness, he had run outside, fallen to his knees and let out a shout of joy that had echoed all over the valley.

"Will!"

Now, at the sound of the name he had chosen for himself, he shielded his eyes from the sun and spotted Jess waving at him from the quay de l'Infante. He waved back, trying to gage her mood. She looked radiant, and that could only mean one thing—Kate Logan had agreed to take the case.

Todd almost wished she hadn't. He had a bad feeling about this, a premonition he couldn't explain. Until now, his life had been pleasant, safe and uncomplicated, and here he was, throwing a monkey wrench into it. How smart was that?

Holding back a sigh, Todd picked up the heavy coil of rope at his feet and tossed it on the dock. Then, with an agility he had developed over the past two years, he jumped off the boat, tied one end of the rope to the concrete cleat reserved for the *Ainara* and ran to meet Jess.

The ride home in Todd's Renault never took more than fifteen minutes, but what a difference those fifteen minutes made. With each kilometer, the landscape changed dramatically. Crowded sidewalks and noisy streets gave way to green hills where flocks of sheep grazed lazily. As they climbed higher, the sea breeze was replaced by the cool, crisp air of the valleys leading to the nearby Pyrénées, the mountain range that separated France from Spain.

"Will?" Both had agreed that to avoid confusion, Jess would continue to call him by his chosen name. "You haven't said much since we left the harbor. Aren't you happy about what I told you?"

"Yes, of course I am." He flashed her a quick smile. "It's just that now that the wheels are in motion, so to speak, I feel...different." He was too damn macho to admit he was scared, but as always, she was totally tuned to his feelings and knew exactly what he was thinking.

"There's nothing to worry about, darling. We'll go about our business as usual, and let Kate do what she has to do."

She made it sound so simple. Maybe it was. Maybe

he was worrying unnecessarily. "You said she wants to talk to me?"

"Yes." She handed him the small piece of paper with Kate Logan's name, address and phone numbers. "She said to call her on her cell phone. It's safer that way." She gave his arm a reassuring pat. "Everything will be all right."

Then, why did he feel as if the weight of the entire world had suddenly settled on his shoulders?

He remained silent until they reached their little one-bedroom house—a *cabanon,* as the French called it—far away from their nearest neighbor. Jess had given it a few homey touches—flower boxes under the windows, an old-fashioned porch swing on the vine-covered terrace, and a bunch of dried *espolette,* the town's famous red peppers, hanging on the yellow front door.

The interior was as cheerful as the outside, furnished with sofas and chairs the color of the sea, and tables they had bought at a local flea market and refinished together. Now that the sun had disappeared, the temperature had dropped sharply, but the little potbelly stove kept the house warm and cozy.

While Jess took a beer and a Perrier from the refrigerator, Todd walked over to the hutch and put Kate Logan's phone number in a drawer.

Jess looked at him anxiously. "You won't forget to call her, will you?"

He took the bottle of Kronembourg she handed him. "Saturday at twelve noon—six p.m., our time. I won't forget." He touched his bottle to hers. "To Kate Logan. And to her success."

*   *   *

As always at this time of day, the terrace at Café Central on Saint-Jean-de-Luz's harbor was jammed. With the evening aperitif hour well under way, waiters were scrambling to keep customers happy with frosty mugs of Kronembourg beer and platters of grilled sardines, a local favorite.

Emile Sardoux sat at a sidewalk table overlooking the seaport and did what he did every evening at this time—sip a Vittel-menthe. He would have much preferred a pitcher of beer or a whiskey, but he was on the wagon now, this time for good.

Watching the fishing boats return to port every evening was a daily routine he had started upon arriving here from Bordeaux two months ago. Usually slow paced, the town suddenly came alive at this time of day as the first *chalutiers*—the sardine boats—started to pull into the harbor. Within moments of their docking, huge baskets of fish were hauled out of the vessels and lined up on the quay, where restaurant owners, shopkeepers and housewives rushed to get the best catch at the cheapest price.

The daily scene had its moments, but there were times when Emile was so damn bored with his new life, he thought he'd go crazy. What other choice did he have? It's not like he was rolling in dough. If he was he would have chosen some other place to spend the rest of his life—the Costa del Sol maybe, or the Canary Islands where life was easy, the sun hot and the liquor cheap.

Instead he had ended up in this sleepy burg where an old friend of his had offered to sublet him an apartment on rue de l'Eglise. The place was no bigger than a postage stamp and had no hot water, but what could you expect for two thousand francs a month?

At times, when he allowed himself to look back, he wondered what might have been if he hadn't let his drinking screw up the two best things he had going for him—his family and his job.

He never thought Antoinette would kick him out of the house, but his being fired from *Bordeaux-Matin*, where he had worked as an investigative reporter for the past ten years, was the final straw. Within twenty-four hours he found himself jobless, homeless and so damn depressed, he actually thought of jumping off a bridge into the Garonne River.

At the last minute, he lost his nerve and climbed back over the railing, shaking like a leaf. When his friend, Jacquo, a Realtor, offered the apartment in Saint-Jean-de-Luz, Emile gratefully accepted. Maybe what he needed to lift his spirits was a fresh start, not in Bordeaux, but somewhere he wasn't haunted by his failures as a man, as a husband and as a father. And if he could stay off the sauce and start working again, maybe Antoinette would take him back.

So far he had managed fairly well. He drank nothing but mint-flavored mineral water and ate three meals a day. He had even found a job in an auto parts store. The pay wasn't great but it was enough to cover food and rent. He was even able to send Antoinette some money every week, something she hadn't expected.

Emile Sardoux was on his way back. He could feel it. Now all he had to do was convince his old boss to give him another chance, and he'd be a happy man. But Maurice's trust was something Emile had to earn back the hard way—by proving he still had what it took to be a first-rate investigative reporter. He had been the best once, going after stories no one wanted to tackle, and often risking his neck to get to the truth. Then the drinking had started, God knows why, and from that moment on, everything had spiraled out of control.

The problem was, except for an occasional bar brawl or a dispute between local fisheries, nothing worth writing about ever happened in Saint-Jean-de-Luz. What he needed was a big story, something that would showcase his talents and bring him national attention.

Holding back a sigh of self-pity, he drained the last of his Vittel-menthe. Time to go home and make dinner. Maybe he'd pick up some tuna on the way. He let out a sigh, thinking how good a cold glass of sauvignon blanc would taste with the seared fish, then shook his head. A Coca Cola would do just fine. He had made a promise to himself, and by God, this time he was going to keep it.

Twelve

Flannery Designs was on the second floor of a four-story town house on K Street that also housed a beauty parlor, a tax accountant and a chiropractor. Lynn had told Kate her receptionist didn't work on Saturdays and to come right up.

A familiar aria, "La Donna e Mobile" from *Rigoletto,* reverberated through the stairwell. Humming along, Kate ignored the elevator and took the stairs to the designer's studio. The door was open, giving Kate an ample view of the large, well-lit room, which was filled with a wild assortment of postmodern furniture in every possible shape and color.

In the center of the room, a woman Kate assumed was Lynn Flannery stood over a three-legged, chartreuse coffee table, applying spiky black lashes to a very large eye painted in the upper-right corner of the table. In her mid-thirties, she was attractive in a sporty, healthy kind of way. Her short brown hair was brushed back from her face, styled simply to reveal strong, razor-sharp features. She wore loose cargo pants and a baggy sweatshirt splattered with yellow and purple paint.

Mesmerized, Kate just stood there for a moment, her gaze sweeping over the furniture. Although postmodernism didn't particularly appeal to her, she had to admit the woman's talents and versatility were truly inspiring.

Perhaps sensing that someone was there, the designer turned, paintbrush in hand. Intelligent gray eyes studied Kate briefly. "Ms. Logan?" She spoke loudly enough to be heard over the music. When Kate nodded, she waved toward a pair of stools next to a workbench. "Why don't you have a seat? I'll just be a minute."

"Certainly." Kate watched Lynn put on the last eyelash, until, satisfied at last, the woman straightened and brushed a strand of hair from her forehead, leaving a smear of black paint on her skin.

"Sorry about that." She turned off the CD player. "I'm entering the National Furniture Design Competition and my entries must be in New York no later than tomorrow evening." She smiled, revealing tiny white teeth. "Preferably dry."

"I'm sorry if I've come at a bad time," Kate said.

Lynn waved the apology aside. "You haven't. Talking to you will be much more pleasant than watching the paint dry. Unfortunately, I can't offer you anything. My partner is in charge of refreshments, and she hasn't arrived yet."

"I don't need anything."

"So." Lynn walked over to a workbench and stuck the paintbrush in a can of turpentine. "You said on the phone that you were investigating Molly's murder."

"Yes. I was hoping you'd be able to help me."

"Frankly, I wasn't sure I wanted to." She turned to face Kate and perched one hip on the other stool.

"Not after I heard you were representing Todd Buchanan."

"You don't like Todd."

"I hate the son of a bitch. He's a spoiled brat, a coward and a liar, so if you expect me to help you find another suspect, you've come to the wrong person. Todd is the one who killed Molly."

Kate winced inwardly. With the picture she was getting of Todd from various people, she was beginning to worry that if the case ever went to court, there wouldn't be a sympathetic ear on the jury. "Why are you so sure he did?"

Lynn smiled. "Because my gut instincts tell me he did, Ms. Logan. Is that good enough for you?"

It was Kate's turn to smile. "I've been known to follow my instincts every now and then. However, a court of law would require something a little more substantial."

"All right. What do you want to know?"

"Tell me about Molly. Was she in the habit of meeting men in motel rooms?"

Lynn didn't reply.

"Ms. Flannery—"

"Lynn."

"All right, Lynn. I know this is difficult for you. Your best friend was murdered, and you think I'm here to help the killer beat the rap. I wouldn't blame you if you had refused to talk to me, but you didn't. So, please don't hold back on me now. I need to know what Molly was all about, what she did in her spare time, who she saw."

"Didn't Mitch tell you?"

"Apparently Molly didn't confide in him as much

as he wished she had. The fact that her body was found in that motel room was almost as much of a shock to him as her death was.''

Without a word, Lynn walked over to a desk and retrieved a shoe box from a bottom drawer before walking back. ''Here—'' she said, putting the box on Kate's lap. ''This will tell you what Molly was all about.''

''What's this?'' Kate asked, lifting the lid.

''Snapshots of Molly I took over the years. I'm a bit of a photo buff.'' She waited until Kate had flipped through several photographs before adding, ''As you can see, she was a free spirit, a tomboy who excelled at any sport—volleyball, baseball, street hockey, swimming. By the time she was thirty, she could fly a single-engine plane, had parachuted in the Arizona desert and kayaked through the Colorado rapids.''

''Nothing dull about her life.''

''No, no one could accuse Molly of being dull, but her antics drove those around her crazy with worry.''

''Was Todd as adventurous as she was?''

''You mean as crazy, don't you?'' she said with a wistful smile. ''The answer is yes. Not only did Todd pay the bills for her little whims, but he was right there with her, doing whatever she was into that week. I expected her to slow down a little as she got older, but she didn't. If anything, she became even wilder, especially after she came back from Colorado.''

''Colorado?'' Funny, Mitch hadn't said anything about that. ''When did she go to Colorado?''

''Eight years ago.''

Kate did a quick calculation. ''That would have made her twenty-two. Wasn't she at Georgetown?''

"In her senior year. Six months before graduating, she announced that she was quitting school and moving out west, to a small town I had never heard of—Singleton, I think it was. Her only explanation was that she needed a change of pace."

"How long was she there?"

"A little over a year, then she came back."

"How did she explain her return?"

"She didn't. Not really. She just said that she missed Washington, the same place she couldn't wait to leave." Lynn shook her head. "Ten months later she was marrying Todd Buchanan.

"I tried to talk her out of it," she continued. "So did Mitch, but as usual, she wouldn't listen. Molly was the kind of person that the more you told her not to do something, the more she wanted to do it. I guess she thought she had found the perfect mate, someone who understood her need for adventure."

"So marriage didn't appease that need?"

"On the contrary, it fueled it, intensified it. She seemed to grow more reckless, almost as if she didn't give a damn anymore. She started to do things she wouldn't have considered doing before."

"Like what?"

"Oh, like racing Todd's speedboat in nasty weather, skiing too fast, bungee jumping."

"What made her do all those things?"

"I asked her that, many times. Her answer was always the same. 'A girl needs a little spice in her life.'"

"Did that spice include going out with strange men?"

Lynn starred at the geometric pattern on the black-

and-white tile floor for a few seconds before answering. "She didn't start with that nonsense until a couple of years or so before she was killed."

"Who were the men?"

"She never told me their names."

As Frankie would say, dollars to doughnuts Molly herself didn't know their names.

"I worried constantly about her," Lynn continued. "Worried about her lifestyle, the risks she took. But every time I tried to reason with her, we'd end up fighting, so I usually backed off."

"If you worried about her lifestyle, why won't you consider the possibility that she may have been killed by one of the men she went out with?"

"Because Todd was insanely jealous." Her voice turned thin and brittle. "And because he had just threatened to kill her. The housekeeper heard him."

"He said that in a moment of anger."

Lynn's eyes glowed with hatred. "You don't know anything about Todd except what he wants you to know."

"I'm not sure I understand—"

"He hit her once. Did he tell you that? He hit her so hard, she was black and blue for days. I took Polaroid shots of her and begged her to press charges against him."

"But there were no photos to corroborate your statement."

"That's because Todd destroyed them."

"Wouldn't Molly have told you if he had?"

She sighed. "Molly was always covering for him, trying to make him look better than he really was."

"Why would she do that?"

"How the hell do I know?" She jumped up and started rearranging a set of brushes on the workbench. "Maybe she was scared of him. Or maybe she liked all the fun and games his money could buy. And then again, maybe she was just a sucker for punishment."

She turned back, her gaze intense. "Whatever the reason for their attraction to each other is immaterial. The bottom line is, Todd killed her. He knew she was going out that night. He followed her to the motel. Maybe he tried to bring her home and she wouldn't go. They had an argument, he picked up the bottle of champagne and he killed her."

A simple scenario, Kate thought. And entirely plausible. No wonder so many people had bought it. "But Molly was obviously waiting for someone," Kate argued. "Wouldn't Todd worry that her date would suddenly show up and catch him in the act?"

Lynn shrugged. "Strange things happen when a man is overcome by blind rage."

Kate started going through the stack of photographs, all candid shots, some dating back more than ten years to when Molly had attended Georgetown.

"I loved taking pictures of her," Lynn said in a voice that was suddenly charged with emotion. "She was such a natural, and she could change her personality at the drop of a hat. I once told her that with a little effort she could become the next Cindy Crawford. She just laughed and said I was crazy."

Kate picked up a shot of Molly standing beside a single-engine airplane, a helmet tucked under her arm. "When was that taken?"

"About three years ago at the Delmarva Air Show. Molly was a very good pilot, but that day, she went a little too far with her stunts and almost crashed. That picture was taken moments after her close call. You wouldn't know it by looking at her, would you? She and I had a terrible fight that day. I accused her of trying to kill herself.''

''Was she?''

''I've no idea. All I do know is that Molly was a tormented soul. And Todd was the reason,'' she added.

The more Kate studied the photographs, the more she realized Lynn was right. Something had happened to Molly between those early college days and the more recent pictures. The transformation was unmistakable, even to someone who hadn't known her. Behind the bravado and the daring smiles, Kate saw something else, a hardness in the eyes that wasn't immediately noticeable, but was there nonetheless.

Two of the snapshots showed Molly in front of a laptop, probably the same laptop the police had taken as evidence from the Buchanans' house after the murder. ''Where was this taken?'' she asked, holding one of the photographs.

''Right here, in the workroom. Sometimes, when I worked late, Molly would pick up some food, bring it over and keep me company. Afterward, I'd go back to whatever I was doing and she'd sit right here, prop her laptop on the workbench and surf the Net. She was an Internet freak, knew every Web site out there—gardening, fitness, health, interior decorating, sports, you name it, Molly had explored it.''

Kate put the picture down and studied Lynn. The woman's eyes appeared suddenly sunken as they seemed to fight back tears. This, and the emotion in the woman's voice, couldn't be mistaken for anything but a deep affection for the friend she had lost. Or was it more than that?

"Please forgive me if I offend you," Kate said, meeting Lynn's gaze straight on. "But I'm sensing something different here. Your feelings for Molly seem to have run much deeper than those one might have for a best friend."

Lynn blinked away the tears. "You're very perceptive." She paused before adding, "And you're right. My love for Molly was different from hers for me, but I never pushed myself on her."

"I see."

Lynn let out a weak chuckle. "What are you thinking? That maybe *I* was jealous, got pissed off and then killed her?" Before Kate could reply, she was shaking her head. "I didn't. I could never hurt Molly, no matter how furious she made me."

They were interrupted by the sound of footsteps— a woman's footsteps. Soon, a stunning, short-haired brunette in black leather pants and a bulky white sweater walked in. She stopped in the middle of the room. "Oh." She glanced at Kate but addressed Lynn. "I didn't know you had company."

"Denise," Lynn said. "This is Kate Logan. She's an attorney. Kate, this is Denise Jenkins, my partner. She runs the financial end of the business."

"Pleased to meet you, Denise."

As the young woman nodded, her eyes stopped on the shoe box on Kate's lap. Her expression cooled instantly. "Did you say you were an attorney?"

"Yes." Kate wasn't one to miss an opportunity, even if it meant stirring a little trouble. "I'm investigating the murder of Molly Buchanan. Did you know her?''

Frosty blue eyes met hers. "Yes, I knew Molly." But it was obvious from the closed expression on her face that her former co-worker hadn't been one of her favorite people. Nor did Kate need a crystal ball to see that Lynn and her beautiful partner were involved in more than business.

"If you'll excuse me," Denise said, heading for a door on the other side of the workroom, "I've got some billing to take care of."

Now *there* was someone else she ought to talk to, Kate mused, but kept that thought to herself. Instead, she turned to Lynn again. "I assume Molly had an office?"

Lynn pointed to another closed door in the back.

"Would you have any objection if I took a look at it?"

"Why?"

She shrugged. "The police may have overlooked something."

"They didn't, believe me. They came here one morning, searched through her desk, took the company's computer and all her files, and returned them two weeks later. They found nothing."

She wasn't going to give an inch, Kate realized. Not if it could help clear Todd of the murder. "I won't stay long—"

"That's not the point," Lynn said sharply. "Molly's office is now being used as a storage room. That's where I keep my drawings—drawings I'd rather not have anyone look at. You understand."

"Of course." Pressing her further would be pointless. Kate flashed a quick smile. "All right if I keep these for a day or two?" She held out the shoe box.

Lynn nodded. "I'll be in New York for the better part of next week, but Denise will be here whenever you're ready to return them."

Thirteen

The burst of spring-like temperatures Washington had enjoyed for the past week vanished as quickly as it had arrived. By noon on Saturday, a blustery wind made its way to the capital, blowing the blossoms off the cherry trees around the Tidal Basin and sending disgruntled tourists scurrying back to their hotel rooms.

Kate sat at her kitchen table with Molly's photographs spread out in front of her. Once again, she went through each snapshot, studying the woman Lynn Flannery had captured on film. Molly Buchanan had been a lovely young woman, with shapely legs, expressive brown eyes that held a touch of mischief and a winning smile. She looked like her mother, Kate decided, remembering a photograph of Elaine Calhoon in Mitch's living room, while Mitch had inherited his dad's Irish good looks.

The longer Kate studied the pictures, the more she understood what Lynn had meant when she had mentioned Molly's many personalities. The girl was a chameleon, playful as a child one moment, a seductive vamp the next. Yet behind the mischief and the seduction, Kate saw something else, though she couldn't quite decide what it was. Sadness? Regret? Longing? Maybe all three?

"Who were you really, Molly?" Kate murmured as she looked at the picture of the young woman standing beside the single-engine Beechcraft. And why had the quintessential girl next door Mitch described turned into someone hell-bent on destroying herself?

Her gaze stopped on one of the two photographs Lynn had taken of Molly in front of her laptop. She had spun around on her stool and made a funny face. The background was out of focus, but Kate could see that, indeed, Molly had been on the Internet, perhaps checking one of those Web sites Lynn had mentioned?

She picked up the second snapshot. There, Molly held one of Lynn's creations, a delicate, round-backed chair painted neon orange, in front of her, peering through it, her eyes exaggeratedly crossed. This time the chair totally blocked the computer screen.

Disappointed, Kate let the photo drop back on the pile, then saw a third picture taken in front of the laptop, one she had missed earlier. This one was much clearer.

Excited, Kate picked up the magnifying glass beside her and took a closer look, not at Molly, but at the computer screen. She was right. Molly had been surfing the Net. Kate leaned closer, moving the magnifying glass around. Wait a minute. This wasn't a Web site. It was a chat room. An *erotic* chat room.

"Well, what do you know." Kate looked at the suggestive logo at the top of the page—two naked women holding a spider's web, hence the chat room's name, *Spider's Web*. Kate could see that two guests had been online. One called herself Tiger Lilly, the other Guinevere. The latter had been in the process of typing a reply, but had been interrupted. It didn't take a genius to figure out that Guinevere and Molly were one and the same.

Kate leaned back in her chair. So Molly had been into cybersex. Not a very safe hobby, judging from the many tragedies that had happened in recent years in the nation's capital alone. No wonder Molly had kept her little activity secret. Mitch would have had a fit if he had known.

Curious, Kate picked up the phone and dialed Lynn's studio. "Lynn," she said when the designer answered, "did Molly ever mention an erotic chat room?"

The furniture designer laughed. "Molly wasn't into that sort of thing."

"Are you sure?"

"Yes, I'm sure. She didn't have to rely on cybersex for stimulation, or on Internet misfits to satisfy her needs. Why do you ask?"

"One of those shots you took of her in front of her laptop shows she was in an erotic chat room at the time."

"Maybe she was surfing," Lynn offered as an explanation. "I told you she was an avid explorer."

"She wasn't surfing, Lynn. I can only read a few lines of conversation, but it's enough to show that Molly was a participant." As an afterthought, she asked, "Do you remember when those pictures were taken?"

"A couple of weeks before she was killed. I remember because I was working around the clock, trying to finish a special order. Molly came in every night to keep me company.''

''Thanks, Lynn.'' Kate hung up. She wasn't particularly knowledgeable in Internet matters, and knew next to nothing about erotic chat rooms, but there had to be a way to track down that Tiger Lilly person. LuAnn Chester immediately popped into her mind.

Kate was about to call her friend, when her cell phone rang. Checking her watch, she saw that it was noon, which meant the caller was probably Todd Buchanan. ''Hello?'' she said.

''Is this...?'' The male voice at the other end was hesitant.

''This is Kate Logan.''

She thought she heard a small sigh. ''Ms. Logan, this is Todd. Is this line safe?''

''Completely.''

''Good.''

She heard hushed voices and assumed Jessica was standing beside him.

''Thank you for taking my case, Ms. Logan. Frankly, I didn't think you would.''

''Your fiancée was very persuasive.''

''Yes.'' He let out a nervous laugh. ''Ms. Logan?''

''Why don't you call me Kate?''

''Yes...thank you.'' He cleared his throat. ''Jessica said you might have some questions.''

''A few. One of them has to do with something Lynn Flannery said.''

''Whatever it is, I'm sure it's nothing good.''

''She told me that you had beaten Molly once.''

"That's a damn lie! I never laid a hand on a woman in my life and certainly not on Molly."

"Lynn is prepared to testify to the contrary."

Todd's tone turned cynical. "Lynn was in love with Molly. I don't think a jury would view her as a credible witness."

That same thought had crossed Kate's mind but she refrained from saying so. "She also claims that she took several Polaroids of Molly the day after the beating. Yet, no such photographs turned up at the time of the investigation. Just to make sure, I asked Detective Sykes if they were placed in a separate file, and he said he never saw them."

"That's because there were no photographs. Lynn made that up to make me look bad. The woman is trouble, Kate. She'll do and say anything to make sure I hang for Molly's death."

"Why does she hate you so much?"

"Molly told me once that Lynn actually believed she would have had a chance with her if I hadn't come along. I don't know whether that's true or not—Molly liked to torment me any way she could, so she might have made that up—but I know one thing, Lynn never stopped trying to split us up."

Kate picked up the photo with the laptop in the background. "Did you know that Molly spent a great deal of time on the Internet?" she asked.

"Yes. The last year of our marriage, the Internet had become her new passion."

"Did you also know that she may have been a regular visitor in an erotic chat room called *Spider's Web?*"

"You're kidding." Kate wasn't sure whether she

heard disgust or disbelief in his voice. Maybe a little of both. "Molly?"

"Yes. Her screen name was Guinevere. I'm trying to track down one of her chat-room friends by the name of Tiger Lilly. Any idea who that might be?"

"I didn't even know Molly was into that kind of stuff." He laughed. "No wonder she had no time for me."

Kate decided to follow another hunch. "What do you know about Lynn's business partner, Denise Jenkins?"

"She's all right. I didn't know her very well."

"Are she and Lynn lovers?"

"Molly said they were. I don't think they made a secret of it."

"I also had the feeling that Denise resented Molly."

He laughed. "Big time. Not only because of Lynn's friendship with Molly but because of the way Molly insinuated herself into the business. I think Denise might have viewed her as a threat." He paused. "You think Denise may have killed Molly?"

"Anything's possible. It wouldn't have taken a lot of effort for an average-size woman to don a man's suit, comb her short hair a different way and appear to be a man, especially in the dark and from a distance."

That thought stayed with Kate long after her conversation with Todd was over.

LuAnn Chester, who had once made her living as a call girl, was one of those street-smart women with a hard-as-nails attitude and a soft heart. Four months ago, she had been instrumental in helping Kate break the prostitution ring that had cleared Eric of a murder charge. Since then, and with Kate's glowing recommendation, LuAnn had found a new job as a filing clerk in a law firm only two metro stops from Kate's office. The short distance enabled the two women to meet for lunch occasionally.

As usual on her day off, the former call girl was busy practicing her newest hobby, *feng shui,* an ancient Chinese method of arranging furniture and accessories in a way that brought harmony to the home and to the soul. LuAnn claimed the philosophy had changed her life, increasing her energy and heightening her mental abilities.

But even though LuAnn's lifestyle had vastly improved, her former profession had left its marks. At forty-five she looked at least ten years older, mostly because of the deep bags under her eyes and a spreading midsection. A good haircut could have taken a few years off her face, but she was a die-hard *Charlie's Angels* fan and still wore her brassy blond locks in an outdated Farrah Fawcett do, which, strangely enough, both suited and aged her.

"Quick," she said, reaching out to pull Kate inside. "Before all that good *ch'i* escapes."

Kate smiled, remembering that *ch'i* was Chinese for energy. "What happened to that beautiful arrangement you had on that table?" she asked.

LuAnn made a face. "Got rid of it. Dried flowers hold dead energy." Then, poking Kate in the ribs, she added, "Don't laugh. I know what I'm talking about."

"I never said you didn't."

"And you could use a little rearranging yourself." Her critical eye moved up and down Kate's body. "I see a lot of green around you, but not much red, which means you need to relax, trust people more and get rid of those negative thoughts."

"I'm a criminal attorney, LuAnn. Trust doesn't come easily to me." She sank into a cushiony wraparound sofa and let the soft pillows envelop her.

"I could give you a few pointers, but I know you didn't come here to hear me praise the benefits of *feng shui*." LuAnn sat on the floor and crossed her legs, yoga style. "You said something about a chat room over the phone?"

"An erotic chat room."

LuAnn's eyes twinkled. "What's the matter, hon? That Irish hunk of yours isn't doing it for you anymore?"

Kate smiled. "No, that's not it at all. I'm working on a new case and I was hoping you'd know enough about those chat rooms to help me out with something."

In her best Mae West voice, LuAnn said, "Honey, me and chat rooms? We talk the same language."

"Let's try this one, then—*Spider's Web*."

LuAnn let out a slow whistle. "Now what would a proper little lady like you know about *Spider's Web?*"

"So you have heard of it."

"Enough to know that it's one of the naughtiest chat rooms on the Net. Definitely not for good little girls." With a grace Kate hadn't expected of a heavyset woman, she stood up and walked over to the dining room table, one end of which was occupied by a computer. "You're looking for anyone in particular in that chat room?"

Kate followed her. "A woman with the screen name of Tiger Lilly. I need to find out if she has information on another regular, a woman who called herself Guinevere. She was murdered a couple of years ago, but I was hoping to find Tiger Lilly by pretending Guinevere is still alive. Is that possible?"

"Sure. All I have to do is take Guinevere as a secondary screen name, provided it's not already taken. It'll only take a minute."

Looking quite confident, LuAnn sat down and logged on. A menu popped up, then another. LuAnn typed her new screen name, chose a password, saved it and gave Kate a big grin.

"Is that it?"

"That's it. Now we go looking for Tiger Lilly. Problem is, two years is a long time. People come and go."

Kate looked with anticipation at the screen. "See what you can do."

With one hand on the table, the other on the back of LuAnn's chair, Kate watched as her friend moved the mouse around, pointing and clicking until the *Spider's Web* logo appeared at the top of a page.

LuAnn glanced over her shoulder, her eyes bright with mischief. This time she did her Bette Davis impression. "Fasten your seat belt, honey. It's gonna be a bumpy ride."

Kate watched in fascination as LuAnn introduced herself as Guinevere, explaining that she had been away from *Spider's Web* and was hoping to connect with some old friends. The conversation heated up quickly, with each guest spicing it up with his or her own brand of teasing. From time to time, an instant message box would appear with one of the guests trying to engage LuAnn in a hot, one-on-one conversation. She brushed them off gently before returning to the chat room, where visitors kept dropping in and out.

No one, however, had heard of Tiger Lilly.

An hour later, LuAnn stretched back and flexed her fingers. "We're not having any luck, hon."

"Could she be elsewhere? In another chat room?"

"There are hundreds of similar chat rooms throughout the Web, but only a dozen or so as shameless as *Spider's Web*. Want me to try a couple?"

"Please."

The next hour brought more of the same erotic banter between perfect strangers, requests for dates, offers of free literature and videotapes. One man even offered to fly LuAnn to Paris for the weekend, sight unseen. She just rolled her eyes and moved on to the next chat room.

At 3:45, after two solid hours of searching and weeding through myriad chat rooms and talking to an endless procession of totally uninhibited men and women, LuAnn let out a little yelp of victory.

Kate, who was on her way to the kitchen to make more coffee, rushed back. "Did you find her?"

"She just logged on in a chat room called *Sex Pals*."

Kate pulled up a chair and sat beside LuAnn, who angled the screen so Kate could read the message.

"Guinevere, you sly one," Tiger Lilly wrote. "Where have you been, girl?"

"Oh, here and there," LuAnn wrote back.

"And they didn't have Internet access here and there?" she teased. Before LuAnn could type a reply, Tiger Lilly wrote another message, this time addressing it to the rest of the group. "Gang, say hello to Guinevere. She's an old-timer from another chat room and a lot of fun. By that I mean she's *very, very* naughty."

"I like naughty," someone by the name of Tom Cat wrote.

The instant messaging box immediately popped up. "We have lots of catching up to do, girl," Tiger Lilly said. "Last thing I heard, you were getting ready for a little tête-à-tête with that sexy man, the one who liked Dom Pérignon and called himself Black Knight. How did it go? Was he everything he claimed to be? Or just another bag of wind? Come on, girl, fess up."

LuAnn looked up at Kate. "Black Knight. You know that name?"

Kate shook her head. "Try to find out if she knows anything about him, and if he's still around."

"I guess I'll have to improvise a little." LuAnn's fingers flew over the keyboard. "As a matter of fact, the little weasel stood me up," she wrote. "That's why I've been looking for you. I wanted to know if you could help me locate him. I felt like renewing old acquaintances."

"Sorry," Tiger Lilly replied. "He pulled a disappearing act, too. We haven't heard from him in ages."

"Any idea where I might find him?"

"Nope. The man just vanished into thin air. About the same time you did, as a matter of fact. I thought you and him had eloped or something."

"No, nothing like that. Oh, well, thanks anyway, girlfriend. Got to go."

"Don't be a stranger."

As LuAnn signed off, Kate couldn't hide her disappointment. "Is there any chance Black Knight is still out there?"

LuAnn shrugged. "Depends. You think he's the one who murdered Guinevere?"

"He could be."

"Then, chances are *if* he's still out there, it won't be under the same screen name, and finding him would be a little like looking for a needle in a haystack. On the other hand, he could be as close as the chat room we were in, watching, listening." She was thoughtful for a moment. "I could ask around. Got a description of the guy?"

"Medium height, medium weight. Drives a dark car."

"You ain't giving me much to work with, hon."

"The murder occurred in an out-of-the-way motel in Fairfax—the Lost Creek Motel. And we know that the killer had a penchant for Dom Pérignon champagne."

LuAnn nodded and pushed her chair back. "I'll talk to a couple of girls I know who do business through the Internet."

"I'm not sure I'm comfortable with that, LuAnn." Kate was suddenly nervous about involving innocent people. "The man is a killer. If he gets wind that someone is snooping around…"

"He won't. Those girls are smart cookies. And real careful. Now…" She stood up. "How about coming into the bedroom with me and helping me move my bed?"

Fourteen

Mitch and Alison returned from Baltimore at six o'clock, still high from the Panthers' unexpected victory against the Falcons and already making plans to attend the next game.

Despite her good intentions to stay up after dinner for a game of checkers with Mitch, Alison was barely able to make it through dessert. At eight o'clock, exhausted, she said her good-nights and went to bed, leaving Kate and Mitch to do the dishes.

As soon as she had disappeared, Mitch turned to Kate. "How did your visit with Lynn Flannery go?"

She hated to tell him what she had learned, but didn't see any way out of it. "It was...interesting."

He gave her an amused glance. "Interesting? That's all?"

"No." She took the glasses Mitch handed her and put them in the dishwasher. "That's not all." She hesitated. "I just don't know how to tell you."

"Tell me what?"

She walked over to the kitchen desk, took the box of photographs and extracted the three taken in front of the laptop. She handed them to him. "Those are three photographs out of many that Lynn took of Molly over the years."

He studied them for a moment before looking up. His expression was blank. "I take it you're not talking about Molly herself but about what's on the laptop."

"That's right." She handed him the magnifying glass. "As you can see," she continued, while he studied the photos, "Molly, who used the screen name Guinevere, had been chatting with another woman—Tiger Lilly. I didn't know how to find the woman, so I went to LuAnn, hoping she knew more about erotic chat rooms than I do." She told him about LuAnn's conversation with Tiger Lilly.

Mitch was silent. His head was down as he kept inspecting the photos, and she couldn't see his eyes, but she knew what he was going through. The sister he had loved and lost, looking for sex on the Internet, taking risks no one with an ounce of common sense should have taken.

After a while, he walked to the window and stared into the night. "He's still out there," he said, more to himself than to Kate. "Under a different name, but he's still out there."

"That's what LuAnn thinks. She's putting the word out on the street. A couple of girls she knows do a lot of business through the Internet."

"This...Tiger Lilly—" He turned around. "What did she tell you about Black Knight?"

"Nothing, other than he sounded sexy and liked Dom Pérignon."

She came up behind him. "I'm so sorry, Mitch. I didn't want to tell you."

"I wish I had known. I could have helped her."

"Lynn tried. She didn't know about the chat

rooms, but she knew Molly was heading down a dangerous path and tried to get her to stop. Molly wouldn't open up to her. I don't think she wanted to be helped, Mitch. Can we find this Black Knight?'' she asked, when he remained silent. ''When all we have is a screen name?''

''Oh, we'll find him.'' His voice was low and harsh. ''It's going to take a court order, and at least a week, but we'll find him.'' He glanced at his watch. ''It's not too late to call Frank. He's the only one who can request the court order.''

''Will he do it?''

''I think so. He said he couldn't reopen the case unless he had a good reason to.'' He picked up the phone. ''This should do it.''

After a few minutes of conversation with his old friend, Mitch smiled and hung up. ''He didn't need much coaxing,'' he told Kate.

''Good.'' With a casualness that was a little forced, she added, ''Oh, by the way, I found out something else today.''

''About Molly?''

She nodded. ''I didn't know she moved to Colorado six months before her graduation from Georgetown. Why didn't you tell me?''

Not a single muscle in his face moved. ''Because it's not relevant to the case. It was so long ago, anyway, I'm surprised Lynn even brought it up.''

''She brought it up because she thought the move to Colorado changed Molly.''

''Changed her how?''

''She said Molly became more reckless, taking risks she'd never taken before. I know you were working for Worldwide at the time and may not have noticed during your short visits here, but Lynn did. And she was troubled by it.'' When Mitch didn't comment, she asked, ''Why did Molly move to Colorado?''

''She was tired of Washington.''

''Is that all she said?''

''I think so.'' He sounded very casual, as if the event had been unimportant. ''I really don't remember.''

Now, that was hard to believe. Mitch and Molly had once been as close as a brother and sister could be, and he hadn't questioned her sudden decision to move clear across the country?

Before she could decide whether or not to challenge him on that answer, a cell phone rang. Both reached for theirs on the counter, but the call was for Mitch. As he listened, he glanced at the clock on Kate's wall. ''All right. I'll be right there.''

''What is it?'' Kate asked, when he hung up.

''An apparent homicide on Embassy Row. I've got to go.''

''Why does it always have to be you?''

He kissed her mouth. ''Because they know I need the overtime.''

''I know *that's* not true.''

She watched him walk to his car while she stood on the front step, still wondering about Molly's temporary move to Colorado.

Fifteen

Sunday morning brought the rain, a steady drizzle that turned the city a depressing shade of gray. The dreary weather seemed like the perfect excuse for Kate, Mitch and Alison to spend the afternoon at the Smithsonian, something they hadn't done in a while. Unfortunately, after only three hours' sleep, Mitch was back on the Embassy Row murder and had no idea when he'd be finished.

Bored, Alison begged Kate to drive her to Eric's house so she could visit with Candace. Not wanting to create another major row, especially now that Alison seemed to have set aside her idea to live with her father part of the year, Kate finally gave in and drove her to Georgetown.

Once back home, she slipped into comfortable leggings, an old college sweatshirt she kept for rainy days and thick socks rolled up at the ankles. Thank God, she had plenty of work to keep her busy, including the preparations for Ed Gibbons's trial, which had been scheduled for June third.

She was working on a list of witnesses when her doorbell rang. She didn't move. Alison was at her father's and Mitch was on a case. Anyone else could come back later.

The bell rang a second time, briefly, then again. Kate sighed. Clearly, whoever was out there had no intention of going away. She laid her legal pad on the sofa and went to answer the door.

When she saw the two people standing on her front porch, she was barely able to hold back a gasp.

"Ms. Logan?" the man asked.

"Y-yes." Kate swallowed as she glanced from him to the elegant, dark-haired woman beside him. She felt as awkward as a rookie attorney in front of a judge for the very first time.

"Justice Buchanan." This time, she managed a smile. Mrs. Buchanan returned it, but her husband did not. "You must forgive me. This is…totally unexpected." An understatement, she thought, as the controversial justice continued to size her up.

She glanced beyond them, expecting to see a couple of FBI agents standing guard, but saw nothing except a gray Town Car parked along the curb.

"We understand," Mrs. Buchanan said. "I hope this isn't a bad time."

"No, not at all." Kate moved aside to let them in, wishing she was wearing something a little more professional.

As they walked in, she assessed them quickly. Lyle Buchanan had seemed bigger on television, but was no less imposing in person. His famous pewter-gray hair was just as thick as it was in those official photos she had seen in magazines. He had strong features— a broad forehead, a square jaw, and eyes that seemed to penetrate one's very soul.

She remembered something Douglas Fairchild had said once when a case he had been appealing had appeared in front of the Court: *No matter how good an attorney you are, or how confident, the moment Buchanan's eagle eyes set on you, you become a bumbling idiot.*

"Are you alone?" Justice Buchanan asked.

"Yes." She led them into the living room, which was always clean and tidy, and motioned toward a pair of wing chairs in a gold-and-cream striped design. "Won't you sit down?"

Mrs. Buchanan sat gracefully, setting her purse on her lap, but her husband remained standing. Hands behind his back, he looked around the room, his unfriendly gaze moving slowly from the large bay window overlooking the street, to the inexpensive watercolors on the walls and the dozen or so family photographs displayed on the mantel. He looked a little like a general reviewing the troops—tough, watchful and fearless.

As the silence began to grow uncomfortable, Mrs. Buchanan picked up a framed photograph of Alison on the table beside her. "Your daughter?" she asked with a smile.

"Yes. Her name is Alison. She's thirteen." Too much information? Not enough? How did one speak to the wife of a Supreme Court justice?

Hallie Buchanan laughed, putting Kate instantly at ease. "Ah, those terrible teen years. I remember them well." She put the picture back. "She's lovely."

"Thank you."

Justice Buchanan, apparently finished with his inspection, turned to face her. "So you're the young woman my son chose to represent him."

His condescending tone made Kate bristle. "You sound as though you don't approve."

"I'm not questioning your abilities, Ms. Logan, but I'll be frank with you. I'm surprised that out of the hundreds of experienced criminal attorneys in this town, Todd would choose someone who is just starting out."

"Lyle!" His wife made no effort to conceal her shock. "How can you be so insensitive? We discussed Ms. Logan's credentials before we came here. You know that she's highly qualified."

He didn't seem to have heard her, or if he did, he just ignored her. "This is a complicated case, Ms. Logan, much too complicated for just one attorney. I would have felt differently if you were still at Fairchild Baxter and had the support of a first-rate criminal team, but you alone..." He pinched his lips together and gave a slight shake of his head. "I can't help wonder if you might be in over your head."

The pompous asshole, Kate thought, struggling to stay calm. He hadn't come here to meet his son's attorney, but to pressure her to withdraw from the case.

"I understand your concerns, Justice Buchanan," she said in her most professional voice. "You want the best possible representation for your son and you're not sure I fit the bill. Believe me, I would like nothing more right now than to prove to you I'm perfectly capable of representing Todd, but as you're well aware, I can't discuss the case. What I can tell you, however, is that I'm making progress."

"That's wonderful," Hallie Buchanan said, but as she looked at her husband, Kate thought she saw something other than relief in her eyes. Or was that her imagination? "Isn't that what you wanted to hear, Lyle?"

Rather than answer her, Justice Buchanan started walking around the room, his hands still behind his back. He stopped in front of the mantel and studied the photographs. Some were of Kate's late mother and father, others were of Alison and her paternal grandparents, Rose and Douglas.

One of the photographs had been taken this past Christmas. It showed Mitch on a ladder, ready to perch the angel on top of the tree. Alison, looking angelic herself, was smiling.

Justice Buchanan studied it for a long time before saying, "What does Detective Calhoon have to say about your decision to take Todd's case?"

"He was as skeptical as you are, at first, though for different reasons."

"And now?"

"He's beginning to accept the possibility that someone else killed Molly."

"Mitch was a very angry man at the time," Mrs. Buchanan said. "I tried to tell him that Todd was incapable of killing anyone, let alone Molly, but his mind was already made up and he wouldn't listen."

"I had a hard time convincing him, myself."

The woman smiled. "I'm glad Todd found you," she said. "At least you believe him. That's more than I can say for his previous attorney. And," she added, slanting a knowing look to her husband, "Syd Willard came from a large, experienced law firm, one of the best in Washington, I believe. Am I right, Lyle?"

While the reproach was hard to miss, Justice Buchanan's face remained impassive. "I made a mistake about Willard," he said, not looking at either woman. "By the time I decided to retain someone else, Todd was gone."

Hallie turned her attention back to Kate. "How is Todd, Ms. Logan? Have you spoken with him?"

"Yes. He wants you to know that he's fine, that he loves you both very much and that he's...engaged." Todd had asked her not to mention Jessica's pregnancy just yet, so she didn't.

Mrs. Buchanan pressed her hands to her chest. "Engaged? Oh, dear." She looked at her husband, who seemed equally surprised, though satisfied to let his wife handle this unexpected turn of events, then back at Kate. "What is she like, Ms. Logan? Have you met her?"

"Yes. She's quite lovely," Kate replied. "In every way. I'm afraid I can't say any more than that. However," she added as Hallie Buchanan started to rise, "since you're both here, I wonder if I could ask *you* a question."

Todd's mother shot another hesitant look at her husband.

"What do you want to know?" Lyle asked.

He didn't seem thrilled, or even mildly accommodating, but at least he hadn't shot down her request with a curt no. "While going over some old newspaper articles," she said, "one of the comments that kept being repeated was the possibility that someone killed Molly and then framed Todd to get back at you, Justice Buchanan. I wonder if you had any thought on that."

"That's a ridiculous assumption, Ms. Logan. If

anyone had wanted to get back at me, they would have killed me, not my daughter-in-law.''

"But if you had to choose one person who might be spiteful enough to kill an innocent person just to make his point, who would it be?"

He smiled without warmth. "I would have to hand you a very long list, Ms. Logan, and by the time you had finished investigating each suspect on that list, you would be old and gray." He turned to his wife. "Hallie? Are you ready?"

She looked up, her smile a little strained. "Yes."

When they reached the front door, the older woman laid a hand on Kate's arm. "Ms. Logan, should..." She drew a breath. "Should the case go to trial, what are Todd's chances that he'll be acquitted?"

"I can't make any guarantees, Mrs. Buchanan. I can only offer to do my very best."

Kate glanced at Justice Buchanan, and for a moment, just a moment, she saw his expression change. For the first time since he had walked into her house, he looked like a father instead of a famous figure. A father afraid for his son.

"What's wrong?" Jess asked, as Todd walked out of the phone booth. "You look upset."

Todd took her arm and led her across the square. As always on a warm Sunday evening, Place Louis XIV was busy with strollers. "My parents went to see Kate."

Jess's face brightened instantly. "Really? What did they say?"

He stopped at a fish stand and bought a half-dozen crisp, grilled sardines before they resumed their walk.

"My mother was a little emotional. She wanted to know how I was, and the news that you and I were engaged seemed to please her."

"And your father?"

Todd took a sardine from the brown paper and started to eat it. "He didn't ask about me."

"I'm sure he wanted to."

"I don't know. I wouldn't blame him if he never wanted to see me again. I hurt him bad, Jess. I thumbed my nose at everything he stood for, everything he taught me."

"Someday, you'll have a chance to make it up to him." She, too, nibbled on a sardine. "Did he say anything at all, or was your mother doing most of the talking?"

"Oh, he said plenty." He let out a short laugh. "He wants Kate off the case."

Jess looked shocked. "He came right out and said that?"

"Not in so many words, but I know my father, he gets his message across."

"Kate isn't quitting, is she?"

Todd laughed. "Not a chance. Apparently, she, too, knows how to get her message across."

Jess licked her fingers and wiped them off with a paper napkin. "Did she say anything more about that chat room she mentioned yesterday?"

"She seems to be making progress in that area. She found Tiger Lilly."

Jess's eyes filled with excitement. "Oh, Todd, that's good news, isn't it?"

He gave her a skeptical look. "I don't know, Jess. The whole thing seems so far-fetched to me. Accord-

ing to that Tiger Lilly person, Molly had been cor-
responding with a man whose screen name is Black
Knight, and had made plans to meet him.''

''Who is this Black Knight?''

''That's where the story gets real bizarre. No one
knows. He entered the chat room every night, took
part in the sexy banter, but never said anything about
himself.''

''How did he and Molly make plans to get together?''

''Probably through private messages. That's why
Tiger Lilly can't supply any information about him.
All she knows is what Molly told her. And the fact
that he disappeared from the chat room at the same
time Molly did.''

''But, I don't understand. Why didn't the police
find that information when they checked Molly's laptop? Didn't you tell me they took it from the house?''

''They did. The hard drive had been purged, wiped
clean.''

''Isn't that difficult to do?''

He shook his head. ''Not for someone with a little
know-how. And these days, most people with a PC
are pretty computer-literate. They would know how
to do something like that.''

Jess stopped walking and turned to him. ''Maybe
this Black Knight killed Molly and then erased the
computer files.''

''Oh, Jess, can't you see what a long shot that is?
He would have had to come into our house. How
would he even know where we lived? Molly may
have been reckless, but she wasn't stupid. She would
never give her address to a stranger.''

"Are you sure, Todd? We're talking about a woman who thought nothing of meeting a man she didn't know in a motel room."

No, he *wasn't* sure. He wasn't sure of anything anymore.

"I think this Black Knight is the best lead we've had so far." Jess linked her arm with Todd and started walking again.

"Detective Sykes seems to think so, too. He's agreed to reopen the case. Kate said he's working on a court order right now. He'll need it to obtain subscribers' information and find out who Black Knight is."

She opened her mouth. "You didn't tell me that."

"I didn't want to raise your hopes too high."

She leaned her head against his shoulder. "They're going to find him, Todd. You'll see."

Todd didn't have the heart to tell her that, in spite of Kate's optimism, he had serious doubts they'd ever find the man. Someone who had eluded the police for so long wasn't about to suddenly make a drastic mistake and get caught.

Instead, he patted Jess's hand. "Let's hope she will," he said.

Sundays in Saint-Jean-de-Luz were for strollers. Entire families came to the harbor to eat, walk around or take pictures of *la maison de l'Infante,* the house Louis XIV and his bride Marie-Thérèse had occupied shortly after their marriage.

With nothing better to do at this early evening hour, Emile Sardoux had come to Café Central for his usual Vittel-menthe while indulging in another local pastime—people watching. Next to him, a customer ordered a cognac, and Emile winced at the memory of what the liquor felt like going down his throat.

He pulled his gaze away and heaved a long-suffering sigh. Sobriety was a drag. If it weren't for Antoinette and the fact that he wanted her back in a bad way, he'd say the hell with it and order a beer.

Trying to divert his thoughts, he watched an American couple as they stood up to leave. Emile, who spoke fluent English, had eavesdropped on their conversation earlier and learned about their plans to visit *Le Rocher de la Vierge* in Biarritz before heading back to Milwaukee the day after tomorrow.

''The Rock of the Virgin Mary.'' Emile felt a lump in his throat. That's where he had proposed to Antoinette. The two of them had walked all the way to the top of the rock, and there, facing the roaring ocean, he had asked Antoinette to be his wife. He would never forget the expression on her face as she said yes, the word barely audible over the sound of the surf.

Emile's gaze fell on the table the American couple had occupied, and the newspaper they had left behind—the *International Herald Tribune*. It was opened to a center page and folded in two. At the top of the page was the photograph of a man, and above it, a headline: Son of Supreme Court Justice in Limelight Once Again.

Intrigued, Emile took the paper from the table and read.

Kate Logan, a Washington, D.C. attorney, has reopened the investigation of Molly Buchanan's murder, the thirty-year-old marketing executive who was found dead in a Virginia motel room two years ago. Still at large is Todd Buchanan, the victim's husband and prime suspect in the murder. Logan, a former associate with the law firm of Fairchild Baxter, has been unavailable for comment.

After Emile had finished reading, he looked at the grainy black-and-white photograph again. It showed a handsome young man with short blond hair, a square jaw and a thin mustache. The white dinner jacket added to his sophisticated look—he was not at all the kind of person Emile would be rubbing elbows with. And yet…

He continued to study the photograph. There was something familiar about the man's face. Was it the eyes? Or that debonair smile, maybe? He read the name again—Todd Buchanan—and shook his head. No, it meant nothing to him.

So why did he feel as though he had seen Buchanan before?

Holding the newspaper, he looked around him and searched the crowd. It was just a Sunday like any other, with tourists reading their guidebooks, children riding the carousel and their parents lining up at the sardine stands for a snack.

Emile took another sip of his drink. Was his imagination playing tricks on him? Was he so anxious for a story that he was seeing things that didn't exist?

In the state he was in, bored beyond belief, anything was possible, but…what if his hunch was right?

What if an American man, a fugitive from justice, was hiding in Saint-Jean-de-Luz?

And Emile was the one who found him?

The thought was so mind-boggling, if he had been drunk he would have sobered instantly. What a story that would make. He could almost see the headlines now: French Reporter Flushes Out Wanted Murderer.

Emile kept studying the handsome features, trying to imagine what changes the man could have undergone in the past two years. He could be sporting a beard. Or he could have shaved his head and his mustache and put on a few pounds. Add a pair of glasses, and no one would be the wiser.

Except Emile. He'd always had an eye for details.

Sixteen

At four o'clock on Sunday afternoon, after working a fifteen-hour-straight shift, Mitch called Kate. He was on his way home for a much-needed shower and a beer. Maybe some sleep—unless she could find a way to meet him there, in which case he'd forget about sleep.

With a couple of hours to spare until she picked up Alison at Eric's, Kate drove to Mitch's town house on Kalorama Road, certain that, in spite of his good intentions, he'd be too exhausted to do anything but sleep. He surprised her.

So did she. Shedding her clothes on the way to the bathroom, where she could hear the shower running, she stepped into the steaming stall, laughing at the delighted look on his face.

"Well," he said, taking her into his arms. "Aren't you full of surprises."

Already aroused, she ran her tongue over his lips. "You like?"

"Oh, I like very much." He kissed her open mouth, his hands running up and down her body, cupping her breasts. Then, pinning her against the shower wall, he gripped her thighs and wrapped them around his hips.

They made love right there, hands and mouths all over each other, their bodies slick, hot, hungry.

Later, exhausted, sated, Kate lay under Mitch's puffy green comforter. He had dozed off and lay on his stomach, one arm across her chest, the other hanging outside the bed. She wanted to cuddle close to him and listen to the deep, even sound of his breathing. But the fact that he had fallen asleep the moment his head touched the pillow proved he was in desperate need of sleep.

Gently she lifted his arm, hoping to sneak out of bed without disturbing him.

Just as she swung one leg out from under the bedding, he gripped her arm. "Don't go."

She turned back and kissed him lightly on the mouth. "You need your sleep."

"I need you more."

Skilled hands slid over her again, awakening a desire she thought she had thoroughly satisfied. Even now, after four months of intimacy, after learning all there was to know about her body, he could still surprise her, still make her feel as if this was their first time together.

"Thought you could sneak out without me knowing?" Holding her waist with both hands, he lifted her on top of him.

"You're beat."

He rose to meet her. "Yeah. Tell me how beat I am, Kate."

Eyes squeezed shut, she bore down on his erection, surrounding him, groaning with pleasure. Then she was off, moving to his rhythm, breathing hard, crying out his name—until the climax tore into her and she collapsed against his chest.

She stayed there for a minute, trying to catch her breath. "I won't be able to walk to my car."

"I tried to warn you, Kate. Absence not only makes the heart grow fonder, it does amazing things for the libido."

"Hmm. Does that mean we should stay apart more often?"

He played with a strand of her hair, curling it around his finger. "Not on your life."

She closed her eyes, so perfectly content and relaxed that she could have easily fallen asleep herself. But that was a luxury she couldn't afford. In another half hour she would have to leave to go pick up Alison. "Justice Buchanan and his wife came to see me today."

He faced her and propped his elbow on the pillow. "You're kidding. What did they want?"

She recounted the conversation and the Justice's barely disguised insinuation that his son would be better off being represented by another attorney.

"The insult aside," Kate said when she was finished, "I have a strange feeling about those two."

"What kind of feeling?"

"Creepy. Suspicious. They know something, Mitch. The entire time they were there, I felt as though the three of us were playing a cat-and-mouse game without being sure who was chasing whom."

"Maybe they were just being cautious."

"No, it wasn't that. I can't explain it. I had the same feeling when I called Terrence Buchanan's office the other day."

"I didn't know you saw Terrence."

"I didn't. His secretary put me on hold, then came back a short while later to tell me that Provost Buchanan was very sorry but he wouldn't be able to see me or even talk to me. Something about this being a busy time for faculty members. I didn't believe her. I think he was avoiding me."

"Hmm."

"What's that look for?"

A mysterious expression on his face, he opened his nightstand, took something from it and turned back, holding a bracelet. "Take a look at this."

Kate took the bracelet, a gold bangle studded with small rubies. "What's that?"

"One of the many little baubles Todd gave Molly over the years. She said this was his first gift to her, and that it had a special meaning."

"It's lovely. So delicate." She turned it around. "There's an inscription."

"I know."

"'Yours forever,'" Kate read. "'*T.*'"

She looked up. "You know something? I think Todd meant those words. I think that, in spite of everything—the fights, the insults, the constant put-downs—he really loved Molly."

"Maybe. In his own way." Mitch took the bracelet back and casually said, "Don't you find it strange that he didn't have his entire name inscribed? Just the *T?*"

Kate shrugged. "I guess there wasn't enough room."

"Or maybe…" His eyes seemed to challenge her. "Todd didn't give her that bracelet."

"But…she told you he did."

"I know what she told me. I just wonder if it was the truth."

Kate held her breath. The implication of what Mitch had just said was so startling, that she couldn't form a coherent thought. "Terrence," she said at last. "You think that's what the *T* stands for."

He shrugged. "It's possible. They knew each other long before Molly married Todd."

"How?"

"She was his student—a student with a rather serious crush on him. I was in Washington for a week right around the Easter break one year, and all she talked about was her International Law professor. When I asked her where that sudden interest in International Law came from, she replied, 'If you saw Professor Buchanan, you wouldn't have to ask.'"

Kate sat up, the sheet barely covering her naked breasts. "You think they had an affair."

"It wouldn't be the first time a handsome professor seduced a starry-eyed coed."

Kate's mind was working furiously. "Do you suppose that's why the Buchanans came to see me? They knew about Terrence's indiscretion and wanted to find out if *I* knew?"

She glanced at the clock and realized it was time to go. "No wonder he didn't want to talk to me." She got out of bed and started getting dressed. "He didn't want to be confronted with what I might know."

Hands crossed behind his head, Mitch watched her step into her slacks. "But he'll have to see me, won't he? Because I'm family. Or was."

* * *

Despite its urban setting, Jefferson University had managed to maintain a distinctive collegiate atmosphere with a seventy-five-acre campus and more than a hundred student organizations, ranging from international and political societies to literary and theater groups.

Mitch had been out of the academic life for several years by the time Terrence Buchanan had been singled out to be the next national security advisor, but he still remembered the euphoria throughout all three campuses when the news leaked out.

The celebration had been short-lived. In a press conference held in front of three thousand somber students, Terrence Buchanan had announced that, although he was withdrawing his name from the nomination, he would be staying on as provost of Jefferson University, assuring students and faculty alike that his contribution to the two-hundred-year-old school was every bit as rewarding as working for the president of the United States.

The press conference had been played and replayed on TV for days after that, until the news of Todd's escape was old news and Washington was concentrating on a new scandal.

But life was turning around for the popular provost. Just last month, the university nominating committee had announced that Terrence Buchanan was one of three men being considered for the position of president of Jefferson University.

Mitch had never had any reason to like or dislike Terrence. The fact that he was a Buchanan was enough to tip the scales on the side of dislike, but the truth was, he really didn't know the man, other than what Molly had told him.

His hands in his pockets, he fingered the bracelet, wondering if his hunch was right. If it was, the investigation of Molly's murder would be going in an entirely new direction. Of course, Terrence would never admit to having given the bracelet to Molly, much less having an affair with her. But unless the man was an accomplished liar, Mitch would see right through him.

Because it was the lunch hour and the provost's secretary was out, Terrence, who was expecting him, had left his office door open.

Terrence was on the phone, his feet on the desk, crossed at the ankle. As Mitch stopped in the doorway, Terrence beckoned him in, never missing a beat in his conversation.

"You're much too generous, Mr. Rodewald," he said affably. "And once again, a mere thank you doesn't seem to be enough."

Trim and fit, he looked like an older version of Todd, with a touch of gray at the temples and deep laugh lines around the eyes. He spoke with assurance, chuckling at all the right places and looking completely relaxed, clearly pleased that Mitch was here to witness his conversation with Samuel J. Rodewald, one of Washington's most generous philanthropists.

As Terrence continued to chat and flatter the famous benefactor, Mitch waited patiently, content to watch a true pro in action. It was easy to see how a young girl like Molly could have fallen in love with him. He exuded charm and self-confidence.

At last, Terrence brought his legs down. "Would

it be presumptuous on my part to ask you to be part of the ground-breaking ceremony next fall?'' he asked. ''Splendid. Yes, I look forward to seeing you again, too. Good day, Mr. Rodewald.''

He put the phone down and stood up, smoothing his tie as he did so. ''Sorry about that, Mitch. Rodewald just bankrolled a new library for the university, and I couldn't very well give the old goat the brush-off, could I?''

''Of course not.'' The two men shook hands.

''It's good to see you, Mitch. How have you been?''

''Busy.'' Mitch sat down. ''By the way, congratulations on your nomination.''

''Thank you, though between you and me, I don't stand a chance. Merv Lindquist is a much more likely choice.'' He shrugged. ''But those are the breaks, aren't they. You learn to take the good with the bad.'' Then, in a direct way Mitch hadn't expected, he said, ''You're here about Todd, aren't you. And the re-opening of his case.''

''That's right.''

He shook his head. ''I don't envy your position, Mitch. It can't be easy to see the woman you love represent the man who killed your sister. On the other hand, Todd is entitled to the best defense he can get. And from what I hear, Kate Logan is an excellent attorney. My mother was very impressed with her.''

But not his father. ''You make it sound as though you believe Todd is guilty.''

''Quite frankly, Mitch, I don't know what to believe. He's my kid brother. I love him and I want him back home where he belongs. Unfortunately—'' he gave a long, regretful sigh "—the evidence against him is so damaging, you'd almost have to be a fool not to believe he's guilty."

"Kate doesn't."

"And I'm glad. Todd needs that kind of support right now." His eyes locked with Mitch's. "What about you, Mitch? The last time we talked, you were convinced Todd had killed Molly. Do you feel differently now?"

"Let's just say I'm trying to keep an open mind."

Contrary to what Mitch had expected, Terrence seemed happy with that answer. Or was that just an act?

Terrence's welcoming smile returned. "So, how can I help you, Mitch?"

Now seemed as good a time as any to bring out his little trump card. "Ever seen this?" He let the bracelet dangle from his fingers.

Terrence's reaction was disappointing. Looking more curious than surprised, he lifted an eyebrow, craned his neck a little as though to take a better look, then shook his head. "I don't believe I have. Whose is it?"

Either Mitch was way off base with his suspicions or the guy was one hell of an actor. "Molly's." He turned it over and read the inscription out loud. "'Yours forever. *T*.'"

Terrence gave a hearty laugh. "Well, no one ever accused Todd of having bad taste—in women or in jewelry. Though I thought we had found all of Molly's jewelry. How did this piece end up with you?"

"Molly kept a few things at my house. This happened to be one of them. It was her favorite piece of jewelry.''

''I'm not surprised. Like I said, Todd had good taste.''

''Actually,'' Mitch said, studying Terrence's face, ''I don't think Todd gave it to her.''

''I thought you said—''

''I only repeated what Molly told me.''

''But if Todd didn't give it to her, then, who did?''

''I thought it might have been you.''

Once again, the reaction Mitch had expected didn't come. Instead, Terrence broke into a big belly laugh that turned into a cough. It was a nice touch, but this time Mitch didn't fall for it. He had seen enough acting to recognize a good show when he saw one.

''Me?'' Terrence asked when he had regained his composure. ''Where in hell did you come up with a crazy idea like that?''

''The *T* sort of clued me in,'' Mitch said simply.

''Yes, *T* as in Todd.''

''Or as in Terrence.''

''You're insane.''

''You did know Molly before she married Todd.''

''That's hardly a state secret. I was a professor at Georgetown at the time and Molly was my student.''

''A student who had a serious crush on you and took your word as gospel. In fact, weren't you the reason she stayed in school as long as she did?''

''I encourage all my students to finish what they start. I'm an academic, Mitch. I believe in a strong education.''

''But she didn't finish school, did she? Six months before graduation, she quit. Weren't you surprised by that? Didn't you feel you had failed her in some way?''

''Of course I did! Molly was very gifted. She just didn't know how to channel her talents, and yes, I did feel partly responsible for her dropping out. Any good teacher would. When I asked her why she was leaving, she said she was bored with college. She wanted to explore other things.''

''That's not my interpretation of it.''

''And what is your interpretation, Mitch?'' he asked coldly.

''I think Molly fell deeply in love while at Georgetown and was later dumped. She couldn't take the rejection and left school.''

Terrence's expression was one of utter disbelief. ''And in your sick mind, you think that man was me? And that—'' he gestured toward the bracelet on his desk ''—I gave her an expensive trinket as a parting gift? Is that it?''

''Not as a parting gift, or it wouldn't say, 'Yours forever.'''

''I didn't give her that bracelet. And I didn't have an affair with your sister.'' He squared his shoulders, his expression somber. ''I resent your accusations, Mitch. I've always been an involved teacher. I believe in reaching out to my students and taking a personal interest in their problems. I am proud of that, proud of the contribution I have made to hundreds of students over the years. So don't you dare come in here and accuse me of taking advantage of one of them.''

At last some of that calm, cool composure was beginning to unravel. ''I'm just a cop, Terrence, searching for answers.''

"I don't give a shit if you're the Dalai Lama. You have no right to even be here. Molly's murder is out of your jurisdiction."

Mitch held his gaze and leaned forward. "Just between you and me, then, where were you on the night my sister was killed?"

Terrence's face turned red as a beet. "How dare you!"

"Are you refusing to answer the question?"

"I was in my bed, dammit! Asleep. With my wife. Are you satisfied?"

"Would your wife swear to that in a court of law?"

"Get out."

"Or maybe she can't substantiate your claim. Elaine has trouble sleeping, if I recall. That's why she takes sleeping pills. Molly once told me that Elaine could sleep through a nuclear attack."

"Get out!" Terrence roared.

Seventeen

Mitch hadn't set foot inside Cromwell Jewelers since an afternoon a year ago when he had stopped two robbers from walking away with a fortune in jewels. He had been about to fly to Orlando for his mother's sixty-fifth birthday and had wanted to give her something special. The diamond teardrop pendant in the window of Cromwell Jewelers on Connecticut Avenue had seemed like the perfect gift.

Mitch had been halfway through his purchase when two armed men burst through the door. While one aimed a gun at Mitch, the other tossed a canvas bag to the frightened owner and ordered him to fill it up.

Mitch only had a split second to react. It had been enough. Before Bruce Cromwell could put a single item into the bag, one of the robbers was on the floor with a bullet in his chest and the other was plastered against the wall with his hands up, screaming, "Don't shoot me! Don't shoot me!"

The grateful jeweler couldn't get Mitch to accept the diamond pendant free of charge, but he had insisted on giving him a handsome discount.

A bell tinkled softly as Mitch entered, and within a few seconds, Bruce Cromwell walked from a back room and into the shop. He was a tall, elegant man with impeccable manners and a slight British accent.

His face lit up instantly. ''Detective Calhoon! What a pleasant surprise.'' He walked around a display case to shake Mitch's hand. ''It's good to see you again. You're looking well.''

''Thank you, Bruce. But what's with this Detective Calhoon stuff? I thought you and I were on a first-name basis.''

Cromwell bowed his head. ''And so we are. I guess you've been away too long.'' He walked behind the case. ''But you're here now, so what would you like to look at today, Mitch? Something for your lovely mother, perhaps?''

''Actually, I'd like to show *you* something, if you don't mind.'' He took the ruby-studded bracelet out of his pocket and laid it on the glass case. ''What can you tell me about this?''

Cromwell picked up the bracelet and inspected it briefly. Then, taking a jeweler's loupe from a shelf behind him, he stuck it to his right eye and bent over the bangle, turning it around as he inspected the stones, one by one.

After about twenty seconds, he removed his loupe. His expression was dismayed. ''Did you intend to sell this?'' he asked.

''No.'' Mitch frowned. ''What is it, Bruce?''

''The stones...'' Cromwell cleared his throat. ''I hate to say it, but they aren't real.''

That was a surprise. What kind of creep gave fake stones to the love of his life and made her believe they were real? ''Don't be,'' he said, brushing Cromwell's apology aside. ''As I said, I'm not interested in selling the piece. I just want to know who bought it. Is there any chance you could find out?''

Cromwell took a receipt book and a pen from a drawer. ''I'm not an expert in fake jewelry, but fortunately this town isn't short of jewelers who make a living copying expensive pieces. One of them may have made this.'' He handed Mitch a receipt. ''I'll give you a call as soon as I know something.'' He dropped the bracelet in a small envelope. ''Is that all right?''

''Thanks, Bruce. I knew I could count on you.''

Alison missed the bus on Monday morning, and Kate had to drive her to school on her way to work. By eleven o'clock, she had worked her way through a ton of paperwork, made an appointment with Ed Gibbons's court-appointed psychologist and taken a call from Mitch as he drove back from Cromwell Jewelers.

She hung up feeling a little bit like a traitor. Mitch had become her unconditional ally, just as he had before. He was going out of his way to unearth information she would never be able to get on her own, and he was sharing it with her. And how was she repaying him? By scheming behind his back.

She glanced at the doodles she had made earlier and the three words in the middle of a large square— *The Colorado Connection.* The more she thought about it, the more she believed that Molly's move to Colorado was much more significant than Mitch wanted to admit. And if she was right, as Todd's attorney, she owed it to him to fully investigate this little mystery.

But what about Mitch? Would he understand if she told him what she wanted to do? Or would her decision build more tension between them? The answers to those questions were all too obvious. She tried to not address them for a while, occupying herself with other matters, but like a nagging headache, they kept coming back. In the end, it was her duty to her client that won.

Just before she left for her appointment with Dr. Eileen Brown, she called Jim Faber, a former Washington cop who had turned private detective. Jim was thorough, dependable and discreet to a fault. And he had done an excellent job finding out the information she needed about Melanie's ex-husband.

The private detective greeted her with his usual affability. "Hey, there, counselor. How are you today?"

She took a deep breath, feeling as shaky as she had the night she had called Jessica on her cell phone and told her she was taking the case. "It depends on whether or not you can fly to Colorado for a couple of days."

"When?"

"Right away?"

"Hmm." She heard him flip through some papers. "I have back-to-back appointments all day today, but I could leave first thing in the morning. Is that all right?"

"I guess it will have to be." She told him what he needed to know, adding, "I have a photo of Molly Buchanan here at the office. I'll send it over with Frankie, along with your retainer. Will you call me as soon as you learn something?''

"You got it."

Dr. Eileen Brown was a petite, soft-spoken woman in her mid-forties with an unexpectedly strong hand-shake and a steady gaze. She came to meet Kate in the reception area of her plush office on M Street.

"Ms. Logan. I've been looking forward to meeting you."

Soon both women were on first-name basis and dis-cussing Ed Gibbons's complex personality and how to best help him.

Impressed by the woman's deep understanding of the human psyche, Kate decided to take advantage of her expertise and ask her a few questions regarding cybersex addiction.

"I've worked extensively with sex addicts," Dr. Brown replied. "And I'll be glad to answer any ques-tions you have, as long as we don't violate my clients' privacy."

"We won't. In fact, my questions are quite general. The first is, can a person with such an addiction func-tion normally? By that I mean, can they have a fam-ily, a job, normal hobbies?"

"Many do," Dr. Brown replied. "Until they reach a breaking point and can no longer handle their dou-ble lives."

"What happens then?"

"Some seek help, while others allow their com-pulsive behavior to take over their lives—lives that eventually spin out of control."

"What kind of person becomes a cybersex ad-dict?"

"All kinds. To understand what brings them to that

stage, we have to return to the person's childhood, and find out if he or she was sexually abused by a parent, or someone of authority. This type of family history is one of the most common I find in my practice. Unfortunately, the problem doesn't manifest itself until the person is well into adulthood.''

''And by then it's too late?''

''No, not at all. The disorder is a little more difficult to treat, but it's never too late.''

''How would you recognize a sex addict?''

''That's not always easy. There's a pattern some follow. A very subtle pattern. Cautious ones will be on guard at all times, while others will be incorrigible flirts. There might even be some touching, though the gesture will seem perfectly innocent.''

''Would that apply to men *and* women?''

''Absolutely.''

Kate wasn't sure why Denise Jenkins, Lynn Flannery's beautiful partner, popped into her head at that very moment. But she did—not because Kate suspected her of being a cybersex addict, but because of the way Denise had reacted the other day. What if she had known about Molly's secret pastimes and had used it to lure her to the Lost Creek Motel? Even if the idea sounded a little far-fetched, it wouldn't hurt to talk to Denise and find out exactly how she had felt about Molly.

And what better time to do that than while Lynn was out of town?

Moments after the receptionist, a perky redhead in a size-two dress, had announced Kate on the intercom, Denise Jenkins came out, looking as unfriendly as she had when they'd first met.

"This isn't a good time, Ms. Logan," she said, making no effort to disguise her annoyance. "I'm very busy."

"I promise it won't take long."

After a quick glance at the receptionist, who was pretending to be busy but was listening to every word, Denise nodded. "I suppose I can give you a few minutes."

Her office was an attractive combination of print fabrics, lush ferns and dark woods. One of the first things Kate saw on the mahogany desk was an eight-by-ten color photo of Denise and Lynn aboard a sail-boat. Their arms were wrapped around each other. They seemed blissfully happy.

Denise sat behind her desk, pushed a stack of invoices aside and took Kate completely off guard. "Are you investigating me, Ms. Logan? Is that it? You found out that I didn't like Molly very much, so you assume I killed her?"

Kate recovered quickly. "Did you?"

"No. I didn't like Molly, but I didn't kill her, though I may have wanted to at times."

"Why the animosity?"

Denise's short laugh was as sharp as a blade. "A smart attorney like you and you haven't figured that one out yet?"

"You saw her as a threat? Competition for Lynn's affection?"

"I didn't see her as a threat. She *was* a threat, in every sense of the word." She picked up a pencil and held it in her right hand, her thumb playing with the point. "Do you know why she came to work here?"

Kate shook her head.

"Her career as an entrepreneur went down the toilet, mainly because she didn't have a clue how to run a business, so she filed for bankruptcy, took a few courses in marketing and interior design and decided she was good enough to come work for us."

"Was she? Good enough, I mean."

Denise snickered. "Don't make me laugh. The extent of her skills was limited to writing press releases and following up with a few phone calls. She had no regard for time and deadlines, she came and went as she pleased, spent hours on the Internet and flirted with everything in pants that walked through the studio's doors."

"Why did Lynn keep her? Or hire her, for that matter?"

"Because she cared about her, not romantically, although she did, once."

"And you didn't like that."

"Hell, no. And I liked it even less when Molly started to make waves about becoming a partner, claiming she brought in a lot of business and therefore she should have a piece of the action." Denise laughed again. "The only business she brought in was from men who wanted to get into her pants. Once they'd done that, most of them backed out of the deal."

"There must have been a lot of tension around here."

"More than you know, but we tried to keep out of each other's hair." She stared at Kate. "I didn't kill her,'' she repeated. "I would never screw up my life because of that tramp. I may be hotheaded and jealous, but I'm not stupid."

"What do you know about the men she saw?"

"Nothing. She didn't confide in me. I only found out what she was up to after I heard how she was killed."

"Lynn believes Todd killed Molly. How do you feel about that?"

Denise shrugged. "Lynn blames Todd for everything—Molly's restlessness, her unhappiness, her deplorable lifestyle. Of course she's going to blame him for Molly's death. Nothing would make her happier than to see him behind bars for the rest of his life."

"What about you? What did you think of Todd?" *Please, God,* Kate prayed, *let her say something I can use on the witness stand.*

Denise gave another shrug. "The first time I met him, I thought he lived up to his reputation as a womanizer and a spoiled rich kid. But I was wrong. For reasons that elude me completely, he truly loved Molly. I don't think he could have killed her."

Kate waited a couple of seconds before asking, "Do you spend a lot of time on the Internet, Ms. Jenkins?"

Denise raised a thin dark brow. "That's a strange question—"

She never had a chance to answer it. The receptionist suddenly burst into the room.

"Denise, you have to come out and talk to Mrs. Waiscott. She's furious. Her new furniture was delivered today, and she claims the fabric on her sofa was put on upside down. I told her Lynn wasn't here, but she won't leave until—''

"I'll talk to her." Denise rose from behind her desk. "I'm sorry," she said, walking quickly. "I have to see this customer."

"Go ahead." Kate made a vague gesture toward the ladies' room, knowing that Molly's office was only two doors down. "You don't mind if I..."

Denise waved a hand. "No, no, go right ahead."

As soon as Denise had disappeared, Kate hurried down the hallway, bypassing the ladies' room. At Molly's door, she gave a quick glance behind her. Reassured that she was alone, she let herself in and quietly closed the door.

Lynn hadn't lied about the office being used as a storage area. Aside from the several sheets of plywood propped against the wall and the cans of assorted paint on the floor, the room was crammed with large pieces of furniture that made it difficult to maneuver.

Kate's gaze stopped on a desk piled high with sketches, some rolled up, some unfolded. At first glance, there didn't seem to be anything in here that could have belonged to Molly, which wasn't surprising. Any personal item would have been returned to the family long ago.

But since she was here, Kate decided, she might as well take a look. It was possible that the police, in their haste to pin the murder on Todd, had overlooked something.

She searched the desk drawers before moving to a credenza, which was equally empty. Three boxes marked Accessories were stacked under the window.

She went through each one, searched through an assortment of candlesticks, bookends and antique frames, and found nothing.

It didn't help that she didn't know what she was looking for. It probably wouldn't be anything blatant, just a small item, a detail so insignificant it had gone unnoticed.

Disappointed, she let her gaze sweep over the crowded room. There were more boxes, this time unmarked, on top of a bookcase. Glancing at her watch, Kate tried to gauge how much time she had before Denise returned. Probably not enough. Rather than dwell on that thought, she climbed on a chair and started going through the first box, ripping the heavy sealing tape and coughing as dust flew all around her. One thing was certain: no one had touched this part of the room in a long time. Maybe not even the police.

The first two boxes were heavy and filled with books on interior design. Kate was pulling a third box toward her when something behind it caught her eye—a glass jar filled with matchbooks, the kind customers picked up as souvenirs in restaurants and cocktail lounges.

Feeling as though she was racing against the clock, Kate grabbed the jar, climbed down and dumped the matchbooks into her purse. Then, her hands clammy and her heart slamming against her ribs, she climbed back on the chair to put the empty jar back where she had found it, pushing the heavy box in front of it. Hopefully no one would be the wiser.

She leaned against the bookcase for a moment to

catch her breath. How did people do this kind of thing for a living? She was a nervous wreck.

Seconds later, she walked out and made her way back to the reception room, where Denise was saying goodbye to Mrs. Waiscott. The crisis seemed to be over. "Is everything all right?" she asked Denise, when the woman had disappeared.

"Temporarily. But I'm afraid I'll have to cut our conversation short. I promised Mrs. Waiscott I'd go take a look at her sofa."

Kate waved her hand. "You go right ahead. I've taken too much of your time as it is."

Out on the sidewalk, Kate clutched her purse to her chest as though she were protecting the crown jewels. Opting not to take the metro, she hailed a cab.

"Hey, what's going on?" Frankie asked, as Kate rushed past her desk without bothering to pick up her messages. She noticed the purse. "Hold that thing any tighter and you'll break a rib." She winked. "What have you got in there, anyway? The Pentagon Papers?"

"Better than that." Kate jerked her head toward her office. "Come and help me."

By the time they'd gone through the more than one hundred matchbooks, they had made two piles—one for those from faraway places, and another, much smaller, from establishments that were within a thirty-mile-radius of Washington, D.C.

Frankie read them out loud. "The Blue Oyster in Silver Springs, Pearl's Bed & Breakfast in Chevy Chase, Pepe's Tapas Bar, in Falls Church, and Bubba's right here in the district, on Wisconsin Avenue." She looked up. "Don't tell me you're going to investigate a place called Bubba's all by yourself."

Kate smiled. "Would you rather do it?"

"Thanks, boss. I think I'll pass."

"In that case, why don't we let an expert handle it? Get me Jim Faber on the phone, will you?"

"I thought you were sending him to Colorado."

"Priorities have changed. Hurry, Frankie. Before he makes his travel arrangements."

Eighteen

"Mom, you're home!"

"I live here, don't I—?"

Kate stopped abruptly. Alison and Candace sat at the kitchen desk, in front of the computer. Both had spun around when she entered, looking very guilty.

"What's going on?" She looked from one girl to the other.

"Candace is here," Alison said a little too brightly.

"I can see that. I meant, what are you two doing?"

"Nothing." Alison, who was a terrible liar, turned beet red and glanced at Candace for support, which was another dead giveaway.

"We're just doing some research on the Internet," Candace said with a shrug. As usual she was dressed like a rock star, in a formfitting sweater the color of lime juice and black spandex pants.

"What kind of research?" Kate put her briefcase on a chair.

"Oh." Another shrug. "It's a school project for Alison. I was showing her how to access a Web site."

Her eyes on Alison, who looked as if she wanted to disappear, Kate marched over to the computer. "Then, you won't mind if I have a look—"

It was too late. With a click of the mouse, Candace had logged off. The screen went blank.

"Why did you do that?" Kate asked sharply.

"Do what?"

"Don't insult me, Candace. I wasn't born yesterday. Whatever you were doing on that computer had nothing to do with a school project, so what was it?"

"Mom," Alison said in a small voice. "She told you. It was nothing."

"Then, why did she turn the computer off just before I had a chance to see for myself?"

"It was an accident, Mrs. Logan, I swear. I could try to get it back if you want."

Kate ignored her. "Where is Maria?"

"Downstairs," Alison said. "Folding the wash."

From the corner of her eye, Kate saw Candace slide something under a stack of books. This time Kate didn't waste time asking questions. Without warning, she pulled the girl out of the way and yanked the sheet of paper from its hiding place.

"Hey!" Candace cried. "What are you doing?"

"Well, well, what do we have here?" Kate held up the black-and-white photograph of a grungy-looking man in his mid- to late-twenties with long, stringy black hair, a five o'clock shadow and a crooked front tooth. Except for a guitar strapped across his chest, he was buck naked, and proudly displaying a very large erection.

Kate wasn't sure how she managed to keep a handle on her anger, but somehow she did, knowing she wouldn't accomplish anything by blowing up. "Is that what you call 'research,' Candace?"

Candace's expression was completely innocent. "I've no idea how that got there."

The girl lied like a spin doctor. How could Megan not see that? Kate turned to Alison. "Can *you* explain this?"

"Uh…" Alison threw a desperate look at Candace, who shrugged as if to say Alison was on her own on that one. "It's a…picture of a boy."

"How did you get it?"

"Dustin sent it to us."

"How do you know this Dustin?"

"I don't really know him. I mean…we just met him." She swallowed. "In a chat room."

Kate saw red. Ever since finding out about Molly and Black Knight, she had been lecturing Alison every night, warning her to never go into a chat room that Kate hadn't investigated first.

"A chat room? After I expressly told you to never do that?"

"I didn't think—"

"Do you have any idea the kind of people who lurk in chat rooms? This man could be a child molester or a rapist. Or a murderer."

Tears welled up in Alison's eyes. "I didn't do anything bad, Mom. I mean…I didn't know he was going to be naked, and then, suddenly there was his picture on the screen and…" She threw another SOS to Candace, who finally came to her rescue.

"We were just kidding around, Mrs. Logan. It was a harmless prank, that's all."

Kate held out the photograph and shook it. "The man is naked, Candace. Does that look harmless to you? Were you going to reciprocate with a photo of your own?''

"Couldn't," Candace said, studying her red fingernails. "You don't have a scanner."

Pushing past her, Kate went through Candace's books, one by one, turning them upside down and shaking them.

"Hey, that's my private property," Candace protested. "You can't do that."

"When you're in *my* home," Kate said, throwing the last book back on the desk, "using *my* computer to download pornography and involving *my* thirteen-year-old daughter, your property becomes my property. You understand that?"

"Mom, please, calm down."

"Go to your room, Alison. You and I will talk about this later."

The door to the basement banged open, and Maria walked into the kitchen, a basket of laundry under her arm and a startled expression on her face. She was a short, round woman with tightly curled black hair and the strong features of her Puerto Rican ancestors. She had been the Fairchilds' maid for nineteen years and had known Alison since she was a baby. When Kate had moved out of her in-laws' house, Douglas had suggested that Maria go with her so Alison would have someone she knew and loved looking after her when Kate was at work. The arrangement had worked perfectly.

"What's going on?" the housekeeper asked.

"I'm taking Candace home, Maria. Would you mind staying with Alison until I get back?"

"Of course not." She looked from Kate to Alison. "What did they do?"

"They were in a chat room." She held the printout for Maria to see. It was clear from Maria's expression that she had no idea what had been going on while she was doing the laundry.

"Madre de Dios," Maria murmured.

"You're not going to rat on me, are you?" Candace asked.

"Oh, Candace." Kate gave her a thin smile. "I'm going to rat on you big time."

"You can't! My aunt will freak out. She'll ground me for a week."

"My recommendation will be one month." She shoved the books into the girl's arms. "Get your coat."

"Kate, I'm so sorry," Megan said after she'd sent her niece to her room. "I had no idea Candace was into that kind of thing. I'll talk to her, I promise. And I'll make sure this never happens again."

"I'll be honest with you, Megan," Kate replied. "I never felt truly comfortable with Alison and Candace being friends. The difference in their ages is just too great. Alison may sound older than thirteen at times, but in many ways she's still a child. I would like to keep her that way a little longer."

"I understand."

Eric, of course, had to put in his two cents. "Why don't you activate the parental control option on your computer?" he asked. "That way you wouldn't have to worry about Alison entering Web sites you didn't approve of."

"I never had a reason to activate that option, Eric. Alison and I had an understanding about the Internet."

While Megan went upstairs to talk to Candace, Eric walked Kate to the door. In a rare moment of complete perceptiveness, he said, "What's got you so bent out of shape, Kate? I understand why you're upset—I am, too—but I've never seen you like this."

"Don't you read the papers, Eric? Chat rooms have become one of the safest places for some men to prey on innocent young girls. Tonight it was just a photo, but what about tomorrow night? Or next week? Will this Dustin ask to see Alison?"

"She would never go!"

"How do you know, Eric? How do you *really* know?"

Eric was visibly shaken. "I suppose I don't."

"And you had the nerve to tell me that my daughter was not safe in my home." She let out a shaky laugh. "Take a good look at what's going on under your own roof, Eric, because until you do, and until I'm a hundred-percent sure that there will be no repeat of what happened tonight, Alison is not setting foot in this house."

"Now just a minute—"

Kate strode off.

Nineteen

"Thank you, Maria." Kate dropped her keys on the kitchen desk. "Did Alison say anything while I was gone?"

"I went up and we talked a little." The house-keeper's face showed her deep concern. "I'm so sorry. I should have watched them more closely."

"Don't blame yourself, Maria. You couldn't have known they'd sneak behind your back and do something like that."

Maria slipped into her coat. "I don't think it was Alison's fault."

"I realize that."

"So…" The housekeeper gave her a sidelong look. "You won't be too hard on her?"

Kate smiled. Maria had always been fiercely protective of Alison, which was one of the reasons Kate felt so comfortable having her around. "I just want to talk to her, make sure she understands what a dangerous game she was playing."

"Then, I'll go. Oh, and Mitch called earlier. He said for me not to cook dinner. He's bringing pizza— half with just cheese for Alison and the other half loaded."

Kate was glad to hear that Mitch would be stopping

by. If Alison didn't want to listen to her, she'd listen to Mitch.

She found her daughter in her room, sitting in a chair, her arms folded against her chest, her eyes full of resentment. Kate sat on the edge of the bed, glad that her outburst on Eric's doorstep had drained all the anger out of her. Surprisingly, it was Alison who spoke first.

"Mom, how could you?"

"How could I what?"

"Act the way you did and embarrass me in front of my friend."

"You don't think I was justified to be upset?"

Alison tightened her arms around herself and stared out the window.

"What you and Candace did was very dangerous." She felt as though she were talking to a wall, but went on just the same. "You and I talked about that, didn't we? How some men use chat rooms to meet young girls like you, how they pretend to be someone they're not and then lure them to some isolated place."

"And you think I would do that?" Alison asked. "You think I would just go and meet someone I don't even know?"

"I would hope not—but there's another reason I'm so upset. Once someone knows your e-mail address, he has access to all sorts of other information—where you live, where you go to school, what you do in your spare time."

"I'm sorry." Alison was starting to mellow a little. "Was Daddy mad?"

"He was furious." Let him be the bad guy for a change.

"Is Candace grounded?"

"For two weeks."

Alison finally met Kate's gaze. "Are you going to ground me, too?"

"No. I realize that going into that chat room wasn't your idea. You should have said something to Candace, tried to stop her, but I understand why you didn't. For your safety's sake, however, I'm going to change our e-mail address. And I want your absolute promise that you will not give it to anyone I haven't approved of."

Alison looked relieved. "I promise. Is that all?"

"Not quite. Mitch is coming over. He knows a lot more than I do about the dangers of chat rooms. I want you to listen to what he has to say. Can you do that?"

Alison nodded.

"How did it go?" Kate asked when Mitch returned to the kitchen.

He stole a slice of pepperoni from the pizza Kate had kept warm in the oven. "She listened. And you were right. She wanted to stop Candace but didn't want to look like a baby. Peer pressure is a tough enemy, Kate. Parents deal with it all the time. You're lucky. Alison learned her lesson, and I don't think she'll let anyone download pictures of naked men in her house ever again. But to make sure, why don't you go ahead and block the sites you don't want her to see?"

"I already have. While you were upstairs."

The rest of the evening was uneventful, with only a trace of tension between mother and daughter. After Alison had gone to bed, Kate and Mitch had one more cup of coffee, then it was time for him to go.

"Thanks," she said, walking him to the door.

"I didn't do anything."

"You were here."

He threw his jacket over his shoulder and kissed her. "Let me know if you ever want it to be more than that."

He left her standing on the front porch, stunned and speechless. What had he meant by that?

On Tuesday morning, Kate spent two hours in court waiting for a ruling on a misdemeanor and another half hour talking on the phone to the clerk at the Lost Creek Motel. Mike Banaki had been promoted to daytime manager since the murder, but he remembered that night well. He was friendly and earnest, but as Kate had expected, he hadn't shed any new light on the case and only repeated what he had told the police two years ago and Mitch last week.

When Kate asked him if the person he had seen coming out of room 12 could have been a woman, he thought for a moment and simply said, "I suppose so, but I couldn't swear to it in court."

His statement might be enough to show reasonable doubt, Kate reflected. At the same time, it could be regarded as a desperate attempt on her part to cast suspicion away from her client.

Elbows on her desk, Kate sank her fingers into her hair. This case was beginning to get to her, making her edgy. The media wasn't helping. Not a day went by without a newspaper or a television broadcast mentioning the murder, speculating on Kate's strategy, even questioning her experience. She didn't get it. Less than two weeks ago, following her appearance on CNN, she had been the darling of the media. Now that she had reopened the Molly Buchanan murder, the news people had made a hundred-and-eighty-degree turn. It was almost as if they expected her to fail. Was Todd more unpopular with the press than she'd thought? Or were they just trying to get back at Justice Buchanan?

She had just lowered her head on the desk, when Frankie buzzed her. "You didn't forget that Alison has a half-day today, did you? And that you promised to take her shopping?"

Kate's head snapped back. "Oh God, is it that time already?" She picked up her purse, thanked Frankie on the way, and ran out of the reception room.

"No," Kate said firmly. "I will not buy you black-berry-colored lipstick. Or black eyeshadow. You look beautiful just the way you are—*au naturel*."

No longer sulking as she had last night, Alison stood at the lipstick counter in Douglas Cosmetics on the second level of the Union Station Mall and pouted. "But all my friends wear those colors, Mom."

"And they all look like vampires. Is that what you want? To look like Dracula?" She didn't wait for a reply. "And, anyway, didn't we come here to buy jeans?"

Alison said something unintelligible as she put the lipstick back on the display board and walked out, leading Kate toward Compagnie Express. Feeling nostalgic, Kate followed her, remembering what a pleasure these shopping trips used to be, a true bonding experience between mother and daughter. But Alison was a teenager now, and makeup introduced a whole new set of emotions on both sides. These days, a trip to the mall was about as much fun as a wake.

Fortunately, Kate had mastered the fine art of compromising. As a trade-off for the black lipstick, she agreed to let Alison add one item that hadn't been on the list—the Backstreet Boys' latest CD.

It was five o'clock by the time they walked out of Sam Goody's. Kate had hoped to finish sooner to avoid the rush hour, but hadn't been that lucky. Struggling with their packages, Kate and Alison ran for the escalator that would take them to the subway level.

As expected, the platform was packed with commuters waiting for their trains. People who rode the metrorail system on a daily basis were the most relaxed group, content to read their newspaper and be jostled. It was all part of the routine. Others, less tolerant, frowned and grumbled at the slightest intrusion on their space.

As more people poured down the escalator, Kate laid a hand on Alison's arm. "Don't stand too close," she warned. Alison had an annoying habit of leaning over the edge of the platform and peering into the tunnel as the train approached. Sometimes Kate suspected she did it on purpose, just to get to her. Today, however, she remained by Kate's side.

A Japanese woman, who had apparently been on a shopping spree herself, was watching her. Kate smiled and rolled her eyes as if to say, *children.* The woman smiled back then let out a small gasp as she was suddenly shoved against Kate. Cursing herself for not taking a cab, Kate steadied her, aware that the crowd had thickened in the last few minutes and was beginning to crush them. A map of Washington, D.C. slipped out of the woman's hand and fell on the platform. Apologizing profusely, half in English, half in Japanese, she bent to pick it up, but Alison, smaller and quicker, beat her to it.

"Here you go." With a smile Alison seemed to reserve for strangers, she handed the woman her map, while in the distance, a train rumbled.

"Thank you." The woman bowed. Giggling, Alison returned the bow.

As the rumble grew louder, the crowd started to move closer to the tracks, and once again Kate was pushed farther toward the edge of the platform. Angry, she turned around. "You in the back," she shouted to no one in particular. "Quit pushing before someone gets hurt."

But as her warning was seconded by a man behind her, another shove sent the crowd forward, dangerously close to the tracks. Kate heard a curse, then a scream. Her arm shot out with the speed of a piston, and she yanked Alison back just as the train emerged from the tunnel.

There was another scream, bone-chilling this time. As if in a dream, Kate saw the Japanese woman stumble. "No!" Still holding on to Alison, Kate tried to grab the woman's coat, but couldn't hold on.

A gasp of horror rippled through the crowd as the woman fell into the path of the oncoming train.

"Mommy! Oh God, Mommy!" Alison's hands

flew to cover her mouth. Her eyes were wide with panic.

Too shaken to speak, Kate gathered her close and held her, while all around them people yelled and screamed.

"Mommy..." Alison's voice was a muffled whisper. "Is she...?"

Before Kate could think of something to say, Alison started to breathe in big hiccuping gasps. Recognizing the beginning signs of hyperventilation, Kate quickly drew her past the crowd and toward a concrete bench. She went through her purchases, searching for a small paper bag, found one and held it over Alison's mouth. "Take a few short breaths," she ordered. "Good. Now do it again."

Eyes closed as if to block the horrible scene that had unfolded right in front of her, Alison did as she was told until she was able to breathe on her own. Her face was chalk white, her body trembling from head to toe.

Kate held her, murmuring soothing words. All around them chaos reigned while alarm bells went off. Then, a strong, authoritative voice shouted an order.

"Let us through. Metro PD. Let us through, please."

The crowd parted as a half-dozen uniformed officers rushed forward, followed by two paramedics carrying a stretcher. Someone must have notified the conductor, or the subway authorities, because the train was moving again, very slowly this time, and backward.

"Nobody leaves," the same booming voice ordered. "You people just stay put, please. We need to get your statements."

The human wave, huddled together now, moved toward the center of the platform where a glassed-in advertisement extolled the benefits of a sugarcoated children's cereal. While the paramedics jumped down and removed the Japanese woman's body, the uniformed officers tried to calm the crowd and get as much coherent information as they could.

"That lady over there would know more than I would." A man pointed at Kate. "She was standing next to the victim."

The officer, a ruddy-faced man with a protruding belly, walked over to the bench, his little notebook already open. "Is that true, ma'am? You saw what happened?"

Kate nodded, aware that a camera crew from a local TV station had arrived on the scene and was filming her. "Everything moved so fast. When I saw the woman lose her footing, I tried to pull her back, but the momentum was too strong. I couldn't hold her."

"Did someone push her?"

"I think so. It started in the back and turned into a chain reaction. We were all propelled forward."

"Did you see who did the pushing?"

"No—"

"I did."

All eyes turned toward Alison, who was looking at the officer with big, wet eyes. She seemed calmer now, and the shaking had finally stopped.

Being careful not to crowd her, the officer moved a little closer. "What's your name, young lady?"

"Alison. Alison Logan."

Kate wrapped a protective arm around Alison's shoulders. "She's my daughter, Officer."

He nodded and wrote something in his book. "All right, Alison. Why don't you tell me what you saw."

"A man, trying to get away, right after that last push. He wore a knit cap, pulled down low, and a black windbreaker."

"Do you see that man here now?"

Alison scanned the crowd and shook her head.

"Can you describe him?"

"I don't know. We were all very close and being pushed around. I didn't get a good look at him, but…" She frowned, concentrating. "I remember that he had something wrong with his ear."

"What do you mean, Alison?"

"One of his ears was missing, or maybe part of it was missing."

"I thought you said he had a knit cap on, pulled down low."

"It was low on his forehead, but I could see that part of one ear was missing."

"Left ear or right ear?"

Alison thought for a moment. "Right, I think. No, left." She sighed. "I'm not sure."

"I saw him, too," a woman nearby said excitedly. But because he'd had his back to her, she could offer no further description other than the black windbreaker, the knit hat and the fact that he had left in a hurry. Nor could she corroborate Alison's claim about the mangled ear.

"Officer," Kate said, "my daughter has suffered a traumatic shock. If you're finished with her, I'd like to take her home."

"In a moment, Ms. Logan. I need to talk to some of the other folks, then I'll get back to you. Until then, no one goes anywhere. There won't be any trains for a while, anyway. The line has been shut down."

"Mitch, come here, will you?"

At his friend's command, Mitch stood up, circled his desk and hurried into the next room, where Tom Spivak and two other detectives stood watching a special bulletin on TV. "What's going on?"

"A woman just got run over by a train at Union Station." Tom pointed at the screen. "Kate and Alison were witnesses."

As the camera panned over a grim-looking crowd, Mitch saw them—two figures, pale and huddled together.

"They were taking the red line to Cleveland Park," Tom said.

Mitch thanked him and ran out.

Maria and Frankie were already at the house, when Mitch arrived with Kate and Alison. He'd gotten to Union Station as they were about to leave and had taken them home.

"God, boss, what a horrible thing for you to see." Frankie gave Kate a warm hug. "And you, pumpkin." She hugged Alison, too. "Are you all right? Do you need anything?"

"I made hot chocolate," Maria said.

"I think her stomach is a little queasy," Kate said. "But thank you, Maria. Maybe later?"

"What about you, Detective Calhoon? Would you like a soft drink? Or maybe something stronger?"

Mitch smiled. "I might take you up on that offer, Maria, but not right now."

"I heard about the accident on the six o'clock news." Frankie took Kate's and Alison's coats and tossed them on the sofa. "I couldn't believe my eyes. It was bad enough to hear how that poor woman died, but to find out that you and Alison had witnessed the whole thing..." She shuddered then looked at Mitch. "Were you there, too?"

Mitch shook his head. "I heard about it the same way you did—on television."

The phone rang. Maria answered it, then handed the cordless extension to Kate. "It's Mrs. Fairchild."

"Kate, dear Lord!" Rose exclaimed. "I just saw the news. Are you and Alison all right? Should I come over?"

"We're fine, Rose. A little shaken, but fine. Maria and Frankie are here. So is Mitch."

"Is one of them spending the night? I don't want you to be alone. Maybe you should come here. Mitch could drive you?"

Though Kate deeply appreciated her ex-mother-in-law's concern, she turned the woman down gently. What she and Alison needed right now was some time alone. "That's not necessary, Rose. Dr. Blackstone, Mitch's friend, will be here shortly to make sure Alison is all right. After that, she's going straight to bed, and I won't be far behind her. I'm exhausted."

"All right." Rose sounded disappointed. "If you're sure."

"I'm sure, Rose."

"Have you called Eric? He should know, don't you think?"

"I'll call him, Rose. Thanks for reminding me."

Moments later, Dr. Russell Blackstone arrived. He was a handsome GP with dark-rimmed glasses and excellent bedside manners. After examining Alison, he told Kate she was still a little shaken but would be fine. The mild sedative he had given her would help her sleep.

It took some time for Kate to convince Frankie and Maria she was fine and didn't need to be looked after. They left, reluctantly and only after Kate promised not to go to work in the morning—a promise she had no intention of keeping.

Mitch was a tougher sell. He kept looking out the window, scrutinizing the quiet street, doing all the things men like Mitch did instinctively. "What are you doing?" she asked. "Why do you keep looking out the window?"

"Don't mind me." He let the drapes fall back. "It's a nasty little habit cops pick up."

"Well, stop it. You make me jumpy. And go home. I'm fine."

He picked up his jacket but made no move to leave. "You're sure you don't want me to stay? I could bunk on the sofa."

She smiled. "If you bunk anywhere, it will be in my bed. But not with Alison here." She took his arm and walked him to the door. "I'll call you first thing in the morning."

"All right. I'm out of here."

She watched him drive away, and didn't close the front door until his car had turned the corner.

Twenty

Kate sat in her family room in her terry robe and fuzzy slippers, sipping one last cup of chamomile tea. Her muscles ached with fatigue. She had been so sure she'd collapse from exhaustion the moment Mitch left, but now that she was alone, she was too keyed up to sleep.

The events of the past five hours kept replaying in her head. The woman, she now knew, was a tourist from Osaka, Japan, and had been in Washington as part of an organized tour. Her name was Kyoko Magasa. She was thirty-three, single, and worked as a travel agent. Her parents had been notified and were on their way to the U.S.

How quickly everything had happened, Kate thought for the hundredth time. A moment in time, suspended, in slow motion, and then it was all over. She didn't think she would ever be able to erase the image of that screaming woman from her memory.

A loud knock at the front door jolted her out of her thoughts. Kate stood up, walked across the foyer. "Who is it?" she called out.

"Eric."

Oh God. She closed her eyes. In spite of her promise to Rose to call him, he had completely slipped her mind. And from the sound of his knock and the sharp tone of his voice, he had heard the news. Bracing herself for an onslaught of reproach, she drew a breath and opened the door. "Hello, Eric."

In lieu of a greeting, he stormed into the foyer and turned on her, his expression furious. "Why didn't you call me? Why did I have to hear from some TV reporter that my daughter was almost killed tonight?"

"Keep your voice down, please. Alison is sleeping." She closed the door. "I meant to call you, but things have been a little hectic around here. That accident—"

"That was no accident, Kate. It was an attempt on your life."

She stood there gaping at him. "You're out of your mind."

"You think so?" He bobbed his head as he always did when trying to make a point. "If you do, then explain to me why the man Alison saw ran away."

"He was probably scared."

Eric gave a stubborn shake of his head. "No. I heard the comments from one of the witnesses. He said the shoving began when the man in the black windbreaker tried to get to the front of the crowd— where you were standing, Kate."

She had heard that same statement. "He was just another rude passenger trying to get ahead of the crowd. The truth is, no one really knows how the pushing started."

"What if I'm right? What if that man was after you?"

"For God's sake, will you stop it?" With one hand, she grabbed him by the sleeve and dragged him into the kitchen so the sound of his voice wouldn't carry straight through to Alison's room. "No one is after me."

"It could have been my daughter under that train. Don't tell me that didn't cross your mind."

"She's my daughter, too! And of course it crossed my mind. Why do you think I'm still up? But it had nothing to do with me. I repeat, it was an accident. Union Station is one of the busiest metro stops in Washington. You've been there at rush hour, you know the pushing and shoving that goes on when people try to get to their trains. That's exactly what happened today. Someone pushed a little too hard and…"

As the image of the woman falling over the edge jumped into her mind again, Kate closed her eyes briefly. She sank her hands into her hair and pushed it back. "I can't even bear to talk about it. It was too horrible."

Eric's expression softened, but only slightly. "All right, look, I don't want to upset you any more than you are. Just…get Alison."

Kate stared at him. "Get her? What are you talking about? I told you she's asleep."

"Then wake her up. I want to take her home, where she'll be safe."

"She's safe right here, Eric. What's the matter with you? How can you barge in here, at ten o'clock at night, demanding to wake her up and take her clear across town. How selfish can you be?"

"Well," he sneered, "isn't that just like you. You're the one responsible for this mess, and now you're turning the tables around, making it appear as if *I'm* the one to blame.''

Unlike Kate, Eric had no compulsion about shouting to make his point. Before she could remind him to keep his voice down, Alison was standing in the doorway. Rosy-cheeked and disheveled, she stood there in her blue nightgown, groggy from the sedative, looking much younger than her thirteen years. And terribly vulnerable.

"Daddy?" She rubbed one eye with her knuckles. "What's wrong? Why are you screaming?"

"Are you satisfied?" Kate hissed.

Then, not waiting for an answer, she rushed to her daughter, Eric behind her. "Nothing is wrong, sweetie. Your dad was worried about you and stopped by to make sure you were all right." She turned to look at Eric, ready to murder him if he didn't back up her story. To her relief, he walked the few steps to where Alison stood, got down on his haunches and hugged her.

"I'm sorry if I woke you, princess," he said, using the nickname he had given her when she was just a baby. "Your mom said you were fine, but I had to see for myself." For a moment, he looked as though he was going to add something else, but after glancing at Kate, who was still glowering at him, he said, "I see that you are, so I'll let you go back to sleep. We can talk about what happened later, okay?"

"Okay, Daddy." Alison wrapped her arms around Eric's neck and hugged him.

"Good night, princess."

"Good night, Daddy."

"I'll go up with her," Kate told Eric. "I trust you can let yourself out?"

Kate lay in bed, unable to get to sleep, cursing Eric for planting that stupid idea in her head.

But what if he was right? What if the incident at the metro station was not an accident, but an intentional act? A warning for her to back off? A chill of unease swept over her as she tried to think of who hated her enough to want her dead, and realized this had nothing to do with hatred. If, indeed, someone had tried to kill her tonight, fear was the motivator. Someone was afraid of her, afraid of what she might find out.

And that someone could only be Molly's killer.

For the past two years, he, or she, had been completely safe. Now everything had changed. The case had been reopened, and under the heat of the new investigation, the suspects were beginning to surface. First there was Terrence Buchanan, who may or may not have had a relationship with Molly. Then came his famous father, the irascible justice, who wanted Kate off the case but had no obvious motive to kill his daughter-in-law. And, of course, there was his wife—sweet, meek Hallie—who, in Rose's words, would do anything for her oldest son. Not the least, there was Lynn Flannery, who loved Molly and hated her lifestyle, and Denise Jenkins, the openly jealous lover.

Had one of them become a little too nervous about Kate's investigation? Or was there someone else? Someone she hadn't thought of yet.

All of a sudden she understood Mitch's earlier behavior, his whispered conversation with the police officer at Union Station, the way he had rushed her and Alison out of there, his lengthy, precise questioning during the ride to Cleveland Park. She had been too shaken at the time, and too preoccupied with Alison, to notice his mood, or understand why he had been so insistent about spending the night.

Now she did.

He hadn't bought the accident theory, either.

She lay in the dark, watching a branch from the old oak tree out in the yard cast strange shadows on the wall. One of them looked like a woman tumbling. It was a long time before Kate finally fell into a troubled sleep.

Twenty-One

While Kate didn't frighten easily, the possibility that Alison could be in danger was enough to force her to take precautions she had never taken before. The following morning, she drove Alison to school and spoke with her teacher, stressing that under no circumstances was anyone, other than she or Eric, allowed to pick up her daughter.

On the way to her office, she called Mitch. "Tell me the truth," she said when he answered. "Do you think Alison or I were the target last night—not that Japanese woman?"

He was silent for a while before asking, "What makes you think that?"

"Eric. He stopped by last night, demanding to take Alison home with him because, in his opinion, *I* was the intended target, not Ms. Magasa."

She heard Mitch sigh. "The thought entered my mind."

"Why didn't you tell me?"

"Because I didn't want to worry you without some concrete evidence."

"And now you have it?"

"No. All we have are two possible suspects. Both live in the immediate Washington area and fit Alison's description. One is a recovered drug addict with several priors. He was born with a deformed left ear. The other is Luther Whorley. In some circles, he's known as Van Gogh, because of an ear he lost in a barroom brawl. He works for his uncle, a notorious crime syndicate figure—Lou Torres.''

Kate knew the name well. Lou Torres had started as a loan shark before moving up the ranks and eventually becoming the head of one of the East Coast's most powerful crime families. Torres's ''clean'' graft practice of paying police and politicians allowed him to run his bookmaking outfits, his loan-sharking activities, his porno parlors and his prostitution setups. Well-connected and smooth as snake oil, he managed to stay out of jail by hiring some of the best legal minds in the country.

''Why would either Torres or his nephew want to harm me?''

''Unlike his uncle, Luther's done time. Did you ever prosecute him?''

''No.''

''I didn't think so. And if he wanted revenge against you, why would he wait so long?''

''I want those two men questioned, Mitch—Luther and that former drug addict.''

''They will be.''

At five o'clock, as Kate and Alison were watching *Little Women* together, Mitch called back. ''Torres's nephew was just brought in.''

Kate glanced at Alison. ''What about the other man?'' she asked in a low voice.

''He died of lung cancer in January.'' He paused.

"I want to put Luther in a lineup. Can you bring Alison to headquarters?"

Kate stiffened. "Why don't you ask that other witness to identify him?"

"I just finished talking to her. She still claims she didn't see his face, only his back."

"Oh, Mitch. Alison has gone through so much already. I don't know if I can ask her to do this."

"We need her, Kate. Without a positive ID, I'll have to let Luther go."

Kate sighed. "All right. I'll ask her. But if she refuses to come, I won't force her. You understand that, don't you?"

She heard the reluctance in Mitch's voice when he said yes.

She had misjudged her daughter. "I want to do it, Mom," Alison had told her. "I want that man to pay for what he's done."

A half hour later, Kate and Alison arrived at the Washington Metropolitan Police Department complex on Indiana Avenue. Mitch, who had come to meet them in the lobby, wrapped a reassuring arm around Alison's shoulders as he escorted them toward the elevators.

"Did your mom explain to you what a police lineup is?"

Looking very grown-up, Alison nodded. "It's five men, standing side by side. I'll have to pick the one I saw in the subway yesterday."

"Exactly. All five men will be of similar height, weight, age, and will be dressed approximately the same."

"Do they all have missing ears?" she asked, looking up at Mitch.

Mitch smiled. "No. In fact, their ears will be covered."

"Why?"

"Because the mangled or missing ear could influence your judgment. We need more than the ear for a positive ID. You did see his face, right?"

"I only had a quick look."

Mitch patted her head. "You'd be surprised how much the subconscious remembers, even after one quick look."

"Is he... Will he see me?"

"No." They entered a small room, and Mitch closed the door, pointing at a window overlooking another room. "This is what we call a two-way mirror. You can see the people in the next room, but they can't see you."

"But they know I'm here."

He glanced at Kate, who nodded. "Yes," he said. "However, the man you identify will be taken away to be questioned before you even step foot outside this room. There's no chance for him to see you."

Praying Alison wouldn't feel the shaking in her hands, Kate anchored them firmly on her daughter's shoulders. Whoever was behind this would have to kill her first, before he got to Alison.

She saw Mitch bend down and speak softly. "If you're ready, I'll instruct the officer you see over there to bring the men in."

Alison nodded. "I'm ready."

Mitch spoke into a mike on the wall. "Bring them in, Josh."

Almost immediately, five men filed in, took their position against a white backboard and turned to face the mirror, their faces devoid of expression. Kate felt Alison shrink back against her.

"It's all right, baby." Kate pressed her cheek against Alison's head. "Remember, they can't see you."

Mitch came to stand beside her. "Take your time, Alison. Look at them carefully and try to remember what you saw on that platform."

Kate felt uneasy. Even for an adult, the experience of having to identify a criminal through a lineup was unnerving. She could only imagine what it could do to a young impressionable girl like Alison.

Several seconds went by, then a few more. Kate glanced at Mitch, who looked down at Alison. "Recognize anyone?" he asked gently.

Kate, who had been watching Alison and not the five men, saw her daughter bite her lip. "I think it's...number 3," Alison said at last.

"You're not sure?"

"I don't know." Her voice was just a whisper. "It looks like him, but..."

"Maybe if I brought him a little closer?"

Alison nodded.

"Number 3," Mitch said into the mike. "Would you please take two steps forward?"

The man obediently did as he was told. His hands behind his back, he stared at the mirror with that same blank expression. Kate tried desperately to jar her memory but couldn't form an image. Everything had happened too fast—the pushing, the woman screaming, Kate yanking Alison back, then trying to grab hold of the woman....

"Is this better?" Mitch asked.

Alison nodded again. She took another few seconds, then looked up at Mitch. "It's him," she said quietly.

"Are you sure?"

She nodded and looked at the man again. "Yes, I'm sure. It's him."

Kate threw a quick inquisitive look at Mitch, but his face was impenetrable. He just gave Alison's head a pat before saying a few words Kate couldn't hear to the officer at the door.

When he turned back to face them, he was smiling. "Why don't you and your mom go wait at my desk," he said. "Officer Dunn, here, will get you something to drink."

Alison looked confused, but Kate had already understood. Alison had failed to identify the perpetrator. "It's not him, is it?" she asked in a whisper.

Mitch shook his head. "The man she identified is one of ours—Sergeant David Bloom."

"All right, Luther. Why don't you make it easy on yourself and come clean?"

In a windowless interview room, Mitch pulled up a chair and sat down, while his friend Detective Tom Spivak, an eleven-year veteran with Metro PD and built like a linebacker, perched a hip on the corner of the wooden table.

Mitch knew the questioning was illegal and so did his friend. That's why Tom had insisted on being present.

"I don't want you to do anything stupid," Tom had told him.

Across from Mitch, Luther watched them with a cocky expression. He was a runt of a man, barely five feet tall and a hundred pounds soaking wet. But what he lacked in stature, he more than made up for in smarts, even though his rap sheet said he only had a seventh-grade education. Part of his right ear had been severed in a bloody barroom fight that had left his attacker dead. Because of several witnesses who swore the other man had thrown the first punch and Luther was only defending himself, he had gotten off.

He had been in and out of foster homes for years, until his uncle had taken him under his wing and taught him everything there was to know about the business. Luther had been a quick study. By the time he turned twenty, he was Lou Torres's right-hand man and an expert at inflicting pain. The word in the street was: *Don't mess with Luther. When he comes to collect, you pay.*

"You two clowns," Luther said in a voice made scratchy by too many cigarettes. "You think I'm stupid? You think I don't know your so-called eyewitness couldn't identify me as your..." He made quotations marks in the air. "Metro killer?"

"It was you, Luther. It's only a matter of time until we prove it. And when we do." Mitch shook his head. "We won't be as inclined to cut you a deal as we are now."

Luther slouched in his chair, his legs spread wide, his arms dangling by his sides. "I don't need you to cut me no deal, Calhoon. Because as soon as my attorney arrives, I'm outa here." His lips pulled in a thin, nasty smile. "And then I'm gonna sue your ass for holding me without cause. You and your Barney Fife patrol are gonna wish they never laid eyes on Luther Whorley."

Mitch ignored him. "Where were you at 4:00 p.m. yesterday?"

"At home, doing what I always do during March Madness."

"Oh, yeah?" Tom said. "You're a basketball fan, Luther?"

"You got a problem with that?"

"Who was playing?"

Luther didn't miss a beat. "Duke vs. UCLA."

"Who won?"

"The Devils, man. Good thing, too. I had ten big ones riding on that team." His grin turned smug. "Want to know how many points Shane Battier scored?"

Mitch and Tom exchanged a glance. The bastard had covered all the bases.

Mitch watched him with an unblinking gaze. "I don't know about you, Detective Spivak, but I smell a rat. Guy's too well prepared, if you ask me. What do you think, Luther?"

Luther leaned forward, his smile gone. "You ask me what I think? I'll tell you. I think you're full of shit, trying to intimidate me with your Dirty Harry routine. I'm a law-abiding citizen now, in case you haven't checked lately. I pay my taxes, I drive within the speed limit and I go to church every Sunday. Hell, I don't even jaywalk. I've been real patient with you, Calhoon. I agreed to let you question me even though I knew you didn't have a leg to stand on, but now

I'm getting pissed off, so either you charge me or you let me go."

In spite of his efforts to keep up a positive front, Mitch knew Luther was right. Without a positive ID, he had no right to keep him here. Still, Mitch forged on.

"Did somebody put you up to this, Luther? Are you in the contracting business now?"

Luther rolled his eyes. "Give me a break, will you? I'm telling you I didn't kill that broad. I don't even know her name."

"Maybe she wasn't your target."

"What the hell does that mean?"

"It means, Luther—" Mitch came within inches of the little man's face "—that you screwed up. It means that the person you were sent to kill is still alive. How did that go over with your client, Luther? I can't imagine he was too happy about it."

"And just who the hell was I supposed to kill, huh, Mr. Big Shot Detective? Tell me that."

"I was kind of hoping you would."

"You're nuts. I'm not saying another word until my attorney gets here." He looked around him, yelling at the door. "Where the fuck is my lawyer?"

Disgusted, Mitch stood up. "Get out of here."

"Gladly." As Luther started for the door, Mitch blocked his path. "I'm watching you, Luther. Don't do anything stupid."

"What the hell is going on here?"

At the booming voice, all three men turned around. Bob Harris, a flamboyant, carrot-haired attorney, who had bailed Luther out of jail more than once, burst into the room.

"Detective Calhoon! Have you lost all sense of ethics? Holding my client without cause, putting him in a lineup without an attorney present and then interrogating him? You're lucky I'm not slapping you and your department with a lawsuit." Behind him, Luther snickered like an idiot.

"Your client signed a waiver of right to legal counsel at lineup, counselor. As for answering our questions, he did that voluntarily, too, claiming he had nothing to hide. I'm finished, so why don't you take him out of here before I do something I'll really regret."

Mitch stood there long enough to see the two men disappear into an elevator. Then, with a bad feeling he couldn't shake, he went to knock on Lieutenant Fennell's door.

"You want to do what?" the lieutenant asked, after Mitch had told him about the lineup. He was a big man with a voice that made rookies shake in their boots and an explosive temper.

"I suspect Kate Logan, or maybe her daughter, may have been Luther's target," Mitch replied.

"Why do you think that?"

"Luther may be involved, directly or indirectly, with my sister's death, which Kate is investigating."

"Then, I suggest you talk to Detective Sykes of the Fairfax police about your suspicions and let him handle the matter." Fennell fixed Mitch with a hard stare. "I'm serious, Mitch. I want you to stay out of your sister's case. I need you here. As for your request to put a twenty-four-hour watch on Luther on the basis that he's lying, that's denied. The man might be a sleaze, but he does have constitutional rights."

He walked back to his desk and started to shuffle through a pile of paperwork, a clear indication the conversation was over. Though disappointed with his boss's reaction, Mitch hadn't held out much hope that he would go along with a twenty-four-hour watch on Luther.

Therefore, he would have to take care of that little detail himself.

Twenty-Two

"I'm sorry, Mommy," Alison said as soon as she and Kate were safely inside Mitch's car. "I really thought it was him."

"Don't worry about it." Mitch met her gaze in the rearview mirror. "These things happen. And considering what you had to witness, it's a wonder you can remember anything at all."

"Which one was he, Mitch?" Alison asked in a small voice.

"It doesn't matter," Kate said firmly. "It's over now, baby."

"But it does matter." She leaned forward, her hands on the back of Mitch's seat. "You let him go, didn't you?"

Mitch maneuvered the Ford around the heavy traffic on Massachusetts Avenue. "I had no choice, Alison. I couldn't keep him."

"So he won't be punished for what he did to that lady?"

Kate and Mitch exchanged a look. "Not right away," Mitch said in a reassuring tone. "But he will."

Back at the house, Mitch took Kate aside. "I called

Jim Faber and asked him to put a twenty-four-hour watch on Luther.''

Kate felt a jolt of alarm. "You think that's necessary?"

"I don't trust that weasel, Kate."

"You shouldn't be doing that. The lieutenant was very clear. You're defying direct orders."

"It's all part of my investigation of Ms. Magasa's death."

"Mitch—"

"I'm not taking any chances, with you, Kate, or with Alison."

"Alison?" Kate's mouth went bone dry. "You think she's in danger?"

"She could be. Maybe what happened at Union Station is someone's sick idea of pressuring you to withdraw from the case."

"But she's just an innocent child! What kind of evil person would want to hurt a child?" She sat down, suddenly drained.

"There is a way to make sure Alison stays safe," Mitch said quietly.

She looked up. "I'll do it. Whatever it takes."

"You won't like it."

"Tell me, anyway."

"Have Eric take her away somewhere—skiing maybe. I know a place in Montana that would be—"

Kate gave an emphatic shake of her head. "I can't do that. I can't let Alison out of my sight. I would be too worried."

"You have more reasons to worry if she stays here, in harm's way."

"I can protect my own daughter, Mitch!"

But could she? Kate listened to the sounds of her daughter walking in her room. Maybe, if she took her out of school, locked her inside the house, surrounded her with armed guards, she might be able to keep Alison safe. But was that what she wanted? For Alison to be a prisoner in her own home?

She pressed the heels of her hands against her eyes. "God, I hate this. I feel so helpless."

"You'd be doing the right thing," Mitch continued. "No one needs to know where Alison is, except you and me. She'll be completely safe."

"What about Megan? Will she go along with all this secrecy? Won't she want to know where her husband is?"

"Megan will understand once we explain the situation to her. The only reservation I have is about Eric. Will *he* do it?"

"Oh, he'll do it," Kate said sarcastically. "In fact, this is what he's been waiting for all along, to prove to me that my job is dangerous and that he should have custody of Alison. I could lose my daughter over this, Mitch."

"You could lose her another way."

Eric arrived at ten o'clock, which surprised Kate since punctuality had never been high on his list of priorities. Maybe he was changing, after all. Maybe all he had needed to get his act together was an adoring woman to keep him on track. A *rich,* adoring woman.

He gave Kate a curt hello and threw Mitch a look charged with venom. It was no secret the two men didn't like each other, though they had learned, for

Alison's sake, to put their differences aside, at least in her presence. And while Eric would never admit it, he was grateful to Mitch for saving Alison from the ape who had kidnapped her four months earlier.

"Are you sure she's all right?" Eric asked Kate when Alison ran upstairs to get her suitcase. "That lineup didn't upset her?"

"A little, but she's fine now."

"I don't understand why you had to put her through such an ordeal in the first place." This time the remark was directed at Mitch. "I mean, there were dozens of people on that subway platform, and the only person you could find to give a description of that killer was my thirteen-year-old daughter?"

Afraid of a confrontation, Kate started to lay her hand on Mitch's arm, but there was no need. In spite of Eric's blatant accusations, Mitch remained amazingly calm. He even managed a smile, which seemed to infuriate Eric even further.

"Yes, there were a lot of people on that platform, Eric. Unfortunately, only one person had a good look at the man. I didn't like putting Alison through the stress of a lineup any more than you would have. It was the only way to ID the man."

Eric let out a sarcastic laugh. "But you didn't ID him, did you. Your perp is still out there, laughing at you."

"He knows I'm on to him. He'll stay put."

"You won't get offended if I don't believe you, will you, Calhoon? This is my daughter we're talking about. If that man is a threat to her, I want something done about him."

"I'll do my job, Logan. You do yours. Unless you

don't feel capable of protecting your daughter for the next week or so. If that's the case, tell me now, and I'll make other arrangements.''

"Why you—"

"Eric!" Kate stepped between the two men, just as Eric, looking dramatically outraged, took a step forward. She wouldn't have put it past him to throw the first punch and knew without a doubt that for all his self-control, Mitch would have hit him back.

"Stop it," she ordered, splaying her palm on Eric's chest to hold him at bay. "Have you lost your mind?"

"He insulted me."

"Oh, cut it out. You asked for it." She dropped her arm. "Pull yourself together, will you?" When he was sufficiently calmed down, she asked, "Where will you be?"

Eric pulled an itinerary from his pocket and handed it to her. "Mountain Peak Lodge in Big Sky, Montana—Mitch's first choice," he added, with another somber look toward Mitch. "I wrote down the phone number."

Kate read the itinerary. "You chartered a plane?"

"There are no flights scheduled at this time of night, Kate. What did you expect me to do? My daughter's safety is at stake here."

And he wasn't missing a single opportunity to rub Kate's nose in it. "You have your cell phone with you?"

Eric patted his pocket. "Right here. You called the school?"

Kate nodded.

"I'm ready." Alison stood in the doorway, her

suitcase in hand. She wasn't perky the way she had been the morning she had left for the Virgin Islands. She was quiet and solemn and looked no happier now to leave Kate behind than she had been earlier.

Kate went to her, adjusted the collar of her blue parka. "You're going to have a great time, sweetie. You'll see."

"I'm going to be worried about you, Mommy."

Mommy. Most of the time now Alison called her Mom. She only called her Mommy when she was frightened. "I'll be fine." Kate forced a smile. "I have big bad Mitch to watch over me."

"But what if that man isn't arrested?" Anxious eyes searched her face. "What if he tries to kill you?"

Kate caught Eric's gaze and his "I told you so" expression. "He won't dare. He's much too afraid of Mitch."

"Then, why are you sending me away? If he won't hurt you because he's afraid of Mitch, then, he won't hurt me."

Kate and Mitch exchanged a wordless glance. Alison had obviously been doing some thinking in the past couple of hours. In that respect she was very much like Kate. "We are sending you away as an extra precaution," she explained. "It's also a lot easier for me to take care of myself if I don't have to worry about you."

"Daddy wouldn't give Megan the lodge's phone number."

"I know. It's safer that way."

"Who knows?"

"Mitch and me. No one else."

"Not even Grandma?"

Later, Kate would have to apologize to Rose for this. "Not even Grandma."

Alison threw her arms around Kate. "I'll call you every day, Mommy."

"I will, too."

She watched the black limousine drive away and had one last glimpse of her daughter, leaning out the window, waving. Kate wiped her eyes and collected her emotions before walking back inside the house.

Mitch was on the phone. His face was grim.

She watched him intently as he hung up. "What's wrong now?"

"Luther's dead."

Twenty-Three

"Dead?" Kate leaned against the kitchen counter. "How? Where?"

"Two teens discovered his body in the Smithsonian Sculpture Garden."

"What happened?"

"We don't have details yet. Jim Faber lost his tail on Luther just before the murder. The police just got there. One of the officers called me because he knew about the lineup earlier today." He took his holster with his gun in it from the top of the refrigerator and strapped it around his shoulder. "Go pack an overnight bag."

"What for?"

"I'm dropping you at the Spivaks' house. I've already talked to Mary Beth. She'll be more than happy to put you up for a few days."

Tom Spivak, a detective at Metro PD, and his wife Mary Beth were old friends of Mitch's and would do anything for him. They were good, generous people, and Kate had no doubt the invitation was sincere, but moving was out of the question. "I won't be chased out of my home, Mitch."

"Kate, don't be stubborn. We don't know who Luther was working for."

"You don't know if he was working for anyone.

What if he told you the truth and had nothing to do with what happened at Union Station?''

"Luther doesn't know the meaning of the word *truth.*"

"What about my job? The cases I'm working on? The people who are counting on me? Am I supposed to drop everything and go into hiding?" She shook her head. "I won't do it, Mitch. I agreed to send Alison away because I believed you were right, but I won't agree to do this. I have a life. I can't just put it on hold when things go a little wrong."

"A little wrong? Someone may be trying to kill you."

"Oh, Mitch, do you have any idea how many killers I put behind bars when I worked in the prosecutor's office? Or how many threats I received over the years? Dozens. I'm still here, aren't I?"

A short, charged silence fell between them. Kate held his gaze, wondering for a moment if he was going to throw her over his shoulder and carry her to his car kicking and screaming.

"All right," he said at last, even though he didn't look convinced. "We'll do it your way. But I warn you. If you let anything happen to you, I'll kill you. You got that?"

"I got it." She gave him a teasing smile. "Should I wait up for you? Or am I being presumptuous in assuming you'll come here after you're done."

"You aren't being presumptuous."

"Good. Wake me up."

"Lock your door."

The traffic was relatively light at this time of night, and it took Mitch only ten minutes to get from Cleveland Park to that section of the National Mall. Two cruisers and an ambulance, their red and blue flashing lights illuminating the night sky, were already there when Mitch arrived.

Hands in his pockets, he walked down the ramp that led into the Sculpture Garden. A yellow police tape encircled a small area of the garden. After checking his credentials, a patrolman let Mitch through.

The body lay at the foot of a bronze sculpture entitled *The Great Warrior Montaubant*. A medical examiner Mitch had worked with before knelt beside the body. Mitch approached and glanced at the man he had questioned less than five hours ago.

"What's the scoop, Abe?"

Abel Moskowitz, a diminutive man with sharp eyes and steady hands, looked up and started to remove his protective gloves. "Two gunshot wounds to the heart, far as I can tell."

"Time of death?"

"Somewhere between 8:00 and 10:00 p.m. I'll have a more accurate time after the autopsy."

Looking around him, Mitch spotted Daniel Rourke, the officer who had made the call, and walked over to him. "Where are the two kids who found him?"

The young officer pointed toward a patrol car. Two teenagers, their arms folded against their chests, walked back and forth and stomped their feet, trying to stay warm. "Did you notify the next of kin?"

"His uncle is on the way."

"Call me when he gets here."

Mitch walked over to the two teenagers, who were watching him apprehensively. "Hi, guys."

Both boys nodded but remained silent. They looked no older than fifteen or sixteen.

"Can you tell me what you saw?" Mitch asked, after he had taken their names and addresses. "From the beginning?"

They glanced at each other, clearly uncomfortable. The first to talk was a tall, rangy kid by the name of Matt Pierce. "Well, me and Andy, we were on our way home from a party."

"Where at?"

"A friend's house near McPherson Square."

Mitch glanced at his notes. "You live on New York Avenue, not far from McPherson Square. So what were you doing in the Sculpture Garden?"

Matt licked his lips and started to say something, but Andy stopped him. "He's a cop, man," he said between clenched teeth.

"So?"

"So shut up, okay?"

"Look—" Mitch leaned against the cruiser. "I don't care what you two were doing here unless it's something illegal, like buying or selling drugs." He looked from one to the other, eyebrow raised.

"No, no drugs!" Both spoke in unison, shaking their heads so hard, Mitch had to smile. "No drugs of any kind, Detective," Matt said. "I swear. Me and Andy, we..." He looked at his friend.

"We came here with our girlfriends," Andy filled in. "It's pretty deserted here this time of night and we thought...I mean we were hoping to..." A light flush climbed to his young face. "You know."

"You two were hoping to score?" Mitch had a hard time keeping a straight face.

The boy cleared his throat. "Well…yeah. Kinda. 'Cept the girls said they were cold and split."

"Is that when you found the body?"

"Yeah. We were sitting on that wall up there, shooting the bull." He pointed at a stone wall about six feet high. "Then I looked down, and there was this dude, flat on his back, staring at the sky."

"Then what?"

"We went down to see if he was sick or drunk, or something. That's when we saw all the blood. He was dead."

"How did you know that?"

"I put my fingers on his throat," Matt said. "Like they do on TV." He showed Mitch, using his own throat as an example. "I didn't feel a pulse."

"Did you see anything suspicious? Someone running away? Or a car speeding off?"

They shook their heads.

Mitch wasn't surprised. As crowded as the National Mall was during the day, it turned into a ghost town at night. "How long were you here?" he asked.

"We got here at ten-fifteen. I remember because one of the girls said she had an eleven o'clock curfew. That's when I looked at my watch."

"Thank you, Matt. And you, too, Andy." Mitch pulled away from the cruiser. "I'll have one of the patrolmen take you home. It's too late for you two to be walking alone."

Matt grinned. "Hey, cool. I mean…thanks."

"Detective Calhoon!"

At the sound of the angry voice, Mitch turned to face Lou Torres, a tall, gaunt man with the sharp Aztec features of his ancestors and an unfriendly demeanor. He wore an expensive dark suit, a white shirt open at the neck and a black overcoat casually thrown over his shoulders. Two bodyguards stood behind him, their eyes scanning the area. It was a scene straight out of *The Godfather.*

"What is this I hear about my nephew getting shot?" Torres's tone was belligerent. "Did you have anything to do with this, Calhoon? You couldn't pin anything on him earlier, so you killed him."

Mitch did his best to ignore Torres's inflammatory remark and watched one of the paramedics zip up the body in a black rubber bag. "When was the last time you saw, or spoke to, your nephew, Mr. Torres?"

"I spoke with Luther a couple of days ago, on the phone. I don't remember when I last saw him. A week maybe." He tugged his coat around him. "Now let me ask you a question. What were you thinking when you arrested Luther earlier today?"

"Luther wasn't arrested, Mr. Torres. He was detained, questioned and released."

"You had no right to do that."

"Why are you so worried about Luther's questioning? Were you involved in that metro death, by any chance?"

"Of course I wasn't involved. What are you trying to pull now?"

"Oh, I don't know. Seems to me you're more concerned about what went down at Metro PD this afternoon than you are about your nephew's death."

"Detective?" One of the Crime Scene Unit technicians held out a cell phone and a foam cup. "We found the phone in his pocket."

With his gloved fingers, Mitch dialed star 69. A

recording from the law firm of Harris & Barton came on. Luther hadn't made any calls since phoning his lawyer earlier. He nodded to the tech. "Bag it."

The tech handed him the empty cup. "We found it about six feet from the victim. Coffee residue inside. It may or may not be his."

Mitch brought the cup to his nose. It smelled like coffee. "Take it, anyway. Anything else?"

"Just his ID, a set of keys, money. The usual."

"All right. File your report when you get back and leave a copy on my desk." He turned back to Torres. "How did you find out about Luther's visit to Metro PD?"

"Bob Harris called me on his way there."

"You didn't hear from Luther himself?"

"I'm not Luther's keeper, Detective. He's a grown man. He knows how to take care of himself."

"Yes...I can see that." Somewhere in the distance, Mitch heard the wail of a siren. "Where were you this evening, say between seven-thirty and ten?"

"Are you accusing me of killing my own nephew?"

"Just answer the question, Mr. Torres."

"I was having dinner at my restaurant—Ariba on 13th Street. My staff will verify that."

Mitch wrote the information in his book. "What has Luther been up to recently?" he asked, still writing.

"What do you mean by that?"

"I mean—" Mitch looked up "—has he done anything that would make someone angry enough to kill him?"

"Luther was my comptroller, Detective. He kept

my finances in order, made sure the bills were paid and the accounts receivable collected. I don't know what he did in his spare time, and I resent your implication that he was anything but an honest, hardworking man. So get off my back and find someone else to harass.'' He paused. ''Or you could become a hazard to your own health. If you get my drift.''

Mitch had about had it. He came to stand in front of Torres, ignoring the two pit bulls who had moved closer to their boss, ready to do what was necessary to protect him.

''Listen to me, Mr. Torres. I may be just a dumb cop to you, but I know who you are. And I know what you do. And while loan-sharking, bookmaking and prostitution aren't any of my business, when those activities are linked to a homicide, it very much becomes my business. So if I find out that you had anything, anything at all, directly or indirectly, to do with that Japanese woman's death yesterday, or Luther's, I'll come after you personally. And when I do, all the fancy mouthpieces in the world won't be able to keep you out of prison. If you get my drift.'' He snapped his book shut. ''In the meantime, don't leave town.''

Torres, who had listened quietly, his face inscrutable, gave him a long, steady look Mitch was certain was meant to be intimidating. Then, holding the lapels of his overcoat, he walked away, his two bodyguards close behind.

Twenty-Four

A̶t a little after midnight, Mitch let himself into Kate's house, using her spare key. He stopped by the bed long enough to listen to her even breathing before going to the bathroom to wash up.

The hot shower helped ease some of the physical tension but did little for his frame of mind. With Luther dead, finding out who was behind the metro incident would be more difficult, unless the killer tipped his hand somehow. And judging from the crafty way the man had eluded the police so far, that wasn't likely to happen.

A search of Luther's apartment had produced little in the form of evidence. Mitch had found a .357 Magnum without a serial number, and a box of cartridges, but no gun permit. The medical examiner had promised to have the results of Luther's autopsy by midday. Once Mitch knew the time of death, he could question the staff at Ariba, but he already knew how that would turn out.

As he let the shower spray work out the kinks in his neck, he thought about his earlier conversation with Lou Torres. The man bugged the hell out of him. He was too cool, too well prepared—just as Luther had been. And then, there was that bodyguard, the one with the brush cut. He had looked vaguely familiar, but Mitch couldn't remember where he had seen the guy before. He made a mental note to check him out first thing in the morning.

His side of the bed was cold, so he snuggled against Kate's back, spoon style. Just wrapping his arms around her soft, warm body was enough to chase away the images of the dead men and women he had seen over the past week. Kate somehow balanced the horrors of his daily life. She was his anchor in a world that had gone mad.

After a disastrous marriage to a woman for whom only money mattered, Mitch had never thought he would fall in love again. Then he had met Kate. Loyal, compassionate and brave Kate, who had changed his thinking about women in general, and lawyers in particular. But the qualities he admired so much in her often brought them head-to-head, both fiercely fighting for what they believed.

To say she often infuriated him was an understatement. Their recent confrontation over Todd's guilt or innocence was a perfect example. They had faced each other like two lions defending their territories, but in the end, he was able to take a step back, re-examine the case and look beyond his hatred for Todd.

He liked to think he brought the same stability to Kate's life as she did to his. Especially where Alison was concerned. Earning the teenager's trust hadn't been easy. It had taken patience and a great deal of understanding on his part, but the results had been well worth the effort. Now Alison called him at work whenever she felt like it, laughed at his jokes, and gave him a glimpse of what it would be like to be part of a warm, loving family.

A smiled tugged at his mouth as he recalled Kate's startled expression the other night when he had tossed that spur-of-the-moment remark at her. Actually, he had surprised himself with that one. As much as he loved Kate, he hadn't given marriage any serious consideration. But the thought that something could happen to her had forced him to rethink his situation. Life was too short to be miserable. Not a very poetic observation, but it made its point.

Groaning softly, Kate turned into his arms. "Welcome home, Detective," she murmured sleepily.

A tender breast pressed against his chest, bringing a ripple of familiar heat. "Thank you, counselor."

"Everything okay?"

"Peachy."

"Mmm. Wanna talk about it?" Her words were slurred, but even half-asleep, she was there for him.

"Not now," he whispered back.

He was about to tell her what he really wanted to do, when she let out a sigh, sank deeper into his arms and began to snore gently.

Closing his eyes, he tightened his hold on her.

By nine-thirty the following morning, Mitch was back at his desk. He had found the bodyguard's name—Carlton Pritchett—and had already requested a complete background check on him.

The M.E.'s report on Luther's death would be on his desk before the end of the day, but Abe had already told him that death had occurred between 8:30 and 9:00 p.m. last night.

With that information, Mitch drove to Torres's restaurant to question the staff. As predicted, the three waiters, the cook, and two kitchen workers—both of them Chinese men who may or may not have been here legally—vouched for their boss. Lou Torres and his two bodyguards had been at Ariba the previous evening. After dinner, they had played a game of gin rummy, as they did almost every night. They had left the restaurant at ten-thirty, when Mr. Torres had received a call from the police.

One of the Chinese men, a dishwasher who spoke fairly good English, was clearly frightened and kept glancing furtively around him as he answered Mitch's questions. Mitch asked him to repeat his name—Yan Wey—and made sure he had spelled it correctly, which seemed to make Mr. Wey even more nervous. Mitch would have to check him out, as well.

From Ariba, Mitch went to Torres's plush apartment in the Watergate Building, but Torres stuck to his story, which coincided perfectly with the various statements members of his staff had made.

When questioned about the .357 Magnum in his nephew's apartment, Torres kept a straight face and told Mitch he had no idea Luther carried a gun without a permit.

Mitch returned to Metro PD as frustrated as he had been the previous night. Frank Sykes was there, waiting for him, but the news he had come to deliver did nothing to improve Mitch's mood.

"I couldn't find Black Knight," Frank said in his slight Southern drawl. "The screen name belonged to a man by the name of Paul DiAngelo and payment to the Internet provider was made with Mr. DiAngelo's credit card. The problem is, this particular Paul DiAngelo doesn't exist.''

''Is the credit card still active?''

''Nope. It was canceled two years ago, and the provider no longer has any e-mail belonging to that subscriber. My bet is that Black Knight not only has a new screen name, but a new credit card, as well. Finding him now under these conditions is a near impossibility.''

Mitch let out an oath. He had been afraid of that. Credit card fraud was growing at an alarming rate, not only with stolen card thefts, but with entire cartels of criminals who manufactured phony IDs and then sold them to whomever could pay the price. If a mother of three in Mexico could provide false identification for drug traffickers, an American counterpart in the U.S. would have no problem doing the same. The scheme worked because the forgers, the good ones, went to a lot of effort establishing verifiable birth certificates, social security numbers, residences and even jobs. At one time, only savvy criminals were able to perform such services. Nowadays, securing a new ID was as easy as applying for a fishing license. All you had to do was log on to the Internet and, for a fee, you could find out exactly how to obtain a new identity.

The problem had become so serious that many police departments had implemented a computer-crime-related division to handle the complaints.

''Are you telling me,'' Mitch said, ignoring the stack of messages on his desk, ''that we're not going to be able to get this guy?''

Frank took a stick of gum from his shirt pocket and

started to unwrap it. "That's the worst possible scenario. One of our detectives is working on a case very similar to your sister's death. The girl's body was found in a roadside motel and there was little in the form of evidence except her e-mail. He'll keep me informed."

Frank rolled the stick of gum and put it in his mouth. "Anything new on Luther?"

"I'm still waiting for the M.E. report. I've also requested a background check on one of Lou Torres's bodyguards."

"Why?"

Mitch shrugged. "A gut feeling. He looks vaguely familiar and it bugs me that I can't place him."

"Will you let me know what you find? If what happened to Luther Whorley is connected to Molly's death, I'll need all the help I can get." He tossed the wrapper in a wastebasket beside Mitch's desk. "How's Kate?"

"Oh, you know her. She forges ahead, no matter what."

Frank laughed. "You two make quite a pair, you know that? Makes me wonder why I even bother, when I could just sit back and let you and her do all the work."

"Because there wouldn't be any fun in that, Frank."

"Maybe you're right." He stood. "Give Kate my best, will you?"

"I'll do that."

Twenty-Five

"You're not listening to me, Maurice." A little exasperated, Emile tried to keep his temper in check. He was, after all, talking to a man he hoped would re-hire him. "This story could be the biggest *Bordeaux-Matin* has done in years. Todd Buchanan is not just anyone, but the son of a very wealthy, very influential Washington family. His father is a Supreme Court justice. Can you imagine the headlines?"

He could tell from the skeptical expression on Maurice's face that he hadn't sold his ex-boss entirely. Not that Emile blamed him. After what he had put his former boss through in the past couple of years, the man had a right to be skeptical. But Emile's crazy benders were over. All he had to do was make Maurice believe it.

The veteran editor, a portly man with a bad stomach and an ugly birthmark the color of Beaujolais on his forehead, popped another antacid tablet into his mouth. "What makes you think Todd Buchanan is in Saint-Jean-de-Luz?" he asked.

"I know I've seen him somewhere. It's true," he added when Maurice's thick, unruly brows lifted. "You know me, Maurice, once someone catches my attention, his face is engraved in my memory forever.''

''Saint-Jean-de-Luz is a small town. Why haven't you already found him?''

''I haven't looked that hard yet. But you give me the word, and I'll start doing some serious investigating. All I want from you is the assurance that if I deliver the story, you give me my old job back.''

''Is that all?'' Maurice asked sarcastically.

Emile cleared his throat. ''I'll need a small advance.''

At Maurice's sharp, suspicious look, Emile put up his hands, palms out. ''Not for booze, Maurice. I've given that up. I need the money to rent a car, buy gas, pay informants. You know what it takes to investigate a story like this.''

Grumbling, Maurice stood up and walked around his small, cluttered office. He ran his hand over his thinning hair, the way he always did when he was trying to make up his mind. ''I don't know about this, Emile. You've let me down so many times before.''

''I'll never let you down again.'' Emile spoke the words as if his life depended on them. And, in a way, it did. ''It's not just my job I want back,'' he continued. ''It's Antoinette. I'm miserable without her, but the only way she'll have me back is sober and working.''

Maurice remained silent.

In one last attempt to win his old boss over, he put his hand over his heart. ''You have my word, Maurice. I know it doesn't sound like much, considering all that has happened, but it's all I've got to give.''

Maurice took a long, noisy breath, sounding like a

rumbling engine. Hands behind his back, he went to stand by the grimy window overlooking the botanical garden. He stood there for what seemed to Emile like an eternity.

When Maurice turned at last, he gave a curt nod. "All right. I'll agree to your deal. But I warn you—" he pointed a stubby finger at Emile "—if you screw up, I'll come after you personally. I'll drag you out of whatever gutter you're lying in, and I'll carve your heart out with my fish knife. Are we clear on that?"

Emile smiled. Maurice hadn't lost his flair for theatrics. God, he'd missed this place.

"Very clear," he said.

Emile left the building, whistling the old refrain of *La Vie en Rose*.

Emile was pleased with himself. Not only had he been given a second chance, but he was actually making progress in his search for Todd Buchanan.

With the help of former colleagues, neighbors, friends, and friends of friends, he had located fifty-two foreigners living within a twenty-five-mile radius of Saint-Jean-de-Luz. Thirty of them were an assortment of Germans, Swiss and Brits, all of whom he had dismissed after careful investigation. That left fourteen Americans. Of those, one was a retired fashion model recuperating from a nervous breakdown, seven were students on sabbaticals and two were World War II veterans who had been in southwestern France for decades.

That left four, all men, of approximately the same age as Todd Buchanan. One was a tour guide who spoke seven languages, another made a living singing American folks songs on street corners, and the last two shared a luxury condo on boulevard Thiers.

It was on those two that Emile had concentrated his attention, even though he had expected Buchanan to be a loner. The younger of the two had blond hair and blue eyes and bore a certain resemblance to the picture Emile had cut out of the *Herald Tribune.* After a few discreet inquiries, he had learned that one of the salesgirls at *Boulangerie Chevalier,* where he bought his bread every day, had a hopeless crush on him.

"He looks just like Brad Pitt," Yvette had told him, blushing as she spoke. "And I just love the way he says, *'Une baguette, s'il vous plait, mad'moiselle'* with that sexy American accent." She had heaved a little sad sigh. "Too bad he doesn't like girls."

Disappointed to hear the man was gay, Emile had scratched the blond Adonis from his list and was left with no prospect. Either he had missed something or he had to accept the possibility that there was no Todd Buchanan. At least, not in Saint-Jean-de-Luz.

Now, sitting at his regular outdoor table, Emile sipped his evening Vittel-menthe, wondering what to do next. He was considering ordering another drink when he saw the girl. She stood on the dock, her brown hair blowing in the evening breeze. She wasn't pretty per se, but there was something arresting about her, a gracefulness of movement and a certain elegance, even in her simple flowered dress.

He had seen her before, though he couldn't remember where. Suddenly, she waved, not at anyone nearby, he realized, but toward the sea where the first sardine boats were starting to return to port after a long day at sea.

Following her gaze, Emile saw that a man stood at the bow of one of the boats and was waving back. Even from this distance, Emile could tell he was tall and well built, with broad shoulders and muscular legs. The thought of such a sophisticated young woman going out with a rugged fisherman made Emile smile. Maybe it was true what they said about opposites attracting.

The waiter stopped by his table, but Emile shook his head and kept his eyes on the girl. That's where he must have seen her before, he realized, right there on the quay, waiting for her man.

Now that the boat was getting closer, Emile could read its name on the hull, painted in big black letters—*Ainara*—"swallow" in Basque. The guy was a looker, with long blond hair held back in a ponytail, and the deep tan of one who spends days in the sun. With the grace of a dancer, he jumped on the dock and gave the girl a quick kiss, before securing the boat to the dock.

Emile's adrenaline started pumping. The man couldn't possibly be a local. Not with that hair and that body. A German, perhaps? Or a Swede? How about an American?

Rising, he put a ten-franc coin on the table and started walking toward the young couple, forcing himself not to look too eager. He needn't have bothered. They were too preoccupied with their conversation to pay the slightest attention to him.

If Todd had one outstanding quality, Kate thought, it was punctuality. The clock on the wall had just struck twelve, when her cell phone rang.

Her first question, before she even mentioned the metro incident and Luther's death, was about Molly's bracelet.

"It doesn't sound like anything I ever gave her," Todd said, after she had finished describing it. "In fact, I don't recall ever seeing her wear anything like that."

Maybe she hadn't wanted him to see it? Kate wondered. And that's why she had kept it at Mitch's house? She saw no reason not to share Mitch's suspicions about Terrence's possible involvement. "Is it possible that your brother gave Molly that bracelet?" she asked.

Todd gave a hearty laugh. "Terrence? Are you kidding? He thought she was a total flake."

"When did he say that?"

"When I told him Molly and I were getting married. He knew her pretty well. She was his student once."

"Yes, I know. So he wasn't happy with the wedding announcement, either?"

Todd laughed again. "Are you kidding? He almost had a heart attack. He was worse than my parents."

There was a short silence while Kate digested this little piece of information. She still had no proof that Terrence and Molly had been romantically involved, but it wouldn't hurt for her to stay on that track and gather as much data as possible on the older Buchanan brother.

"Did Terrence and Molly have a lot of contact with one another after you were married?" she asked. "I mean, did the family get together for Sunday dinners, or birthday celebrations, cookouts? Or did Terrence dislike Molly so much that he actually avoided being around her?''

"I don't recall my brother trying to avoid Molly." Todd's voice had turned sharper. ''And I didn't mean to give you the impression that he disliked her. Like my parents, he didn't think she and I were suited, that's all. As for family gatherings, at first, there were a few occasions when we all got together, but Molly was never comfortable around my folks, so we stopped going unless it was absolutely necessary.

"Look," Todd continued, "I don't know who this *T* person is, but believe me, Kate, it's not Terrence. My brother is a good man, and as straight an arrow as you'll ever meet. He would never fool around with a student. And he's a very happily married man.''

"Happily married men sometimes stray, Todd."

"Not Terrence," he said firmly.

Kate gave another high mark to Todd for being a good brother, but that didn't mean he had sold her on Terrence's godliness.

Emile watched the blond man as he walked away from the public phone, wrapped one arm around the girl's shoulders and headed toward the little park that doubled as a parking lot. Emile increased his pace, coming close enough to the couple to catch bits and pieces of their conversation.

When he heard the man's voice, Emile felt a prickle of excitement crawl up his back. The guy spoke English but with an accent Emile recognized immediately. After spending his senior year of college at Columbia University in New York, he had no problem distinguishing an American accent from a British accent, and this one was definitely American.

But if the man was a Yank, how could he have slipped through Emile's meticulous search? Before he could think of an answer, the couple got into a gray Renault. Emile cursed himself for having left his rental car at the apartment. But since he couldn't follow them, he did the next best thing—he wrote down the license-plate number.

"All right," Jess said, as Todd pulled out of the parking lot. "No one can hear us now, so tell me. What did Kate say to upset you so much?"

Todd turned south on Route 918 and headed toward Ascain. "She thinks Terrence and Molly may have had an affair."

Jess was speechless for a moment, then asked, "Did they?"

"No! Of course not. Mitch must have planted that idea in her head."

"Why would he do that?"

"I don't know." He glanced in the rearview mirror. "Apparently, Molly left a rather expensive-looking bracelet at Mitch's house. It was inscribed with the words 'Yours forever. *T.*' Kate thought the *T* stood for Todd, but when I told her the bracelet wasn't from me, she wanted to know if Terrence could have given it to her. I'm afraid I lost my temper a little, Jess."

"Oh, Will, she's only trying to help you."

"I don't want her to help me at my brother's expense. I've caused him enough grief as it is."

She kept watching him. "You were on the phone a long time. What else did she say?"

He didn't answer right away. He hated to worry her, especially in her current condition, but she was as stubborn as he was protective. She wouldn't let up until he had told her everything.

"Someone may have tried to kill her—or her daughter."

Jess let out a gasp. "Todd, that's terrible. What happened? How? Where? Were they hurt?"

"No, no one was hurt. No, that's not true. A Japanese woman was killed." He repeated what Kate had told him, including Luther's unexpected death, which Kate now knew was a homicide.

"Do you know this Luther Whorley?" Jess asked.

"I've heard of him. And I've heard of his uncle, Lou Torres. Both are very dangerous men."

"Does Kate think one of them is behind what happened at Union Station?"

"Too soon to tell. Mitch is investigating." He noticed Jess's sudden pallor and said quickly, "I don't want you to worry, Jess. It could be nothing more than what it appears to be—an accident."

For the third time in the last ten minutes, Todd glanced in the rearview mirror. Ever since leaving the harbor, he'd had this nagging feeling that he was being watched, but so far he hadn't spotted anyone following.

Jess turned around in her seat. "What is it? Why do you keep looking behind you?"

Like a man with a nervous tick, he glanced in the rearview mirror again. The several cars that were behind him had all turned off, heading for various destinations. "I don't know. I had a funny feeling earlier."

"About what?"

"I felt as though someone was watching us."

Jess turned around again. "When?"

"A little while ago, at the harbor."

"Did you see who it was?"

"No." He negotiated a hairpin curve before getting onto the straightaway that would take them home to Ascain. "It's probably nothing. I'm just jumpy over what happened to Kate, that's all."

They didn't talk until they reached the house. Jess brought drinks out to the terrace, as she did every night—a beer for him, a Perrier for her—and they sipped quietly. He gazed at the spectacular view of the rolling hills, while listening to the sound of bells as a shepherd took his sheep home for the night.

When they were finished with their drinks, they went back inside. Todd settled at the kitchen table to read the paper, but found himself watching Jess instead. She had wrapped an apron around her still-very-small waist, and was taking bundles of vegetables from the refrigerator in preparation for tonight's *piperade,* a local specialty that included tomatoes, green peppers, hot spices and eggs.

He smiled as she began slicing the peppers into thin strips. She had adapted so well to the local lifestyle and spoke French so fluently that she easily could have passed for a native. His French wasn't as good, but he, too, felt a connection with this area of the world. In fact, it never failed to amaze him how detached he felt from his former life, and how meaningless and superficial those early years now seemed.

Oh, sure, he had accomplished a few things he was proud of. He had finished college, had gone to broadcasting school and turned his passion for sports into a lucrative career. Romantically, however, his life had been a series of disasters, a procession of beautiful women as shallow as he was.

Molly had been like a breath of fresh air. He had met her when the TV station had sent him to cover a much-publicized bicycle race, which Molly had won hands down. After the interview, he had asked her to dinner, and by the time he took her home that night, he was head over heels in love with her.

He wasn't sure when the discord began, or why. Suddenly nothing was the same. They stopped having fun together, and Molly started going out on her own, claiming the zest had gone out of their marriage. Like a lovesick puppy, Todd had tried everything. He had whisked Molly away on romantic trips, bought her jewelry, and told her he couldn't imagine life without her. He even saw a marriage counselor. Nothing helped.

And now here he was, two years later, a new man, happy, in love again—and this time forever. Soon, with the arrival of their first child, his happiness would be complete.

Why was he risking it all by reopening the case against him?

Suddenly, Jess glanced over her shoulder. "Everything all right?" she asked.

Not trusting his voice, or his emotions, Todd just nodded.

Twenty-Six

After a small delay due to a snowstorm, Eric and Alison had arrived in Big Sky without any problems. Alison was still asleep when Kate called, but Eric had promised to have their daughter phone home the moment she woke up.

"Is Mitch making any progress investigating this Luther Whorley?" Eric asked.

"Luther is dead." Tucking the phone between her ear and her neck, Kate took the glass carafe from the coffeemaker and filled it with tap water. "Someone shot him a few hours after he left the police station."

She now knew that Luther had been shot at close range and died from two .9-mm caliber gunshot wounds to the chest. Both bullets had gone through the heart, punctured a lung and torn a main artery, causing a massive hemorrhage. She refrained from giving Eric those details, however. He didn't have the stomach for such graphic description.

"That's not good, is it, Kate? Luther being dead, I mean."

"Oh, I don't know," she said, trying to downplay the situation. "At least I'll no longer have to look over my shoulder every time I enter a metro station."

"I wouldn't stop looking over my shoulder if I

were you, Kate. The fact that Luther is dead doesn't mean you're off the hook.''

''Thank you for that thought, Eric,'' Kate said dryly. ''I feel so much better now that I've talked to you.''

''I didn't mean it the way it sounded.''

''Just make sure Alison calls me.'' She hung up.

She had just turned on the coffeemaker, when the phone rang again. Certain it was Eric, calling to apologize, she started to say a sharp ''what?'' Then she caught herself just in case it was Alison. ''Hello?''

''Ms. Logan, this is Lyle Buchanan.''

The shock of hearing his voice on the phone was almost as great as having seen him on her doorstep. ''Good morning, Justice Buchanan.'' Semiconsciously, she brushed a strand of hair from her face.

''I just heard about the incident at Union Station. I was out of town or I would have called earlier. I'm sorry about the ordeal you and your daughter had to go through.''

''Thank you.'' He sounded different than he had the other day. Was it possible that he was truly concerned about Alison and her?

''How is your daughter?''

''Better. You know children. They're very resilient.''

''Yes, I do know. I'm a parent, too, which is the reason I called. I'm quite concerned about this incident.''

''You needn't be, Justice Buchanan. I—''

''Please hear me out, Ms. Logan. I know you and I didn't have the most auspicious start, and for that I apologize. I'm not an easy person to deal with, but I would like you to put that aside for a moment because I want to talk to you as one parent to another.'' He paused. ''In view of what happened at Union Station, I think it would be best if you withdrew from the case and allowed me to hire another counsel.''

Kate let out a small sigh. He wasn't giving up, was he. Although, this time there was no contempt in his voice, no innuendo about her experience, or lack of it. He sounded genuinely concerned. ''Todd will never agree to work with someone else,'' she said.

''He will if you tell him what happened to you and your daughter.''

''He already knows, and what happened at Union Station was just an accident.'' She didn't add that she believed his fears were probably founded, or that she had sent her daughter away.

''I don't think it was just an accident, Ms. Logan,'' he said as if in answer to her thoughts. ''Men like Luther Whorley don't hang around metro stations, waiting to cause an accident. I know all about that man and his uncle. They're dangerous individuals who never do anything without a clear motive. And that's the one thing lacking in the killing of the metro incident. They had no reason to kill that Japanese woman. They may have had a reason to kill you.''

In spite of her good intentions to keep a cool handle on her emotions, Kate was shaken. Mitch had more or less told her the same thing, but somehow, coming from Lyle Buchanan, the words had the effect of an icy shower.

''If Lou Torres is somehow involved in my daughter-in-law's death, he will stop at nothing to protect himself. Think about that, Ms. Logan.''

"I can't abandon Todd now," she said, annoyed that her voice shook. "He's counting on me."

"Call him. Will you do that? Will you explain my concerns to him? And if he wants to call me, tell him I'm available. Day or night."

"I'll give him the message."

She hung up, just as Mitch walked into the kitchen, a smile on his face, his hair still wet from the shower.

One look at her and the smile faded. "What's wrong?"

"Justice Buchanan just called."

"What has he done now?"

"Actually, he apologized for his behavior the other day."

"That's a first, but encouraging."

"Then he asked me to quit so he can retain another attorney."

"Oh."

She took two mugs from the cupboard and set them on the counter. "He wasn't nasty about it, though, or insulting, or patronizing. He was almost…humble."

Mitch laughed. "Humble? Justice Buchanan? What did you put in your coffee this morning, darling?"

"I mean it, Mitch. He just wanted to talk to me as one parent to another. He was truly concerned about what happened at Union Station."

Mitch took the mug she handed him. "He'd better be careful. He'll tarnish his image." He took a sip of his coffee. "So…are you going to do it?"

"Do what?"

"Withdraw from the case."

"In a pig's eye."

"Thata girl." Mitch was about to say something

more, when the phone rang a second time. This time it was Jim Faber.

"The parking attendant at The Blue Oyster remembers Molly," the private detective said. "He also remembers the guy she hung out with. He drove what kids call a muscle car—a yellow 1971 Cuda convertible."

Kate didn't know much about cars, but she was familiar with that particular make. "Isn't that what Nash Bridges drives?"

At her reference to the popular TV series character, Jim laughed. "Exactly."

"Who's the man?"

"You've heard of him. Victor Harlow, better known to TV viewers as Uncle Vic. He owns a Dodge dealership in Bethesda."

Kate had an instant image of a large man in outrageous costumes, doing silly commercials. Depending on the time of year, he could be seen on the small screen as a jolly Santa, an Easter bunny or a big, red Valentine heart. He was loud, tacky and obnoxious, but somehow he managed to make all that unpleasantness work for him. His business was enormously successful.

"I could pay him a visit if you want," Jim offered. "See what he has to say."

"Thanks, Jim, but I think I'll talk to him myself."

"Okay. What about Colorado?"

The unexpected question threw her, and for a moment, she couldn't think of anything to say.

"Kate? Do you still want me to go?"

She glanced at Mitch, who hadn't taken his eyes

off her. "ASAP," she said, barely able to get the words out.

Kate hung up. "That was Jim," she said. "One of those matchbooks from Molly's collection paid off. A parking attendant at The Blue Oyster remembers her and a man she apparently saw on a regular basis."

"Who was he?"

"Victor Harlow of Uncle Vic's fame."

"The owner of the Dodge dealership?"

"The one and only." She struggled to regain her composure and prayed he wouldn't see through her. "That may be the break we've been waiting for. With any luck, he could be Black Knight. Wouldn't that be something? If we stumbled onto him out of sheer serendipity?" She stopped, aware that she was babbling like an idiot.

"Indeed it would." He continued to observe her. "What is it you want Jim to do ASAP?"

Her heart jumped in her throat. She searched for an answer he could believe, but could only think of a line from a Sir Walter Scott poem: "Oh, what a tangled web we weave when first we practice to deceive."

To her surprise, the lie slid off her tongue with the amazing ring of truth. "Oh, that. He hadn't checked on the other matchbooks yet. I told him he should— right away."

Turning around so she wouldn't have to look at Mitch, she dumped the rest of her coffee into the sink.

Harlow Dodge sat on a busy stretch of Wisconsin Avenue, all strung out with red, white and blue foil garlands and a poster-size picture of Uncle Vic mounted at the entrance.

She spotted him right away, a big man in brown pants, a loud yellow jacket and no tie. His thick hair, much too black to be natural, framed his ruddy face like a helmet. He was talking to a salesman, but when he saw Kate, he gave the man a pat on the arm and hurried over immediately, his arms swinging.

"Hi, there, little lady." The loud, patronizing tone was as grating here as it was on television. "Looking for a car to shlep the little ones to and from school?" Before she could reply, he took her elbow in a rather possessive way. Kate was reminded of something Dr. Eileen Brown had told her about casual touching.

"You've come to the right place," Harlow continued. "I've got the perfect vehicle for you—a Grand Caravan with power-activated sliding doors, side air bags and great stability. Prettiest minivan around, too. Candy-apple red," he stated proudly. "Why don't I—"

Feeling her patience slip, Kate quickly disengaged her arm. "I'm not here to buy a car, Mr. Harlow. My name is Kate Logan. I'm an attorney and I need to ask you a few questions about your relationship with Molly Buchanan."

The phony smile froze for a second before disappearing altogether. "What the hell are you talking about?" he said in a low growl. "What relationship? What are you trying to pull?"

Kate leaned against the trunk of a dark green Durango. "Are you denying that you and Molly Buchanan knew each other?"

He studied her through unfriendly narrowed eyes.

"A few drinks together doesn't constitute a relationship."

"Did you ever see her outside The Blue Oyster?"

"No." But the word lacked conviction.

"Would you swear to that in court?"

"Of course I would," he said, a little too indignantly.

A middle-aged couple that had been walking toward them suddenly stopped to peer at the price tag of a Dodge Ram pickup truck. "Look," he said, probably hoping to cut the conversation short. "I bought the lady a few drinks, okay? And I shot the bull with her once or twice, but that's it." He tucked his shirt collar inside his jacket. "Now, if you don't mind, I've got customers."

He started to walk away, but Kate blocked his way. "We can do this two ways, Mr. Harlow. You can answer my questions right here, or in a court of law. And believe me, by the time I get you on that witness stand, I'll know everything about you, including what you have for breakfast every morning." She gave him a sweet smile. "So, what will it be?"

Harlow was silent for a moment. With his teeth clamped over his bottom lip, he studied her as if he was seeing her for the first time. Having apparently made up his mind, he snapped his fingers at a salesman who had come out of the showroom for a cigarette break, and gestured toward the middle-aged couple. The salesman immediately dropped his cigarette on the ground, stubbed it with the toe of his shoe and hurried across the lot.

After another few seconds, Harlow nodded. "Okay,

but I'm telling you right now, I didn't kill her, so don't try to pin that on me.''

"How well did you know Molly, Mr. Harlow?''

"Not well. She didn't talk much about herself. And I certainly had no idea she was the daughter-in-law of a Supreme Court justice, or God be my witness, I would have stayed the hell away from her.''

"Did you have sex with her?''

His nervous eyes raked the lot. "Is any of this going to come out? I mean...I'm a married man, and the father of three teenage girls. If my family gets wind that I...'' He looked scared, not at all the overbearing, overconfident man who had greeted her a few minutes earlier.

"This is a murder investigation, Mr. Harlow. If the case goes to court, I will probably have to subpoena you.''

The color left his face.

"Mr. Harlow?''

"Yeah, I had sex with her,'' he said reluctantly.

"How often?''

A shrug. "Who counts? A few times, I guess.''

"Where did you meet?''

"I have a summer cabin on Lake Anna. That's about a hundred miles south of here.''

"How about the Lost Creek Motel? Ever been there with her?''

He shook his head. "I never heard of the place until I read about Molly's murder in the papers.''

"You go on the Internet a lot, Mr. Harlow?''

He seemed startled by the question, just as Denise Jenkins had been. "Sure. I have a Web site I update regularly. And I do some shopping on the Net.''

"Do you ever venture in chat rooms? Erotic chat rooms?"

He laughed. "That's not my bag." Of course it wasn't. His bag was to pick up strange women in bars.

"When was the last time you and Molly were together?"

"Long before she was killed—maybe six months before."

"Whose decision was it to break off? Yours or hers?"

"There was nothing to break off," he said with a touch of exasperation. "I'd walk into The Blue Oyster. If she was there, we'd have a few drinks together, maybe drive down to the cabin, maybe not. That's how it was."

Kate caught him licking his lips and knew there was more to his statement than he wanted her to believe. "Why do I have the feeling you're not telling me everything?"

His gaze shifted away. "I don't know."

She returned his shrug. "Okay, I guess I'll see you in court, then."

She started to turn, but he stopped her, taking her arm and holding it so tight, she winced. He realized what he was doing and let her go. "I'm sorry. I didn't mean to do that."

Looking clearly uncomfortable, he jammed his hands in his pants pockets. The salesman and the middle-aged couple were engaged in an intense conversation, and Harlow watched them for a few seconds, but Kate didn't think his mind was on a sale.

"I'm taking a big chance here," he said.

Kate just waited.

"Molly and I... We got carried away one night."

"What do you mean?"

"She..." He moistened his lips again. "She liked it rough sometimes."

Kate got the picture. "Go on."

"Like I said, one night we got carried away, or rather *I* got carried away. She asked me to stop, but I didn't and—"

"What were you doing to her?"

"I was squeezing her throat," he said, his voice so low she could barely hear him. "That was her idea, by the way. I didn't want to do it. I was scared, but she kept insisting. She had heard that partially cutting off someone's oxygen supply during sex heightened the pleasure, and she wanted to experiment. She threatened to walk out if I didn't go along." He looked down as though inspecting his shoes. "I guess I squeezed a little too hard, because all of a sudden she was scratching and kicking, until I finally came back to my senses and let go of her."

"And then what?"

"She took my car and drove away. The following morning she called to let me know where she had left it. I never saw her again."

"She never returned to The Blue Oyster?"

"I wouldn't know about that. *I'm* the one who never went back. I had no desire to, believe me."

"Were you afraid of Molly?" Maybe she had threatened to tell his wife.

"No, but I sure as hell was afraid of her friend, who told me that if I ever came within a hundred feet of Molly again, I'd be facing criminal charges."

Well, what do you know, Kate thought. Lynn Flannery had known about Harlow and hadn't said a word. "What's her friend's name?"

Harlow shook his head. "I've said enough."

"Here or in front of a judge, Mr. Harlow. The choice is yours."

Several seconds ticked by. Then, his shoulders slumping, he said, "His name is Ted Rencheck. The D.C. assistant U.S. attorney."

Twenty-Seven

As Kate drove back toward the city, she kept thinking about what she had just learned from Victor Harlow. Molly and Ted had been friends. Good enough friends, apparently, for Molly to confide in Ted in ways she had never confided in anyone else. Not even her brother.

Why? Had they been secretly involved? Kate shook her head. That made even less sense. Four years ago, Ted's beloved wife of eighteen years had lost her long battle with cancer and died. To Kate's knowledge, Ted hadn't looked at another woman since, and had filled the void by totally immersing himself in his work.

Kate wasn't even aware that he and Molly knew each other. Mitch certainly had never said anything.

Was that friendship the reason Ted had acted so peculiarly in her office last week? Could it be that his interest in the reopening of Molly's case was more than professional curiosity? There was only one way to find out, wasn't there? And that was to ask him.

She spent the rest of the morning catching up with her paperwork and going over a handful of bills with Frankie. At four o'clock, she called the prosecutor's office, found out that Ted was in court and told Frankie she was leaving for the day.

Half an hour later, she slipped quietly into Judge Messner's courtroom, where a bail hearing was in progress, and took a seat in the back. When the defendant's request was denied and court was adjourned, Ted closed his briefcase and headed for the door, looking pleased with himself. He held his head so high as he walked by, he didn't see her.

"Ted!"

He turned around, looking surprised. "What are you doing here? Getting a few pointers?"

"From you, Ted?" She scoffed. "Hardly."

The insult didn't seem to faze him. "Then, may I assume you're finally ready to concede on the Gibbons plea?"

"No, I want to talk to you about Molly."

He gazed back at her, his eyes black and watchful. "What about Molly?"

"Why didn't you tell me the two of you were friends—very good friends?"

He looked away for a few seconds, as though searching for an answer. She wondered if he was going to lie. He didn't. "How did you find out about that?"

"I talked to Victor Harlow."

This time he didn't hide his surprise. "You found Harlow?"

"You always did underestimate me, Ted. Yes, I found Harlow."

The courtroom was empty except for a young man in a front row—probably a law student—taking notes.

"Why don't you buy me a hot dog from that nice vendor outside?" Kate suggested. "Then we'll talk."

"I've already had lunch."

"I haven't, and I happen to know that you always have a snack at this time every day—a hot dog with everything on it."

"Don't you have anything better to do than to spy on me?"

"This may break your heart, Ted, but I don't spy on you. Your habits are common knowledge around here. Come on," she said, when he didn't reply. "Let's go, before he runs out. I'm starved."

They walked out in silence. Once outside, the vendor, an older man with an engaging smile, gave Ted a big grin. "The usual, counselor?"

"Make that two, today, Charlie."

"Sure thing." The man glanced at Kate and touched a finger to his forehead in a little salute.

A minute later, Kate and Ted were walking toward the National Law Enforcement Officers Memorial.

"So," Ted said, "what do you want to know?"

"Why don't you start with your friendship with Molly. When did that begin?"

"A few weeks before Debra died." Ted took a bite of his hot dog and chewed it slowly. "Actually I had met Molly the previous summer, at one of the barbecues Debra and I gave each year. She came with Mitch instead of Todd, and spent the entire afternoon talking to Debra and making her laugh. I didn't see her again until several months later. She had found out that my wife was in a bad way, and she started coming to the hospital. She would read to Debra, fix her hair, do her nails, all those little things that Debra could no longer do for herself.

"Afterward, she would stop at the house and try to cheer me up. She seemed to know exactly what I was going through. I don't know how, but she did. After Debra died, Molly was there for me. She brought me food, cleaned my house, did my laundry, talked when I felt like talking and left me alone when I didn't."

A new picture of Molly Buchanan was slowly emerging—the Molly her brother had described, kind and caring.

Ted took another bite. "I never forgot what she did for me during those first few months. But don't get any ideas," he said, throwing her a sideways glance. "We were friends, nothing more."

"I believe you." She didn't know why, but she did.

"I honestly don't know what I would have done if it hadn't been for her. I missed Deb so much, I wanted to die. Molly was there to make sure I didn't."

"Did Mitch know about your friendship with his sister?"

"No. He and I never really hit it off, and Molly knew that. She figured it was best if he didn't know. He wasn't around much in those days, anyway. By the time he returned to Washington and joined Metro PD, I was back on my feet, so to speak, and Molly and I didn't see that much of each other. We talked on the phone occasionally, met for a drink, but that was about it."

Kate licked mustard from her lips. "Tell me what happened that night with Harlow."

"I thought you talked to him."

"I did. I'd like to hear your account."

"You mean you want to know if he killed Molly."

"Among other things."

"He didn't. I checked him out myself, thoroughly. He and his wife were attending a chamber of commerce function along with about two hundred other guests. I have it from a reliable source that the Harlows didn't leave the Windminster Hotel until after two that night."

He wiped his mouth with a paper napkin, crumpled it and dropped it into a waste receptacle. They had entered the memorial where the names of more than fourteen thousand policemen and women killed in the line of duty were inscribed on a low marble wall.

"On the night of June second," he continued, "Molly called me from an all-night diner in Louisa, a little town not too far from Lake Anna. She sounded scared, so I got out of bed and drove there. I found her sitting at a booth, wearing sunglasses and a scarf that covered the left side of her face." Kate saw his jaw harden. "She had been beaten up. At first she wouldn't tell me who did it, and I thought it was Todd, but it wasn't. Todd was in Chicago all week, covering the basketball playoffs. She had been seeing a guy, Victor Harlow, and that night she had been in the mood for a little experimenting." He met her gaze. "He told you about that?"

Kate nodded.

"The whole thing turned sour. When he realized she was going to leave, he got angry. Somehow, she managed to get away. She grabbed his car keys, drove to the nearest diner and called me."

"He never said anything about beating her up."

"Take my word for it, he did. And he hurt her bad. She was bruised for days."

"Lynn Flannery told me Todd had done it."

"That's what Molly wanted her to think."

"Why didn't she tell Lynn the truth? Lynn was her best friend."

"She didn't want anyone to know what she was into. She wouldn't have told me, either, but she was scared Harlow would come after her."

They walked slowly along the wall, stopping every now and then to read a few names before resuming their slow stroll. "So you went to see him."

He nodded. "I had a concealed tape recorder in my pocket, and the photos Lynn had taken of Molly. I told him I was keeping the tape and the pictures for insurance and that if he ever came near Molly again, I'd make sure he'd rot in jail for a long, long time. What I really wanted was for Molly to press charges against the son of a bitch, but that would have meant exposing her secret. She didn't want that, so I just made sure Harlow would never be a threat to her again."

Little by little, layers of Ted Rencheck were being peeled off, revealing a side of him Kate had never suspected. This man, whose arrogance and ruthlessness in the courtroom were legendary, actually had a heart. The discovery didn't completely change her mind about him. It just made it easier to overlook his less admirable traits.

"Did Molly ever tell you why she was being so promiscuous?" Kate asked.

He shook his head.

"Did you ask her?"

"Dozens of times. I was scared for her, just as Lynn was. Molly always gave me the brush-off. Once, she even threatened to end our friendship if I didn't stop lecturing her. So I decided to just be there for her, like she had been for me."

"Why couldn't she tell Mitch?"

He shrugged. "He would have freaked out. Besides, she had already put him through the wringer once—to use her own words—and she didn't want to do it again."

Kate was suddenly alert. "What did she mean by that?"

"She wouldn't tell me. Molly had lots of secrets, if you haven't already realized that."

She had. This was just one more to add to the long list of pieces that didn't fit. "Mitch needs to know, Ted."

He kept his gaze on the wall. "Why? What's the point now? I told you Harlow didn't kill her."

"He still has a right to know."

"Know what?" a voice behind them said.

Kate spun around. Mitch stood behind them, looking from one to the other.

"Looking for me?" Ted said in lieu of an answer.

"No, actually, I was looking for Kate. The hot dog vendor told me the two of you might be here." He gave them both another look, then glanced at the wall, obviously puzzled. "You changed the subject, Ted. What is it that I should know?"

Kate crumpled her napkin. "Why don't I leave you two alone," she said. "I have to get home." She squeezed Mitch's arm. "I'll be waiting for you."

Twenty-Eight

Mitch and Ted ended up at Stoney's, a neighborhood bar with sports memorabilia on the walls, more than a hundred beers to chose from and the juiciest burgers in town. It was too early for beer, too late for lunch and too damn noisy to talk.

Mitch couldn't remember the last time he and Ted had gone out together. Although, technically, Mitch worked for the prosecutor's office, his relationship with the assistant U.S. attorney was less than amicable. In Mitch's opinion, Ted was a prick and always would be.

It was five o'clock and Stoney's was already packed. To Mitch's surprise, however, Ted said a few words to one of the waitresses, and a minute later, they were settled at the bar, with two Cokes and a bowl of cashews in front of them.

Mitch popped a nut into his mouth. "When did you become the big man around town?"

"It's my charm," Ted replied with a straight face. "Try it sometime."

"I will." He chewed another nut. "I don't want you to think that I totally hate your company, but why did you bring me here when we could have talked at the wall?"

"I figured you wouldn't make an ass of yourself in a public place."

"What is this all about, Ted?"

"First, give me your word that you won't go off on me."

"Will I have a reason to?"

"Give me your word, dammit."

"All right, you have my word. Now talk."

"You will not make a scene."

Mitch narrowed his eyes. "You're beginning to annoy me, Ted. If you have something to tell me, tell me. Otherwise, I'll get it out of Kate."

"I don't think so."

Mitch turned around on his stool. "Is it about Todd?"

"No," Ted replied. "It's about Molly."

As Ted started to talk, Mitch listened, not interrupting him once. He just sat there, stone cold, staring into his Coke, as images of his sister being hit repeatedly by that ape engraved themselves into his mind.

When Ted was finished, Mitch drained his glass as if it were a shot of whiskey. "You let him get away with it," he said.

"I didn't want to, believe me, but I had Molly to think of. She didn't want anyone to know."

"So the bastard got off with a slap on the wrist and a warning to never beat up a woman again."

"My hands were tied, Mitch."

"Mine aren't." Mitch stood up and kicked his stool back.

"Mitch?" He heard the alarm in Ted's voice but ignored it. "Mitch!" Ted shouted as Mitch strode toward the door. "Dammit, Mitch, you gave me your word."

Mitch left him there, scrambling for his money.

Victor Harlow lived in McLean, in a three-story Tudor big enough to house three families. The businessman opened the door himself, a tumbler of whiskey in his hand. "Yes?"

"You're Victor Harlow?" Mitch asked, just to be sure.

The big man gave him his TV smile. "Living and breathing."

"Not for long." With one hand, Mitch grabbed him by his shirt collar, and with the other, he closed the door.

"What the fuck—"

"Shut up and walk." Mitch shoved him toward the back of the house and pinned him against the wall. The glass slipped out of Harlow's hand.

"Who the fuck are you?" he barked. At the same time, he tried to pry Mitch's grip loose but couldn't.

"Name's Calhoon. I'm Molly Buchanan's brother."

The man's mouth went slack. "Now, look here—"

Mitch sank a hard fist into the man's startled face. "This one is from me." He hit him again. "And this one is from Molly."

He had the satisfaction of seeing Harlow's fat bottom lip split in two. Blood gushed out, soaking his shirt collar. Harlow started to slide down, grimacing with pain, but Mitch held him up. "What's the matter, Harlow? You don't hit men? Only women?"

"It's not what you think." Harlow wiped his

mouth, which was swelling up fast, stared at all the blood on his hand and looked as if he was going to pass out.

Mitch slammed him against the redbrick siding. "What did she ever do to you to deserve what you did to her? Tell me that."

Harlow was breathing hard and glancing from left to right as if hoping someone would come to rescue him. "I'm sorry," he said, talking through the blood that bubbled out of his mouth. "W-what more do you want me to say?" His gaze fell on the ground, and a flicker of hope he couldn't quite hide flashed through his eyes.

Mitch glanced down. A pair of large garden clippers lay on the grass, partially hidden under a rhododendron bush. Bending slightly, Mitch picked them up with one hand.

"How about your prayers?" he said in answer to Harlow's question. "You want to do that?" He snapped the blades open and shut a few times. "Let's see now, what should I hack first? Your hands or your balls?" He kept snapping the blades, enjoying watching the helpless man jump and blink with each sound. "I'm torn here, Harlow, though I'm leaning toward the balls. What do you think?"

"You're a lunatic!" But Harlow was truly terrified now. Whether by design or because his legs couldn't hold him any longer, he slid down the brick wall and wrapped his arms around his knees, as if to protect himself from Mitch's madness. "My wife and kids are inside, for God's sake."

"Why don't you tell them to join us? That way

you can tell them what a pervert you are, before they read it in the papers.''

''Mitch!'' Quick footsteps sounded, coming up the driveway. ''Goddamn it, Mitch, drop that thing!''

Two hands grabbed him and pulled him back, hard enough to send the two men tumbling onto the grass.

Mitch was back on his feet in an instant, Ted a microsecond later. ''Fuck off, Rencheck.''

''Give me this—'' Ted yanked the clippers from Mitch's grip and threw them out of reach.

''The man's a maniac!'' Harlow shook an accusing finger at Mitch. ''You saw what he did, how he attacked me. He would have killed me if—''

''Shut up, Harlow.'' Ted gave Mitch another shove and went to stand in front of the slobbering man. ''Shut up and listen good, because I'm going to say this only once. You're going to get up, brush yourself off and forget Detective Calhoon was ever here. Do we understand each other?''

Harlow wiped more blood from his mouth. ''I'm not going to forget anything. I'm going straight to the chief of police with this. We play golf together. I'm sure he'll be very interested to know the bully he has working for him.''

Rencheck squatted in front of Harlow. Mitch had to strain to hear him. ''And when you do talk to the chief, don't forget to tell him about that tape I have, and the photos of Molly. Because if you don't, I will.''

''You'll lose your job.''

''It'll be worth it, just to see you end up on death row.''

"For beating up a slut?" He gave a shaky laugh. "You're out of your mind."

Mitch sprung forward, but Ted held out his hand. "No," he said mildly. "Not for beating her up. For killing her."

"I didn't kill her!"

Ted shrugged. "Maybe you did, maybe you didn't. Doesn't matter to me. Once I'm done introducing new evidence against you, there won't be a person in Washington that won't believe you killed Molly Buchanan."

Harlow stared at him in total disbelief. "What new evidence? What are you talking about?" Then, as he finally understood what Ted was saying, he looked from one man to the other. "My God, you're as crazy as he is. You would actually lie?"

Ted gave him a thin smile. "I'm an attorney. Lying's what I do best."

Kate missed Alison terribly, more so now than when Alison was in the Virgin Islands because this time she had no idea how long her daughter would be gone. They talked every day, twice, sometimes three times. The skiing was fun, and Eric took her on sleigh rides every evening and out to fancy restaurants. But Alison was worried and wanted to know why Mitch hadn't yet implicated the one-eared man in that metro death. Kate didn't have the heart to tell her Luther was dead. She and Eric had agreed that their daughter didn't need to hear about that.

She glanced at her watch. Eight o'clock. Two hours had passed since she'd left Ted and Mitch at the Police Memorial, and she hadn't heard from either one.

She was thinking of trying Mitch on his cell phone again, when she heard the front door open.

"Mitch!" She ran to the foyer and stood there, her mouth open. His suit was muddy and rumpled, his shirt streaked with grass and blood. An ugly scrape stretched across his cheekbone.

Comprehension dawned. "Harlow? You two had a fight?"

"Wasn't much of a fight." Mitch walked past her, went straight to the kitchen and filled a glass with tap water.

"Let me give you some ice for that cheek." Kate started for the freezer, but he stopped her.

"Don't." He took a long gulp of the water. "I'm fine."

She made him sit down. "How bad did you hurt him?" She needed to know how badly he had damaged his career.

"Not bad enough. Ted showed up and ruined everything."

"What do you mean, Ted showed up? I left you two together."

"I got away." He drained his glass and set it down with a bang. "I have to hand it to our prosecutor, though. He's full of surprises. And he's got more balls than I ever gave him credit for."

"What did he do?"

"He convinced that jackass that he could get him convicted of Molly's murder. By the time Ted was finished with him, Harlow was ready to sell his own mother for a deal."

"Does that mean you're not in trouble?"

Mitch let out a harsh laugh. "I almost wish I was,

just for the satisfaction of seeing that miserable louse pay for what he did to Molly. But Ted would be in worse trouble. I don't want that.''

Kate smiled. "When did you become president of his fan club?"

"There's a lot people don't know about Ted."

"True." Gently, she pushed that stubborn strand of hair from his forehead. He was disappointed and so was she. Harlow had seemed like an excellent suspect at first, but now… "This case isn't getting any easier, is it."

"Oh, I don't know." He pulled her onto his lap. "I've got some interesting information about Torres's bodyguard."

"The one you thought you knew?"

He nodded. "I was right. His name is Carlton Pritchett. He's an ex-FBI agent."

"What?"

"He was with the bureau's National Crime Information Center for three years. His job was to assist local and state authorities with stolen vehicles that had been transported interstate."

"Why did he leave the FBI?"

"He didn't. He was fired, tried for grand theft and sentenced to four years in prison. He got paroled after eighteen months."

"What did he do?"

"He stole the cars he was supposed to find and sold them on the black market."

"How did he end up with Torres?"

"That's what I plan to ask him. Offhand, I'd say he and Torres knew each other while Pritchett was still with the bureau." He started to play with the button of Kate's blouse. "I also had a chance to question the staff at Ariba a second time."

"Someone changed their statement?"

"No, but I found out that the dishwasher, who is from China, entered this country illegally. I let him know, discreetly, that I was aware of his status and could make things difficult for him."

"Did he change his story?"

"Unfortunately, no. He still maintains Torres and his two watchdogs were at the restaurant the entire night. Maybe after he's had time to realize he could be deported, he'll come around. I slipped him my card. Unless I'm way off on this, I think I'll be hearing from Mr. Wey very soon."

He ran a finger along the contours of Kate's bra, making it difficult for her to concentrate on what he was saying. "Right now, I'm too tired to worry about it." His other hand slipped behind her back and unhooked her bra. "Why don't you tuck me into bed?" he said, filling his hands with her breasts.

"I thought you said you were tired."

"Never too tired for you, Kate."

Twenty-Nine

The following morning, as Kate was preparing to leave for the office, LuAnn called to say that she had good news and would be stopping over on her way to work.

"Oh, hon," she said when she arrived. "You've got to let me do something with this house." She closed her eyes and shook her hands as if to fend off evil forces. "I can feel the negative energy from a mile away."

Kate gave her friend a hug. "The energy can't be all bad. You're here, aren't you? And with good news."

LuAnn accepted the cup of strong, steaming, French roast coffee Kate handed her and took a noisy slurp before sitting down at the kitchen table. "Ah, I needed that."

"Don't keep me in suspense," Kate said, sitting down, as well. "What did you find out?"

"My friend Charlene Meyers, who spends hours in chat rooms, met a john through the Internet that seems to fit the description you gave me. He wanted to know everything about her, but told her nothing about himself. She'll tell you what you want to know when she sees you. Oh, and the information is free, by the way.

She was going to charge you because she might lose a john over this, but I told her you and I were friends, so the scoop is on the house.''

Kate smiled. ''Thanks, pal.''

''What are friends for?'' She added a few drops of cream to her coffee. ''The only thing she wasn't sure of was the kind of champagne he liked, so, yesterday, in an e-mail, she asked him what his favorite bubbly was. She'll let you know if he says Dom Pérignon.''

Dismayed, Kate put her cup down. ''I wish she hadn't done that.''

''Why? What's wrong?''

''What's wrong is that this man could be a killer. So far, he's been very successful at keeping a low profile, but a question like this, out of the blue, could tip him off.''

LuAnn threw her a worried glance. ''You think he's on to her?''

''Let's hope not. When did she send the e-mail?''

''Sometime yesterday afternoon. Maybe early evening.''

Still troubled, Kate nodded. ''Am I supposed to call her? Or meet her somewhere?''

''She said you can stop by her apartment anytime between nine and nine-thirty this morning. After that she's busy.'' LuAnn took a small piece of paper from her purse. ''Here's the address. She usually works out at that time of the morning, so if she doesn't hear the doorbell over the loud music, just go in. She'll leave the door open.''

Charlene Meyers lived a block from the Franciscan Monastery, in a newly renovated building that fronted several acres of gardens and woodland. In spite of the warning about loud music, not a sound came from behind the door of apartment 4B on the second floor.

Kate rang the bell. When there was no response, she rang it again, then started knocking, gently at first, then louder. Silence. A turn of the knob produced no result. The door was locked.

Kate knocked again. "Charlene," she called out. "It's me, Kate Logan. LuAnn's friend?" It was no use. Either the woman wasn't home, or she had changed her mind about ratting on a john. Kate didn't want to think about the third possibility.

"Hey," someone shouted from the floor below. "What's all the racket up there?"

Kate leaned over the banister and saw a beefy man in a T-shirt and low-riding jeans come up the stairs. "I have an appointment with Ms. Meyers," Kate said, as he reached the second floor, puffing loudly. "But she doesn't answer."

The man gave a low chuckle. "You ain't her kind of appointment."

"Are you a neighbor?"

"I'm the building super. Name's Bellamy. As in Ralph."

Kate had no idea what he was talking about and didn't ask him to elaborate. "Mr. Bellamy, I'm a little concerned. Ms. Meyers told me she would be working out and that I should come right in. But the door is locked, and she doesn't answer."

The man scratched his head. "Strange. She usually has her CD cranked way up high at this time of day."

"Would you mind checking her apartment, please? To make sure she's not ill or something."

He scratched the other side of his head. "I don't know. She could have somebody in there."

"If she did, she would have come to the door and said something. Or she would have taped a note on the door."

The super walked past her and pounded his fist on the door, loud enough to make it rattle. "Yo, Ms. Meyers! You in there?" He stuck his ear to the door and waited a few seconds.

At last, as if convinced the silence warranted some kind of intervention on his part, he gave a curt nod. "I'll go get my keys."

He was back within a few minutes, carrying a large key ring with more than a dozen keys attached to it. He selected one, inserted it into the lock and gave the knob a quick turn.

The door opened onto a living room that was anything but subtle. A semicircular leopard-covered sofa occupied center stage and was surrounded by floor cushions in the same motif. Two art deco table lamps were turned on, suggesting that either Charlene wasn't concerned about her electric bill, or she hadn't come home yet.

"Ms. Meyers!" the super called again as he walked in. There was still no answer.

After a quick glance into the kitchen, Kate walked past him, down the hall and into the bedroom, where the jungle theme continued. The king-size bed, with its tiger-skin spread, hadn't been slept in, but a black, silky nightgown was draped over a chair.

The super shook his head. "She ain't here. And I could get in plenty of trouble—"

Kate didn't wait for him to finish. With a cold feeling in the pit of her stomach, she pushed the bathroom door open and came to a dead halt. "Oh my God."

A naked woman in her early twenties lay on the floor. Judging from the lacerations on her body, she had been stabbed repeatedly. Blood was everywhere—on the floor, the tub, the sink and the wall, where several bloody handprints indicated that Charlene may have tried to stand up.

"Aw, Jesus." Behind her, Kate could hear the super's ragged breath.

"Don't touch anything," she warned, as he started to reach for the sink for support. "The police will have to dust for prints."

He looked at her suspiciously. "Who are you?"

"My name is Kate Logan. I'm an attorney." She started looking for her cell phone, then stopped herself in time. "I don't have a phone with me," she lied. "Would you mind going back down and calling the police? I'll stay right here."

Kate sat in Ted Rencheck's office, waiting for him to finish signing a stack of letters his secretary had brought in. A homicide detective she knew had already questioned her about the body in apartment 4B, but she hadn't been surprised to hear that the assistant U.S. attorney wanted to question her, as well. One of the reasons Ted Rencheck was good at his job was that he always investigated a case personally and thoroughly.

Kate had been in his office too many times to count, and not always under the most pleasant circumstances. Because of her dislike for the man, she had never really taken the time to study his surroundings. But after their recent conversation at the Police Memorial, she was more than a little curious about the man beneath the legal veneer.

The office hadn't changed much since its last occupant. The same scarred desk, littered with files, still occupied the center of the room and was surrounded by dull gray walls. On a bookcase, photographs of Debra in happier days shared shelf space with law books bound in red leather.

Ted scrawled his signature on one last piece of correspondence, thanked Clarice and asked her to hold his calls. "So, Kate," he said, as soon as they were alone. "What is it with you and ladies of the evening? First there was Gina Lamont, your ex's one-night stand, who got herself strangled, then LuAnn Chester, who was foolish enough to help you with the Lamont murder and was almost beaten to death, and now I hear you are a witness in the stabbing of a third prostitute. Are you going for some kind of record here?"

"A woman has died, Ted. This is hardly the time for bad jokes and insensitive wisecracks."

"You're right. Let's get down to business." He flipped through some notes before leaning back in his chair. "How do you know Charlene Meyers?"

"I don't. I never even met her. This meeting was arranged by LuAnn Chester."

A smile flickered across Ted's lips, and he shook his head as if to say, *Some people never learn,* but he didn't. "Tell me what happened when you got to Charlene's residence."

She repeated what she had already told Detective DiLuca. "She may have had information about Molly's killer."

"What kind of information?"

"I can't tell you that."

He knew better than to push, so he didn't try. "What *can* you tell me?"

"Charlene had agreed to meet me at her apartment between nine and nine-thirty this morning. She told LuAnn she would be working out and that she may not hear the doorbell. She would leave the door open, so I could go right in."

"But the door was locked."

"Yes. I knocked and rang the bell several times, and called her name. The super, George Bellamy, heard me and came up. I told him I was worried—"

"Why were you worried?"

Kate hesitated, wondering how much to tell him without compromising her case. "I was afraid someone may have found out she was about to give me information. And when she didn't answer her door, I thought the worst. Mr. Bellamy opened Charlene's apartment, and we went in together."

"I understand you're the one who found her."

She knew what he was thinking, that she may have searched the apartment and found evidence that could help his detectives find the killer. "Yes. I didn't touch the body. It was obvious she was dead. Some of the blood had dried, so I assumed she had been dead for some time."

Ted glanced at his notes again. "There's just one thing that's not quite clear." He pursed his lips as though puzzled, but she knew him better than that. He was just trying to throw her off. "Detective DiLuca told me the super made the call to 911 from his apartment down on the first floor."

"That's right."

"Why not you? Since you found the body."

"I couldn't find my cell phone."

"The super said you didn't have a phone with you. Which is it?"

"I had it," she said, keeping her cool. "I just couldn't find it. I guess I was pretty badly shaken."

He flipped to another page, where more notes were scribbled in his illegible handwriting. "Okay, let's see if I've got this right. You found Charlene's body and you stayed at her apartment, while Mr. Bellamy went downstairs to call the police."

Kate nodded, already knowing what his next question would be.

"And you didn't take a little walk around the place, peek into a closet or two, hoping to find what you came for?"

What attorney worth his or her fee wouldn't jump at the chance to do just that? Unfortunately her time had been too limited to search more than a couple of dresser drawers. Mr. Bellamy, as in Ralph, was back within minutes, and had stuck to her like glue until the first officer had arrived.

"I took a quick look," she admitted. "And if you're worried that I may have contaminated the crime scene, I didn't."

"I'm more interested in finding out if that quick look paid off."

She shook her head. "No."

He flipped his pad shut. "Then, you might be interested to know that Detective DiLuca did find a few pieces of evidence. One of them is Ms. Meyers's little black book, with more than two dozen names and phone numbers of men in and around the Washington area. Some of them might surprise you.''

Knowing what she knew about Washington, she doubted it. ''What about her computer?''

''He's working on getting a subpoena right now.''

She hadn't even tried to boot up the machine. More than likely, whoever had killed Charlene had wiped out any compromising e-mail, just as had been done with Molly's laptop. ''Would you have any objection to giving me a copy of Charlene's black book?'' she asked mildly.

The request was probably useless. Rencheck was famous for his unwillingness to cooperate with defense counsels.

''Oh, I might be able to do that—after I've finished with it, of course.'' He seemed to enjoy the look of surprise on her face. ''Contrary to what some people think about me, I do, occasionally, cooperate with fellow attorneys.''

''Really, Ted?'' She smiled. ''I guess that's something else about you I never noticed.''

It was a little after twelve noon when Kate walked out of Ted's office and found Mitch entering the reception room.

He rushed to her. ''Kate! I just heard. Why didn't you call me?''

''I didn't think of it. There was so little time to do anything.''

''Clarice said you were in Ted's office for over an hour. Why so long? Did he give you a hard time? Because if he did—''

''No, no.'' She shook her head. ''He was fine. He

was just…Ted." She took Mitch's arm. "Come on, let's get out of here. I'll tell you everything as we drive."

On the way home, Kate called Frankie to brief her, as well, and tell her she would be taking the rest of the afternoon off. The skies above Cleveland Park had turned a steely gray and the streets smelled of spring rain. Any other time, Kate would have suggested a walk, but today her heart wasn't in it. She kept going over the events of the past couple of hours, wondering what she could have done to prevent Charlene's murder.

Detective DiLuca had wasted no time in locating the girl's next of kin, an elderly aunt who lived in Pennsylvania and was too sick to travel—or to even know how her niece had earned her living.

Kate had refused to eat lunch, a quarter-pounder with cheese that Mitch had picked up at the local McDonald's. She sat on the sofa, her knees drawn up and her arms wrapped around them.

She felt emotionally drained, and was beginning to have serious doubts about whether she was tough enough to be in this kind of business. Maybe Eric was right. Maybe this job had become too dangerous—not for her, because she could take care of herself, but for her daughter. How often would she have to send Alison away because some maniac threatened her life? How many more innocent people would have to die?

Maybe civil law was a safer occupation. She pressed her forehead to her knees. Or maybe she was too damn tired to think straight.

She felt Mitch's hand on the back of her neck. He

started rubbing out the tension that had built up at that very spot over the past two hours. She closed her eyes. "She was so young," she said, partly to Mitch, partly to herself. "Only twenty-two."

"I know. Don't think about it anymore."

"I can't help it. I feel as though her death was my fault."

"There was nothing you could have done to prevent what happened today."

"If only I had stopped her from sending that e-mail."

"How could you? By the time LuAnn told you about it, Charlene had already sent it."

"I shouldn't have enlisted her help," she said stubbornly.

"That was LuAnn's idea. You had reservations about the whole thing, remember? LuAnn didn't. And neither did Charlene."

"That's because she didn't realize what she was getting herself into."

"Don't be so sure. Girls like Charlene like to live on the edge. Maybe she saw an opportunity to do something exciting, something a little out of the norm, and she took it."

Kate turned to look at him, her cheek resting on one knee. "How can you be so matter-of-fact, Mitch? So...detached. Is this just a routine death for you? Another case number?"

He shook his head. "No death is ever routine, Kate. There are times when I'm sure I'll never be able to witness another autopsy, or face another grieving family, or attend another funeral. From the moment you enter the police academy, one of the first things that is hammered into your head is to never let a death affect you, or your investigation, but it always does. You just learn not to show it. I do feel bad that a young girl is dead, but at the risk of sounding hard, I'm more concerned about you. If you had been at Charlene's apartment at the wrong time, her murderer could just as easily have killed you.''

That thought had occurred to her, too. And what would happen to Alison if Kate died? Who would take care of her daughter, protect her, make sure she didn't grow up too fast?

She fell asleep in Mitch's arms, but was haunted by dreams that forced her to relive the awful moment in Charlene's apartment. In her restless sleep, she caught the glint of a blade and saw a faceless man on a horse. He wore a black knight costume and rode back and forth through the apartment, his shiny sword slashing everything in his path.

''Stop that man!'' Kate screamed, as he and his horse galloped down the stairs. ''He's a killer. Stop him!''

She awoke with a start, in the middle of the night, drenched in sweat, fighting Mitch, as he tried to calm her.

''Shh, it's all right,'' he murmured, as she pummeled his chest with her fists. ''It's all right.''

She pressed her cheek against his shoulder and let his strength surround her. ''Don't go,'' she murmured.

''Never.'' He kept talking to her in that soft, soothing voice, until she fell asleep again.

Thirty

The young fisherman hadn't been on the list because, according to Emile's friend Michel at the *Gendarmerie,* the Renault was registered to William Adler, a native of Manchester, England, now residing at 13, chemin de Teileria in Ascain. Adler's girlfriend was an American. Her name was Jessica Van Dyke, and she taught English at the Grégoire high school here in town.

The information had cost Emile a rather expensive lunch at Brasserie du Port, but he wasn't complaining. Without Michel's help, finding out Adler's identity could have taken days.

Emile had spent the next two days studying the couple's respective schedules, which, fortunately, didn't vary much. Adler was at sea Monday through Saturday, from 6:00 a.m. to 6:00 p.m., and Ms. Van Dyke taught from nine to four every day except weekends. That would give Emile more than enough time to search their house and find proof that Adler was, in fact, Todd Buchanan.

Today was the day Emile had chosen to do the search. Earlier this morning, he had called his boss, claiming to have *une crise de foie,* that old but dependable liver ailment every self-respecting Frenchman had, at one time or another, experienced. Monsieur Laborde had told him to get plenty of rest, drink lots of liquids, and come morning he'd be like new.

At ten-thirty, forty-five minutes after Ms. Van Dyke drove off in the Renault, Emile got into his rented Opel and headed for Ascain, a hilly village just south of Saint-Jean-de-Luz. He already knew that the property Adler rented was a couple of kilometers from its nearest neighbors, a smart precaution to take when you were on the lam. Still, Emile approached the house cautiously, surveying the surroundings to make sure he wasn't being observed.

Getting into a strange house was always risky, even though locked doors were no obstacle for him. Fortunately, this one was equipped with a rudimentary lock that took him less than thirty seconds to open.

He found himself in a large, sunny room that was part kitchen, part living area, with a table and four chairs, a woodstove, a sofa covered in a bright blue fabric, and a television set. A bedroom and a bathroom occupied the back of the house.

Because most people kept their important papers in the bedroom, he started there, not entirely sure what he was looking for. He would know when he found it. But after going through an armoire with its lavender-scented linens, two bedside tables and a desk, all he found was a passport belonging to Jessica Van Dyke of San Diego, California, and another bearing the name of William Adler of Manchester, England.

At first glance, the passport photo bore only a vague resemblance to the one Emile had cut out of the *International Herald Tribune*. On the official photo, Adler's hair was darker and longer. He also wore a beard he had since shaven, and black-rimmed glasses that added years to his face. But the thick straight brows, the square jaw and broad forehead were the same. And if Emile looked closely at the right cheek, just above the beard, he could see part of that little dimple Emile had noticed on the man's face.

Leaving both passports opened at the photo page, Emile removed a camera from his backpack and snapped several shots before putting the documents back.

The bathroom was next, and then the kitchen hutch. He didn't think he'd find anything there other than dishes and pots and pans, but he was wrong. Tucked among forks and knives, corkscrews and cheese graters, candles and matches, he found something that brought a smile to his face—a piece of paper from a Washington, D.C. hotel with a name and address written on it: Kate Logan, attorney-at-law, 300 Michigan Avenue, Washington, D.C. There were also two telephone numbers and a fax number.

Kate Logan was the attorney who had reopened Todd Buchanan's case. Now, what would Mr. Adler be doing with her name and phone number? he thought as he took another photograph. Unless he wasn't Mr. Adler at all, but Mr. Buchanan?

Emile tapped the small sheet of paper against his chin. What was that expression Americans always used when they found something? Ah, yes. He smiled. "Bingo."

A thin drizzle had begun to fall. Through the mist, the small funeral procession made its way to the tiny

Catholic cemetery in Laurel, Maryland, where Charlene Meyers's parents were buried.

The autopsy had revealed that Charlene had been stabbed six times and had probably died a slow and horrible death. Detective DiLuca had called it a cold-blooded, brutal murder, and Kate had no doubt that whoever had ordered it had meant to send a clear message to all the girls on the street. You talk, you die.

"Just what do you hope to find here?" Kate asked, as she, Mitch and LuAnn stood beside the freshly dug grave.

"Didn't you learn that in Law 101?" Mitch replied. "Killers love funerals. Some come just for the kicks, while others want to make sure the victim is really dead. Cops attend funerals because they hope the killer will show up and give himself away."

"Well, you're right on one count." With her chin, Kate motioned toward a tall, lanky man in a raincoat who was standing at a distance, surveying the area. "Isn't that Detective DiLuca?"

"Yep. Right on time."

Next to Kate, LuAnn whispered, "This is just a little too familiar, Kate."

Kate nodded. She and LuAnn had met at the funeral of Gina Lamont, the call girl Eric had been suspected of killing. Only three people had been there—Mitch, LuAnn—who knew Gina—and Kate. "I'm sorry about Charlene, LuAnn."

"It wasn't your fault. I had warned her to play it cool, but Charlene had a mind of her own."

And she had paid dearly for it. Just as Molly had.

Holding back a sigh, Kate looked around her, at the few people gathered around the grave—a minister, reading from the Bible, a man LuAnn had told Kate was Charlene's pimp, and two young Asian women, both hookers, who stood beside him, their eyes downcast. Off to the side, attended by a uniformed nurse, a woman Kate assumed was Charlene's aunt sat in a wheelchair, looking bemused, as though she had no idea why she was here.

If the killer was also in attendance, he remained well out of sight.

Kate and Mitch dropped LuAnn off at work and were back at the house in Cleveland Park by two o'clock. "I think I'll call Alison," Kate said. "After a morning like this, I need to hear the sound of my little girl's voice."

But before she dialed, she pressed the play button on her answering machine to listen to her only message. Too late, she realized it was from Jim Faber.

"I'm afraid I've struck out in Colorado, Kate," the detective said.

Kate's insides twisted into a knot. She started to shut off the machine, then stopped, her hand in midair. Mitch had heard enough. Aware of his eyes on her, she listened to Jim tell her that no one in Singleton had heard of Molly Buchanan or Molly Calhoon.

"She must have been there under an assumed name," Jim continued. "Let me know if you want to pursue this any further. Or if I should come back. You can reach me at the Hillside Inn. You have the number."

Kate pressed another button to rewind the tape, and only after the machine had completely shut off did she find the courage to look at Mitch. She wished she hadn't.

"You sent Jim to Colorado?" he said, his voice dangerously low. "Behind my back?"

"I was going to tell you, but, with everything that's happened..." She sighed. "No, that's not true. I didn't tell you because I knew you'd be angry."

"But that didn't stop you, did it."

"I had to check it out, Mitch."

"Why?" He slammed the palm of his hand on the island, sending a fruit bowl rattling. "We talked about this. I told you there was no connection between my sister's move to Colorado and her death. Why couldn't you leave it at that?"

"And why couldn't you trust me?" she snapped back. "All you had to do was tell me why Molly went to Colorado."

"That's none of your business!"

She flinched at the harsh words. "I'm only doing what any good attorney would do—follow a lead. Is that so hard to understand?"

He regarded her steadily for a long time, making it difficult for her not to fidget, or feel guilty. "All right," he said after a while. "You win." He took the tweed jacket she had worn at the funeral and handed it to her.

"Where are we going?"

"You'll see." He walked out of the kitchen in his long, brisk stride.

They had been driving for almost an hour, and Mitch still hadn't said a word. Respecting his silence, and feeling a little awkward for forcing his hand this way, Kate kept quiet, her eyes on the road.

At first she had thought they were headed for the airport and maybe Colorado, but when they sped past a sign for Dulles International, that theory went out the window. Mitch drove fast and expertly as they sped down I-95, past Alexandria, Woodbridge and Quantico. At Fredericksburg, Mitch merged onto a divided highway and drove past a historical battle-field. Just after the battlefield, he turned onto a private road, where a wooden sign told them they were en-tering Rustling Willows and to please drive slowly.

The winding drive meandered past green lawns, streams and fields of wildflowers. Soon Kate realized this wasn't a resort, as she had first thought, but some kind of medical facility for children. Men and women in Hawaiian print tops and white pants walked around, pushing wheelchairs, playing ball, or just sit-ting under a shady tree reading to a group of attentive youngsters.

Mitch pulled under the arched entrance of a low stucco building and stopped the car. "I'll be right back," he said.

She watched him walk through the double glass doors and into what looked like a reception area. The woman behind the pink-and-blue wraparound desk looked up and smiled at Mitch as though she knew him.

Moments later, he was back, holding two visitor badges. He handed her one. "You'll have to put this on."

She clipped the badge to her tweed jacket, as Mitch put the car in gear again. He kept driving until they reached a one-story building with black wrought-iron balconies and flower boxes hanging from every window.

Taking his lead, Kate got out of the car and followed him through a courtyard, past another smiling receptionist and down a sunny corridor with Disney prints on the walls. At the end of the hall, he stopped and just stood, looking inside the room.

Kate held her breath. A little girl, no more than six or seven years old, sat in a wheelchair in front of the open window, watching children play. Though Kate only saw her profile, she could tell that the child was lovely, with shoulder-length blond hair, a peaches-and-cream complexion and long, dark lashes. She sat very still, with her hands in her lap but held stiffly, and at an odd angle. Beneath the pink skirt, her legs were painfully thin, as was the rest of her.

Kate didn't have to ask whose little girl she was. She knew.

Mitch's eyes never left the blond child. "Her name is Hope," he said in a husky voice. "And if you haven't already guessed, she's Molly's little girl. My niece. She's seven years old."

"She's beautiful."

"Yes, she is. Molly adored her."

"What's wrong with her? Why is she in a wheelchair?"

"She was born with spina bifida."

Kate was familiar with the disorder, which was brought on by the inability of the fetus's spine to close properly during the first month of pregnancy, causing an incomplete development of the brain as well as of the spinal cord. "Any chance she'll get better?"

Mitch shook his head. "The nerve damage is permanent and irreparable. Sadly, Hope's type of SB— the most severe—has created the kind of complications that make it necessary for her to be monitored daily. That's why she's here. Rustling Willows is the ideal place for her. The facilities and the medical staff are the best there is."

Kate's gaze returned to the little girl, and her eyes filled with tears. "She can't walk at all?"

"No. She's completely paralyzed from the waist down. Therapy has helped improve the use of her hands. She can draw a little and she can hold a doll, but that's about it."

"What's the prognosis?"

"Poor. With continued care she could live well into adulthood, but she developed a heart condition shortly after birth, so now her chances are severely diminished."

"Molly must have been devastated."

"She was inconsolable, and certain Hope's condition was her fault."

"Why did she think that?"

"She fell from her bike during a ten-K race sponsored by the university, and had to be taken to the hospital. That's where she found out she was pregnant. She had a few bruises and some internal bleeding, but other than that, she was fine. It wasn't until later in her pregnancy that the doctors realized there was something wrong with the baby. They assured Molly that her fall hadn't caused the condition, but she didn't believe them. She never stopped blaming herself.''

His lips curved at one corner in a sad smile. ''At first she thought she could take care of Hope herself. She took the baby out of the hospital as soon as it was safe, and rented a house in Singleton, where she had moved to when she found out she was pregnant. Three months after Hope was born, she developed an irregular heartbeat and had to be hospitalized. The condition worsened, and Molly was told that her baby would be better off in a facility equipped to take care of her needs on a long-term basis. She wanted to be back in this area, so I did some research and found Rustling Willows.''

''So Hope has been here since she was three months old?''

He nodded. ''Molly came to see her every day, but although she loved her more than her own life, Hope's illness took a terrible toll on her, maybe not physically, but emotionally. Every time I came to Washington on a visit, I could see that one more piece of her spirit had chipped away.''

Kate spent a moment collecting her thoughts before speaking again. ''Does Todd know about Hope?''

''No. She didn't want him to know.'' He continued to watch his little niece. ''I didn't realize how much and how drastically Hope's illness had changed Molly until I moved back to Washington. I did what Ted tried to do—reason with her. It was useless. She claimed that living on the edge helped her forget what she had done to Hope, and nothing I said to her could convince her to stop. She even got angry once and told me to butt out. She was a big girl and didn't need

a watchdog looking after her. So I left her alone.''
He jammed his hands in his pockets. "That was the
biggest mistake I could have made.''

It took Kate a few seconds to find her voice. "I'm
so sorry, Mitch. I didn't mean to hurt you by pry-
ing—''

"I know that.''

She glanced back at the child. "Aren't you going
to let her know you're here?''

He shook his head. "I always bring her a present
when I come, and a big lollipop. I don't want to dis-
appoint her by showing up empty-handed.''

He turned away and started back the way they had
come. Kate waited until they were in the car before
asking the question that had been on her mind since
finding out about Hope. "Who's the father, Mitch?''

"I don't know.''

"Molly never told you?''

"She didn't want me involved. All I wanted was
to make sure he was providing for Hope. Molly assured me that he was, though not with monthly child
support.''

"Then, how?''

"When Molly found out Hope would need to be
institutionalized, she asked the father for one million
dollars. At first, he refused, claiming he'd never be
able to get his hands on that kind of money. When
she threatened to put his name on the birth certificate,
he changed his tune.''

"I take it he was married.''

"Yes.''

"Did she love him?''

"Very much. I don't think she ever got over him.

That's probably why she married Todd—to forget Hope's father, though I'm not sure the ploy worked.''

Kate turned in her seat. ''My God, it's all beginning to make sense.''

Mitch didn't answer.

''You know what I'm thinking, don't you?''

''That Terrence is Hope's father?''

''Yes! That would explain what Todd told me the other day—that Terrence, like his parents, had tried to discourage Todd from marrying Molly. Don't you see, Mitch? He must have been terrified to have her in the Buchanan family, terrified of what she could let slip, either inadvertently or intentionally.''

''I guess we'll know soon enough. I talked to the jeweler, Bruce Cromwell, today. He hopes to have something for me before the end of tomorrow.''

''I was just thinking...'' Kate waited until he had merged onto I-95 again. ''A million dollars is a lot of money, but...what if it wasn't enough to take care of Hope?''

''It was enough. Molly was a shrewd investor. And if she needed more money, she knew I was there.''

''But what *if* it wasn't enough, Mitch? And what *if* she didn't want to come to you?'' Kate felt like a wound-up toy that couldn't be stopped. ''She could have gone back to the father and asked for more money. He may have gotten scared. Maybe he thought she'd keep coming back and back....''

She didn't finish her sentence. She didn't have to. When Mitch's gaze met hers, she knew the thought had already occurred to him.

Thirty-One

On Monday morning, true to his word, Bruce Cromwell called Mitch. The bracelet had been designed by a jeweler who had gone bankrupt five years ago, following several complaints about a phony stones scam. After serving eighteen months in prison, Dave Frankel had retired to Cape May, New Jersey, where, according to the grapevine, he spent his days fishing.

"You're aware that you're still under strict orders not to investigate your sister's death, aren't you?" Kate asked, as Mitch pored over a map of southern New Jersey.

"Of course." He traced the route from Washington to Cape May with his finger. "Today's my day off. I'm just coming along for the ride." He refolded the map and gave her a grin. "And to watch you in action. You know how that always turns me on."

"All right, Romeo, let's go, then. I wouldn't want to deprive you of a few thrills." She took her purse from the desk. "I'll need to stop at the bank on the way."

"What for?"

"If we're going to convince a bankrupt, retired old man to give us the kind of information we want, we have to be ready to pay for it."

"Homicide detectives don't pay for information."

She tweaked his cheek. "That's why cops never get anywhere and attorneys do. Now, stop frowning and let's go. It's going to take us more than two hours to get there."

Her estimate wasn't too far off. A little before eleven o'clock, Kate and Mitch stood on a dock facing the Delaware Bay. A sharp drop in temperature had kept fishing enthusiasts away, except one—an old man in a rowboat.

Mitch cupped his hands around his mouth. "Mr. Frankel?" he called out.

The old man looked up, squinting. "Who wants to know?" he asked crankily.

"I'm Detective Calhoon of the Washington, D.C. police. I'd like to ask you a couple of questions, if you don't mind."

"What about?"

"A bracelet you designed a few years ago."

Taking his time, Frankel reeled in the line, brought the pole back over his head and cast again. "I've made dozens of bracelets in my lifetime."

Having no intention of carrying on a conversation from thirty feet away, Mitch dropped the Mr. Nice Guy routine. "Let's talk up here, Mr. Frankel, shall we? Unless you'd rather come to the police station."

Kate jabbed him in the ribs. "Are you crazy? Why did you say that? What if he takes you up on it?"

"He won't."

Frankel pushed back his hat and looked at Mitch and then at Kate, as though reassessing them. "All right, all right. No need to get testy, son." He reeled in his line again, laid down his rod and started to row back to shore. "Give me a hand, will you?" he said when he docked.

Mitch helped the old man out of the boat. Looking at those rough, calloused hands, it was difficult to imagine him doing work as delicate as the bracelet in Mitch's pocket.

Frankel gave Kate a quick appraising glance. "And who might you be?"

"My name is Kate Logan," Kate replied. "I'm an attorney."

"Bah." He made a disgusted gesture. "Lawyers. They're the reason I left Washington. Damn town's infested with 'em."

He waved toward a small blue rancher with white trim. "Let's go inside. I've got nosy neighbors. Not 'nough to do when you're old, I guess."

Mitch and Kate followed Frankel inside. The house was clean, small and functional, with a galley kitchen on one side and a living room on the other.

"So," Frankel said, inviting them to sit down, "what's this about a bracelet?"

Mitch took the bangle from his pocket. "I understand you designed this."

Frankel took the bangle and inspected it closely, his eyes in a squint. "I guess it could be one of my designs."

"You're not sure?"

He gave Mitch a sly look. "The old eyes aren't as good as they used to be, if you know what I mean."

Knowing Kate was probably smiling inwardly, Mitch kept his eyes on the old man and reacted appropriately. "You wouldn't be trying to sell me the information, would you, Mr. Frankel? Because if you are—''

As if they had rehearsed the scene a dozen times, Kate jumped in. ''Mr. Frankel,'' she said sweetly, ''what Detective Calhoon is trying to say is that for the sake of time, we should come to a quick understanding.''

Frankel's little beady eyes lit up as he glanced at Mitch. ''Should let the little lady do all the talkin', son. She's a lot brighter than you are.'' He returned his attention to Kate. ''How big an understanding?''

''How does two hundred and fifty sound?''

''Not as good as five hundred.''

Kate opened her purse and rummaged through it. ''What do you say we split the difference and make it three hundred and seventy-five? That's all I have.''

She was getting off cheap, Mitch thought. She had expected to pay him twice what he was asking.

''Do we have a deal, Mr. Frankel?'' She held a roll of bills just within his reach.

The old guy was almost salivating. ''Yes.'' He took the money and counted it, not once, but twice. Satisfied it was all there, he nodded. ''What do you want to know?''

Kate closed her purse. ''Did you design that bracelet?''

''Sure did. One of my best pieces, if I say so myself.'' He looked at Mitch. ''I hope you didn't come here to hassle me about the stones being fake. That's water under the bridge. I paid my dues.''

''We're not interested in the stones,'' Mitch said. ''Just the person who bought the bracelet. You do remember him, don't you?''

The sly smile returned. "I'm trying to, but you know what they say. After the eyes, the memory is next to go."

Kate's good humor seemed to fade. "And you know what they say about lawyers, don't you, Mr. Frankel? They like to get value for their money. In my book, three hundred and seventy-five dollars to hear you admit you designed the bracelet, which we already knew, is not good value, so unless you give me the name of the man you swindled..." She snatched the money from his hands. "You can kiss the loot goodbye."

His face fell. "Now, now, there's no need to get hasty."

"Is your memory improving?"

He sighed. "Yeah. I reckon it is." He licked his lips, his eyes on the money. "Name's Buchanan. Terrence Buchanan."

Thirty-Two

"I'll be damned," Kate murmured. "It was Terrence all along." She buckled her seat belt. "But why did he lie? Didn't he realize that you'd be moving heaven and earth to find out who gave that bracelet to Molly?"

"We're talking about something that happened eight years ago. Frankel went bankrupt and then vanished. Terrence never thought I'd find him. And I wouldn't have, if it weren't for Bruce."

"It's not looking good for Terrence, is it."

Mitch shook his head. "Not only could he be Hope's father, but if your blackmail theory is correct—" he met her gaze "—we may have found our killer."

"You don't think he'll make trouble for you, do you? Call Lieutenant Fennell and tell him you're investigating a case out of your jurisdiction?"

"He can't afford to."

After dropping Kate off at her office, Mitch went straight to Jefferson University, where the same pleasant receptionist who had greeted him two days earlier told him that Provost Buchanan was in a meeting and couldn't be disturbed.

"Get him out, please," he said.

She looked bewildered. "I beg your pardon?"

"This can't wait. Get him out of the meeting."

Less than thirty seconds later, Buchanan was walking down the marble-floored hallway, his expression clearly hostile. "Are you insane?" he said between clenched teeth. "Bullying my secretary into interrupting one of the most important meetings of the year? Who the hell do you think you are?"

Mitch didn't bother with an answer. "You want to talk out here or in private?"

Without a word, Buchanan marched into his office. Mitch followed him and closed the door. This time there was no handshake, no pleasantries exchanged.

"Well?" Buchanan folded his arms. "I'm listening. What have you come to accuse me of now?"

"Ever heard of a man by the name of Dave Frankel?"

Terrence blinked but remained unruffled. "Can't say that I have."

"Funny. He remembers you."

Buchanan let out a snicker. "A lot of people think they know me."

"Stop playing games, Terrence. Besides being an excellent craftsman, Frankel was also a meticulous record keeper. Not only does he remember you, but he was able to produce an invoice for the bracelet you commissioned, with the inscription Yours forever, T., in your own handwriting. He expected you to file suit along with a dozen other angry customers—but you never did, did you, Terrence? Because that would have meant exposing your affair with my sister. It was easier to kiss twelve thousand dollars goodbye than to face a scandal that would have destroyed your career.''

The man seemed to deflate like a punctured balloon, right before Mitch's eyes. He opened his mouth to say something—then, perhaps realizing that any protest would be a waste of time, he closed it again.

Mitch felt no compassion for the man, only contempt. ''What's the matter, Buchanan? Feeling a little queasy?''

Terrence walked over to his desk and sat down. ''It's not what you think.''

''Really? Are you saying you didn't seduce my sister? Or have an affair with her? Or father her child?''

''We had an affair, but I'm not the one who did the seducing. From the moment Molly walked into my classroom, she made it clear that it was me she was interested in, not international law. I did everything I could think of to discourage her, but she wouldn't take no for an answer. Late one night, I came out of the law library where I had been doing some research and found her waiting by my car.''

Looking like a man beaten, Terrence clasped his hands and held them against his mouth. ''I make no excuse for myself. I could have driven away, or threatened to turn her in. She…made it impossible for me to do either.''

Mitch didn't want to believe him. This was his kid sister the scum was talking about, the little girl he had taught to play baseball and who had later helped him build his tree house. But he also remembered another Molly, the wild teenager with a hopeless crush on Duke, Mitch's best friend, and the outrageous antics she had pulled trying to catch Duke's attention. There had been signs of the woman she was becoming, and he hadn't seen them.

"How long did the affair last?" he asked.

"Six months. Until she told me she was pregnant. We had a terrible fight that day. I wanted her to have an abortion. She didn't. When I realized I wasn't getting anywhere on that subject, I told her I'd pay child support, whatever she needed, just as long as she kept my name off the birth certificate."

He sighed. "Then she found out about the baby's illness and everything changed. She wanted money— a million dollars. I told her she was crazy, that I couldn't give her that kind of money without my wife finding out."

"But you did give it to her."

He lowered his hands on his desk and gazed at them. "It wasn't easy, but yes, I gave her the money. I had no choice. She was threatening to go to the newspapers."

Mitch decided to follow Kate's hunch. "When did she start coming back for more?"

Terrence looked surprised. "How did you know about that?"

"I didn't. Kate Logan thought of it."

"Oh." A few seconds went by. "She came here to the university a couple of months before she was killed. She wanted another million. I was furious. I told her to get off my back and go to you for the money, because I didn't have it. She didn't want to do that. She said Hope was my responsibility, no one else's."

"So what did you do?"

"I gave her a hundred thousand, and even that took some doing."

"Was she satisfied?"

He barked a laugh. "Molly was never satisfied. She always wanted more."

"So you found yourself trapped," Mitch continued. "You didn't have the money, and at the same time you knew that one word from Molly and everything that mattered to you would be lost—your brilliant career, your marriage, the respect of your peers."

"No. You've got it all wrong." He could no longer conceal the panic in his voice.

"She was going to destroy you, Terrence. What other choice did you have?"

Terrence fell back against his chair. "I guess I'd better call an attorney before I say another word."

"That wouldn't be a bad idea." As Terrence picked up his phone, Mitch took his out of his pocket and dialed Frank Sykes's number in Fairfax.

His shoulder against the lamppost, Emile pretended to be reading the evening paper, while watching Todd Buchanan walk over to the same public phone he used almost every evening at this time. He was probably conferring with Kate Logan, keeping abreast of the latest developments on the other side of the Atlantic.

Emile had done the same, logging on to the Internet almost every night before he left the auto parts store and reading the headlines of a half-dozen American newspapers. Several incidents had taken place recently, and while they may or may not be directly related to Todd Buchanan, they had helped Emile write his story, which was now finished. He couldn't wait to see the look on Maurice's face when he read the completed draft.

His eyes still on Buchanan, Emile folded his paper and started walking toward the bakery where, every day at the same time, he bought a half baguette for his dinner. Tonight, however, *Madame* Millet was behind the counter, not her daughter. Yvette was in the back room—Emile could see through the open door— urging a woman to sit down.

''Here—'' Emile heard her say. ''Drink this. It'll make you feel better.''

''What is it?'' The woman's voice was accented and vaguely familiar.

''Plain water with a little sugar in it. My grandmother's instant remedy for an upset stomach. Drink up.''

As Yvette straightened, Emile gave a little start. The woman Yvette was fussing over was Jessica Van Dyke. Trying to look inconspicuous as he waited his turn, he stole another quick glance into the back room. Ms. Van Dyke was unusually pale, and her forehead was covered with perspiration.

''Feeling better?'' Yvette asked.

Jessica smiled and nodded. At the same time her right hand slid down to her belly, a gesture that didn't go unnoticed by Yvette.

''I don't mean to be nosy,'' she said, lowering her voice a little. ''But...are you pregnant by any chance?''

Jessica beamed at her.

Pregnant. Emile almost needed a chair himself. Of course. He had seen those same symptoms in Antoinette—the nausea, the light-headedness, the pallor. Jessica Van Dyke was pregnant.

Dear God.

"*Monsieur* Sardoux?" Yvette's mother was smiling at him, her head cocked to the side. "A half baguette, as usual?"

Suddenly lost for words, Emile nodded, took the bread, paid for it and hurried out, but not before he heard Yvette say, "Oh, Ms. Van Dyke. I'm so happy for you."

Emile walked away, the half baguette under his arm. After a minute or so he realized he was walking in the wrong direction and had to turn around. He never even glanced toward the phone booth to see if Todd Buchanan was still there. He was remembering the day Antoinette had told him she was expecting a baby. Laughing like a crazy man, he had twirled her around and around until she had begged him to put her down.

Eight months later, Julien was born, a chubby little boy with Emile's dark eyes and lungs like Caruso. Two years later, they'd had Magalie, their darling daughter, who, at the tender age of twelve, was already turning heads.

He loved his children dearly, and let them know every night when he talked to them on the phone. Those calls, though they made him happy, left him longing for the day when the four of them would be a family again.

A family. That was something Todd Buchanan's baby would never know. By the time he was born, his father would be in jail. Or on the run again.

Back home, Emile took a pot of soup from the

refrigerator and started to reheat it on top of the two-burner stove. It had just started to simmer, when he realized he wasn't hungry. His mouth was dry and his stomach was in knots. What the hell was the matter with him? Maybe he was coming down with a real *crise de foie.* That would teach him to lie to his boss.

He sat at the kitchen table and tried to go over his story one more time before he turned it in, but he couldn't concentrate. With a groan of frustration, he threw the pages aside and walked out of the apartment. He needed to clear his head, and more importantly, he needed to remember the things that mattered—like getting his job back. If he kept repeating those words like a mantra, he would be fine.

The wind had kicked up, bringing with it the sharp smell of the sea. He could already hear the happy squeals of children riding the merry-go-round on the town square. That, too, brought back a few memories. He may not have always done the right thing by his kids, but there had been some good times. There would be again.

That's more than he could say for Baby Buchanan.

Todd knew something was wrong the moment Jess walked out of the bakery.

"What happened?" he asked, studying her features. "You're shaking. Are you sick? Is it the baby?"

"I'm fine." She looked around her. "Let's get out of here."

"Jess, you're scaring me."

She didn't speak until they were both inside the

car. "Someone knows about you," she said in a shaky voice.

He tried to control the panic that washed over him. He had to, for Jess. "Who?"

"His name is Emile Sardoux. He works for an auto parts store here in town."

"How do you know all this?"

She kept playing with the pendant around her neck, the little Basque cross he had given her for her birthday. "Yvette at the *boulangerie* told me. The man has been asking questions—at the *boulangerie* and maybe elsewhere."

"What did Yvette tell him?"

"Nothing. She's too discreet to talk about her customers."

"Does he know who I am?"

"I don't know. He called you *Monsieur* Adler. All Yvette said was that you were a customer, and nothing more."

"What exactly did he want to know?"

"How long you had been in town, where you came from. That kind of thing."

Todd glanced in the rearview mirror. "What does he look like?"

"Mid-forties, slim, light brown hair, well-dressed, well-spoken." She turned around in her seat and glanced behind her. "He must have been watching us, Will. What if he's following us right now?"

"He's not."

"How do you know? Only a couple of days ago, you thought someone was watching you, so how can you say no one is following us now?"

Todd could tell from the sound of her voice that

the control she had been hanging on to since leaving the bakery was beginning to fray. He took her hand and held it. "I've been watching, Jess. There is no one behind us."

She didn't seem reassured. "I'm scared."

"Jess, just think. Why would an auto parts salesman be interested in us?"

"I don't know! Maybe he's an American undercover cop, pretending to be French."

"Yvette would have known if he was a foreigner."

"Should I go back and ask?"

"No! We don't want to bring attention to ourselves."

"What are we going to do?"

He wished he knew. He had felt so safe here, so certain that no one would ever find him.

"It's all my fault," Jess said, staring out the windshield. "If I hadn't insisted we contact a lawyer, none of this would have happened."

"It's not your fault." Todd gave her hand a firm shake and tried to speak with all the conviction he could muster. This was no time for Jessica to be torn with guilt. Not in her condition.

"Yes, it is," she said stubbornly. "Kate warned us that reopening the case could bring some unpleasant surprises, especially once the foreign press picked up the story. And that's exactly what happened. Maybe someone offered a reward for your capture. Or maybe this Emile Sardoux is some kind of bounty hunter."

Todd had no answer for her.

Jess's voice was a bare whisper when she murmured, "Oh, Will, what have I done?"

Thirty-Three

"Emile." The editor in chief looked up, his eyes bright with anticipation. "Is it all done?" He rubbed his hands together. "Let me take a look."

With a sinking feeling in his stomach, Emile met Maurice's earnest gaze. "There is no story."

Maurice's expectant smile faded. "What?"

"There is no story," Emile repeated. "I made a mistake."

"Mistake?"

The fact that a man as eloquent as Maurice Varnier was speaking in one-word sentences was not a good sign. Anytime now he would explode, and when that happened, it wouldn't be pleasant.

"The man I thought was Todd Buchanan is in fact a German," Emile lied. "From Stuttgart. I'm sorry, Maurice. I feel like such a fool."

Maurice kept staring at him. His face was turning purple, and in his right temple, a little vein pulsed erratically. Emile took advantage of the heavy silence to forge on.

"I know you're disappointed. I am, too. That story was going to change my life—"

"You son of a bitch," Maurice hissed. "You're selling the piece to another paper, aren't you."

Emile hadn't expected that. After ten years with *Bordeaux-Matin,* he hadn't thought his integrity would be questioned. "No! My God, Maurice, I would never do that. I came to you, didn't I?"

"Because you knew I was the only fucking idiot in this country that would fall for your sob story. Then, when you realized that maybe you could do better elsewhere, you went looking, figuring that if it didn't work out with the big papers, you still had the old sucker here as a backup."

"No." Emile was too hurt to come up with a strong defense. He doubted he could have convinced Maurice, anyway. "I never wanted to write for any paper but *Bordeaux-Matin.*"

Maurice stood up and walked around his desk, toward Emile. "Are you telling me that if *Le Figaro* or *Paris-Match* came to you with an offer, you'd turn them down?"

"Yes, because I made you a promise."

"And that's supposed to be worth something?" Maurice yelled, pushing his angry face into Emile's. "The promise of a drunk?"

The words stung. "That's hitting low, Maurice."

"What about what you're doing to me? I went out on a limb for you. After you left the other day, I spent two hours trying to convince the big guy upstairs that we could trust you. My integrity is on the line here. Maybe even my job."

"I still have some money left," Emile said pitifully. He started to take three thousand francs from his pocket. "I'll pay the rest back, I swear—a little each week, even if I have to take a second job."

"Oh, shut up. Don't insult me by compounding

your lies with a noble gesture.'' He flicked his hand at the money. ''This isn't appeasing me. I want the story, dammit.''

''I told you, there is no story. Todd Buchanan isn't here.''

''You're lying.'' He pointed a finger at Emile, the way he had the other day, but this time the gesture and the words were not amusing. ''I don't know what kind of game you're playing, but I know you're up to something. I'm going to find out what it is. And I'm going to find Todd Buchanan if I have to go after him myself. And then I'm going to destroy you, Emile, do you hear me? I'll make sure you never work as a journalist again. I'll make sure the whole damn country knows what a back-stabbing, double-crossing snake you are. And that includes Antoinette.''

He walked back to his desk and sank into his chair. ''Get out,'' he said, without looking up. ''Just get out.''

Quietly, Emile let himself out.

''I think you should call Kate,'' Jess said.

Todd didn't answer. After spending half the night pacing back and forth, wondering what to do, he was no closer to finding a solution to his problem than he had been at ten o'clock the previous night.

At dawn, instead of getting ready for work, he had called the captain of the *Ainara,* and asked permission to take the day off.

Now sitting at the kitchen table with his bowl of *café au lait* growing cold in front of him, he slowly nodded. Jess was right. Kate had to be told. Maybe she would know what to do, because he sure didn't.

Before he could decide whether to go into town or take a chance and call from the house, there was a knock at the door. Both he and Jess jumped. Touching a finger to his lips, Todd walked over to the small window overlooking the driveway and peered through the blue-and-white gingham curtain. A man he had never seen before stood on the other side of the door, his head down, his hands behind his back.

Jess let out a small gasp.

"You know him?" Todd asked in a whisper.

"Yes. I mean no. I think that's Emile Sardoux. I recognize him from Yvette's description."

"What is he doing here? How did he find out where we lived?"

"I don't know." She held on to his arm. "Maybe if we don't answer, he'll think we're not home and go away."

But the Renault was there, big as life. "He saw the car, Jess. We have to let him in. If I don't, he'll only grow more suspicious." He took Jess's cold hands in his. "Don't worry," he said, trying to fight off his own panic and not doing a very good job. "It's going to be all right."

"How do you know?"

"Just think. If he was a bounty hunter, or someone after a reward, he wouldn't be here. He'd be at the police station, turning me in."

"Maybe he's hoping you'll pay him more than the reward."

Todd was silent for a moment, considering that option. If money was what the man was after, then there was no problem. The three hundred thousand dollars he had deposited in a Swiss bank two years ago had grown into a tidy sum. Even after Kate's retainer, there was still enough in the account to cover any emergency.

So whatever the man wanted, within reason, Todd could give it to him.

Before he could lose his nerve, he opened the door. *"Oui?"* he said, hoping his French would be good enough to carry on a conversation.

To his surprise, the man answered in English. "Good morning," he said, with a slight bow of his head. "My name is Emile Sardoux. I'm sorry to bother you so early, but the captain of the *Ainara* told me you had taken the day off, so I decided to take a chance you might be home. It's urgent that I speak with you and..." He glanced above Todd's shoulder. "With the young lady."

Todd's throat was so dry, he could barely swallow. He let the man in, but not without making sure he had come alone, though he had no idea what he would have done if a contingent of French *gendarmes* had suddenly jumped from behind a bush.

"You speak English well," he said, slowly assessing the man. He was just as Yvette had described— average in every way, and seemingly unthreatening.

Sardoux's hazel eyes looked at him without flinching. "I studied at Columbia University for a full year." He turned to Jess. "I hope you are feeling better, mademoiselle."

"Why wouldn't I be?"

"I saw you at the bakery yesterday evening, when you took ill."

Todd wrapped a protective arm around Jessica's shoulders, aware of the strange tableau they must make. Three people, two of them hiding from the law, the third ready to turn them in.

"I understand that you've been asking about me," Todd said, watching the man's face for a reaction.

"Ah. So you heard about that."

"What do you want?"

Sardoux gave him a level look. "I know who you are, Mr. Buchanan."

Thirty-Four

Although those dreaded words didn't come as a surprise, they hit Todd hard. He glanced at Jess, who had turned white as a ghost. "I don't know what you're talking about," he said, making sure he continued to speak with a British accent. Someone as fluent in English as Sardoux would know the difference between a British accent and an American one; therefore it was important to stay in character. "My name is William Adler."

Sardoux didn't contradict him. "Let me explain who I am," he said instead. "At the moment, I sell auto parts on rue Gambetta, but I'm a reporter by profession. I was employed at *Bordeaux-Matin* for the past ten years. Then things started to go badly for me, and I lost my job."

He told them about his drinking, his move to Saint-Jean-de-Luz, his return to sobriety, and the hope that he could get his old job back, along with his wife, whom he loved very much.

"I don't understand why you are telling us all this," Todd said, still reluctant to admit the truth even though he knew that denying it was useless. This man was no fool. He wouldn't be here if he didn't have solid proof to back up what he was saying.

"I'm telling you, *Monsieur* Buchanan, because I want you to understand that I'm not a bad person, just a desperate man trying get his life back together. But I didn't know how to do that. Then, last week, I picked up a newspaper and I read about this Todd Buchanan from Washington, D.C., a fugitive who was suspected of having killed his wife, and how an attorney by the name of Kate Logan was reopening the case. Your picture was in the paper, and when I saw it, I knew I had seen you before. I spend a lot of time at the harbor, you see, watching the boats come in. So, I did a little investigating, and what I learned confirmed my suspicions. I knew this would make a great story and with that story, I could get my life back."

Next to Todd, Jess stiffened. "And for a story," she said calmly, "you are willing to destroy us?"

"Jess," Todd warned.

She shook her head. Her expression was sad but resolute. She had realized, just as he had, that the game was over. "No, Will. There's no need to pretend anymore."

Todd was silent. What could he say? She was right.

His gaze returned to the man who now held their lives in his hands. How much did he want for his silence? Ten thousand francs? A hundred thousand? More?

"I'm not as bad as you make me sound, *mademoiselle*," Sardoux said gently. "In fact—"

"Look—" Todd cut in, dropping the phony accent. "Why don't you just tell us how much you want and be done with it?"

"I beg your pardon?"

"I said how much do you want to keep quiet?

That's why you're here, isn't it? For a shakedown?'' Aware the man may not understand that expression, he rubbed three fingers together in that universal gesture everyone understood. "Money?"

The man looked insulted. "I'm afraid you misunderstood me, *monsieur.*"

"I don't think so. I can smell a shark from a mile away."

"Then, your sense of smell is off, *monsieur.* I don't want your money. I came here to help you."

Todd let out a sarcastic laugh, and was annoyed when Jess squeezed his arm and said, "Help us how, *Monsieur* Sardoux?"

"I have no intention of writing the story. I did, up to yesterday, but when I saw you at the *boulangerie* last night and realized you were expecting a baby..." He shook his head. "Something happened to me. It's one thing to turn you in, *Monsieur* Buchanan, but to put the life of a little baby in jeopardy." He shook his head again. *"Non, ça je ne peux pas."* That I can't do.

"You expect me to believe that?" Todd asked.

"It's the truth. I spent a sleepless night trying to talk myself out of the idea, knowing that the job I wanted back so badly would be gone forever."

Todd felt Jessica's fingers dig into his arm and knew what she was thinking. Sardoux was letting them off the hook. Still, something wasn't adding up. "I don't understand. If you're not going to do the story, what are you doing here?"

"When I told my boss that there was no story, no Todd Buchanan, he didn't believe me."

"What does that mean?"

"It means that he's going to do the story himself. Or he will assign it to his best investigative reporter. Either way, you will be found. Don't get me wrong— Maurice is not a bad man, but his job is at stake, so now he must do whatever is necessary to save it."

"How much time do we have?" Todd asked.

"If he sends his best reporter, maybe forty-eight hours. If Maurice comes after you himself, less than that. He is a very good reporter. And he has excellent contacts."

"How much have you told him?"

"Only that I thought I had seen you in the Saint-Jean-de-Luz region. Of course, that covers a rather large area—Ciboure, Anglet, Biarritz, Bayonne—but he'll start in Saint-Jean-de-Luz because that's where I live."

Todd knew what would happen once the story broke. The international press would pounce on it like vultures, turning Jess and Todd's idyllic life into a circus. Then the French police would arrive, handcuff him and throw him in jail, while they decided whether or not to extradite him.

"If I were you," Sardoux continued, "I would leave right now. You have enough time to board a plane for anywhere in the world. By the time the story breaks, you will be thousands of miles away."

"Yes." Todd nodded. "I suppose I could do that."

Sardoux stood up. "I'm sorry about everything. I hope you understand why I did it."

"We do." Jess extended her hand. "And we appreciate your coming here, *Monsieur* Sardoux, knowing what it cost you."

"Bonne chance." Good luck. He shook her hand. "To both of you."

Todd and Jess stood at the front door, watching the green Opel disappear down the winding road. When they could no longer see it, they went back in and locked the door. Todd laughed at the futile gesture.

"What do we do now?" Jess asked softly.

He wished he knew. If he were alone, the solution would be simple. He would pack whatever he could carry with him and hit the road. But there was Jess to think about. How could he ask her to lead the life of a nomad, moving from town to town, country to country, always looking over her shoulder?

They could go to Geneva, he thought, since that's where his money was. They would be safe there, at least for a while. He might even be able to get a new set of ID, though that might take time. Or they could take Sardoux's suggestion and go as far as possible— New Zealand, perhaps. Or Australia. Who would think of looking for them there?

"I don't know, Jess," he said truthfully. "I honestly don't know."

"I screwed up in a big way, didn't I." She rested her head on his shoulder.

"Stop saying that."

"How can I?" She stood up abruptly, her arms wrapped around her middle, and started to pace. "If I hadn't insisted we contact Kate, the story wouldn't have made the international papers and we wouldn't be in this mess."

"And if I hadn't thought that clearing my name was a good idea, I wouldn't have agreed to do it."

"You agreed because I pushed and pushed. You

did it for me. You risked your freedom, and look what it brought us.''

''I did it for the three of us.'' He turned her around, and as he did, she collapsed against his chest and broke into huge sobs.

Todd held her, his mind racing as he tried to come up with a solution they could both live with. His main preoccupation at the moment was Jess and the baby. He had to keep them safe and send them somewhere where the press wouldn't be able to touch them, where they would be cared for, even pampered.

He knew of such a place.

He waited until the sobs had subsided before saying, ''Come. Let's sit down for a moment.'' He led her back to the little sofa where they and Sardoux had sat moments earlier. Then he went to get her a glass of water, and waited until she had taken a few sips before sitting down beside her.

In as calm a voice as he could manage, he told her the options they had, none of them acceptable. ''The truth is,'' he said, ''I don't want to run anymore, Jess. Especially now that we're about to have a baby. He or she deserves better than that.''

''Then, what...?'' A dry sob shook Jess's shoulders. ''What can we do? You heard Sardoux. We have forty-eight hours, maybe less. What can we do in such a short time?''

''We can go back.''

Mouth open, Jess fell back against the cushions. ''Back?'' she repeated. ''To the States?''

''It's the only way I can be sure that you and the baby will be safe.''

''What about you?'' she cried.

"I'll turn myself in."

"No!" The cry seemed to have come from her very soul. She would have jumped out of her seat, if Todd hadn't held her down. "I won't let you do that! They'll put you in jail!"

"For a while. Hopefully a short while."

"What if you're wrong? What if they lock you up for months? Years."

He continued to hold her. "You've always had faith in Kate," he reminded her. "Don't give up on her now."

"She's just an attorney, Will. Not God. And if you're arrested…"

She didn't have to finish her sentence. He knew what she was thinking, that the baby would be born while he was in jail. That thought had occurred to him, too. He didn't like it, but he had no choice. He had to go back. For Jess. For his family.

"I'm going to call my parents," he said. "And ask them to take you in."

"Oh, Todd, no." She shook her head. "They don't know me. We have no right to expect them to open their home to a stranger."

"You're not a stranger. You're my fiancée. The mother of my baby."

"They don't know me," she said stubbornly. She dried her tears. "Maybe I could go to San Diego— to my parents' house."

"They'll never be able to protect you from the media the way my father can. And you'll be three thousand miles away. Is that what you want?"

"No." But she was still resisting, still considering other options.

It took Todd another five minutes to convince her to let him make the call. When she finally agreed, he dialed quickly, amazed he could still remember the number. He had expected Lizzy, his parents' maid, to answer, or his mother. To his surprise, it was his father who took the call. The shock of hearing the man's voice was so great that for a moment Todd was speechless.

At the other end, the voice turned impatient. "Hello? Is anyone there?"

Todd swallowed past the knot in his throat. "It's me, Dad."

The line went silent, and Todd could only imagine the range of emotions his father was experiencing. When Lyle Buchanan finally spoke, his voice was low and husky. "Is that really you, Todd?"

"Yes." Todd blinked the tears away but one rolled down his cheek. He took a swipe at it. "It's good to hear your voice, Dad."

"And yours." Several more seconds ticked by. "Are you all right, son?"

Todd wished he could have reassured his father. "Not exactly."

"What's wrong?" His father's voice was filled with concern.

"I need you to do me a favor, Dad."

"Name it."

Todd laughed. "That's a dangerous thing to say to a fugitive, don't you think?" It seemed like the wrong time to attempt a little humor, but he was so damn nervous, he blurted out the words.

"You're my son," Lyle said simply. "I would have helped you before if you had given me the chance, but you didn't. So if I can help you now, I want to."

"It's not for me, actually, but for Jessica."

"Your fiancée. Kate Logan told us about her."

"She...we're going to have a baby, Dad."

There was another silence, longer this time. "A baby." Lyle cleared his throat. "Congratulations, son. That's wonderful news."

"The baby is the reason I called, Dad. We're no longer safe here." As briefly as he could, he told his father about the reporter's visit and what would happen if they stayed. "We only have forty-eight hours, maybe less, to make a decision—to leave or to stay," he added. "I don't want to run anymore."

"What other options do you have?"

"I want to come home."

"That's crazy! You'll be arrested the moment you set foot on U.S. soil."

"That's why I called. I need to know that Jessica will be safe, that the press won't be hounding her night and day." He hesitated. "Dad, can she stay with you and Mom? Until this whole mess is over?"

The reply came quickly, without the slightest hesitation. "Of course she can, but, Todd, listen to me. You can buy yourself some time. In order for U.S. authorities to have you extradited, they must first apply for the extradition. That will take time, and even after extradition is granted, you can appeal the order in a French court. That could take months."

"I won't do it, Dad. I won't put Jess through that ordeal."

He heard the sigh at the other end of the line. "Are you absolutely sure?"

"Yes."

"In that case, you have another option."

"What?"

"Run, Todd. I have friends all over the world, people who can help you and Jessica."

He hadn't expected that. His father, this great guru of justice who had sworn to uphold the law, was not only telling him to run but offering to help him escape. That was one more thing Todd could blame himself for—corrupting a Supreme Court justice. "I've destroyed my brother's career because of what I did two years ago. I won't destroy yours."

"The hell with my career!"

"Don't say that! It won't change my mind. Jess and I are taking the first flight out of here tomorrow. Air France flight 28 from Paris. It arrives at Dulles at four-ten in the afternoon."

Lyle let out another sigh. "All right, son. If you're sure that's what you want to do, I'll be there."

"And you'll take care of Jessica?"

"Yes." He paused. "With one condition."

"What's that?"

"I want you to fire Kate Logan."

Thirty-Five

"I'm sorry, Mitch." Frank Sykes shook his head. "I can't hold him. As much as I agree with you that Terrence Buchanan had one hell of a motive for killing Molly, I don't have a shred of evidence against him. And he's got an alibi—not airtight, like Victor Harlow's, but an alibi just the same."

"Then, work on that alibi, Frank. Talk to Elaine Buchanan."

"I already have. She maintains that Terrence was in bed with her, all night."

"How the hell would she know? She has a sleeping disorder. She takes pills to sleep."

"That's where it gets cute. She claims she didn't take one that night. She forgot. As a result she spent all night drifting in and out of sleep. And every time she woke up, Terrence was there."

"And it never occurred to her to get up and take a pill?"

"She kept hoping she'd fall asleep without it."

"What a crock. Don't tell me you fell for it, Frank."

"I didn't. And I don't think his attorney believes him, either, but you know Jacob Winters. He could make Benedict Arnold look like a choirboy. Don't worry, I'm keeping my eye on Terrence and his wife. I just wanted you to know that, for the moment, I can't do much more than that.''

He gave his black string tie a little tug. ''About Victor Harlow—'' he said, studying Mitch. ''He looked as if he had been put through the fast-spin cycle of my Maytag.''

''No kidding.''

''No kidding. He had a broken nose, one eye swollen shut and a split lip. You wouldn't happen to know anything about that, would you?''

Mitch assumed his most innocent expression. ''Me? Why would I?''

''Oh, I don't know. I just thought I'd ask.''

''Maybe you should ask Harlow.''

''I did.'' Frank leaned back in his chair. Mitch could have sworn he saw amusement in those shrewd eyes. ''He says he fell down a flight of stairs.''

''Well, then, there you go.'' Mitch stood up. ''Mystery solved.''

He walked out of Frank's office, aware of his friend's gaze on his back.

Kate was working on Ed Gibbons's pre-trial conference, when Frankie announced she had a call— from Todd Buchanan.

''Why didn't you call me on my cell phone?'' Kate asked when she had him on the line.

''The connection wouldn't go through for some reason.'' He sounded different, subdued.

''You're taking a chance.''

''It doesn't matter anymore, Kate. It's all over.''

She sat up. "What's all over? What are you talking about?"

"A French reporter found out who I was. I won't go into details. The bottom line is, the news that I'm here is about to break."

Kate couldn't find her voice for a few seconds. She had been afraid something like this would happen. "Todd, listen to me—"

"No, Kate, let me speak because I don't have much time. I called to let you know that I'm coming back. I'm turning myself in."

"Oh, Todd. Do you really want to do that?"

"Jess and I discussed it. It's the right thing to do—the only thing to do." He paused as though gathering his thoughts. "You've been great, Kate. Regardless of what happens, I want you to know that I'll always be grateful for what you've done."

Kate laughed. "You're talking as if coming back means the end of our professional relationship. It doesn't. If that's what you really want to do, I'll make the necessary arrangements so your return can take place with the minimum of attention. I'll be with you every step of the way, Todd. You can count on that."

"That's not what I want, Kate."

She frowned. "What do you mean, that's not what you want?"

He took a moment to answer. "I've retained another attorney."

Kate's mouth opened to say something but she couldn't get the words out.

"Kate?"

"Yes, I...I heard you." She fought to pull herself

together. "I don't understand. Have I done something wrong?"

"No, I told you, you've been great."

"Then, what is it? The other day when I relayed that message from your father, you didn't want to hear anything about another attorney. What happened to change your mind?"

"The other day I didn't fully realize the danger you were in. Now that I do, I can't allow you to go on. I would feel terrible if something happened to you."

"I'm not in any danger, Todd."

"I know you're upset—"

"Just tell me why you're doing this, dammit. I have a right to know. Is it your father? Did he talk you into letting me go?"

"I want you to keep the rest of the money," he said, as though he hadn't heard her. "You've earned it. Goodbye."

After Todd hung up, Kate just sat there, staring at the phone as if the instrument could give her an explanation.

"Boss?"

Kate looked up to see Frankie standing in front of her desk. "God, boss, you look awful. What did he say?"

Kate put the phone back in its cradle. "I believe I've just been fired, Frankie." She repeated her brief conversation with Todd. "He finally got what he wanted."

"Todd?"

"His father. He never wanted me on this case. He didn't think I was good enough, so he talked Todd into letting him hire another attorney."

"I thought the two of you had patched things up, more or less."

"I thought so, too, but I guess now that Todd is coming back and will most likely have to face a trial, Justice Buchanan feels he needs to pull out the big guns—like Jacob Winters."

"I'm sorry, boss." Frankie looked crestfallen. "You worked so hard on this case. Not to mention all the other crap you had to take."

Kate stood and paced over to the window and back, arms folded against her chest. "I don't get it. The other day Todd wouldn't hear of another attorney, and today, he couldn't wait to get rid of me."

"I wouldn't waste my time worrying about it," Frankie said, giving a dismissive shrug. "Those people treated you like dirt. I say, good riddance."

"There's more to that call than meets the eye."

"And sometime a cigar is just a cigar."

Kate stopped her pacing. "Meaning?"

"Meaning maybe the kid really is worried about you, just like he said. He wouldn't be the only one, you know. I'm scared to death for you, too. I keep wondering what will happen next." She picked up a stack of signed letters from Kate's desk and flipped through them. "Now I don't have to worry anymore."

She started to leave, then walked back to Kate's desk. "Uh...I don't want to sound crass or anything, but..." There was a beat of silence. "What about the money?"

"What money?"

"Todd's retainer."

"Oh." Kate laughed. "He said I could keep it, that I had earned it."

Frankie let out a sigh of relief. "Good."

"I'm not keeping it," Kate said, and watched Frankie's face fall. "In fact, I want you to go over the account right now, see how much we've spent, how many billable hours I have, etcetera. Then I want you to make a check for the balance to Todd Buchanan. I'll give it to him when he returns."

"But, boss—"

"Just do it, Frankie."

"Kate, you have to eat something."

With the prongs of her fork, Kate speared a morsel of pepper-crusted tuna, done rare, the way she liked it, held it poised over her plate for a second, then put it back. "I'm not hungry."

Hoping to cheer her up, Mitch had brought her to her favorite restaurant for lunch—Bistro Français, in Georgetown. But, although the service was as impeccable as ever, the glow from the flower-shaped wall sconces soothing and the food wonderful, she couldn't appreciate any of it.

As Frankie would put it, she was in a funk.

She had never been fired before, and the experience had left her angry, humiliated and worried about her future as an attorney. Not necessarily in that order.

Mitch must have sensed her mood because he made no further comment about the food, or her appetite. He seemed content to glance at her from time to time while devouring his venison medallions and chestnut purée.

When she couldn't stand to watch him stuff his

face anymore, she pushed her plate away and folded her arms on the table. "How can you eat at a time like this?"

His fork stopped midway to his mouth. "A time like what?"

"You're not funny, Mitch."

"Not even a tiny bit?" He crossed his eyes, and she was reminded of that photo Lynn Flannery had taken of Molly. In spite of her determination not to be entertained, Kate smiled.

"That's better." Mitch took another bite of his food. "Now, please eat or I'll be forced to play 'Open your mouth, here comes the 'choo-choo' with you."

"Airplane. Open your mouth, here comes the airplane."

Mitch shook his head. "Choo-choo. It was one of the best promotional campaigns the Long Island Railroad engineered."

This time she laughed. And tasted the tuna, which was excellent. "Thank you, Mitch."

"For what?"

"For putting up with me today, for making me laugh, for feeding me."

"Consider it a small reward for reaching a new milestone in your life."

"Are you going to crack jokes all night, while I suffer?"

He put his fork down and turned serious. "No, Kate. The truth is, I'm furious. I'm furious with Justice Buchanan for interfering and I'm furious with Todd for being so damn spineless."

"What happened isn't Todd's fault. Something we don't know went on between him and his father."

"I admire your loyalty, Kate. Personally, I find that entire family totally unworthy of your efforts. Now, what do you say we stop trying to ruin our lunch and order dessert? Gérard told me the almond-amaretto tart is not to be missed."

Thirty-Six

Emile stood on his balcony on this bright Sunday morning and looked up toward the cloudless blue sky. Right about now, Todd and Jessica's plane would be taking off from the Bayonne-Biarritz airport, bound for Paris. From there the couple would board another plane for the United States, and Emile would probably never hear from them again.

The previous afternoon, Todd had come to the auto parts store and asked Emile to deliver a letter to their landlord, along with two months' rent, in cash. He hadn't been sure that was enough compensation for breaking a year's lease, but Emile had assured him that it was. The house had been well maintained, and the owner wouldn't have any problem renting it, especially since Todd was leaving it completely furnished.

Emile would take it himself if he could afford it. But with his journalistic career over and no hope of getting his family back, that garret on rue de l'Eglise was all he needed. All he would ever have.

Refusing to give in to self-pity so early in the day, he walked back inside, took the envelope Todd had given him and slid it into his jacket pocket. An hour later he was back from the landlord's house, his mission accomplished. He hadn't had to go far, but everything took a little more time now that he no longer had a car. Fortunately, it was a beautiful day and the walking took his mind off his problems.

He had just reached the third floor of his apartment building, when he stopped abruptly. Maurice stood on the landing, that familiar scowl on his face.

Startled, Emile said nothing. One hand on the banister, he waited for the other man to make his move. He already had a pretty good idea why Maurice was here.

"Where are they?" Maurice asked. "Where are Todd Buchanan and Jessica Van Dyke?"

So the old fox had already found out their names, and apparently their address. This had to be a record, even for Maurice. "Why ask me?" he said cautiously.

"Because they're gone, Emile. Todd called the captain of the *Ainara* and told him he was taking an extended leave of absence and didn't know when he'd be back. And Jessica Van Dyke did the same at the school where she teaches. And you, my traitorous friend, know where they went."

He pulled away from the wall and came to stand in front of Emile. This time, however, he looked more puzzled than angry. "You warned them, didn't you. You knew that once I started my own investigation, I'd find out Todd's real identity faster than you did, so you warned them."

Emile didn't answer.

"Where are they, Emile? Did you help them escape? There are laws against that, you know. Very harsh laws."

Emile remained quiet.

Maurice shrugged. "Oh, well, it doesn't matter. The story will be in tomorrow's paper, anyway—front page. It won't be as detailed as yours would have been, or as personal, and of course, I won't be able to deliver Buchanan to the police, which would have been a nice touch. But thanks to my friends at Interpol, I have enough to guarantee *Bordeaux-Matin* national attention."

So Maurice had called Interpol. Well, that wasn't surprising. Maurice and the elite international police had always been on good terms. Just last year, *Bordeaux-Matin* had been instrumental in helping Interpol nab a notorious art thief. The problem was they would be knocking at his door any moment now, demanding Emile's full cooperation in apprehending Buchanan, or else.

Maurice studied him intently for a few seconds. "Why, Emile? You could have had it all back—your job, your family, the respect, even the admiration, of your peers—and you gave it all up. Why?"

"I guess I'm getting soft in my old age."

"Those people were nothing to you. What was there to be soft about?"

"You're the ace reporter, Maurice. You figure it out."

As soon as Maurice left, Emile let himself into his apartment, found the number for Charles de Gaulle airport and dialed information. He had to warn Todd that Interpol had been brought into the picture. How the young American eluded them would be up to him.

After talking to three airport employees, he was finally put through to someone who operated the paging system. He heard Todd's name being announced on the loudspeaker, with the request for Mr. Adler to proceed to the nearest courtesy phone. The announcement was repeated three times. No one answered it. A call to France-Inter, France's national airline, confirmed that the Biarritz-Paris flight had touched down an hour ago.

Either Todd had already boarded the U.S.-bound flight or Interpol had picked him up.

Emile sighed. It was out of his hands now.

By Sunday morning, news that Todd Buchanan was on his way back to the U.S. and planning to turn himself in had spread across the nation's capital like a wildfire.

Emile Sardoux, the French reporter Todd had mentioned to Kate during their brief phone conversation, had been arrested for aiding and abetting, and threatened with prison unless he told them what he knew, which he had.

From time to time, local television stations interrupted their regular programming to bring the public the latest news. Speculations were rampant as so-called experts in the field—criminologists, trial lawyers and even a former judge or two—gave their views on the case and what would happen to Todd once he turned himself in.

Frank Sykes had made a brief statement to the press, explaining that Todd would be met at Dulles, taken into custody and formally charged with the murder of Molly Buchanan. His new attorney, Jacob Winters, had been notified of Todd's arrival. While Frank had refused to give Todd's exact time of arrival, Winters, a shameless publicity hound, had leaked the information to the press.

"Dulles will be turned into a circus," Kate murmured, as she and Mitch watched the latest bulletin.

She had calmed down considerably since Todd's phone call and was now more frustrated than angry. She also felt sorry for Jessica. Those first few months of pregnancy were terribly critical, requiring the least possible amount of stress. Yet the young woman had been forced to leave her home, her belongings and everything that was dear and familiar to her. How much more stressful could her life be?

"If his new attorney is smart," Mitch commented, "he'll pull a few strings and have Todd's plane diverted to another airport."

"He'll never do that. Look at him. He's turning this press conference into a self-promoting opportunity. He doesn't care about Todd, or Jessica, or their baby. He's only concerned with himself. You want to bet he'll be on *Larry King* before the end of the week?"

"He won't be able to talk about the case."

"So what? He'll talk about himself, the cases he's won, his humble beginnings, his important clients."

She expelled a long breath. "I shouldn't be bitter. I may not like Winters, or his tactics, but he gets his clients off. In the end that's all that matters."

"He hasn't contacted you?"

She shook her head. "I expected him to. I was willing to tell him what I had so far, but I haven't heard a word. I guess he doesn't swim with little fish."

Mitch wrapped his arm around her and brought her

close. "Put the case behind you, Kate, and look at
the bright side. Alison can now come home."

"Yes, though not yet. I just talked to Eric. The
entire southwestern corner of Montana is buried under
twenty-two inches of snow, and the blizzard is still
raging. All the airports are closed."

"When will they be able to fly?"

"Tomorrow, if it stops snowing."

"Hmm. It's going to be mighty boring around here
with nothing to do." He bent to kiss her. "Unless
you have a suggestion how we could pass the time?"

Todd sat in his seat and gazed out the window as
the Airbus sped through the clouds. Beside him, Jess
slept, something she hadn't been able to do much of
in the past forty-eight hours.

Before leaving Saint-Jean-de-Luz, he had asked
Emile Sardoux to deliver a letter and two months' rent
to his landlord, along with the permission to sell or
keep whatever was in the house. He doubted he and
Jess would be back. Maybe for a visit, if he was
cleared. Never, if he was sent to prison.

He had tried not to think about the possibility there
might be a trial, but now, sitting here with nothing
but that eventuality ahead of him, he could do little
but think.

He wanted to have faith in his new attorney, whom
his father swore was the best talent money could buy.
But Todd still had a bitter taste in his mouth over the
cold-blooded way he had dismissed Kate. Someday
maybe, he would try to explain to her that the only
reason he had gone along with his father was to protect Jess.

"Mr. Adler?"

Todd looked up to see the first-class flight attendant smiling down at him.

"I'm sorry to bother you," she whispered, glancing at Jess. "The captain would like to have a word with you."

Todd's heart picked up a beat. "Me?"

"Yes, sir."

"What does he want?"

"He'd rather tell you himself. He's waiting in the galley."

Jess stirred, opened her eyes. "What's wrong?" she asked. "Are we there?"

"The captain wants to see me."

Her eyes were quick to register panic. "Why?"

"I'm sure it's a mistake, Jess." He gave her a strained smile. "I'll be right back."

It was not a mistake. The captain, a tall, lanky man with silver hair and a serious expression, watched him approach. "Mr. Adler," he said. "Or rather, Mr. Buchanan."

Todd felt as if he had been sucker-punched. The captain knew. But how? Who had tipped him off?

"I just received a call from the Fairfax Police in Virginia," the captain continued. "Informing me that you and your fiancée were aboard this plane."

"How did they find out?"

"They didn't give me any details. They simply wanted you to know what will happen once you land."

So the quiet arrival he had hoped for would not be. He nodded. "All right. What will happen?"

"You and Ms. Van Dyke will be allowed to disembark first. As you know, Dulles uses mobile lounges rather than a Jetway to get you into the terminal. The passengers will not board those mobile lounges until you and Ms. Van Dyke have left. You will be met by uniformed officers, airport officials, immigration and the FBI. That's standard procedure in cases such as these," he added, when Todd looked at him questioningly. "Justice Buchanan will also be there. As will your attorney. No press. At least, not here."

Todd felt as if his life was spinning out of control, no longer his own. It had begun with Sardoux's startling visit, followed by his father's request to fire Kate, and now this. "Thank you, Captain. How long until we land?"

"We'll begin our approach in about twenty minutes." He paused before extending his hand. "Good luck, Mr. Buchanan."

He shook the captain's hand. "Thank you."

Todd returned to his seat, aware that some of the first-class passengers were watching him.

"You were there a long time," Jess whispered. "What did he want?"

"To warn me that a welcoming committee will be waiting for us."

"What does that mean?"

He repeated his conversation with the captain but could offer no explanation how word of their arrival had leaked out. "Maybe Sardoux's boss was an even better journalist than Emile thought." He shrugged and returned his attention to the view out the window. "It doesn't matter now."

Thirty-Seven

"You've got a visitor," the desk sergeant told Mitch, when Mitch returned from lunch.

Mitch walked over to his desk and was pleased, though not surprised, to find Yan Wey waiting for him. The man looked nervous and kept turning a small hat, similar to a sailor's hat, around and around in his hands.

"How are you, Mr. Wey?"

He bowed his head.

Mitch pointed to a chair beside his desk. "Please sit down. Can I get you anything? Some tea, perhaps?"

Wey shook his head. "No, thank you."

Mitch nodded, knowing he would have to proceed slowly, at the man's own pace. "Do you have something to tell me, Mr. Wey?"

The man threw a furtive look around. "Not good for me to be here, Detective Calhoon."

"You're frightened."

Wey nodded. "I have wife and children. I worry."

"I understand. How long have you been in this country, Mr. Wey?"

"Eighteen months."

"And you've been working at Ariba the entire time?"

He inclined his head.

The long employment meant that he was in a position to have witnessed other suspicious activities in and around the restaurant, all of which could help build a case against Torres.

"If you give us the kind of information we could use in court," Mitch said, "and you have to testify, we could offer you and your family protection, before, during and after the trial. Do you understand?"

Wey nodded vigorously. "Witness protection program."

He had already checked. He must be scared. "Yes," Mitch said. "Would you be willing to do that, Mr. Wey? Relocate to another city?"

"With family?"

"Absolutely."

"No trouble for me about...entry to United States?"

"No," Mitch told him. "No trouble of any kind. That's part of the deal."

Wey nodded. "Okay."

Mitch leaned forward so the man could talk as quietly as he wished. "All right, then. Why don't you tell me what you know?"

Wey's statement was straight and to the point. Lou Torres and his two bodyguards—Carlton Pritchett and Leo Iminez—had been at Ariba and had just ordered dinner, when one of the waiters came into the kitchen and said to cancel the veal *saltimbocca*. The boss had just received a phone call, and he was sending Pritchett out on an errand. The ex-fed didn't return to Ariba until 9:45, at which time he re-ordered his dinner and proceeded to wolf it down.

They had all lied—Torres, the bodyguards and the restaurant staff. All Mitch had to do now was pick up Pritchett and get him to talk. But before he did that, a conference with Lieutenant Fennell and the assistant U.S. attorney was in order.

Tom Spivak, who was assisting Mitch in the Luther case, was already in the lieutenant's office when Mitch arrived, as was Ted Rencheck. The meeting lasted only ten minutes, then Mr. Wey was brought in and asked to repeat his story one more time.

"Mr. Wey," Ted said, when the man was finished, "are you afraid of Mr. Torres? And that's why you lied to Detective Calhoon the first time he questioned you?"

"Yes."

"Then, why are you here now?"

For the first time Wey's gentle eyes showed a flash of anger. "I have daughter. Twelve years old. Last week, Mr. Torres took her to massage parlor, to work. I said no. He said if I said no, great harm would come to family, and other daughter."

A hush fell over the room. The vice squad had raided Torres's massage parlors many times in the past. But because of the cops he paid to protect him, the police had never been able to find anything but licensed masseurs and masseuses in any of his establishments.

Ted was the first to speak. "Thank you, Mr. Wey. Go back to Ariba, and don't mention this conversation to anyone. For the time being, we won't have to say where the information came from. When and if we do, you and your family will immediately be put in protective custody.''

"And daughter?" Wey asked, twisting his little hat.

"Your daughter won't have to stay at the massage parlor much longer, but for the moment, everything must appear normal, as if you were never here. You understand?''

He bowed his head. "Understand."

When Yan Wey left, Ted looked from Mitch to Tom. "You two, do what you have to do, but get me Torres. I don't want details. I just want Torres. This department has waited a long time to nail that bastard and, by God, this time we've got him."

"Pritchett will want immunity."

"Give it to him. Give the scumbag anything he wants, as long as he delivers Torres."

The first person Todd saw when he stepped off the plane was his father. Lyle Buchanan stood at the bottom of the ramp, his hands jammed in his overcoat pockets, his expression one of anxiety and expectation as he watched the cabin door.

Still holding Jess's hand, Todd walked down the steps; then, unable to hold back, he ran and threw himself into his father's open arms. They stayed locked in a fierce embrace for almost a minute, neither one capable of uttering a word.

When Todd finally disengaged himself, tears were streaming down his face and his voice shook. "I can't believe they let you come here." He glanced at the motorcade he had first seen from the plane window, four cars in all. Two uniformed officers stood outside an unmarked vehicle. Next to them, Detective Sykes watched him with a dispassionate expression.

"The captain told me you'd be here," he continued. "But I didn't believe it."

Lyle smiled. "Being a justice has its advantages." He inspected Todd from head to toe. "You look good, son. Different. Taller, maybe?" He laughed as though to break the tension. "Or have I gotten shorter?"

Todd pressed his lips together in an effort to control the rush of emotion that threatened to burst. "I'm so sorry, Dad. For what I put you and Mom and Terrence through."

Lyle's eyes glinted with moisture. "I know you are, son. Let's not talk about that now, all right?"

"Where's Mom?" Todd looked around him. "I thought she'd be here, too."

"You'll see her later." Lyle glanced behind Todd. "Is that lovely young woman who I think she is?"

Todd turned, smiled at Jess, who had been waiting at a distance, and extended his arm, pulling her toward him. "Dad, meet Jessica. Jess, this is my dad."

"How are you, sir?" Clearly intimidated, Jess took Lyle's hand and shook it.

"I should be asking you that question, my dear, but since I was requested to make this conversation brief, let me just say welcome. Hallie and I are looking forward to having you in our home. And please, try not to worry about Todd. He's in excellent hands. Jacob is waiting for us at the immigration office, where we'll have to stop for a few minutes. Then Detective Sykes will ride with you and Jacob to the police station in Fairfax."

"What about Jess?" Todd asked.

"She and I and two FBI agents will follow in another car."

"Dad, how did the authorities know I was on this flight? Who told them?"

"Interpol arrested your reporter friend."

Todd's heart sank. "They arrested Emile?"

Lyle nodded. "Apparently he didn't have much choice but to tell them what he knew. They made it pretty tough for him." He gave Todd's arm a squeeze. "Don't worry, son. Everything will be all right."

Todd nodded. He desperately wanted to believe that.

Though Todd had expected a crowd at the Fairfax County police station, he wasn't prepared for the chaos that greeted him. Dozens of reporters and news vans filled the parking lot, while a cordon of uniformed officers did its best to keep the crowd from getting through the barricades.

Cameras flashed as Todd got out of the car. All around him, reporters shouted his name and hurled questions at him.

"Did you kill your wife, Mr. Buchanan?"

"Why did you run?"

"Why did you change attorneys?"

"Will you plead guilty?"

"Will you plead not guilty?"

To his relief, there was no hostility from the crowd. In fact, many carried signs that read, Todd Is Innocent and Set Todd Free. A group of teenagers tried hopelessly to touch him. "We love you, Todd!" one screamed. Right on cue, several young voices began to chant. *"We love you, Todd, we love you, Todd."*

This kind of demonstration was not foreign to him. He had once been one of the most popular broadcasters in the Washington area, and every night when he left the television station, screaming fans waited by the back door, calling his name, professing their love, shaking their autograph books at him. He had loved the adulation then, the notoriety, the high ratings. Now the attention only embarrassed him.

Suddenly, his new attorney, whom Todd had met years earlier during a fishing trip on his father's boat, was by his side. "Smile at them, Todd," Jacob Winters urged. "Make eye contact. Remember that everyone in this crowd is a potential juror."

The thought of playing up to his supporters made Todd ill. He was trying to find a polite way to turn down Winters's suggestion, when he heard someone call his name again. This time the voice was vaguely familiar.

Both he and Lyle turned. Lynn Flannery stood less than six feet from Todd. Her face was white, her jaw tight, her eyes filled with such hatred, Todd's heart did a flip. She mouthed something to him, a silent word Todd couldn't quite read.

Die? Is that what she had said?

The rest happened so fast, no one had time to react, not even the two FBI agents who had stayed close to his father.

Lynn whipped a gun out of her raincoat pocket and, holding it with both hands, aimed it at Todd, just as Lyle shoved him out of the way.

The gun went off. Simultaneously one of the federal agents threw himself on Lyle and Todd, while the other opened fire on Lynn. Lyle's full weight slammed against Todd.

"Dad!" Instinctively, he wrapped his arms around his father's waist to prevent him from falling. "What's wrong?" He felt something wet and sticky on his fingers. "My God, he's been shot." He looked up. "My father's been shot!"

Forceful hands pulled him away, while a line of uniforms formed a human barricade to protect the justice from a further attack.

"We'll take care of him, Mr. Buchanan," one of the FBI agents said. Then nodding to Jacob Winters, who was visibly shaken, he added, "Take him and Ms. Van Dyke inside, quickly."

Thirty-Eight

Mitch and Tom Spivak hadn't wasted any time in picking up the former federal agent. They found Carlton Pritchett in the bathroom of his Massachusetts Avenue condo, bathing in a sea of scented bubbles with a stunning black girl washing his chest.

"You people are in so much trouble," Pritchett growled, as Tom read him his rights. "You can't arrest me. Where the hell is your warrant?"

"We don't need a warrant, Pritchett. We have probable cause."

In the car, Mitch and Tom let him rant and rave, and didn't say another word to him until all three were in an interrogation room.

"All right, Pritchett." Mitch sat down. "Here's the deal. We know you killed Luther. We've got two eyewitnesses that place you just outside the Sculpture Garden at the time of Luther's death." The lie would keep Yan Wey out of the picture, at least for now.

"I don't believe you," Pritchett spat. "You guys lie. You think I don't know that?"

"You don't have to believe me, Pritchett. All you have to do is stand in a lineup and get ID'd."

The two "witnesses" were nonexistent. This kind of deception was an interrogating technique Mitch used occasionally, and only when he had probable cause to believe a suspect had committed a felony. Sometimes it worked, sometimes it didn't.

This time it did. Pritchett became visibly nervous and stopped threatening them with legal action.

Mitch glanced at Tom, who nodded. "I won't lie to you, Pritchett," Mitch said. "You're in one hell of a mess this time. Not only have we two witnesses, but those three handguns we found in your apartment have been turned over to Ballistics. You want to bet one of them will match the bullets that killed Luther?"

Pritchett licked his lips and said nothing.

"As I said, you're in a heap of trouble." He paused, long enough to heighten the tension in the room. "Unless you agree to cooperate."

The ex-fed looked from Mitch to Tom. "Cooperate?"

"That's right. You tell us what we want to know, and we'll give you complete immunity. We've already cleared the offer with the U.S. attorney's office."

"What good will your immunity do me if I'm dead?"

"Not much, but you're not going to be dead because we're going to protect you."

"Says you."

"Come on, Pritchett." Tom laughed. "Give us a little credit, will you? It's not like we've never done that before."

"I don't know." Pritchett ran a hand over his mouth. He was beginning to sweat profusely.

"Sure you do. Ask yourself this question: Where

would you rather be right now? In a cell where one of Torres's men can put a knife in your back? Or in protective custody?''

This time Pritchett was shaken, and he had good reason to be. Torres's ability to reach inside prison cells and silence witnesses was not something to be taken lightly.

"Oh man." The bodyguard closed his eyes and leaned back in his chair.

Mitch and Tom exchanged a wordless glance.

"Ready to talk?" Mitch asked.

His eyes still closed, Pritchett nodded.

Mitch leaned toward the tape recorder on the table and pressed a button.

After stating his name and address, Pritchett began talking. At seven-thirty on the evening of March twenty-ninth, Lou Torres had received a second phone call from his attorney. Bob Harris and Luther had just left Metro PD and were on their way to a bar on First Street to discuss the possibility of any further questioning by the police, and how that eventuality should be handled.

Torres, already upset with his nephew for allowing himself to be spotted at Union Station, became enraged when he found out that Luther had agreed to be in a lineup without an attorney present. The fact that Alison could not identify him did not appease the mob boss. Luther had made an inexcusable mistake and would have to pay for it. Torres, as most people knew, was not a forgiving man. And he had zero tolerance for incompetence. He had made exceptions with his nephew before, but not this time.

He called Luther on his cell phone and told him to

meet him at the Sculpture Garden at nine o'clock. Luther didn't argue. He was used to Lou's little lectures, which he had to listen to whenever he screwed up.

After Lou hung up, he took a sip of his wine and calmly instructed Pritchett to go to the garden and kill Luther.

The metro incident was a little more complex. Originally, it had been decided that either Pritchett or Iminez, the other bodyguard, would carry out Kate Logan's execution, which had to look like an accident.

After following her for a couple of days, both Pritchett and Iminez had suggested doing the hit in the subway, which Kate used frequently. There was only one alteration to the plan. Both bodyguards were much too large and conspicuous to do the job and get away without being seen. Luther, on the other hand, had an amazing ability to blend with the crowd. He was small, fast and agile. All he had to do was cover his deformed ear, and no one would be able to identify him.

And then everything went wrong, as things sometimes did. For reasons Pritchett hadn't fully understood, Luther was unable to get to the front of the platform where Kate was standing. Then, in his haste to get out of there, his hat slipped, enabling Kate Logan's daughter to have a good look at him.

Pritchett, who by virtue of his status as a former FBI agent had become Torres's confidant, also told Mitch that the contract on Kate had been ordered by a third party who wanted her investigation of Molly Buchanan's murder stopped. But that's as far as

Pritchett's knowledge went. He swore, repeatedly, that he had no idea who had ordered the hit. Torres never told him, and Pritchett knew better than to ask. But he was able to give Mitch and Tom incriminating evidence against the mob boss that would make Ted Rencheck very happy.

"What about Charlene Meyers?" Tom asked. "Was that also your doing?"

Pritchett moistened his lips and nodded.

"Why did she have to be killed?"

"Torres didn't tell me. He just said to kill her and to use a switchblade this time, to throw the cops off."

"You must have enjoyed it." Mitch's tone was scathing. "To stab her repeatedly the way you did."

"She fought me, man." The ex-fed touched an ugly red scratch on the left side of his throat. "That slut had claws like a witch and ripped the hell out of me. You'd be pissed, too."

Mitch was so disgusted he was tempted to throw the bastard out in the street and let Torres have a little fun with him. Unfortunately, he needed Pritchett alive. "Who ordered the hit?"

Pritchett shrugged. "No idea. Maybe the same person who wanted Kate Logan dead."

After Pritchett was finished, Mitch shut off the recorder. They had enough, not only to put Torres away for a long time, but to shut down his operations for good.

Thirty-Nine

Kate was thoroughly enjoying Alison's vivid description of the blizzard that had paralyzed most of Montana, when her call waiting beeped.

"Let me see who this is, sweetie. I'll be right back."

"Kate!" a familiar voice cried. "Oh, Kate, you've got to help us."

"Jessica?"

"Please help us—"

"My daughter is on the other line," Kate said, hearing the hysteria in the woman's voice. "Let me say goodbye to her and I'll be right with you."

She was back within two seconds. "What happened? Where are you?"

"At the Mayflower Hotel. Todd is in custody and...and..." She let out a strangled sob. "Justice Buchanan has been shot."

"Shot? Dear God. Is he...?" The thought that he might be dead was too impossible to put into words.

"He's alive, but I don't know what his condition is. They rushed him out of there so fast, I didn't have time to ask any questions, and now they won't tell me anything."

"Who shot him?"

"Lynn Flannery. She was waiting for Todd outside the police station. She came to kill him, Kate."

"But Todd isn't hurt?"

"No. Justice Buchanan pushed him out of the way and took the bullet that was intended for him." Kate heard another sob. "She shot him in front of all those people—the police, the FBI..."

"Where is Lynn now?"

"She's dead. They opened fire on her and... Oh, Kate, this is a nightmare."

"Jessica, you have to calm down."

"I will. Just say you'll help us."

"I don't know what you want me to do. I'm no longer Todd's attorney—"

"But I have no one else to turn to."

"What about Hallie Buchanan? Isn't she there with you?"

"No! She went away. On a trip. Can you believe that?"

No, she couldn't believe it. What mother would go on a trip at a time like this? With her son facing a murder charge?

"Have you talked with Todd's attorney?"

"I don't like him." Jessica's panic was tapering off. "And I don't trust him. He keeps saying stupid things like 'leave everything to me,' and 'follow my lead.' You've got to get back on the case, Kate. Todd never wanted to fire you in the first place. He did it because his father asked him to."

"He didn't have to agree." Kate regretted the words as soon as she said them. This wasn't the time or the place to be petty.

"He did it for me," Jessica replied. "He wanted

me to stay somewhere where I would be safe, where the press wouldn't be able to get to me. Justice Buchanan agreed to let me stay at his house and watch over me, on one condition—that Todd fire you.''

Kate could understand Todd's dilemma. As a mother, she would go to any lengths to protect her child or those she loved. ''If Todd's father agreed to take you in, what are you doing at the Mayflower?'' she asked.

''I can't stay at the Buchanans' house now, with only the maid there. I would feel like an intruder.''

''Does Mrs. Buchanan know that her husband was shot?''

''She must by now. Todd asked me to call Lizzy, the maid, and tell her what had happened—and I did. She would not, however, tell me where Mrs. Buchanan was.''

The entire household, even the maid, was shrouded in mystery. ''I'm sorry about what you're going through, Jessica, really I am. But Jacob Winters is Todd's attorney now. You must have faith in him.''

''You wouldn't say that if you knew what he was planning to do.''

''What do you mean?''

''Earlier today, at the airport, we had to stop at the immigration office to fill out some forms. When I was done with mine, I went to find a ladies' room, and overheard Justice Buchanan and Jacob Winters talking. They didn't know I was there. They couldn't see me, but I heard every word they said.''

''What did they say?'' Kate couldn't help asking. She was curious.

"Winters is planning to frame Todd's brother for Molly's murder."

This time Kate had to sit down. "Terrence? How?"

"By pressuring Terrence's wife, Elaine, to change her story and admit she did take a sleeping pill that night and has no idea if her husband was in bed with her or not. Apparently Elaine has some kind of emotional problem in addition to her sleep disorder, and convincing her to change her story won't be too difficult."

"And Justice Buchanan went along with that?"

"Yes, but he also told Winters that as far as Hallie was concerned, the attorney had acted completely on his own, without Lyle having any knowledge of his plan."

A heavy silence fell over the line as Kate absorbed this latest bombshell.

"We can't let that happen, Kate," Jessica continued. "If Terrence is guilty, then yes, he should be punished, but I don't want him framed for something he didn't do. I haven't had a chance to talk to Todd, but I know he would feel the same way. He would never want his brother to be made a scapegoat, after all Todd put him through already. He loves Terrence. You have no idea how much."

Kate did. She had gotten a glimpse of Todd's affection and loyalty for his big brother during their last phone conversation. Even after she told him about Terrence's affair with Molly, Todd had refused to accept the possibility that Terrence had killed Molly.

"I wish I could help you, Jessica," Kate said truthfully. "But my hands are tied. As long as Todd is being represented by someone else, I can't be his attorney. It would be unethical. I could be disbarred.''

"Then, be *my* attorney! That day at the Mall, you made me give you a dollar. You remember that? You said that could be considered a retainer.''

"The situation was different then.''

"Do you want more money, Kate? I have it. Tell me how much, and I'll give it to you.''

"I don't need anymore money.''

"Then, help me.'' Jessica sounded exhausted now, so close to a breakdown that Kate was actually worried for her, and for the baby.

Torn and more indecisive than she had ever been before, she looked out the window. In the past hour, the light drizzle that had been falling over the entire Washington area had turned into a downpour that made the city streets slick and dangerous. It was definitely not a day to be driving around, searching for clues.

"Kate,'' Jessica said in a small voice. "Will you help me?''

Kate drew a long breath. God, what was she getting herself into? "Yes,'' she said at last. "I'll help you.''

As Kate drove toward McLean, where the Buchanans lived, she kept flipping through a half-dozen radio stations, trying to get the latest update on Justice Buchanan's condition.

She found it on WKZ. The bullet had hit the justice in the upper arm, missing a main artery by a fraction of an inch. Although he had lost some blood and would have to stay in the hospital for a couple of days, there had been no nerve damage and the prognosis for a full recovery was good. His eldest son was by his side.

Not a word about his wife.

Where was Hallie Buchanan? Kate wondered as she made her way through the traffic-clogged streets of Washington. And why would the woman choose this time to go away? She had seemed so concerned about Todd that day at Kate's house, so determined to be there for him. At the same time, Kate remembered the woman's nervousness, the ambiguous questions, the glances she and her husband had exchanged. Something had been going on, even then. Something creepy. That was the word Kate had used later to describe her impressions to Mitch.

And then, there was Rose's remark about Hallie and Terrence's relationship. "He is *her* favorite, you know. She would do anything for that boy."

Anything?

Even commit murder?

The thought had occurred to Kate before, but at the time it had seemed too outlandish to consider seriously, let alone pursue. But what *if* Hallie had known about Terrence and Molly? And Hope? And the blackmail? Would she just stand by and allow her son to be exposed as the father of an illegitimate child? To have his political future destroyed? Or would she find a way to remove the threat from his life?

It was an interesting theory, except for one flaw. How did Hallie know where Molly would be that night?

The answer came to Kate in a flash that was so staggering, she nearly lost control of her car.

What if Hallie had hired a killer?

Kate shook her head. Talk about outlandish. The wife of a Supreme Court justice putting a contract on her daughter-in-law. Who would buy that?

She had just about rejected the idea, when the Buchanans' house came into view. Instead of the palatial home she had expected, she saw an elegant, turn-of-the-century Victorian, complete with turrets, stained-glass windows and an old-fashioned wrap-around porch.

Kate parked as close to the house as she could, threw her hood over her head and made a dash for the front door, her boots sloshing through the puddles that had already formed.

"Good afternoon." She smiled at the pretty young maid who answered the door. "You're Lizzy, aren't you?"

The girl returned the smile. "Yes, I am."

"I'm Kate Logan. Mr. and Mrs. Buchanan may have mentioned my name?"

"I'm sorry. They didn't."

"I'm Todd's attorney." Kate would worry later about the consequences of that lie.

The girl didn't contradict her, which was good.

"I know that Mr. Buchanan is in the hospital," Kate continued. "And that Mrs. Buchanan is away, but I have something very urgent to discuss with her. Unfortunately—" she made a helpless gesture "—she forgot to tell me where she would be."

"Don't stand in the rain," the girl said, moving aside to let Kate in. "You'll drown."

"Thank you." Kate gave her a grateful smile. "If you could just tell me where Mrs. Buchanan is, I won't waste any more of your time."

"I'm sorry, Ms. Logan, but my instructions are to tell no one."

Tell no one? Why should a harmless trip need to be kept secret? "But this is terribly important. You see, it concerns Todd's fiancée. You're aware that she was supposed to be staying here?"

The girl nodded. "In the Blue Room. I made it up myself. Then, a little while ago, Ms. Van Dyke called to say she wouldn't be coming, that she was staying at a hotel."

"And that's exactly why I need to see Mrs. Buchanan. Jessica doesn't want to stay here because with both Mr. and Mrs. Buchanan out of the house, she would feel like an intruder."

"But that's wrong. She shouldn't feel that way at all."

"I tried to tell her that, Lizzy, but she won't listen. She's very distraught over all that has happened— Todd being arrested, Mr. Buchanan getting shot." Now was a good time to play her trump card. "Frankly, I'm worried about the baby."

"Baby?" The young girl's eyes went wide with shock. "What baby?"

"You don't know?"

She shook her head. "No one said anything about a baby. I was told to get just one room ready."

"There's no baby—yet." She smiled. "But Jessica is pregnant. That's why Todd wanted her to stay here, where she would be safe."

"Then, that's where she should be. I can take care of her, and Conrad—that's Mr. Buchanan's chauffeur—can drive her anywhere she wants."

"I spent the past hour trying to convince her to do

just that. But I've given up. Mrs. Buchanan is the only one who can set Jessica's fears to rest.''

The girl chewed on her bottom lip for a few seconds. ''I wish I could call her,'' she said, glancing toward a table against the foyer wall. ''But in her haste, Mrs. Buchanan forgot to take her cell phone with her. There's another phone on the boat, but I don't know the number. I have no way of contacting her.''

Thank God for small mercies. ''Then, please tell me where she is and I'll go there.'' She lowered her voice. ''I would never forgive myself, and neither would you, if Jessica miscarried.''

The girl looked truly worried now. With no one to advise her, she had to make up her own mind, and fast.

''Mrs. Buchanan would want Jessica here.'' Kate threw that in as one last incentive.

Finally the girl gave a decisive nod. ''Mrs. Buchanan is at Tilghman Island, on the family boat.''

Tilghman Island on Chesapeake Bay? What was she doing there in this weather? And why had she left in such a hurry, forgetting her phone?

Setting her questions aside for now, Kate did a quick calculation. On a good day, you could make the trip to Tilghman Island in under an hour. In this downpour, she'd be lucky if she got there in twice that time.

''What's the name of the boat?'' she asked.

''*Sweet Melody*. They keep it at the Sea Breeze Marina. I'm not sure where that is, exactly.''

''I'll find it.'' She reached over and squeezed the

girl's hand. "Thank you so much. You did the right thing, Lizzy."

Kate gave her one last reassuring smile and sprinted toward her car.

Forty

Even though for many die-hard boaters early April marked the beginning of the boating season, today's nasty weather and threats of high tide had kept everyone away.

Standing under her umbrella, Kate looked around the marina, hoping to see a security guard who could direct her to where *Sweet Melody* was berthed. No such luck. The place was deserted.

A little shiver, either from the cold or apprehension, coursed through her. She would have much preferred to have Mitch here with her, but after calling the station twice and finding out he was interrogating a suspect, she gave up.

A strong gust almost tore the umbrella from Kate's hand. She gripped the handle a little tighter and walked down one pier after another in search of the Buchanans' boat.

She found it after a fifteen-minute search that left her soaked to the bone. The boat, a forty-foot cruiser with a flybridge and a large deck for entertaining, was berthed in a sheltered area, between two larger boats that were tightly covered.

Kate approached *Sweet Melody* as she called out

Hallie's name. "Mrs. Buchanan! It's Kate Logan. I need to talk to you."

Silence.

Being arrested for trespassing wasn't something Kate looked forward to, so she tried not to think about that possibility as she stepped onto the gleaming teak deck.

The sliding glass doors that separated the deck from the cabin were covered with steam, confirming what she already knew. Hallie was inside. Kate knocked on the glass, only too aware that the last time she had knocked on someone's door, a dead body had been waiting for her inside.

"Mrs. Buchanan!" she called again. "Please let me in. I'm not going anywhere until you do."

She jerked back as Hallie's face suddenly appeared on the other side of the glass. After a few seconds, Kate heard a *click* and the door slid open, just far enough to let Kate in. Hallie was pale and unsmiling. She wore black slacks and a cream-colored turtleneck, and didn't look at all like a killer. But, then again, neither had Ted Bundy.

"Thank you." Kate stepped inside.

"Is something wrong with Lyle?" Hallie asked anxiously. "Is he worse?

"Not to my knowledge. I came here because I need to talk to you about Todd."

"You shouldn't have done that, Ms. Logan."

Kate removed her raincoat and glanced around her. A wraparound sofa in white leather on one side, and a low teak divider on the other separated the lounge from the dining area and galley. Low-level lighting created a cozy atmosphere, and a mug of what looked like tea sat on the white marble coffee table. Kate would have loved something hot to drink, but Hallie didn't look as though she wanted to play hostess.

Spotting a coat hanger just inside the door, Kate hung her wet raincoat on one of the hooks. "Could we sit down, Mrs. Buchanan?"

Hallie motioned toward the sofa. "I can't talk to you. You realize that."

"Why can't you?"

"Because my son is about to stand trial, and anything I say could damage his defense."

She had been well rehearsed, either by her husband or by Jacob Winters. "I would never use anything you tell me to hurt Todd, or his chances for an acquittal."

"You would if the prosecution called you as a witness. And they will, now that you're no longer Todd's attorney."

"Mrs. Buchanan, the only reason I'm here is because Jessica wants me to stay on the case."

Hallie's expression turned suspicious. "Does Jacob Winters know that?"

"He doesn't need to know. I'm here as Jessica's attorney, not Todd's."

"Jacob warned me you might pull something like that."

The attorney's opinion seemed to matter an awful lot to the Buchanan family. "Like what?"

"Try to talk to me. Make trouble for all of us." Her voice had risen sharply, but other than that she was calm.

Pretending to be looking for a tissue, Kate glanced into her purse, which she had left on the coffee table, open. The tape recorder she had placed there before getting out of the car was taping every word, its little red light blinking. "Is that why Jacob Winters sent you away? So I couldn't talk to you?"

"He had nothing to do with my coming here. I did it on my own, to escape the publicity. You don't know how it's been since the news of Todd's return broke."

Was she lying? Kate couldn't tell. She would have to push a little harder. "Forgive me, Mrs. Buchanan, but as a mother myself, I find that a little difficult to believe. Your son, whom you haven't seen or heard from in more than two years, is in jail for murder, and you're sitting here, in this deluge, instead of being with him? That's not very motherly, don't you think?"

"You're a fine one to talk," Hallie retorted. "Most mothers I know wouldn't put their child in the path of a killer just so they could solve a murder case. My husband had more consideration for your daughter's safety than you seem to have."

The observation hurt, but Kate let it pass. "Is that why he had me fired?"

"Yes. The value of life is not something Lyle takes lightly."

"What about you, Mrs. Buchanan?" Kate asked quietly. "Do you value life?"

Hallie held her gaze, but only for a moment. "Of course I do." She picked up her mug and wrapped both hands around it. "What are you getting at?"

"I was trying to decide how far you would go to protect your son. Your eldest son."

"Why would Terrence need protecting?"

"Aren't you concerned that he was brought in for questioning the other day? That he had a much stronger motive to kill Molly than Todd had?"

"No," Hallie replied, as though she truly wasn't concerned. "I knew that once the story of his affair with Molly was out, he would have to answer a few questions. What matters is that he was released. Terrence was in bed that night, as we all were. His wife has already attested to that fact."

"What if I were to tell you—" Kate leaned forward "—that there is a very strong possibility Terrence will be arrested and charged with Molly's murder before the end of the day?" That was a bit of a stretch, but she couldn't think of anything else that would cause this very cautious, very secretive woman to slip up.

As expected, Hallie's face registered shock. "That's insane. Why would they arrest Terrence? He didn't kill Molly."

"Maybe not, but that's not going to stop Jacob Winters. At this very moment, he's making plans to have Terrence's wife admit she *did* take a sleeping pill that night and has no idea whether her husband was in bed with her or not."

Hallie jumped to her feet. "You're lying! Lyle would never permit that to happen."

"Your husband has given Winters's plan his complete approval."

"How do you know?"

"Jessica called me shortly after your husband was shot. She had overheard an earlier conversation between your husband and Jacob Winters. That's why she called me—to tell me she didn't want Terrence framed for something he didn't do.''

Hallie kept shaking her head. "I don't believe you. Or Jessica. You're both lying.''

Kate took her cell phone from her purse, being careful not to disturb the position of the tape recorder—the recorder that, so far, had failed to record a single incriminating word. Maybe the notion that Hallie had hired someone to kill Molly was too improbable to be true. Hallie wasn't that sophisticated. If she was guilty of a crime, she would have given herself away by now.

In one last attempt to keep her theory alive, Kate handed Hallie the phone. "Why don't you call Todd's attorney? He's probably still at the police station. And if you don't mind, turn on the speaker. I'm very interested in hearing what he has to say.''

Her hand shaking, Hallie took the phone and punched several numbers. Winters answered it on the second ring.

"Jacob, this is Hallie.''

"Hallie?'' he said in a jovial tone. "How's my best girl?''

"Not well, I'm afraid. I just heard some disturbing news, Jacob.''

"You can't mean Lyle. He's doing splendidly.'' He laughed. "And driving those nurses crazy—''

She cut him off. "Is it true that you're planning to have Todd cleared by having Elaine change her story about the sleeping pills?''

Winters didn't answer. The man the legal community called the silver-tongued devil was at a loss for words.

"Answer me, Jacob."

"Who told you that?" Winters asked at last.

"Never mind who told me. Is it the truth?"

"Hallie, listen to me. We all know Elaine lied—"

"So it's true."

"Yes, but—"

"How dare you do something like that behind my back," she said with a forcefulness that took Kate by surprise. All of a sudden, the meek little wife was in full command. "What kind of sick game are you playing?"

"Hallie, you're overwrought—"

"Is Lyle in on this scheme of yours?"

There was another silence, followed by a single word. "Yes."

"And the plan was supposed to be your idea? Not Lyle's?"

"Hallie, who have you been talking to? Is someone there with you?"

"Is that the scenario, Jacob?"

Winters cleared his throat. He wasn't used to being put on the defensive this way, especially by someone he had probably never considered much of a threat. "Yes," he said. "That was the plan."

"Thank you, Jacob."

"Hallie, wait—"

Hallie pressed the off button. Slowly, she put the phone on the table next to Kate's purse. She no longer looked angry, just unbearably sad. "I'm sorry if I was rude to you earlier," she said, unaware that she was speaking directly into the recorder. "I'm sorry for everything."

Kate didn't want to rush her, but the tape was rolling. Any minute now she would have to flip it over. How was she going to do that without Hallie noticing?

"Who killed Molly, Mrs. Buchanan?" she asked.

Hallie didn't seem to have heard her. "I've known Jacob all my life. We grew up in New Hampshire together—next-door neighbors. I almost married him." She looked at Kate. "Did you know that?"

Somewhat startled, Kate said, "No, I didn't."

"Then, during a trip to Washington, I met Lyle and I was swept off my feet, as they say. Jacob was a good sport. We stayed in touch, and then later, he attended Georgetown Law and eventually opened a practice in Washington. The four of us became close friends—Lyle and me, Jacob and Theresa. We did everything together. And more importantly, I trusted Jacob. More so than I trusted my husband. Isn't that ironic?"

What was she saying? That Jacob Winters had killed Molly? "Mrs. Buchanan—"

"Terrence didn't do it," she cut in. "Oh, he's made some mistakes, I'll grant you that. Like getting involved with a student and then turning his back on his child. But he could never kill anyone, any more than Todd could."

"Then, who did kill Molly?" Kate asked again.

"Lyle," Hallie said in a clear voice. "Lyle killed Molly."

Unable to say a word, Kate could only stare at her.

"He's an even bigger bastard than I thought." Hallie pressed the back of her head against the cushions. "I kept his dirty little secret all these years while I played the dutiful wife, planned his parties, served on the board of his favorite charities and stood by his side, year after year after year.''

Lyle. It had been Lyle all along.

"Why didn't I see it coming?'' she said, talking to no one in particular. "He never liked Terrence. He never appreciated his qualities, his academic excellence, his political ambitions—ambitions that could have been fulfilled if it hadn't been for Lyle's... deviant behavior.''

Kate wasn't sure how she managed to find her voice again. "Is your husband...Black Knight?''

"So he was right. You did find out about that.'' She nodded. "Black Knight was just one of his many aliases. The Internet had become a new way for him to indulge in his weakness for sex and debauchery.''

"Did you always know about those online activities?''

"No. I found out on the night of Molly's murder.'' She stood up and walked over to the sink to pour herself a glass of water. Quickly, Kate reached inside her purse, opened the recorder and flipped over the tape.

Seconds later Hallie was walking back into the lounge. "I heard a noise that night,'' she continued. "Lyle wasn't in bed, so I got up and found him in the bathroom, fully dressed, washing his hands. There was blood on the edge of the sink and on the cuff of his shirt.''

She sat down again. "I asked him where the blood came from, and where he had been. He said he had cut himself changing a flat tire, but when I checked his hands, they were perfectly fine. He wouldn't answer any more questions. He said he was tired and he was going to bed. The following morning, I heard that Molly had been killed, and that's when I started putting two and two together.

"At first Lyle denied any involvement in the murder, but when I threatened to go to the police, he told me everything—how he had met Molly in a chat room, their plans to get together, his shock when he walked into that motel room and saw her."

"And you didn't say anything? You didn't go to the police to clear Todd?"

"I wanted to. For a while, I even thought Lyle would turn himself in, because I knew how much he loved his son. Then Todd did something neither of us expected. He fled."

"You had it in your power to bring him back."

"Lyle talked me out of it. He said Todd was safe. All I had to do was keep quiet and our lives would go on as before." She set down her mug. "I know what you're thinking, Ms. Logan, but I had to do it, you see. I had to agree to keep quiet because Lyle held something over my head, too, something that could have destroyed Terrence."

"What?"

"Terrence is not Lyle's son."

That came as a surprise. In all the research Kate had done on the Buchanan family, she hadn't come across anything regarding a first marriage for Hallie. "You were married before?"

"No." She met Kate's gaze. "I had an affair, not too long after Lyle and I were married. My husband was working long hours as an attorney at the time. I was always alone, bored and feeling neglected. I allowed myself to get seduced, and became pregnant. I didn't know until it was too late that the man I was involved with was wanted in the state of Oregon for killing a state trooper. He was later arrested, and no mention was made of my name, but Lyle never forgave me. I'm not sure what made him more furious, the fact that I cheated on him or my choice of a lover.''

''But he stayed with you. And he gave Terrence his name.''

''Lyle enjoyed the fact that I came from an affluent, influential family. And despite my brief indiscretion, I loved him very much. I thought the affair would somehow improve our marriage. It seemed to, for a while, but Terrence was a constant reminder of how I had dirtied the Buchanan name.

''He started cheating on me, a year or so before Todd was born. I didn't say anything because I figured it was my fault. I had done it first. I didn't realize his infidelity had turned into a sickness until I learned about his obsessions with chat rooms. I wanted him to go to therapy, but of course he wouldn't hear of it. So I tried to talk to him, hoping I might be able to help. I knew he'd had a difficult childhood. His father was very strict and his mother was hardly ever home.'' She shook her head. ''That didn't work, either.''

Kate remembered something Dr. Eileen Brown had said about sexually abused children becoming dysfunctional, but now didn't seem the right time to bring up that subject.

''So I kept quiet,'' Hallie went on. ''Because if I didn't, Lyle would expose Terrence as the son of a cop killer, and my son's academic career would be over. How could I do that to him, knowing all he had already lost?''

But she'd had no qualms about letting her other son go to prison for a crime he didn't commit.

Hallie gazed into her glass. ''Everything is different now. I won't allow my husband to frame Terrence for something Lyle did. No matter how much mud this family is dragged through before this mess is over, the truth must be told.''

''And what makes you think I'm going to let that happen, Hallie?''

As Hallie cried out in alarm, Kate spun around.

Lyle Buchanan stood just inside the sliding doors, a gun aimed at them.

Forty-One

If the situation hadn't been so serious, Kate would have laughed.

With rain dripping from his face, his famous pewter hair all matted down and his left arm in a sling, Lyle Buchanan looked more like a reject from a bad gangster movie than the sophisticated man she had met a week ago.

"You should have stayed out of our lives, Ms. Logan," he said quietly. "It's not as if you weren't warned."

Kate stared at the gun. "How did you know I was here?"

"Lizzy called me at the hospital. She wanted to make sure she hadn't done anything wrong in telling you where my wife was." He looked at Hallie. "Then, as I was driving down here, Jacob called to say you, my dear, were on to us."

A streak of lightning flashed across the gray sky. "I don't understand," Hallie said. "How did you get out of the hospital?"

"You should know by now that my powers of persuasion are far above those of the average person."

"Yes," she replied coldly. "You were always a master at lying and manipulating."

He turned his attention back to Kate. "How much did she tell you?"

Kate tried to affect a calm she was far from feeling. "Enough."

He shrugged. "Oh well, it doesn't really matter now, does it? Neither one of you will live to tell her tale."

Kate's cell phone rang. She instinctively reached for her purse, but Lyle stopped her with a wave of his gun.

"Don't answer it."

It had to be Mitch. He would start worrying. He might even think of calling Jessica, who would tell him about their conversation and Hallie's sudden trip. Would he guess that she had gone looking for Hallie? Would he think of going to the Buchanans' house and questioning the maid? Maybe. But even if he did, even if he found out where she was, by the time he got here, she and Hallie would be dead.

Hallie didn't seem to be able to take her eyes off Lyle's gun. "Put that gun away, Lyle. Please."

"She's right," Kate interjected. "You have enough problems without adding to them by killing two more people."

He gave them both a thin smile. "But I'm not going to kill you. Well, in a matter of speaking, I will, but as far as the rest of the world is concerned, you will simply have disappeared."

"Your maid knows I came to Tilghman Island."

"But you never got here, you see. Your car will be found on the road, twenty miles from the marina, with a flat tire. We will all assume you were the victim of foul play. And you, my dear Hallie—'' his arm made a wide arc ''—will commit suicide.''

''You're insane,'' Hallie said under her breath. ''Who will believe that?''

''All the people who love you dearly and have witnessed your growing anxieties over the past two weeks—Lizzy, Conrad, Jacob, me, of course. You were so distraught that you couldn't even bring yourself to visit your son in jail.''

''That was Jacob's idea!''

''But no one knows that.''

''What about your alibi, now that you've checked yourself out of the hospital? Won't the police be suspicious?''

Lyle looked pleased with himself. ''No, because Jacob will swear we were together.''

''Is Jacob your partner in crime now?''

''He always was. To whom do you think he owes his successful practice?''

''You both make me sick.''

Every time Lyle took his eyes off Kate, she glanced around the cabin, desperately searching for a weapon, something she could use against him. Or use to defend herself when it became necessary to do so. There didn't seem to be much point in counting on Hallie. She was white as a sheet, her back pressed against the divider, her eyes glued to the gun in Lyle's hand. At the moment, words seemed to be her only weapon, and they weren't doing much good.

''How will you arrange for me to kill myself?'' Hallie asked. ''You don't think I'm going to put a gun to my head and pull the trigger, do you?''

Lyle shrugged. ''Oh, I don't know. I have a feeling

you'll be much more cooperative once your nosy friend here is out of the way.''

"What, exactly, are you planning to do with me?" Kate asked.

Lyle smiled. "Feed you to the fish, Ms. Logan. I'm told they're particularly hungry this time of year.'' He tossed a set of keys to Hallie, who caught them in midair. "Go up and start the boat, Hallie. We're going for a ride.''

"What?" She glanced out the window, where the storm still raged. "In this weather? Are you insane?"

"We won't have to go far." He waved the gun again. "Come on, come on. We don't have all day."

But Hallie wasn't going anywhere. She was slowly moving along the divider, one inch at a time. She was up to something, Kate realized. And whatever it was, she would need help, or some kind of distraction.

"I can't." Hallie's voice shook, and if that was an act, the woman deserved an Oscar. "I'm too afraid. Small crafts advisories have been issued for the entire east coast.''

"We're not so small, and you've taken the boat out in bad weather before. Do it, Hallie!''

"Why? Why should I do what you say?"

"Because if you don't, I'll put a bullet through your head.''

"You're going to do that, anyway."

Kate's gaze fell on the mug on the coffee table, the only object she could reach without attracting attention. It wasn't much of a weapon but desperate situations called for desperate measures.

Saying a quick prayer, Kate grabbed the mug, aimed it at Lyle's head and threw it.

The justice saw it coming and ducked, but the action was enough to throw him off balance. In a move that would have made the football coach at Kate's old high school proud, she rushed him, shoulders low, her head aimed at his midsection.

This time he couldn't escape the collision. As Kate's body connected with his, he let out a grunt of pain. They both fell on the plush white carpet with a dull thud, but Kate's hopes that he would drop the gun died quickly.

As Lyle rolled up to a sitting position, the revolver was still firmly anchored in his right hand. "That was a mistake, Ms. Logan." He pressed the barrel of the gun against her ribs and gave a little jab. "A very bad mistake. Maybe I should shoot you before I toss you overboard. Just to teach you a lesson."

Kate didn't answer. And she didn't move. Unfortunately, he was still calling the shots.

"Let her go, Lyle."

Kate looked up. Hallie's back was still pressed against the teak divider. Her hands were out of sight.

"I'm losing my patience, Hallie. Go start the boat, or I swear I'll shoot her."

"Not if I shoot you first."

And with those words, she whipped out a gun from behind her back, aimed and fired.

The sound of the gunshot exploded, filling the lounge and echoing through Kate's head.

There was a moment of complete silence while all three people in the cabin seemed frozen in place— Hallie with her arms extended in front of her, her hands around the gun; Kate and Lyle on the floor, staring at her in total disbelief. Then, without a sound, Lyle fell back.

"Did I kill him?" Hallie lowered her arms.

Kate bent over the justice, trying to see where he had been hit. She caught his gaze, and this time there was a look of defeat in those hard eyes.

"No, Hallie," Kate said, feeling the situation warranted a little familiarity. "He's just wounded. In the right shoulder this time. Now he'll have both arms in a sling." She stood up and went to retrieve his gun, a .38 Special, that had slid under a chair.

"Why did you do it, Hallie?" Lyle winced as he lifted his head. "Why did you have to ruin everything?"

"I didn't do anything!"

He tried to get up, but Kate stopped him, the same way he had stopped her, by waving the gun. "Uh-uh. Don't move a muscle. I like you just where you are."

Their gazes held. He kept watching her, as she backed away. At the coffee table, she took her cell phone out of her purse. The message icon was blinking on the display screen. Kate retrieved her message, and Mitch's baritone filled the cabin.

"Kate, I swear, if I don't hear from you in the next five minutes, I'm going to send the National Guard after you. Where the hell are you? Why haven't you called? And why aren't you answering the damn phone?"

Kate dialed his number.

He answered on the first ring. "Kate?"

She closed her eyes briefly, realizing how close she had come to never hearing his voice again. "I'm fine, Mitch. I'm at the Buchanans' boat—*Sweet*—"

"I know. That's where I'm headed. I'm halfway there. Kate, listen to me. Lyle Buchanan checked out of the hospital—"

"He's right here." She smiled at Lyle, who was watching her intently. "But don't worry. He's in no condition to hurt anyone."

"What happened?"

"I'll tell you when you get here. Hurry."

She hung up and dialed 911.

Forty-Two

Not since Watergate had the nation's capital seen such headlines. It would be weeks before this latest scandal was put to rest and became part of Washington's colorful history. The press had been quick to point out certain similarities between this case and the case of the Washington Madam, where another powerful local figure had resorted to murder in order to cover up his sexual activities. Coincidence? one reporter had asked in his morning column. Or was Kate Logan intentionally taking her one-woman practice in a new direction by going after the high and mighty? He had called to find out, but Kate hadn't told him anything. She had no idea in which direction her career would be going. Well, maybe she did, but she wasn't about to discuss it with him.

Only hours after the incident aboard *Sweet Melody*, Todd had been released from jail and cleared of all charges. Lyle Buchanan was back in the hospital. Hallie's bullet had done considerable damage to his shoulder, shattering the humerus and part of the shoulder blade.

Not surprisingly, he hadn't been very cooperative with the police. In fact, he hadn't said a word either in his defense or to explain what exactly had hap-

pened in that motel room two years ago. It didn't
matter. Lyle's self-incriminating words and his clear
intent to kill Kate and Hallie had been duly recorded
on Kate's tape recorder.

As for Jacob Winters, he had emphatically denied
any knowledge of Lyle's guilt in the Molly Buchanan
murder. His job had been to get Todd out of jail, and
that's what he had tried to do.

More information about Justice Buchanan had been
supplied by Lou Torres, with whom Lyle had had a
long relationship. Faced with eighteen counts of felony, ranging from murder to illegal gambling, the
syndicate boss was still trying to make a deal with
the U.S. attorney, even though bail had been denied.

He and the justice had met more than twenty years
ago, when Lyle was just a district judge and a regular
at one of Torres's massage parlors. Unfortunately for
the judge, Torres always made it a point to know the
true identity of the men and women who frequented
his establishments.

When he found out who Lyle was, he had approached him and suggested a sort of partnership—
Lyle's use of his best girls and complete discretion,
in exchange for leniency in the courtroom whenever
Torres or one of his associates needed it.

He hadn't known about Lyle's Internet activities,
until the justice came to him and told him he was in
trouble. An attorney by the name of Kate Logan was
reopening the investigation of Molly's murder and
had become a threat. Torres had taken care of the
problem the only way he knew how—by ordering a
hit on Kate Logan. He admitted to providing the jus-

tice with phony ID from time to time, but claimed to have no idea what it was for.

Because Charlene had been one of Lou's girls, he had been surprised to learn she was doing a little moonlighting on the side and had never mentioned it to him. He had been even more surprised to hear she was snooping into a john's private life. She should have known better. When Lyle, concerned about Charlene's e-mail, had called him, Torres had had no choice but to have the girl killed, not only to help his old friend, but to teach the other hookers that, in this business, the only way to survive was to keep your mouth shut. Fortunately, he kept spare keys of all his girls' homes, and making the hit look like the work of an angry client hadn't been difficult.

Hallie, too, would be facing charges. Not for shooting her husband since she had acted in self-defense, but for her participation as an accessory after the fact in Molly's murder. Her bail had been set at a hundred thousand dollars, which Todd, more grateful than angry toward his mother, had paid.

In the wake of the scandal, Terrence had resigned as provost of Jefferson University, but had made no statement to the press about his involvement with Molly or the young daughter he still refused to recognize. The latter was just fine with Mitch, who didn't want Terrence within a hundred feet of his niece.

On a bright note, the Montana blizzard had finally ended and Alison had come home. At the airport, when Kate and Mitch had met their plane, Eric took Kate aside.

"I'm sorry I gave you such a hard time about the joint custody thing," he said, looking unusually apologetic. "The truth is, Alison doesn't really want to live with me. She thought she did because of Candace, but having to leave you behind while a killer was on the loose really shook her up. She loves you a lot, Kate, and she belongs with you. I know that now."

He hadn't given Kate a chance to reply, and that was just as well, because she had been too emotional to say much of anything.

Earlier today, Todd and Jessica had stopped at Kate's house to give her a proper thank you. Though clearly upset over his father's wrongdoings, Todd was trying to be cheerful, for Jessica's sake. The good news from France helped a little. Before coming to Kate's house, Todd had called Emile Sardoux and found out that the French reporter was something of a national hero, if not in the eyes of Interpol, at least in those of the public. As well, *Le Journal du Soir,* which happened to be *Bordeaux-Matin*'s only serious competitor, had been so impressed with Emile's investigation, they had offered him a job. He hadn't yet worked things out with his wife, but he was hopeful.

Shortly after Todd and Jessica left, Frankie showed up, carrying a huge cake with the words *To the greatest criminal attorney in D.C.* written on it.

"Thank you, Frankie," Kate said. "That's very thoughtful of you. However…" She glanced from her assistant, to Alison, to Mitch. "I've decided to quit criminal law and go into civil law instead."

"What?" Frankie and Alison spoke at the same time.

"Boss, you don't mean this." Frankie looked as if she was going to cry.

"Mom, you're joking, right?" Alison was equally stunned.

Mitch wasn't saying anything. He just watched her, looking skeptical.

"I'm not joking at all. Civil law is an exciting, lucrative alternative, and with my criminal experience, I think I'll be good at it."

She threw a smile at random and went in to get plates for the cake. Mitch followed her into the kitchen.

"Did you mean that, Kate? About switching to civil law?"

She took cups and saucers from the cupboard. "Yes, I meant it. I almost lost my daughter over a criminal case, Mitch. I don't think I'll ever forget how close she came to..." She shook her head, unwilling to finish her thought.

"You realize that the incident at Union Station was an isolated case and nothing like that will ever happen again. Especially with Luther and Torres out of the way."

"You're probably right."

"You're a gifted attorney, Kate, and I'll support you no matter what you choose to do. But you love your job, and you have a very special talent for it, so before you turn your back on criminal law, why don't you take some time off and think your decision through?"

She put down the cups. "I might do that."

"No 'might' about it. Let's do it, Kate. Let's go somewhere together. Just the two of us."

"You mean...on a trip?"

"Yes. Eric already offered to keep Alison."

Kate's mouth dropped open. "Wait a minute. You had a conversation with Eric about this?"

"I can be civil, you know, when properly motivated." He held her a little closer. "And believe me, having you all to myself on a deserted, sandy beach is all the motivation I need."

"A deserted sandy beach." She was beginning to warm up to the idea, but not about switching to civil law. Her mind was made up about that. "Where did you have in mind?"

"I don't know. It doesn't matter. Somewhere warm and exotic where you'll be able to wear this." He pulled a hot-pink string bikini from his pants pocket and dangled it in front of her nose.

She laughed as she took the flimsy triangle from his hand and inspected it. "Not much to it, is there."

"Not even a top."

"I see you've really thought this through."

"A trip to the islands isn't the only thing I thought through."

"Oh?" Because of that remark he had dropped on her lap a few nights ago, she had a pretty good idea of where he was leading with this conversation, but she decided to play dumb. Some men had very definite ideas on how and when to propose. "What is the other thing?"

He shook his head. "You won't know until we get to our beach."

She picked up the stack of cups and saucers and put them in his arms. "In that case, I can hardly wait."

"Does that mean I can book the trip?"

"Yes." She started to walk out of the kitchen, carrying the dishes. At the door, she turned around and gave him her sexiest look. "And make it Rio, will you? I hear they have some of the best topless beaches in the world." She was about to add something really naughty, when she heard the doorbell. "That will be Rose. I asked her to come over so she could spend some time with Alison."

She walked into the family room to find her ex-mother-in-law talking to Alison and Frankie. "Hello, Rose."

"Hello, Kate." Rose looked a little dismayed.

"Is something wrong?" Kate asked.

"No, nothing's wrong. I'm just...surprised. Alison tells me you're quitting criminal law?"

"That's right." Kate put the dishes on the coffee table.

"I can't believe you would do that. Criminal law has been your life since you graduated from law school. What will you do?"

Kate laughed. "I'll still be an attorney, Rose—"

She was interrupted again, this time by the phone. As Alison started to pick it up, Kate stopped her. "Let the machine take a message, sweetie. It's probably another reporter requesting an interview I have no intention of giving."

She was starting to slice the cake, when a woman's shaky voice made them all look up. "Ms. Logan," the caller said. "My name is Carly Williams. My ex-husband was just found stabbed to death, in my house, and his new wife has identified me as the killer. I'm at the police station. Ted Rencheck, the assistant U.S. attorney, said you might be able to help me. Can you, Ms. Logan? Please?'' She left a number before hanging up.

The line went dead. Kate put down the knife and slowly straightened, only to find the other four people in the room—Rose, Alison, Frankie and Mitch—watching her with amused expressions.

Frankie leaned toward Mitch and said in a whisper, but loud enough for Kate to hear, ''Dollars to doughnuts, she returns the call.''

''Who gets the doughnuts?''

''The winner, of course.''

''And you think that will be you?''

''I know her better than anyone in this room.''

Kate gave them both an irritated look. ''Will you two stop talking as if I wasn't here?''

Alison giggled. Rose gave one of her knowing smiles. Frankie waved a paper napkin. ''I wrote her number down in case you want it.''

After a slight hesitation, Kate walked over to where Frankie stood and snatched the napkin from her hand. Then, without a word, she crossed the room again, picked up the phone and dialed the number.